THE ISLANDS

THE ISLANDS

Carlos Gamerro

Translated by Ian Barnett
in collaboration with the author

Introduction by Jimmy Burns

First published in English in 2012 by
And Other Stories, 91 Tadros Court, High Wycombe, Bucks, HP13 7GF

www.andotherstories.org

Originally published as *Las Islas*
© Carlos Gamerro 1998, 2007, 2012

English language translation © Ian Barnett, 2012
Introduction © Jimmy Burns

ISBN No. 978-1-908276-08-7

A catalogue record for this book is available from the British Library.

Supported by the National Lottery through Arts Council England.
Work published within the framework of "SUR" Translation Support
Program of the Ministry of Foreign Affairs, International Trade and
Worship of the Argentine Republi

LOTTERY FUNDED

CONTENTS

INTRODUCTION

In nearly four decades of journalism, few articles have proved more challenging than the one I was obliged to write in the early hours of 2 April 1982, when Argentine forces occupied the British South Atlantic colony of the Falkland Islands.

Typing in my office near Avenida Corrientes, my only point of reference was an editorial by the English-language *Buenos Aires Herald*, the newspaper that, during the worst periods of Argentina's 'Dirty War' following the military coup of 1976, had religiously published daily lists of the 'disappeared'.

The *Herald* discerned an element of tragicomedy in the news that the Argentina junta had ordered a full-scale military invasion of the Falkland Islands. The colony was better known for its penguins and other wild life than for any member of its tiny population: just over 1,200, sheep farmers mainly. Yet the junta invoked a 150-year-old disputed sovereignty claim to justify its action and in the process divert domestic attention away from its appalling human rights record. The ensuing war lasted just 74 days and led to the death of over 1,000 soldiers, more than 600 hundred of whom were Argentine. Mrs Thatcher emerged victorious. Humiliated in defeat, the junta disintegrated.

Carlos Gamerro's *The Islands* is a novel about the distorted logic and the bizarre endurance of Argentina's militarised society, viewed through the inevitably distorted gaze of a veteran of the war. Felipe Félix inhabits a world where the lines between reality, dreams and fears are hopelessly blurred, a world dominated by torturers and megalomaniacs, where fear and violence rule. This literary excavation is both a nightmare and a fair reflection of grotesque national trauma.

For the war of the Malvinas – as the islands are known in Argentina – cannot be understood outside the context of Argentine reality and mythology and their convergence in a historical narrative as conceived by scheming military officers and their collaborators. General Galtieri and his junta took society and myth to another level by fighting a war over Las Malvinas as if the islands held a magical key to national identity, a kind of Holy Grail in Argentina's aggrandising quest. As one character in this novel puts it: 'Argentina is an erect prick ready to breed, and the Malvinas, its balls.'

The lunacy of the Falklands War, and the brutality and self-delusion of the militarised society that brought it about, define the personality and motivation of Felipe Félix, Gamerro's protagonist: he is a one-time Argentine conscript, forced ten years later to recall his experience of the conflict, who finds the elements that first provoked still festering like a resistant cancer. These elements endure in the torturers and assassins that continue to inhabit the urban landscape of Buenos Aires.

Felipe is doubly haunted: by the humiliation of the Malvinas and by the memory of that 'dirtier war' that predated the invasion of the islands, during which the military kidnapped, tortured and killed thousands of political dissidents in the name of 'national reorganisation'. But Felipe is more than just a war veteran. He is also a computer geek, a ruthless hacker, an inventor of state-of-the art video war games and, crucially, an agent in the employ of the sinister magnate Fausto Tamerlán, whose tower-block headquarters is located in the city's supposedly regenerated harbour.

Sex is everywhere in *The Islands*, but it is as brutal and extreme as that described by V. S. Naipaul in his essay 'The Return of Eva Perón', written shortly after the 1976 coup that promoted officers like those seen torturing their own soldiers in the novel. Naipaul analyses Argentine history as if it were fiction, suggesting that we 'Outline it like a story by Borges'. What follows is a devastating examination of the rottenness underlying the past and present of a 'flat desolate land' where the quasi-religious figure of Perón's legendary wife Evita provides the only space for emotion in the midst of militarised terror. Twenty years after Naipaul's essay, in 1998, Gamerro's novel first appeared in Spanish. Now, in this fine if somewhat belated translation, it is Gamerro's turn to invoke the spirit of Joseph Conrad and his *Heart of Darkness*.

Conrad wrote: 'The destiny of . . . all nations is to be accomplished in darkness amidst much weeping and gnashing of teeth, to pass through robbery, equality, anarchy and misery under the iron rule of a military despotism.' In Gamerro's *The Islands*, we see how Conrad's words fit the madness of Argentina during those years: they encompass the schizophrenic mood and the moral vacuum of a peculiarly Argentine moment of dream-fused reality.

The River Plate, watched from Tamerlán's window, is as murky as the Thames, where, in *The Heart of Darkness*, Conrad's

Marlow begins his journey in search of Mr Kurtz, a man corrupted by power and wealth, a militarised businessman who has lost all sense of moral value and even of reality. As Felipe seeks out Tamerlán, through his past, present and future, he finds everything corroded and corrosive. In this world where the dead coexist with the living, Felipe's love for his girlfriend must be played out under the influence of hallucinogenic drugs. A rare glimpse of common happiness is engulfed by the horror show.

Conrad may have crept uninvited into *The Islands*, but his presence will guarantee the novel its place in literature and among readers around the world. Gamerro acknowledges the influence of William Burroughs and of Michael Herr, whose Vietnam novel *Dispatches* merged with Conrad's *Heart of Darkness* to form the matrix of Francis Ford Coppola's seminal film *Apocalypse Now*. Perhaps due to Gamerro's practised dramatic eye – he is also a successful playwright – there is a powerful cinematic aspect to this black satirical novel, whose dystopian elements cry out, if not for a Coppola, then certainly for a Terry Gilliam.

Another important literary influence here is what Gamerro himself describes as 'baroque fiction', in which reality and illusion are easily transmuted: fiction in which neither protagonist nor reader can tell whether events are fantasy or reality. With roots in the works of Spanish Golden Age writers like Calderón and Cervantes, as well as in Shakespeare, Gamerro's novel marks him out as a worthy member of the impressive academy of the 'Argentine fantastic', alongside Borges, Bioy Casares, Cortázar and Ocampo. If there is a method in the madness, it is one that should be familiar to fans of these great writers, for in the Argentina of Gamerro's narrative, history is written by individual imagination as much as it is by external 'facts'.

Appropriately made available in English on the thirtieth anniversary of the Falklands War, *The Islands* demonstrates a powerful literary imagination, opening doors of perception beyond tragicomedy, onto the nightmare society that made this conflict possible. Gamerro's novel is as rich as it is ambitious, confirming him as one of today's most exciting and courageous Latin American writers.

Jimmy Burns
London, January 2012

The inferno of the living is not something that will be; if there is one, it is what is already here, the inferno where we live every day, that we form by being together. There are two ways to escape suffering it. The first is easy for many: accept the inferno and become such a part of it that you can no longer see it. The second is risky and demands constant vigilance and apprehension: seek and learn to recognise who and what, in the midst of the inferno, are not the inferno, then make them endure, give them space.

Italo Calvino, *Invisible Cities*

Trans. William Weaver

THE ISLANDS

Chapter 1
ACRYLIC & GLASS

A fly caught in the web, while the spider, replete from its last meal, takes a while to reach him, can have a pretty good time of it if he relaxes while he waits. The threads are an almost intangible gossamer: they accompany the movements of his body without hampering it – as long as they aren't too violent. It's like stretching out in a hammock on holiday, with nothing to do but swing in the breeze and gaze at the blue of the sky through the cracks of your eyes. Yeah, you bet, I could lie here like this my whole life. And if I don't squirm too much, I can't even feel the threads, they're so fine, it's like floating on my back in the air. Yes, they only become real when I try to wriggle free.

I hadn't been able to get the image of the fly out of my head all morning; it had been haunting me for hours as I rolled in the bedclothes, which somehow always dragged me back at the last; and whenever I was on the brink of persuading myself there was nothing to worry about, that it was just another job interview, the image of the fly would alight on my brain again.

Maybe it was the time I got the message – eleven at night – or the fact that, rather than summoning me by phone or sending me an e-mail, they came all the way to my apartment and rang the bell – not the entryphone down on the street, but my actual doorbell. The piece of work I opened the door to was broad-shouldered and muscled, looking not unlike a horse's rear end in a two-piece, complete with cropped, grey-ing hair, bristling moustache, mirrorshades (despite the un-godliness of the hour) and Italian shoes, one toe of which he discreetly jammed in the door to stop me slamming it in his face. A spook for sure, but too well-groomed to be Intelligence or the Army; he looked more like one of the many who had been privatised in recent years. He handed me an open enve-lope and I pulled out a card: Sr Fausto Tamerlán requests the pleasure of your company at 10.00 a.m., 1st June 1992, at his offices in the Golden Tower, Tamerlán & Sons, Puerto Madero. It looked like a wedding invitation.

'Be there,' grunted the sharp-suited thug when I looked at him inquisitively. 'Or I'll have to come and fetch you.'

The telephone had been ringing all morning, a sec-retary's voice vying with the buzzing of the fly in my sleep-addled brain, leaving messages on the answering machine every fifteen minutes from ten o'clock sharp – urgent at first, then imploring, until she broke off in mid-entreaty and was replaced by a familiar voice: 'Fifteen minutes,' was all it said before putting the receiver down. Before they were up, I was combed and dressed and navigating the streets on the 22 bus, whose chrome-plated handrails felt like they were wrapped in sticky threads, as if a candyfloss seller had just disembarked, and for a moment I wondered if I wasn't still in bed dreaming of the spider-web.

Four blocks before my stop I got a seat, which I grabbed to

be rid of those tacky rails, and then, through the green glass
of the closed window, they hove into view: the twin towers of
Tamerlán & Sons, cutting through the sky above the captive
water of the docks and the empty, red-brick storehouses and
the defeated cranes. I'd seen them countless times, but it was
always like the first: they were less unreal in memory than
face to face, as if only the imagination could conceive of the expanse of muddy waters that is the River Plate crystallising into
those two immaculate ice palaces. For a city that hasn't managed to raise itself from the oppressive horizontality of pampas
and river in over four hundred years an elevation of any kind
takes on a faintly sacred character, shielding its inhabitants
from the crushing gravity of the two interminable plains and
the vast sky that bears down on them; and I was now about to
become one of the few mortals ever to enjoy the privilege of
seeing the famed towers from the inside.

I got off at the entrance to Puerto Madero and set off
across the long esplanade leading up to them. From a distance
the profusion of winter suns reflected in their mirrored panes
confused them into a single block, a monolithic structure that,
instead of a building erected by men, looked at times like a newborn mountain, unblemished by erosion, forced through the
tender, green skin of the pampas by the subterranean agonies
of some colossal cataclysm. But as I drew closer, the uniform
summit of ice divided into two identical needles: two razors
lined up blade-to-blade, leaving between them an intolerably
narrow space through which the rebounding sunlight burst
with blinding, almost supernatural violence. They were so perfectly alike it was easy to imagine they were a single building
leaning against a gigantic mirror: a golden mirror in which

the silver tower was reflected gold, a silver mirror making the golden tower's silvered sister.

This was nothing to what I found inside. There were mirrors on the walls, mirrors on the ceiling, mirrors on the floor, mirrors on the mirrors – although 'on', strictly speaking, is inaccurate: there were no walls or ceilings or floors other than mirrors; there was nothing but mirrors, and I floated in their midst as if the law of gravity and the points of the compass had all of a sudden been overruled. I'd barely ventured a few steps before I was turned into some proliferating, tangled polyp, a Hindu god with ten legs, a hundred arms and a planetary system of heads. If I looked down, the black stone floor, polished to the point of dementia, wanted to swallow me in an unfathomable lake; if up, the ceiling burned with white fire, heightening rather than alleviating the gloom of the lake, one spotlight multiplying the next in a blossoming of reflections that stopped me dead in my tracks. (There is something appalling about a black mirror: your reflection stares back from an impossible distance, the other side of death.) Enveloped in a whirlwind of motion, like the only one moving in slow-mo through a film on fast-forward, I crossed the paths of men and women scooting left and right like tracer bullets, in and out of invisible doors, swiftly converging on their reflected forms and at the last moment, instead of shattering, melting into them and vanishing. They performed complex greeting rituals when they met, circling around each other in complicated dance patterns like social insects, some taking off the dark glasses most of them wore and waving them in the air as they spoke. There seemed to be hundreds of them, although it was difficult to decide if there were so many people or simply the image of a few, repeated ad infinitum in the deceptive panes. One person alone stood motionless, staring in my direction through mirrorshades.

'Got your message,' I said in a friendly tone.

'So where have you been?'

'Overslept,' I answered pulling a sleepy face, even though the excuse rarely worked after midday.

'Sr Tamerlán is very strict in matters of punctuality,' he informed me. 'He won't stand for his employees being late.'

'I'm not his employee,' I reminded him.

'But I am,' he retorted, and without saying another word he began to walk towards the lifts, while I trotted after him, the familiar taste of slippers in my mouth again. By the time I caught up with him, he was inserting a card between two panels, one of which slid aside to reveal a lift made entirely out of glass. 'Only for people with direct access to Sr Tamerlán,' he muttered, leaving me barely a chink to squeeze through. 'A lot of them wait a lifetime and never get to use it,' he added, burdening me with a vague and, in my view, rather unfair sense of guilt for the thirty floors of our ascent.

On our way up, one stratum of the glass beehive after another passed before my eyes, and I looked on in astonishment at how the tower began to organise itself as the demented confusion of the mirrors gave way to the geometric order of translucent glass. I suddenly understood why: the mirrors were all one way, the mirrored ceiling of each level becoming the transparent floor of the one above, whereby the tower seemed to grow as floor after floor unfolded beneath our feet. At the speed I was going it was difficult to grasp the general layout, the organising idea: it must have been something very simple to have produced such complexity.

The lift deposited us – quite literally: the floor slid forward on arrival – in a sealed vault where rainbows of triangular mirrors crept over each other at the speed of molluscs, slowly overlapping in a shifting kaleidoscope. My chaperone inserted his card into an invisible slot between them and they fell into line smoothly and noiselessly to form a long corridor, which, from the warmest to the coldest, glowed with all the colours of the spectrum.

'Don't worry about how to get there. The walls will lead the way. Oh, and by the way, send my regards to Verraco when you see him: Freddy's the name,' he added, and before I had time to get my question out, he'd disappeared like a fly on the tongue of a toad.

As I walked down the corridor the walls laced shut behind me; I had no alternative but to go on. I came out into a lobby where the aggression of the mirrors was tempered by thick Renaissance tapestries in which a hart, comic-strip fashion, was by turns startled, pursued, harried and felled by the hunters' hounds and arrows. When it spoke to me, it did so in the emotionless, electronic voice of a computer.

'Lie down please.'

I lay back on a couch upholstered in black leather so soft it felt freshly skinned, and a seated figure materialised in the matching armchair at my head. His smell reached me before his shadow did, a smell of dust blown off old books, of ash and dead insects in a spider-web. Then I saw him reflected in the mirror on the wall. He was a man of indefinite age, greying hair and Freudian beard, thick glasses and hands gnarled like the branches of a rose tree. His torso was sturdy, a block of wood, but his arms and legs were as thin as matchsticks, four more and he'd have looked just like a spider. He was wearing coarse woollen trousers and a dull-coloured tweed jacket, unbuttoned to reveal the butt of an automatic weapon peeping out against the stiff, light-blue cotton of his shirt.

'Turn away please,' he said, and I realised the electronic voice was his natural one. I did as I was told. Two minutes elapsed in total silence.

'I've come to see Sr Tamerlán,' I explained finally.

'Why?'

'He sent for me.'

'What for?'

'I suppose he must be in need of my services,' I ventured.

'What services?'

'Security systems specialist. Networks. Viruses. Um . . .'

'In a word.'

'Hacker,' I answered without hesitation.

'The metal detector,' I saw him glance at a console built into the arm of his chair, 'has registered a foreign body in your head. Show it to me.'

'I can't. It's inside.'

'Explain please.'

'A piece of helmet. A soldier's helmet. A memory . . .'

'We'll get round to your memories some other time,' he cut in. He didn't move his eyes when he wanted to look at something, but turned his entire head the way a mantis does. The staring eyes met mine.

'Don't look at me. The appointment was at ten. It's twelve thirty. Explain yourself.'

'I have trouble getting up in the morning,' I told him. 'So I wait till noon. Mornings give me the fear. Every night I go to bed thinking "Tomorrow. Tomorrow I'll make it," but the alarm clock goes off (actually, it's a voice program I designed) and fills me with dread.'

'What fills you with dread?'

'The feeling that the worst night-terrors pale into insignificance beside the horror of a routine morning. The burden of the day. Having breakfast. Looking out of the window. Going outside. Taking a bus. Once I get moving, the fear goes and I find it enjoyable, even elating. But when I'm fighting with the sheets, it all looks terribly threatening, and I lie there suffering for hours before I can get up.'

'Consequences.'

'The later I get up, the more real my fears become, and I spend the rest of the day in a fog of puffy eyes, with a bad taste in my mouth and a feeling like I'm walking on dirty hospital swabs. Once I cross a certain threshold, I know the day's a write-off and I reason to myself that the later I get up, the less of that write-off I'll have to bear, although of course every hour I subtract from the horror intensifies the dull ache of the ones still to go. By night-time I have insomnia from it all and can't get to sleep before daybreak . . . when the whole cycle starts again. Umm . . . can I ask you a question?'

'Yes.'

'You're Sr Tamerlán's bodyg— head of security, I take it?'

'Yes, I'm his psychoanalyst.'

'What's with the weapon then?'

'What weapon?'

'Not the word. The other one.'

'Oh. That's to protect him from his own fantasies.'

'It isn't for killing real people?'

'You'll discover that in Sr Tamerlán's case that distinction is quite beside the point. Follow me,' he said, and when he stood up, I realised he was barely five feet tall. Swaying unsteadily on two of his legs – probably because he was used to eight – he led me through a mirrored panel, which opened and closed so smoothly and silently it was like stepping through a wall of mercury.

As a boy, one of my favourite bits in the Road Runner was when Wile E. Coyote, in his enthusiasm to catch the mocking bird, would confidently go on running on thin air without realising, until the Road Runner pointed out the void beneath his feet, and only then – as if things only happen when we become aware of them – would he start to fall. I took my first steps into Sr Tamerlán's office in the same spirit of innocence and immediately had to cling to the nearest column. Through the thick glass on which I stood yawned the other twenty-nine storeys of the tower, growing in chaos and complexity, and diminishing in clarity level by level, just the way, when you peer into a crystal sea, the waters get murkier the deeper you look. This office was apparently the point of maximum visibility: the one place from which the rest of the building became transparent – the one place with no mirrors. It was difficult to decide which was worse: the towering chaos below, or this unbearable order into which it finally resolved itself.

'Remain standing, please,' said the bodyguard, whose presence I'd momentarily forgotten about, in the voice of someone inviting me to take a seat, and, gliding fearlessly along the threads of his web spread across the void, he squeezed into a tiny side-room, whose transparent door spun on its axis as he went through, and turned its mirrored face to me.

He hadn't said anything about not walking, so, as the minutes ticked by and I was getting bored, I sauntered over to the imposing desk: a half-moon of thick, tempered glass driven into three supports of living rock positioned in the centre of the room. At one end was a small city of monitors and video-screens, computer terminals, phone and fax switchboards, printers that, chirruping like cicadas, fed now and then on walls of continuous feed. The other half of this great arc was given over to more personal objects: a riding-crop with an ex-quisitely fashioned Creole-silverwork handle; a black stone tray full of white sand raked into sinuous and harmonious furrows around three little grey rocks; a well-trained bonsai ombú – save for the leaves, which were almost normal size – set in an astonishingly faithful replica of a fenceless pampas. But what caught my eye was an acrylic prism about the size of a gold ingot, with a long, opaque object inside. This object must have been about a foot long and as thick as my wrist, bluntish with a pebbly relief at one end and tapering slightly to a little tail at the other, all of an even coffee colour. I held it up to the light, rotating it in my fingers the better to appreciate its shifting, iridescent sheen. That's strange, I thought, looking at it in this light you'd swear it was a . . .

'. . . turd.'

I turned without flinching, still holding it in my hand. I gazed at it admiringly. A truly impeccable piece of work. Not a bubble or a burr to interrupt the perfect union of crystalline and opaque matter. Smiling, I handed it to Sr Tamerlán.

'An admirable piece.'

'And a useful one,' he replied. 'Anyone that puts it back on the desk in disgust when they realise does little to earn my respect. It's a detector. I read the language of the body, and the hand that holds the turd never lies.'

He held it aloft, turning it round and round in his deft fingers the better to appreciate its purity of form. Then, for the first time, he looked at me.

'You've passed the test.'

'What if I hadn't?'

He put the ingot to his cheek to feel its coolness, and dreamily closed his eyes. They were as blue as the flame of an acetylene torch.

'This isn't any old turd, you understand.' He put it back on the desk and leaned on it with his full bulk. 'It's of great sentimental value to me. You might say it's worth its weight in gold, if it weren't for the fact that its value is incalculably greater. Don't bother putting a figure on it. Everything you see, my castle, was born from it as from a germinated seed. I should make it clear first of all that this is my turd, the product of my body, my blood, my cells, my bowels – that perfect and bafflingly complex machine. Not even your most state-of-the-art computer could come close to simulating the miracle our body performs silently, humbly, day in day out. But we're not talking about any day or any turd. It is the indelible memory of the night that made me that's preserved in here. This prism is the treasure chest of my most precious memories. As you can appreciate it, I shall open it for you. My partner – you've heard of him I take it. It took me years. It wasn't simple, the way it is for you lot, altering reality by pressing a few keys without getting your hands dirty. No. It was long and gruelling and complicated. First, I had to get him out of the way for a while, so that the running of Tamerlán & Sons – it had another name in those days – would temporarily be in my hands. Then I had to bury myself up to my neck in papers and papers and more papers, and win over people and people and more people, selling cheap and buying dear, shelling out for favours I hadn't received to people who deserved no better than a bullet in the head. Never had I stooped so low, never had I lived with the taste of humiliation for so many days and nights on end. But it was worth it – I relished it – because it was the last time. When I succeeded, when control of the company had, like barely tilting scales, shifted unquestionably and permanently into my hands, I celebrated with a huge feast, on my own. In the course of the meal – I was on dessert I think – the news of his death reached me. Then, and only then, did I call for the golden chalice. Gold, Sr Félix, was the source of our family fortune, which goes back only to my father. When we came to this country, just the two of us, fleeing from a devastated and hostile Europe, we brought it over with us, all of it. Most was spent immediately, establishing the roots of the empire you can now view from these heights, but we decided to keep a tiny amount as a souvenir, so as never to forget where we came from – in the chalice that I used, on that night of nights, to drink to my victory. The bottom of the chalice was full of . . . let's call them gold nuggets, that had passed into my hands like a torch when an accident took my father's life and delivered me defenceless into the hands of his partner – my own until that night – who took advantage of my grief and youth to lay his greedy hands on everything, including my body. The only thing he respected was my chalice. I drank its contents in one, washing them down with the most expensive champagne, and felt a pleasure inconceivable for anyone who hasn't experienced it in the flesh, that of the polish and caress of pure gold nuggets sliding down my throat to my stomach as if borne on the crystal waters of a stream. A few hours later, and for the first time in years – all the years that I'd lived in that monster's clutches – I loosened my bowels and shat, shat that magnificent, prolonged turd you now behold, instead of the timid, constipated little pellets that always used to drop into the toilet bowl with that pebbly plink that brought tears of humiliation to my eyes.'

He opened them to look at me.

'My son's killed someone,' he said. 'In this very room. Threw him out of that window.' He pointed to the one immediately behind me. 'Five nights ago. To explain what your job will be, you've been allowed a privilege reserved for a happy few: to penetrate to the heart of the diamond.'

I thought this would be the moment to show I was worthy of the honour.

'You want me to erase all the data from the police files. Hold up the investigation. No big deal. There are lots of people who could do it.'

'You are a piece of trash, aren't you.'

'I beg your pardon?'

'You have the eyes of an insect. Dead eyes, only connected to your brain. The eyes of the living throb with the beating of their hearts, they light up, they die away. Yours don't. They have a constant, mechanical frequency. A continuous hum. Like mine. That's why I make my less fortunate employees wear mirrored sunglasses when speaking to an inferior. It makes them more ruthless.'

'In the war . . . ,' I began.

'I haven't got time for cheap soaps,' he interrupted, turning away. 'Besides, that wasn't a war. In a real war fortunes are won and lost. If it was so easy,' he went on, without warning me we'd never dropped the original subject, 'we'd already have done it ourselves. They aren't connected to the Web. You have to go in person, do it on their machines. Getting the picture? Now, you tell me about your war and maybe I'll listen to you. I know you haven't lost your contacts.'

'It's been ten years since I . . .'

'Two years ago there was an epidemic of money vanishing from cash dispensers. The work of some word-perfect digital thief. And the pockets of a mysterious patriotic fund miraculously began to bulge. But it was all sorted out behind closed doors and no one went to gaol.'

'I was only carrying out orders,' I explained.

But Sr Tamerlán wasn't listening. He'd taken a cigar out of a transparent drawer and rested it on the acrylic prism in which his turd was embarked, like an insect in amber, on its centuries-long sleep. I tried to make out the secret presence of the gold nuggets in the suggestive twinkle of this or that irregularity, but on the outside it was indistinguishable from a pauper's turd. Indifferent to my craning neck, Sr Tamerlán compared their lengths and trimmed the excess off his cigar with a silver guillotine, chewing on it before he lit it. Measuring his domains, he strode around and stopped in front of the window of the crime, silhouetted in photomontage against the metallised strip of the River Plate. The only things moving on the backcloth of the frozen landscape were a cargo boat chugging in from the sea and the yellow bulldozers shovelling mountains of refuse up to the edge of the Ecological Reserve.

'The bulldozers,' he said without explaining himself, and fell silent to watch them.

'Are they yours?'

'Yes,' he answered, as if to someone else. He exhaled a puff of rich, blue smoke. Then he remembered my absurd presence. 'Mine, yes. A childhood memory.'

'A family of builders?' I ventured.

He stared at me for a few seconds without saying anything. I understood what his top executives must have felt, accustomed as they were to hiding behind their mirrorshades, when they had to take them off in his presence.

'Thirty floors,' he said eventually, exhaling. 'The body fell thirty floors and left a crater in the new lawn. We had to returf it. And change the glass. From over there,' he pointed, 'they saw it all. He did it on purpose. So everyone would see him.'

I followed the line traced by his finger. Sharp as a knife poised to slice it open, the straight edge of the silver tower seemed about to come down on top of us. If there'd been any people in there when Tamerlán Junior pushed his victim through the glass, they must have seen it as clearly as if they'd been watching it on TV in their living rooms.

He gestured disparagingly towards our neighbour.

'The idea of the twin towers was my partner's, may he rest in peace. He never got to see them started. He thought they'd symbolise our partnership; I'd get the silver one of course. In honour of his memory I respected that side of the original project, as it fitted in very nicely with my plans for my two sons, but, as it did on him, fate pulled a fast one on me: my eldest died before he could see them completed, and now it's his contemptible brother – that was all we needed, him turning murderer – who's going to walk off with the lot. Most of that tower's been let, but we'll get it back when the New Capital scheme's complete. Have you seen the model?'

Yes or no, I was clearly going to now. I looked in the direction he was pointing. Like an oriental city, as shapely and meticulous as a Chinese sculpture carved out of an elephant tusk, a new Buenos Aires rose in a halo of light at the far end of the room. In the model, the structures of the new city radiated out from Tamerlán Towers to the four points of the compass: there was a layer of gardens as kempt as golf courses, out of which sprouted the various groups of buildings, dotted about here and there like polite obstacles to the game; towards what was left of the old City stood the ethereal and diaphanous structures of the new financial and business district, continuing north in convention centres and gated communities with their winding streets and barriers and guardhouses (you could even make out the snarling Dobermans and shotgun-girded guards inside, placed there for the subliminal peace-of-mind of potential buyers). The south contained what might be called the public area: four shopping malls with hanging gardens, connected to each other by aerial gangways, defying families to exhaust them in a single weekend – cinemas, museums, amphitheatres and public footpaths, a sea-world and an amusement park. Last, the marina, which occupied the space between the chain of docks and the riverside, included a polo field and a golf links, jetties bristling with white yachts accessed straight from the offices, artificial lakes and white sand beaches. You didn't have to look very far to see what would become of the Ecological Reserve: its marshlands of snakes and toads transformed into princely gardens by a kiss from the lord of the realm. I caught sight of his reflection, as hieratic as a Byzantine emperor, in the mosaic of mirrors on the twin towers, driven into the heart of the model like the standards of a conquistador arriving on these shores to found the city anew.

'You have no idea what's happening,' he assured me, raising his arms to look taller. 'The bulldozers are paving the way. The Third Foundation of Buenos Aires. The city of the Third Millennium. I won't allow twenty-five people who couldn't look the other way at the right moment to jeopardise this dream. You will retrieve their names and any relevant data from the files in Intelligence and hand them over to me. In return . . .'

'How do you know Intelligence has got them?' I interrupted. 'Your son . . .' I hesitated, then changed tack. 'If this is just an ordinary crime . . .'

'We don't commit ordinary crimes,' he said, pursing his lips in contempt, 'and it's me they're coming after. They'll try and finish off the queen to check the king. I have enough influence to keep a lid on everything for now. But I know they're trying to dig up something to use against me, or against him, when he succeeds me – they know he's easier to bend.'

'What are you going to do to them?'

He raised his arms to the heavens, tracing an arc of flickering ash.

'What a question! What can you do? If I get rid of them, others will come. When you don't do everything yourself, you end up depending on the servants. And they hoard up their secrets, making a voodoo doll out of the scraps they pick up off the floor, and then, with the doll, they think they can influence . . .'

'I meant the witnesses,' I clarified, walking back to his desk two steps behind him.

'What about them?'

'What do you want their names for?'

'To bribe them. I'll give them money, green cards for the good ol' US of A, government posts . . . When my enemies need them, they'll be nowhere to be found. I'll find out who they are, what they need to be happy, and give it to them. Like Father Christmas. It'll be cheap and easy. Only losers go to those meetings,' he said, sitting down on his revolving throne.

'Can I interrupt?' I said, interrupting. 'What meetings are you talking about?'

'Aren't you asking too many questions?'

'If I'm going to take this job . . .'

'If you've heard this much, you have no alternative. The meetings,' he went on, 'are for one of those pyramid sales scams. Small-time cons. They rent out the most luxurious offices in town for a few months, get a load of suckers to invest their pathetic life savings and shower them with all the useless, overpriced junk they can't palm off on anyone else. Spanish Surprises I think this outfit call themselves. They've crossed the Atlantic for the Fifth Centenary Celebrations. A few days ago they started hammering away at that fucking caravel out there, for Expo América '92.' He faked a smile, blowing air through his closed lips. 'How the mighty are fallen! But we still have to raise the money for the Third Foundation, and I think it's only natural the Spaniards should chip in, like they did for the first two.'

I peered out. At the edge of the dock, as if, once complete, it was to be lowered into the outsized bath-tub beside it, sat the bowed ribs of a short, strangely squat wooden vessel, with several tiny figures clambering over it and covering it in planks.

So this was the *Santa María*. What will it discover this time, I wondered, then turned to Sr Tamerlán, who was impatiently doodling what looked like erect pricks among the rocks of his Zen garden.

'Computer graphics unnerve me. The day they manage to simulate stillness like this . . . I've fixed a price.'

'On the garden?'

'On you. A hundred thousand dollars.'

I'd been told on several occasions I might be worth that much in the States – maybe more. But this was the first time I'd been made a solid-gold offer. I tried to turn it into a piece of abstract data in my head, a simple six-digit figure on the screen of my bank account, something that could be erased at the touch of a key. Only because I felt that this figure was about to draw a yes from my lips as easily as a dermatologist pops a blackhead. Because the figure was more than the mind could ignore, more than my powers of decision-making could cope with. A hundred thousand dollars was enough to do my thinking for me.

'There's no need to answer now,' my owner's voice went on, 'or later, because I know what you're going to say.'

'I wasn't expecting so much,' I said in all honesty.

'You have no motivation in life,' he said. 'People like you can't be tempted with the mere image of material goods or the security that money would temporarily buy you. Only the pure, brute presence of gold can make any impression on the likes of you. And money only acquires that kind of purity in large amounts.'

He stopped playing with his Zen rake and made a pyramid of interlocking fingers over the acrylic prism, his cigar smouldering at the summit like the crater of a volcano.

'Part of the sum will be paid in advance. Twenty-five names,' he specified, 'will get you the rest. It doesn't matter how you come by them. A single missing name could mean my son's downfall and, in all probability, your own as well.'

With his silver guillotine he pruned an ombú leaf that had exceeded the limits of what was advisable. The healthy leaf fell onto the glass top of the desk. He picked it up between thumb and forefinger and twirled it round, a green flame bursting from the friction of his fingertips.

'My first son was cut down in his prime. He had everything it would take to be my successor, to extend my dominion over these lands and prolong it in time. My other son, on the other hand, has nothing, as you'll find out as soon as you meet him. He's but a pale reflection of his brother, who had become a faithful reflection of myself, allowing for the imperfections that any act of copying entails. This other one's the product of an inane whim of his mother's, who insisted on having a plaything of her own while I was moulding my son and heir. A happy whim, a lesson in life that it's always useful to have a spare handy – even if it isn't the right one.'

He got up and crossed the resonant, reinforced-glass floors, standing with his back to me, his gaze lost in the shoreless river.

'I won't let the chain be broken at the second link.' He went over to the window through which someone had fallen to their death and touched it as if his hands were touching heaven. 'These walls, Sr Félix, were raised with human blood.'

'Hundreds of labourers . . .' I mumbled politely.

'Don't be absurd,' he broke in. 'We're not in ancient Egypt. This place was built with cranes. No. I'm talking about mine.

At the centre of this organism of mirrors and pipes and phone cables and optical fibres and computer networks beats a single heart: mine. The whole building is merely a multiplication of my own body. Every heartbeat sends out orders that are felt in its furthest reaches; every distant organ goes on functioning even when I'm asleep, because, even then, I am the heart that never stops beating. Problems of logic are your department: surely you've guessed what the guiding principle is.'

When I'd first walked in, I could only have suggested chaos and madness, but the longer I spent in there, the more I was persuaded that this madness was order run rampant, unfettered to reality, the mania of purely mental order yearning for the eternal perfection of the diamond.

'It's all mirrors,' I stated. 'There are no opaque walls.'

'One-way mirrors,' he came to my assistance. 'Translucent glass for the bosses . . .'

'. . . and mirrors for their subordinates,' I concluded. 'Clever.'

I looked down: here and there, meetings were being held; office workers were typing away, their eyes intent on their screens; a waiter was pouring coffee; a weary secretary had kicked off her high heels and was scratching the sole of her foot. On the level below that were more identical meeting rooms and offices and their occupants, and below that another, and another, until they were lost from sight in the depths.

'There's a certain loss of clarity,' I pointed out.

'That's functional, of course. Wherever you stand, everything you can see below you or to the sides is under your command, and the clearer the image, the more direct that command is. Why do I need to see what's happening on the tenth floor when I can see the people who can see the people who can see what's happening on the tenth floor? Directly or indirectly, the boss's eyes are everywhere.'

'Wouldn't it have been cheaper to install television cameras?'

He smiled, and I realised it was just the kind of question he'd been expecting.

'You're confusing hierarchy with surveillance. There are cameras everywhere, but they're only for effective control. They haven't been with us very long.' I looked left and right until I realised by 'us' he meant the human race. 'Mirrors, on the other hand . . . They've had millennia to infiltrate our souls. They're primitive, elemental . . . Their power isn't delegated. A camera can generate discomfort, fear perhaps; but not terror. Mirrors can, and do. The more so when you know there's always someone behind them, behind what you see in them. The master looking at us through our own eyes.'

'Except up here.'

'I am the lord of the mirrors,' he said flatly. But what about that little annex his bodyguard was watching us from? I didn't dare ask, so I tried something more trivial.

'Who did your son kill?'

He looked at me in amazement as if I'd just landed in his lobster thermidor and was lying there buzzing away to myself.

'Eh?'

'Your s-s-son,' I stammered. 'You said he'd committed a murder. Who was the fortu— I mean . . . unfortunate soul?'

'What's that got to do with anything?'

'Um . . .' At first I'd thought the question was fairly logical, but now he made me wonder. 'I thought it might help me to find the witnesses, to . . . Perhaps your son's name isn't in the files, sometimes when it's someone influential they use codes, and it'll be easier to trace the dead man,' I blurted in conclusion, congratulating myself mentally on my cleverness. But he didn't look impressed. He tutted once.

'Nobody knows who it was. My son's natural perversion led him to commit the crime in front of all those people,' he said, pointing at the nearby windows of the other tower. 'There's no point looking in the police records. They don't know who it was either. That, among other things, has allowed me to delay the investigation. But the body could come back to us any day now: swollen like a dead seal with river water, or half-decomposed in the garbage churned up by the bulldozers, but with those tell-tale cuts on its face and its broken bones and its organs ruptured from the fall. And then there are the anonymous letters, of course.'

He held out a sheet of paper. I took it. It was a piece of continuous feed, and the only thing on it was a short poem printed in the middle.

> *Give me a map, then let me see how much*
> *Is left for me to conquer all the world,*
> *That these, my boys, may finish all my wants.*

'The blackmailer – or blackmailers – left it on my desk. It isn't the first. It appears to come from some poem or other, but my people haven't been able to trace the author. They're not exactly literary types, for sure.'

'What makes you think it's a blackmailer?'

'Who else would leave a poem on my desk? I found it under my acrylic prism the morning after the crime. Whether they have access to the body or not, whoever wrote it clearly thinks they know enough to intimidate me. My people are already on the case: maybe, as well as neutralising the threat, they'll find a clue that leads to the dead man. My son maintains that he came in with him from the street and that it never occurred to him to ask him his name. None of the witnesses, it seems, managed to get a clear view of him. Apparently he went through the glass backwards: a man, a well-dressed man, that's all they can tell us. The strangest thing is that, when security arrived on the scene, the body wasn't there anymore. Get the picture? Someone was waiting for him and took the body. Anyway, identity aside, you won't win any prizes for guessing he was a fucking homo.'

'Oh,' I remarked, wondering where I'd missed the clue.

'Like my son,' he went on. 'Must have brought him up here to get buggered. Likes doing it in my office for some reason. One night I came back up and found him dressed as a Mambo Queen. Something to do with humiliation, I suppose: it's always more intense at the top. Masochists have always been a mystery to me, one I never tire of exploring.'

Something about Sr Tamerlán's appearance, barely perceptible at first, had changed. His eyes had turned inwards, as if they'd find more pleasing images there than in the world outside. His jaw had slackened slightly, his fleshy tortoise tongue protruded from between his horny lips, a constant ripple ran through his limbs. With a dreamy tremor in his voice, he said:

'If you want to talk to him I can call him. There he is.'

My eyes followed the line of his pointing finger. In the adjacent office was a young man, clearly unable to see us, standing staring in our direction, the way blind men do when they sense someone's presence. I nodded, knowing it was what was expected of me.

'César, I want you to come in here right away.'

Sr Tamerlán had taken a folded piece of silver foil out of his drawer and, opening it, tipped its contents out onto the glass desk-top. I hoped I'd have better luck than with the cigars, but no. With a single swipe of his Zen rake he combed the gram of gleaming, crystalline, snow-white cocaine into four perfect lines and hoovered them up through a gold tube into his greedy membranes, which were practically hanging out of his nostrils in their haste. A loudspeaker spoke.

'Leave me alone, I'm busy,' was all it said, too late to halt the careering Sr Tamerlán, who, riding-crop in hand, charged at the wall, which slid aside a split second before he went through it. He'd divested himself of his lovely opaline silk shirt, which had slid from his shoulders to the floor like a waterfall; I wondered if I should pick it up. I decided to stay where I was and mop up any stray crumbs left on the desk with a moistened fingertip. The intercom was still on, so, invisible in my front-row seat, I settled down to enjoy the show.

Sr Tamerlán's son had climbed up onto his desk and, jumping up and down like a spooked chimpanzee, was doing his best to dodge the lashes his father was aiming at his shins.

'That is the limit,' he screamed, climbing the peaks of his snow-capped frenzy, 'Here I am trying to save your eight-lane arse and this is how you thank me!' he bellowed as he flogged César's buttocks. 'Get those pants down, boy!'

César leaped off the desk and made a headlong dash for the door, but his father was too quick for him and locked it with a few taps of the keys. Panting and smiling, he advanced upon his son. They sized each other up, circling each other – a choreography of duelling gauchos.

'Daddy, please,' murmured the son. 'Not here,' he begged, but this only intensified his father's agitation.

'On your knees!' he yelled in a strangled voice. 'I'll teach you to bring perverts into my office! You're going to be riddled with AIDS before you give me a healthy grandson! You know you've got a year! Otherwise I'll milk you myself and inseminate some bitch, and you can sing for your inheritance! You'd like that, wouldn't you!'

'Daddy, I don't deserve . . .'

'Shut up! Your brother was the one who deserved things here! You . . .' He made as if to spit. Then he pointed straight at me and I jumped in fright. 'You'd like to be in there one day, wouldn't you. You know what you have to do then.'

Biting his lips and fighting back the tears, the son went down on all fours and undid his belt buckle with uncontrollably trembling hands. With one tug his father impatiently pulled his trousers down to his knees.

'You' – thwack – 'play silly buggers' – thwack – 'and then' – thwack – 'Daddy has to come and save your arse, doesn't he. Tell me what happened! Tell me what you were doing in there, you and that pervert! You always have been a big nancy!'

Unable to contain himself, he unfastened his own trousers and, grasping his son by the hips to adjust his position slightly, mounted him as if he were a bitch on heat.

'Stop clenching, damn you, stop clenching!' His breathing was laboured and he began each sentence with a pant, his tongue protruding between his teeth, making him lisp faintly. 'It isn't enough, is it. It isn't enough!' he screamed in his ear, and his son replied by gritting his teeth and shaking his head from side to side the way a female tortoise does when penetrated by the male. 'As if shoving it into that sewer of your mother's every night wasn't enough, drugged to the eyeballs so I could bear it, only for you to pop out! As if squeezing my testicles into that bottomless barrel till they looked like two raisins wasn't enough! You're still you! God damn you, you're still you!' Possessed with a ferocity, he clutched his son's flowing locks and began to advance on his knees, forcing his mount to crawl, foaming at the mouth, across the glass floor. 'You never go where I tell you to, you're always pulling against the reins, subtly deviating! What a humiliating joke! Genetics! Genetics isn't enough! There's a lot more to cram in here! A lot more! Who, for fuck's sake, is content with smiles and eye colours! And sometimes not even that comes out right! You stupid cook,' – heave – 'learn to mix' – heave – 'the ingredients' – heave – 'properly!'

His son tried to unsaddle him by crawling under the desk, perhaps in the hope that the edge would catch him in the forehead like a cowboy on horseback in a western. He caracoled and his father, a hero on an equestrian statue, raised one hand in the air and roared, 'I'll refound you as often as it takes! I don't give a damn what the doctors say, they've already failed me once! I'm going to conceive you again and again until I get you right!'

Something strange had begun to happen to my eyes. Perhaps they'd been under too much strain since I'd taken my first step into this mirror-world, and had relinquished their grip on reality, which was now melting and dissolving before them. Sr Tamerlán's fingers grew like roots and sank into his son's flesh; black bubbles gurgled and burst forth from the wounds, popping in the swampy air; his son's clawed at the carpet in paroxysm, gouging out furrows down to the glass, and through it they could see their shared empire glittering like a cut diamond with more facets than the sky has stars. The window panes all around me had begun to ooze and drip like molten glass; the computers and other appliances melted like vanilla ice cream into pools of bubbling plastic; the land-scapes in the pictures poured out of their frames like water from a broken fish tank; the very beams that supported the thirty floors I was standing on bowed and buckled like the legs of a reeling drunk. Sailing over the general viscousness, the two bodies had lost their original human shape and were now expanding and contracting like exposed organs in a vivisection, swelling transparent to bursting point one moment and collapsing into voided, crumpled bags the next, and, like decomposition in time-lapse, they quickly mingled and merged. And no sooner had they melted than they began to boil, shuddering like thickening stew, spouting furious geysers of steam, which gradually invaded the whole room, making the events inside quite invisible. The lights went out as at the end of a performance. I closed my eyes for a few seconds and felt a terrible itching, as if all my eyelashes had turned inwards.

When I opened them, the gun-toting psychoanalyst was at my side, smiling like a dog trainer on a field day whose pets have just made him look good.

'Nice trick, but I still think you can't beat pulling rabbits out of hats,' I remarked.

'You've had a rare privilege. An Annunciation.'

'Oh. They don't go through all that for all their visitors?'

'If you knew how to look, you'd have seen a great comet passing through the firmament, heralding the dawn of a new age.'

'Do you think it's wise?' I asked. 'A lot of people are going to find it hard to stomach.'

'The gates to the castle of the mind will only open for the chosen ones,' he announced. 'The Viennese doctor was wrong to try to keep the powerful forces of the unconscious under lock and key. In the course of evolution it is the destiny of the unconscious to become real, to step out into the world and go wherever it pleases. It's what we became rational for. That's what he couldn't read in Greek tragedy. Look what he bequeathed us as the keystone of Western consciousness: not the hero, but the wimp.'

'Let's see if we understand each other. You're suggesting that what Œdipus should have done instead of plucking out his eyes was to say to the people of Thebes, "Sure, I fucked my old lady. So what? If you've got a problem with that, I'll fuck you too."'

He answered coldly, as impervious to irony as the printed circuits of a computer.

'The interest of that myth is merely human. As human as the psychoanalyst who invented it.'

'And what's your interest?'

'I thought you'd realised,' he said evenly, staring at me impassively through the concentric spirals of his milk-bottle bottoms. 'Sr Tamerlán is the superman.'

* * *

Back at ground level, I was curious to visit the spot where the body would have hit the ground, but to get there I had to run the gauntlet of the mind-bending central canyon. From a distance I could have sworn that, stretching out both arms, I could touch the sides, but it turned out to be just another optical illusion: standing halfway between the towers I realised they were much wider apart – a good five metres at least. I couldn't stay there for more than a few seconds: they generated a force-field between them, as if someone were driving two powerful magnets as close together as possible; it was an unpleasant feeling like seasickness, and to make matters worse, when I reached the other end of the canyon I was hit on the head by an empty detergent bottle. Furious, I spun round to see where it had come from: emerging from a stiffened sleeve, a leathery hand covered in blackened wrinkles poked out from round the next corner and beckoned to me with a worm-like wiggle of its hooked finger. By the time I got there, it had disappeared, only to reappear a few metres further on and vanish again. I pursued the elusive reflection – a hand, the flapping heel of a boot, the tip of a yellow-and-grey beard – until I reached the tower's east face, as smooth as the surface of a frozen lake standing on end. But whoever it was I was pursuing had vanished as if they'd fallen into it. Curiouser and curiouser! I lit a cigarette. White against the tower's golden skies, a flock of egrets sailed across the sheer grid of video-wall, bound for the reflected marsh-lands of the Ecological Reserve. Only when I looked down from the living frieze encircling the heights did I see it: poised on a mosaic of recently planted sods (this must have been the spot) by the tower's marble base was a broken supermarket trolley, from which rose a pretty good likeness of the golden tower, in-geniously hashed together out of corrugated cardboard, thick wire, tin cans, tin foil, polystyrene containers, drinks cartons and plastic bags. It was less perfect, of course, than the model in Tamerlán's office, but friendlier and softer, probably because its flimsiness reminded me of the ones we used to build at school, of the first foundation of Buenos Aires, the Cabildo or the Casa de Tucumán; but I had trouble getting a close-up view of it because it receded as I advanced. For a moment I thought it might be remote-controlled, but then I spotted the mangled shoes among the four wheels of the trolley, shuffling along as if their laces were tied together. I sprinted after them, grabbed the trolley by the handle and wheeled it around as if heading for the checkout.

'I can see *you* but you can't see *me!*' said a voice from inside the tower.

Peering into two of the windows I discovered that, while they looked at first glance as if they were made of sweet wrappers like the rest, they were in fact made of cellophane. Two eyes peered back at me in fright, blurry through misted breath. I lifted up the trolley in both hands, tower and all, removing it from him like a hat. In the middle of the grass, looking as disconcerted as a hermit crab out of its shell, stood a profusely bearded tramp with drooping lower lip and bloated body, cowering beneath his dirt-caked jacket. He pointed to somewhere behind me, his eyes gleaming, so I turned round and saw our reflection.

'There's no getting back from the other side!' he exclaimed.

I tried to approach him, but he wheeled the trolley between us.

'Why?' I asked.

He put his finger to his lips like a nurse on a hospital poster and, looking around him, bared two rows of peg-like teeth that reminded me of the corn on a well-gnawed cob. Then he whistled.

'The way up's the same as the way down,' he said, and opened his eyes wide in panic. A white cloud enveloped us and, when it began to disperse, I could see him in the distance, manœuvring his trolley and its teetering tower across the lawn, making a break for the nearest stack of containers. Standing beside me was a man in a red uniform with a still-smoking fire extinguisher hanging from one hand.

'Been bumming around here for two or three weeks, he has,' he remarked. 'They never used to leave their caves before. We tried to winkle him out a few days ago, but the containers are all interconnected and he moves through them like a mole. Should get them fumigated,' he said, lowering his gun, and immediately vanished into a side door, which, when it closed, was just another piece in the wall of mirrors.

Chapter 2

THE CORDOBESE ARMADILLO

Back at home I tossed the first ten-thousand-dollar wad onto the bed, where it bounced with the unbeatable elasticity of nice, crisp notes, and after taking a deep breath I dialled the number on which the whole deal hung.

'Hullo,' I said when someone answered. 'I'd like to talk to Lieutenant Colonel Verraco.'

I heard the familiar chuck-chuck of the bugged phone line. Years of ripping off the phone company had sharpened my ears, a talent shared by all us night-hunters. The operator at the other end took a few seconds to connect the tape-recorder, a couple of breaths to give the trackers a head start, and then said commandingly:

'Identification.'

'Private Felipe Félix, Class of Sixty-Two, Regiment Seven, Company B, posted in La Plata, Puerto Argentino and Mount Longdon,' I reeled off in a single breath.

'Please hold,' he said, and a muzak version of 'The Peronist March' popped up over the line. I waited about ninety seconds (they'd obviously put a rookie on me: they cut their teeth tracing trivial calls) and a doleful voice crept into my ear.

'Who is speaking?' it lowed.

'Conscript Private, Class of Sixty-Two, Felipe Félix, Regiment Seven . . .' I reeled off the litany, but was cut off by a muffled snigger, and the elevator music came on again. I was about to hang up and start again when Verraco answered.

'Argentina's by the year 2000!' he said instead of 'hello', which threw me for a second, until I realised he was talking about the Islands.

'Argentina's, sir, Lieutenant Colonel, sir. Private Felipe Félix reporting for duty, sir.'

'Been a while since we heard from you, Félix. You haven't even been coming to the reunions. What can your old Commander do for you? Shove off, hop it, he's a friend,' he suddenly yelled at some obscure cranny of the telephone network in a different voice. 'Go and practise some shooting if you've got nothing better to do!'

'Wondering if you were still interested in the video game, sir,' I began, and in five minutes I had the whole thing wrapped up. Years ago Verraco had come and asked me to design him a video game of the Malvinas War to be installed in his offices in the new SIDE building. He hadn't had much luck with promotion after the war until somehow he managed to wangle his way into Intelligence. He now had the clout to call the shots and the time to spend on his big hobby: winning the war he'd lost. He'd been luring me into designing the game with special favours – getting the police off my back like fleas off a dog for one thing; it was to be the envy and admiration of his colleagues and would add to his standing in the demanding ex-combatant community. By delivering the game I'd repay these favours and make him a happy man, and I'd also be able to walk right into the impregnable edifice of the State Intelligence Secretariat, sit down in an office specially put aside for me and, while *personally* installing the video game (my condition), I could quietly run through their files and take whatever I needed. A hundred thousand dollars, like falling off a log, I told myself, and moved on to the next level.

Kevin was surprised when I called. I usually sent him an e-mail telling him to call me, because it's easier to phreak from the US.

'Hullo, Kevin. Am I interrupting?' I said to him in English.

'I was working on *Reptiles*,' he answered.

'What's it like?' I asked him.

'Get a load of this. You have to manœuvre a lizard through landscapes constantly shifting between two and three dimensions, and choose your best options as you go. If you put your 2D lizard in a 3D landscape, it can slide under a door or survive a steamroller, but it can't go up stairs; likewise, a 3D lizard can avoid being captured in a photo or dragged along by the wind like a dead leaf or interlocked in an infinite mosaic of identical lizards, but will splat against a flat landscape like a bluebottle against a windscreen,' Kevin explained to me excitedly, clearly still in the throes of his Escher period. His passion was for counterfactual worlds where everything was contrary to experience or indeed reason: objects stood out sharply in the dark and disappeared in the light; it was possible to walk on air and fall through cement; a sudden gesture would break down into more and more detailed planes without ever being completed, and hurrying would only increase the distance to be covered; the lightest brush, on the other hand, could knock down whole buildings if you weren't quick enough to make it violent. An egg could be concave outside and convex inside, containing the universe on its surface; cubes with different-sized faces, labyrinths that led you straight to your goal and straight lines that forced you into interminable detours were the norm. Empty space was as dense as mercury, yet you could grasp interstices with your hand; the faintest of shadows inevitably crushed anyone approaching them, and the densest of bodies could be traversed like early-morning drizzle. Kevin's games deployed a succession of worlds created according to incompatible rules that altered as soon as you got the hang of them, and you had to have quick reflexes and a mind capable of processing mountains of information to survive such extreme shifts. His ultimate goal was to design virtual worlds that could be *inhabited*.

'This is *real* anarchism, buddy,' he told me. 'Anyone can dream of changing the laws of society, but the laws of reality . . . well now, that's a whole different ball game! Don't you think it's a criminal waste what simulators do? Corporations want to restrict their use to imitating the real world, when they know perfectly well they were invented to replace it. We're ready for a new existence outside time, outside the body, and they want to keep us prisoners in here! When personal virtual reality exists, we'll all be able to live in any world we like and write its laws. Only then will we be free!' he concluded and fell silent, perhaps anticipating the kind of canned applause you'd expect from a cheesy US sitcom.

'What is it?' I asked him, envying the altered state he was in.

'Piracetam and choline. What are you calling for?'

I gave him a general picture of the situation and a more detailed idea of my plan, including specs.

'So I have to have an almost perfect video game in three days max. Any ideas?'

'Breaking the codes to any war game's gonna take forever; you know how well protected they are,' he said discouragingly. 'But I think I have what you need. Sega are bringing out a series of DIY video games and they're kicking off with a war game. They're apparently based on military intelligence programs, with all those guys here in California who lost their jobs after the Cold War . . .'

'I want that!' I said, unable to believe my luck. 'That one!'

'They haven't finished it yet. It's supposed to be a total secret. Cloning it won't be easy.'

'How much.'

'Five grand now, five grand later. Cash.'

'Make sure you write a counterfactual world where you don't need money to get things,' I snarled after agreeing to his terms, and I could hear the electric sparks of his laughter before he answered 'What would be the point of writing them then?' and hung up. Ah well, Tamerlán had promised to take care of the eckies.

It might be a while before the game arrived and in the meantime there was something else I needed to do before I got down to work, but I had to move fast if I wanted it by today. I got out of my smart interview clothes and, munching on a swiftly microwaved sausage and half a boiled egg, I donned my war veteran's uniform from the Malvinas campaign, which I'd bought a few years after getting back in the subway at the junction of Avenida 9 de Julio and Corrientes (I never learned the fate of the one I wore over there). The subway-stall owner was one of us and always managed to find some that were virtually identical. I threw on a long overcoat to cover it on my way to the Association and stepped out into the cold of the small hours.

* * *

The offices of the Argentinian Viceregal Association occupy two rooms on the third floor of an early twentieth-century building on Calle 25 de Mayo. You reach the first floor of business offices via a long, curved marble staircase; from there you go up some more-conventional straight stairs to the second floor; the ascent to the third floor is made by negotiating the loose, uneven boards of a little winding wooden staircase that leads on all the way up to the roof. The Association was originally founded with the aim of restoring Argentina's national borders to the historical boundaries of the Viceroyalty of the River Plate (for which it proposes, among other things, the reconquest of Bolivia, Paraguay and Uruguay, and the invasion of Chile and Brazil), but had gone into serious decline in these rather unepical early '90s, and, to finance its minimal costs, it runs courses on national history, national politics, national folklore, national music and any other discipline they can slap the adjective on. They have an agreement with ex-combatants whereby we're given free courses (certificates and all), and everyone from the group was taking them for the third time around, except me.

As I snuck in, trying not to be noticed, Prof. Citatorio, who single-handedly taught all the courses, had got to the bit about the Serpent's progress around the Mediterranean, from which I deduced that it wouldn't be long before he'd be finished. I waved at Ignacio, and tried to attract Sergio and Tomás's attention, but they were so busy whispering that all I got was a furious glare from the Professor, so I sat down by the door to avoid making things worse, while he picked up the thread of his disquisition.

'The Serpent was born in Palestine in the year 909 before Christ, and its cradle was the Temple of Solomon, although some scholars quite rightly trace its origins back to the Serpent that tempted Woman with the First Sin and brought about our Fall. There, with that patience typical of the Landless Race, it grew fatter and stronger until it was ready to strike out. Far from being the result of persecution, as they would have us believe, the Diaspora was the signal for Hebrew armies to embark on their conquest of the world. The Serpent accomplished its first stage in Greece in the year 429 before Christ, where, with the help of traitors like Pericles, it managed to impose democracy in order to undermine the foundations of the cradle of our civilisation. The second stage . . .'

He was interrupted by some voices at the back. Two veterans in naval uniform were arguing, elbowing each other and hissing emphatically as if trying to put themselves in the Serpent's shoes and guess what its next steps would be.

'I said A-7. Hit and destroyed! I win!'

'E-7! It wasn't A-7, it was E-7! And it's a miss! E-7!'

Ignacio had mentioned to me that a lot of Navy types had been showing up of late. Despite never having set foot on the Islands, they'd pushed for honorary ex-combatant status and were now entitled, after a split vote, to bask in our dubious glory and reap its paltry rewards.

'Perhaps the two of you can give us a better idea of this second stage than I can,' Citatorio shrilled at them, like a secondary-school teacher emphasising – as if it needed emphasis – the fact that he was being ironic.

41

'Err . . . dunno. Villa Kreplaj?' said the self-proclaimed winner, triggering general mirth.

'No, sir,' Citatorio hastened to add. 'The Rome of Augustus.'

'Augustus who?' asked a Correntino from R12 whom I knew by sight.

'The only one in Rome, sir. How many others do you know?' He cleared his throat and soldiered on: 'After murdering Our Lord Jesus Christ, who was the first to see the danger and rise up against it, it crawled across the Mediterranean to Spain, where, in the year 1522, it swallowed the empire of Charles V whole.'

'What did they get up to in the meantime? I mean, it's a thousand five hundred years between the two,' asked the Correntino, who'd been writing everything down in his notebook.

'I don't know. You tell me. They sold cloth. I've told you they're patient. Anyway, after that the Serpent marched on in leaps and bounds. Paris in 1796, London in 1814, Berlin in 1871, Russia in 1905 and, of course, in 1917. Wherever a great empire teeters on the brink, you'll see the bald helmet of the Circumcised Serpent peeping out of the rubble. Kiev, Odessa and Constantinople were the last stages before reaching its goal, Jerusalem, and completing its journey, joining its head with its tail to forge the Mystic Ring that will keep Europe under its yoke for ever: the Ouroboros, the Eternal Serpent without beginning or end. And they nearly succeeded!'

This was the cue for the bit about Hitler and how he'd severed with the sword the knot no one could undo, unselfishly laying down his own life and those of millions of Germans to save the world. But, like the Hydra, when you cut off one head, the Serpent sprouts two, and so, pre-emptively, it had forked off to America. I seized the opportunity when he turned round to change maps, and went and sat next to Ignacio.

'Don't you get tired of listening to the same old shite all the time?' I whispered in his ear.

'There's a roll call, you know. Besides, Sergio and Tomás have got something up their sleeves for today,' he said, giggling behind his closed fingers. 'Can't say anything. So what are you doing here?'

'I came to look for you. I need to see the model. I'm making the video game.'

'No! For Verraco?'

I nodded. I was about to explain, when Ignacio nudged me.

'Shhh. He's watching us.'

Professor Citatorio glared at us for a few seconds over the top of his glasses and ploughed on.

'The report that the first Jew arrived in America on the ships of Christopher Columbus is not without foundation. And it was this Jew that incited the previously docile sailors to mutiny. Soon they were swarming all over the place, instilling hatred of the Spaniard and our Church in the natives. Haven't you ever wondered why Spain, which had the vastest empire and the greatest reserves of gold and silver ever discovered, had ended up poor and backward four hundred years later? By the proximity of the Hebrew will ye know the location of the gold!' He always worked himself into a lather when he got to this bit, the colour rising in his cheeks, and would even start waving his goblin hands in the air. 'They were responsible for the failure of our city's first foundation, speculating with the provisions until everyone died of hunger! The first two English Invasions of Buenos Aires were financed by the moneyed

Jews of London with the complicity of our local tribe. Why do you think Viceroy Sobremonte seized his chance and fled to Córdoba with the Viceregal jewels? His real name was Sobremonski – a false convert if ever there was one! And what became of the treasure?'

I especially liked this bit about Sobremonte. I'd never heard it before. The old codger sometimes managed to pull an ace from his sleeve and surprise you for a few seconds. Satisfied with the effect he'd created, he launched into the more theoretical part of his tirade.

'Examined from any other perspective, history appears to us as a series of apparently sporadic and spontaneous events; but viewed in this light it acquires another dimension, one that reveals the intelligence hiding behind the *apparent* events and leaders. There are those who doubt the authenticity of the *Protocols of the Elders of Zion* and the Andinia Plan. We must answer them in the words of our own Hugo Wast: "The *Protocols* may be fakes . . . but they have been amazingly fulfilled."'

In an attempt at theatricality he tore aside the map of the Americas to reveal one of Patagonia and the Malvinas Islands below it, but, getting carried away, he went sprawling on the floor enveloped in both. The whole class hee-hawed helplessly as he struggled there, wrapped in the arms of history.

'Zionist Saboteurs,' he muttered as he picked himself up and put the new map back in its place. We all knew it by heart: a swarm of Stars of David marking the location of the enemy-occupied towns in Patagonia and the Islands, a quiver of missiles tracing their arcs north from them and selected Chilean cities, straight for what remained of the Argentinian Republic.

'Thirty years later, repulsed on the mainland by the

heroic resistance of our forebears, the English got a foothold on our beloved Austral Isles. The expedition was financed by Jewish bankers, the same ones that would later launch hordes of immigrants against us, ready to drown the very roots of our nationality in their blood. Jewish Gauchos! The ultimate bad joke! But in 1920 many people were laughing on the other side of their faces. In the clear light of day, under the sun of our immense southern skies, the enemy, with the aid of the traitor Chile and perfidious Albion, attempted to seize our Patagonia and found the New Jerusalem there. But they weren't reckoning on our army of Patriots! We drove them out in 1806, and in 1920 . . . and again in '82!' he shouted, pulling out his trump card. 'Ten years ago we achieved the full liberation of our national territory for the first time in our history! Never have they been so far from fulfilling their objectives as they were then.'

Some people got to their feet. They'd only come to savour this moment.

'Our Islands! Our beloved Islands! The Serpent that stretches the length of the Andes tried to lay its eggs on our shores, but they smashed on the hard surface of the ocean!'

'What *is* he on about?' I asked Ignacio.

'He's got this theory that at the start of '82 the English were withdrawing from Malvinas so they could be populated by Chilean and Israeli settlers. The first stage of the Andinia Plan. They'd then invade us on two fronts. According to him, foiling the Andinia Plan meant we actually *won* the war.'

'Wonders will never cease.'

'Well . . . if you look at the map of Chile, it does actually look like a snake. Look, Tierra del Fuego's the tail. It laid its eggs in the Atlantic after the Chileans took the Beagle Channel off us. And you're not going to tell me the Islands don't look like two splatted eggs.'

It sounded ridiculous, but it did have a certain logic to it. And it was more interesting than the dry theories of historians.

'Two eggs, yes!' exclaimed Citatorio, and everyone settled down for the juiciest part of his routine. He began stomping about the classroom cowboy-fashion, with legs akimbo and fist clenched on groin. 'Argentina is an erect prick ready to breed, and the Malvinas, its balls. When we recover them, fertility shall return to our lands and we shall become the great nation our founding fathers once dreamed of! A potent country! Our wheat shall flower anew, and our cattle shall ply our oceans of grass; our trains shall run laden with the produce of the land to every corner of the country. Buenos Aires shall be the New Paris, the envy of all the cities of the globe. The Argentine name of the Argentinians shall ring pristine in the ears of the world with peals of wealth and progress! From our recovered Islands an Argentinian sun of unimaginable grandeur shall mark the birth of the day on which the former colony becomes the world power we all long for!'

At that moment someone turned the lights out. Some asked what was going on; others, forewarned, started up a sombre psalmody.

'An attack! Enemy commandos!' came Citatorio's voice in the darkness.

A torch came on, lighting a sinister face from below: black, broad-brimmed hat, hooked plastic nose, black beard that was lost in the dark, and long, dangling side-curls. Tomás had certainly done his homework.

'Oooh . . . I'm the Wandering Jew,' he wailed.

'The Kingdom of the Serpent!' squawked Citatorio. 'The Coming of the Antichrist!'

No one could hold themselves back any more, and the flood of cackles sent people rolling about on the floor among the chairs. Tomás took out a kitchen knife and made it glint in the torchlight.

'Ernesto, our prodigal son. Come with me to the synagogue. Jehovah claims that part of you that belongs to him.'

The shaft of light fell on Citatorio, who, foaming at the mouth, was chasing round and round on all fours, faster and faster, like a dog after its tail, perhaps in the belief that he was aping the Serpent and thereby acquiring the strength to fight it.

'There's no escape,' he hawked from the floor. 'Everything's run by Jews, everything's always been run by Jews! The economy, governments, the press, culture . . . it's *all* Jews! Even anti-Semitism was invented by Jews! They pass themselves off as a persecuted race to escape actual persecution! Everywhere you look there are Jews! Even *we* are Jews: they left us uncircumcised to trick us about their numbers! There is *nothing* but Jews!'

I took advantage of the confusion and led Ignacio, still limp with laughter, by the arm out onto the street. He sat down on the narrow pavement of 25 de Mayo to get his breath back, while buses and taxis roared past in front of our noses, filling the humid air with thick, black fumes. The corroded mouldings of the buildings dripped with soot; long, brown smears ran down below the pigeons' nests in the niches; the sky had gone livid and cold. I looked at the hands on my watch, which moved faster and faster, infected by my anxiousness.

'The model,' I told him.

'Right. Wait, I can't even walk.' He went on laughing a bit longer. 'The model, right.'

But, before I could get him away, Sergio appeared, and then Tomás, gripping the hair-slides he'd used to attach the curls to his head in a clenched smile. They decided to go to the bar to celebrate my return and catch *Titans* while we were there, so I couldn't say no.

We were served by Patán, our usual waiter.

'It's great to see you back again, Don Felipe,' he said, practically hugging me. 'What'll it be for our heroes today?' he asked, polishing the scratched tin of his flat tray until it gleamed.

'An R7 for me,' Tomás answered without a moment's thought, flexing a bare biceps and stroking the outline of the Islands on it. He'd been wounded in the arm by some shrapnel during the bombing of the airport and had had the Islands tattooed around the two star-shaped scars. He was so proud of his work that he'd taken to wearing sleeveless T-shirts, even in winter ('Cold? You're asking me if I feel cold? I'll tell you what real cold is. The two months we spent in those trenches ...') and had started doing weights to beef them up.

'You were great!' Sergio still hadn't stopped laughing and was pounding his back with his fist. 'Citatorio's Oratorio!' he kept shouting, while at his side Ignacio laughed whenever required, copying every one of the others' gestures a split second later, like some mirror with a delay mechanism. It could be hours before I got him out of there.

'Poor old Citatorio, we're always picking on him,' said Tomás, all of a sudden reflective. 'But you've got to admit he's got a point. The other day he was telling us that after they take

Patagonia the Zionists plan to monopolise national food produc-
tion and use Antarctica as a gigantic natural freezer, while the
rest of the country, in the grip of hunger, lays itself at their feet.'

'Interesting,' I remarked. 'And they could always use the
Sandwich Islands as a bar.'

'We could get old Patán here a job,' said Sergio, shaking
him and making him spill the drinks he was carrying.

'It makes me mad to think we handed them to them
on a plate,' Tomás went on. 'We had them in our hands like
two tame doves and we let them get away. And all those little
crumbs in the sea,' he added, eating a few off the table. 'You
didn't come to the landing, did you?' he asked me, jogging my
whisky glass.

'Which one?' I coughed.

'The second of April, of course.'

'No. I didn't get there till the sixteenth,' I answered.
'Thought you knew.'

'Oh, we thought you were here,' he said, getting me even
more confused. 'It was fantastic. We hired like five boats in Pal-
ermo Park – at the little jetty, you know the one – and invaded
the island in the middle of the lake. You know, where couples
go to neck,' he clarified, and only then did I realise he hadn't
been talking about the landing in '82 but the mock one they'd
prepared to celebrate the tenth anniversary. 'Too bad there are
so many trees; looks more like Vietnam than Malvinas. We
planted the flag and did a bit of target practice. Then had a
lamb barbie,' he said, smacking his lips. 'You don't know what
you missed.'

Last 2nd April – the tenth anniversary of Argentina's recovery of the Islands – had been my longest marathon surfing

the Web, utterly immersed in utterly absorbing conversations with hackers in West Germany and Holland. I hadn't answered the door or the phone or turned on the television or set foot outside all day. And I knew it would catch up with me sooner or later.

'Yes.' I smiled at him, mentally muting the rest of the story and leaving Tomás to open and close his mouth in silence like a fish out of water.

'How's the tyre-repair business?' I asked him when I noticed he'd finished.

'Not good, man, not good. There are times I'd like to jack it all in and piss off to a desert island.'

'We already have,' I quipped.

'That's what I mean,' Sergio interjected. 'It was a mistake to invade Malvinas. If we'd invaded Aruba and Curaçao, we'd be sitting around drinking piña coladas now,' he said gazing wistfully into the bottom of his glass.

'Let's be realistic,' said Tomás. 'The logical thing would have been to invade Chile first. A real country, I dunno. Meet other people, another culture, know what I mean? Go out to bars, restaurants . . . Go dancing at the weekend. There are some really pretty Chilean girls.'

'And the fruit!' piped up Ignacio, who only ever did so when he was confident he wasn't contradicting anyone. 'Have you seen the fruit in Chile? The size of the peaches! And it's not frozen.'

'Yeah, right. Chile's something else,' I said.

'And anyway, we'd definitely beat them,' added Tomás.

'We missed a gilt-edged opportunity there. Thanks to that old meddler, the Pope,' Sergio concluded.

Sergio was passionate about alternative history. He pored over every event with an obsessive attention to detail, always looking for the knot that might have led to things turning out differently, always taking a different path from history's at every fork. It was easy to spot unsigned articles by him in the ex-combatants' magazine because seven out of every ten verbs were in the conditional. He claimed to be working on a book called *A Thousand Different Outcomes to the Malvinas War,* but he'd never shown a single page to anyone, perhaps fearing that, if he did, one ending or another would become fixed for ever. I'd never come across anything like that in the English bibliography on the Malvinas war . . . The winners, it seems, reach their destination believing they've walked a straight line to victory; it's us losers who are always left to fret over the multiple possibilities of history.

Tomás, on the other hand, proceeded in rigorously retrospective fashion, projecting the film of Malvinas in reverse so that everything would be back the way it was in the early days of the campaign. The ten thousand prisoners were released from the ships and pelted back to the Islands' capital, which they recaptured, pushing the English back, street by street, hill by hill, earth flying of its own accord to fill in the craters and repair the walls of the trenches, blood trickling back to the bodies of the wounded and the dead, who picked themselves up and returned to the fray, forcing the enemy to retreat to their ships and scuttle back to England arse first. Then all you had to do was stop the film to freeze the image one sunny day back in April 1982, when the Islands were ours again for ever and the enemy so distant that nobody really believed they existed. I glanced at Ignacio, who'd now started on about the landscape in the south of Chile without realising the rest of us had tired of the subject, and wondered how building his model had helped him to deal with the facts.

'Going to Hugo's birthday party on Saturday?' Tomás asked me suddenly as Patán brought over the second round.

I loathed Hugo, but, since everyone else worshipped him, I tried not to let it show. I loathed his razor-back buzz-cut and the way he talked at the top of his voice and the weapons that lined the walls of the dinky apartment, which the big fella still shared with his mum, and most of all I loathed the way he deliberately and obscenely thrust his stumps out over his wheel-chair whenever he held forth about the commandos' performance in the war, particularly if he spotted someone who wasn't nodding vigorously enough at his categorical assertions. I said yes I was, definitely.

'Besides, we've got something to celebrate.'

'The sinking of the *Sir Galahad*?' I asked innocently. As these months marked the tenth anniversary of everything, the list of things to celebrate was as long as your arm.

'No,' he said to me, pausing for dramatic effect. 'They've found some pages from the *Diaries of Major X*. You'll never guess which ones.'

'No,' I replied. It was my turn to play hard to get.

'The full text of the Legend of the Cordobese Armadillo. You can imagine our reaction,' Tomás went on. 'The only version we had till now was Emilio's and you know what that's like: you can't understand a word of it. We saw him not long ago when we went to visit Petete.'

'He's back in hospital again, isn't he?'

'Emilio? Never left.'

'Petete.'

'Oh. It's standard practice.' He finished his second and sat there staring through the whorls in his glass, training it around the bar like field-glasses. 'If you do anything weird, and I mean *anything*, it's off to the madhouse with you. You were in Malvinas.'

'What happened?'

'He'd apparently gone to the supermarket and the Korean at the till looked at him funny through those peepholes of eyes they've got, or asked him for something in Korean and Petete got it all wrong, nobody really knows, but anyway he dropped all his provisions and began backing away and pointing at him, shouting "Gurkha! Gurkha!" He ended up hiding behind the tinned-foods gondola, defending his position with cans of beer – he was even pulling the ring-pulls; he may be off his head but he never forgot his training – till the coppers came to take him away. He tried to explain to them that all the Koreans in Buenos Aires were actually Gurkhas in disguise preparing the third invasion and that they'd be sending commandos to silence him, but they carted him off anyway and kicked his sorry arse all the way to the Borda. It's easier to write him off as a madman. One day, when we have a Korean president and they paint the Pink House yellow, they'll remember. Didn't you hear what Citatorio said? The Koreans are one of the lost tribes of Israel. Haven't you noticed they're like the Jews in everything! They always do well in business, they're tight-fisted, they intermarry, they talk different so you can't understand what they're saying, they hire legitimate Argentinians to do the legwork . . .'

'Yellow Jews. I never thought of that.'

'Well, if there are Black Kikes . . .'

'The Gurkhas too, eh?' I muttered, tutting in disappointment. 'You can't trust anyone these days.'

'The guile of the Serpent knows no bounds.'

I'd only ever seen a few odd pages of the legendary *Diaries of Major X*, recounting the mythical commando leader's early days in Puerto Argentino; the new ones covered the first days of his stay on the Isla Gran Malvina, which we'd only had Emilio's account of up until now, the sole member of the 'phantom platoon' to make it back to the mainland and an irreplaceable witness – if it weren't for the bullet suspended in the jelly of his brain rendering anything he said quite unintelligible. In visit after endless visit before we finally gave up on him we salvaged vague and indecisive references to the unfathomable enigmas of the unexplored moorlands of the Isla Grande, supernatural apparitions, spectral battles and the story of a mysterious entity that started out as 'Conqueror Caterpillar' and subsequently fluctuated between 'Consular Chatter Pillow' and 'Cantonese Armoured Killer', before finally settling on the improbable but consensual 'Cordobese Armadillo'. Here, at long last, was its legend.

The story began in 1806 during the first English invasion of Buenos Aires, when Sobremonte fled to Córdoba with the Viceregal treasure and hid it inside a stuffed *Priodontes maximus* of gigantic proportions, got up in heraldic fashion: an armadillo rampant. Incapable of recovering the city by force himself, the Spanish Viceroy offered to bribe the invaders with the contents of the beast, which he'd secretly had sent to Buenos Aires. But the very day the English laid their greedy hands on the treasure, Captain Liniers's troops were landing at Quilmes and, with the aid of its valiant citizens, the city was recovered and the enemy captured. The treasure, however, had been stowed away and the ship carrying it soon made the windy waters of the River Plate. The vessel in question was the schooner *Fortune*, which, lacking the provisions and crew needed to undertake the long voyage to England, sailed instead to the first safe port of call: the Malvinas Islands.

At that point I began to read with greater attention:

The Islands being in the hands of their rightful owners at the time, the ship anchored in a cove of the less carefully guarded Gran Malvina, where they hoped to make contact with English whalers and seal hunters plying those desolate shores. But they found nothing more than mounds of whale-bones and patches of wet ash, and, exhausted from their gruelling voyage, they decided to go ashore and take on supplies. Faced with scant prospects of success, the wild cattle having been wiped out by the seal-traders, they decided that half the crew would try to reach as far as Brazil, while the rest would remain on the island to guard the treasure, which couldn't be risked on such a perilous voyage. Five men remained behind in the bay and survived all that summer on a diet of penguin eggs and oil, and the bitter flesh of gulls.

With the winter came scarcity of provisions, despair, ambition, and derangement. They had no way of knowing that the *Fortune* had sunk off the coast of Tierra del Fuego, but they must by then have begun to suspect it. The simple, unspoken conclusion must have passed through the minds of all: people will believe the treasure went down with the ship; nobody, save myself and the other four, is in possession of the truth. Two of them avoided a worse fate, inadvertently removing themselves from the scene: less enfeebled than the others by fever and scurvy, they set off one day along the shoreline in search of food and never came back.

The other three did not long endure. We know what happened to them from the diary kept by one of their party, a cabin boy barely sixteen years of age, who had never fully recovered from the burns he suffered in the retreat from Buenos Aires. He had become lost in its unfamiliar, identical-looking streets while fleeing from the boiling oil falling maddeningly from the rooftops, and wandered almost blind around the port for many hours slipping about in slicks of mud until he was picked up by one of the *Fortune*'s boats.

The party's last days were inconceivable: towards the end it seems they began to worship the bristly shadow of the rampant armadillo projected by the fire on the walls of the shelter, its raised claws reaching out towards them like those of the Devil himself, promising to each in turn that only the presence of the other two prevented it yielding up its treasure to him.

We can only speculate as to what happened next; the cabin boy must have stopped writing after he had killed the other two and fled on foot (on an island of all places!), dragging the heavy armadillo stuffed with gold. Guided by the survivors of the wreck of the *Fortune*, the members of the belated rescue expedition came across his remains only some two hundred metres inland. He had eventually eaten the jewels in a last-ditch effort to make the useless treasure his, and, poking their fingers between his ribs into the peat of his intestines, they recovered a few coins. For several days, they searched unsuccessfully for the rest of the treasure: in all probability, one of the Islands' wolf-like foxes had made off with the armadillo's hide and the jewels were lying at the bottom of its burrow somewhere. A long, well-organised search would clearly be needed to recover the armadillo and this could not be conducted in these conditions. And so it was that, thirty years later, the English invaded the Islands and drove out its rightful rulers.

I broke off from my reading to have a word with Sergio, who was on his fourth by now and speaking with furred tongue.

'Seen this? It says it was because of the armadillo that the English occupied the Islands in 1833.'

'Course,' he replied. 'Didn't you know?' There's no surprising some folk, I thought to myself, and went back to my reading.

But all attempts to recover it were in vain. The most significant one was contemporary with the invasion. In 1833 and again in 1834, an English ship, the *Beagle*, visited the Islands, allegedly to chart its coastline. On board was a young naturalist who would later become famous for very different reasons: Charles Darwin.

In his *Voyage of the Beagle*, there is a plethora of evidence, from allusions to his never-specified 'purpose', to his lively interest in the behaviour of the Falklands wolf-like fox (especially its habit of approaching human encampments to steal food). Omission is sometimes the soundest of proofs, and his detailed description of the eastern island only makes conspicuous the total absence of references to the western one, the true goal of his secret mission. The world doubtless has cause to lament his failure: the heinous and misanthropic theory of evolution would never have been formulated by a man upon whom fortune and riches had smiled.

Since then attempts to recover the treasure have been as frequent as they have been fruitless. Interest in it goes beyond the merely material: according to the legend, whoever recovers the armadillo and its contents will have a legitimate right over the Islands, and until that day the question of sovereignty cannot be settled. Like all legends, this last one has a ring of truth about it: according to calculations of its worth (a cargo of incalculable value just arrived from Peru was what sparked the invasion of 1806), the treasure alone would have been enough to tip the scales of the war in favour of its owner. The enemy's interest in the western island – of almost zero strategic value – only points to the veracity of this legend, as does the sophisticated equipment they use to 'detect mines' in areas that our troops had never even set foot in. If after more than a century and a half they have been unsuccessful, it is because the Almighty has ruled that the Cordobese armadillo and its treasure are destined to return to the hands of their rightful owners.

I handed the pages back to Tomás. There was an argument on the boil, but I had no idea what about: the five shots of Scotch were starting to kick in. The voices sounded more and more remote, and mingled with the wailing of wind in cliffs and the melancholy lapping of waves on pebble beaches. The terrain had become slightly undulating, and the advance was frequently hampered by rocky outcrops and hidden crevices.

Even so, I managed to reach the bathroom, the green pipes of whose urinal had calcareous outgrowths on them. Stalactites and stalagmites, I thought to myself. Another tourist attraction for Buenos Aires. When I got back to the table, which had drifted like an unmoored ship in my absence, Sergio was trying to explain to Ignacio, with the aid of a serviette, whose pitted surface perfectly mimicked the choppy waters of the Argentinian Sea, his specular theory about the war.

'They're identical, see?' he explained. 'The Isla Gran Malvina looks like the other one reflected in a mirror. It's the same, but in reverse, get it?' he yelled down his ear. 'If we'd invaded it instead of Isla Soledad, everything would have been exactly the other way round. It would be *our* flag that waved over the peat bogs now. The *Belgrano* would be proudly plying the southern seas. The Task Force would be an underwater scrap heap. We were pursuing a mirage: it was the other island that was the real thing. We mistook the reflection for its object. The name itself announces it: "*Great* Malvina". That should always have been our target! Major X always knew it.'

'Still out there fighting the English, is he?' I asked out of politeness. There was a gap between two chairs and I stretched my legs out between them to keep myself from sliding floorwards. For a moment I imagined it was the San Carlos Strait and tried to stand still and not disturb the waters too much. Better make this the last one.

'He swore never to return until he recovered them!' Tomás interrupted, awakening from a momentary slumber. 'The Isla Grande was never defeated. Menéndez only signed the surrender for the other one.'

'Any news?' I asked.

'In March they apparently captured a jeep loaded with explosives and ammunition. And they're holding two prisoners. English,' he added. 'Course we only hear rumours. No news agency – not even one of ours – would ever admit that there's an Argentinian platoon out there in the Islands, still fighting ten years on. And the silly Brits can't find them!' he laughed in delight.

'If only we had the complete diaries,' murmured Sergio, his mind roving free across boundless fields of supposition.

'Whoever gets hold of that diary,' Tomás now mumbled as he stared into space, 'will unearth the secret of the war. It holds the key to the future of the Islands, which is the future of Argentina. We have to prevent it falling into enemy hands at all costs.'

Ignacio was staring hard at the fraying shoelaces of his army-surplus boots, his lower lip drooping under the weight of four gins. It was as good a chance as any to try and get him to come with me.

'Ignacio!' I shouted in his ear. 'Ignacio! The model!'

'Nearly finished,' he answered automatically.

'No, we've got to get back before it gets too late.'

It was working. Worried by the thinly camouflaged threat in my innocent phrase, he made an effort to stand up.

'Are you off? It's only . . .' Sergio looked at the clock on the wall and exclaimed '*Titans of the Ring*! It's time for *Titans*! Patán, switch the telly on, will you!'

Patán reached up to the television and switched it on, while Ignacio sat back down and I saw the model recede into the distance as if from a toy plane that had just taken off from its runway.

We caught the end of the fight between The Mummy and

Don Quixote, and spent the adverts settling down for the one we were all looking forward to: the bout between the English para and the Argentinian conscript.

Whistled, booed and bombarded with plastic bottles, the Englishman made his entrance, roaring at the stadium: Union Jack T-shirt and hooligan mask, bowler hat, pint mug sloshing . . . He stomped about the ring like Godzilla, swiping at the air and laughing with anticipated pleasure on discovering how weedy his adversary looked, who stood with his feet planted firmly at the centre of the ring. The Englishman towered above him, perhaps in emulation of the English Tower, and beat the flag on his chest and bellowed, pointing at the little man with the defiant expression as much as to say that making mincemeat of him would be a walk in the park. When he saw that the other man didn't bat an eyelid, he roared and mocked some more, until the audience tired of him and shouted at him to just get on with it, let's see what you're made of. The Englishman's first clumsy drop kick was inevitably dodged by the Argentinian conscript with a nimble flick of the waist – a mere shimmy – and the Englishman went flying into the ropes and toppled out of the ring under his own momentum. 'Out, out, out,' yelled the ecstatic audience, 'we've thrown them out!' But the Englishman realises the wee man isn't such a pushover and, after squatting at the side of the ring, climbs back in toting an SRL rifle, and, paying little heed to the audience's horrified cries, starts pounding the defenceless Argentinian soldier with the butt; he eventually goes down on the canvas under the impassive gaze of American referee Bob Whitehouse, who starts the count as if nothing out of the ordinary were taking place. Seven . . . eight . . . and always, just before the count of ten, when the stadium's filled with howls of disapproval, comes the miracle. The Argentinian soldier, who looked to be unconscious, is suddenly flying through the air and landing with all his might on the Englishman's expression of bestial delight . . . Yes, it's the Argentinian commandos' famous secret flying kick: the Pucará Punt! To a man the stadium rises to its feet, the screams threatening to blow the distended dome off and into the night! The Englishman staggers and, before he recovers his balance, another drop kick, and another, until once again he topples out of the ring! The Yank tries to hold the soldier back to give the Englishman a fighting chance to recover, but the Argentinian starts laying into the referee and knocks *him* out of the ring too! Then he tears off the canvas and the Malvinas Islands appear, emblazoned on the floor beneath! One foot on each island, he raises his fists and proclaims himself the victor. The stadium erupts with happiness the way it does every week.

'So when do we get to see the video game?' Sergio asked when we were finished celebrating.

'Two or three days tops. The sooner I get to see the model, the better,' I said to Ignacio, who was miles away and went 'Eh?'

'The model.'

'Not much more to go, honest,' he said, thinking I was complaining.

'You've been telling us the same thing for ten years,' Tomás chipped in. 'And there's always more to go. We were supposed to be able to *use* it. That's why we've put up with you.'

Ignacio looked at him with the expression of a frightened child, then at Sergio and me, his head turning this way and that like a sparrow on the ground.

'You've got to be patient, lads,' he begged. 'It isn't ready yet.

I want it to be perfect for the great day. And there are so many details. I'm working on it at night too.' He began to calm down when he realised nobody was insisting, not so much because they were convinced, but because they'd heard it all before. 'It'll be better than the original, you'll see,' he concluded, smiling, realising he'd got away with it yet again.

* * *

His smile was the last thing I saw before the darkness of his cellar swallowed him up.

'Bulb's gone.' His voice reached me over the noise of his feet taking two steps at a time before I'd even dared to set foot on the first. I was still groping my way down along the peeling wall when I heard him reach the bottom and flick the switch, filling the enormous chamber with the light of a sudden dawn.

Sometimes when, after a sleepless night rocked by the constant shuddering of the bombs, we'd see the first blue light of day from the hill washing across the implacable sky and gratefully drop dead for a measly hour's sleep, we'd awaken later in the morning to see the same view that greeted me now, as if the ten intervening years had been just a passing dream of that brief hour of peace. Before my eyes, as I looked on from the top of the stairs, nestling between the smooth, stretched sheet of the bay and the semicircle of hills that surrounded it like plumped pillows, were dotted the two hundred-odd houses of the Islands' ephemeral and eternal capital, the town of Puerto Argentino, as it might have looked to a passing gull one quiet late-April morning, when there were still no craters, no gutted buildings with their insides on view, no torn-up trees heralding the arrival of history in the town.

'Whoa!' I exclaimed. 'It's exactly the same.'

Ignacio turned round and smiled. He'd gone red.

'Looking good, isn't it,' he said, gazing at it again, as if in its presence he were only allowed to take his eyes off it for a few brief seconds.

Descending the remaining stairs, I put my arm round his shoulder and once again we gazed upon it together. He'd reproduced the houses identically one by one, erecting walls of cardboard or glued matchsticks, painting them white or yellow, roofing them with aluminium from beer cans in blue, red or green. 'Corrugated,' he explained proudly, 'with a fork.' Between each garden – or rather, vegetable patch – he'd set up fences of foam rubber, which also grew in the tops of the town's few trees – the only ones on the island. I could easily recognise the two churches, the dance hall, the post office, the Governor's house . . . Tiny soldiers stood guard in defences camouflaged with gauze, dyed – as he eagerly pointed out – with coffee dregs and surrounded by snarls of wire knotted at regular intervals to simulate the barbs, or directed their still sceptical eyes at the virgin sky painted on the basement ceiling and walls, at the neat foxholes dug in the papier mâché hills, or from the snaking contour of the Avenida Ross and its three straight jetties to the calm, corrugated-nylon waters of the shipless bay. He'd managed to find jeeps and tanks and anti-aircraft cannon that looked almost identical to the originals, models of plastic or lead that he'd carefully hand-painted himself. A Lockheed Hercules, like the one that flew us to the Islands, was unloading military supplies at the southern tip of the airport, and on every hill, following either orders or routine, the conscripts were digging trenches: the Correntinos of R4 among the crags of Enriqueta and Dos Hermanas; the marine infantry on Tumbledown, William and Zapador; the R7 perched on the edges of Wireless Ridge and Longdon. It was just like being back in the Islands.

'Remember?' Ignacio said to me as he ran from one end to the other. 'This was where Diego got hit.'

'You've got the peat just right,' I said pointing to the open ground between the town and the rocky hillsides.

'Touch it,' he said to me with the smile of a proud father.

I touched it, and my finger sank in the soft terrain, the hollow immediately filling with brackish water.

'Ohh! It's just like the real thing! How did you do it?'

'Foam rubber, covered by a layer of soil and yerba maté. I spray it occasionally to keep it waterlogged. The yerba's for luck,' he winked at me. 'Says the land's one hundred per cent Argentinian.'

He ran beside me as I strolled around it, eagerly drawing my attention to any details I might have overlooked, pointing and gesticulating at every rock, every dry stream, every flock of sheep, every minefield. Ignacio wasn't built for generalities; everything was fiercely individual, every element had been created by his own hand and was unique and irreplaceable. 'Was that the shape of those rocks, the hotel windows, this corner?' he kept asking me and I kept repeating yes, yes, yes, as if it were possible to remember. No one, not even the Kelpers themselves, knew this area of the Islands better than he did. 'I'll be an invaluable aid when we go back,' he kept repeating while I committed the layout of the coastal defences, the approach roads to the town, the radar stations to memory. 'They'll have to put me in charge of strategy. We could bomb Stanley into the ground and rebuild Puerto Argentino from my model, with the added advantage that we'd get rid of all the changes it must have suffered over the last ten years. I've even put Kelpers, look.' All that differentiated the little figures were tiny daubs of red or yellow that stood out against the general olive green, but Kelpers they were. 'They'll be replaced by Argentinian settlers one day.'

At first we'd thought it was absurd that he should go to so much trouble to build something that would be razed to the ground in a mock battle in a single day, but he was so enthusiastic that we just let him get on with it. 'It'll be much better if you wait a bit, lads. What's the fun in doing it all in a rush like that?' he'd say, but by then it was obvious he was trying to buy time. His excuse was always the need to extend the model. 'What do you mean we aren't going to include Dos Hermanas, eh? They earned it R4 did.' The four walls of the cellar soon left him without an argument. He spent a couple of desperate months planning how to saw to pieces what he'd done so far and rebuild it somewhere with unlimited potential for territorial expansion, but everyone suspected that the project would be prolonged indefinitely that way, and no one gave him any support. 'Be realistic,' we told him. So then he tried another tack. Until then it had been a vague scheme, with cardboard boxes instead of houses, and plasticine vehicles: a three-dimensional model that was only of any use for replaying the war and reshuffling alternatives. His new undertaking was on a far vaster scale: he wanted to exactly reproduce every stone, every window, every fence, every participant; to capture, as in a high-res satellite photograph, every detail of that April morning when war was still a remote possibility, and hold up the perfection of his model as a lucky charm against its arrival. Ignacio had discovered quite intuitively that space is infinitely divisible and that, as long as you keep on dividing, you can make time stand still. There would always be some detail to add to the increasingly perfect reproduction of that eternal 30th April, and until that day reached its fruition, 1st May would have to wait. He became obsessive. He began to read book after book, to visit the houses of ex-combatants one by one asking them for photos or letters and grilling them for hours: 'So there were two cypresses here, this high? And this house's vegetable patch was well tended? What colour was the store sign?' He'd spend hours mixing pigments on a palette to get the exact tones; he rehearsed for weeks with filters and spotlights to achieve 'the precise effect of shadows and reflections created by the southern light at that time of day.' And when he suggested reproducing the houses' *interiors* through the cellophane windows, we had to threaten to cut off his funding. 'But what sense does it make to retake the town, lads, if it isn't the *same* one?' he'd argue, but we were adamant. 'Two more years waiting for you to touch up some fat Kelper bint on the crapper? You're losing yourself in the details, mate. Can't see the cunt for the pubes,' we'd reply. 'You don't understand, you don't understand,' he'd mutter, but I had begun to understand. He'd come to love his town so much that the real one had ceased to matter to him.

'If you'd give me unlimited funds and a team of men under my command,' he repeated now, resting his hands on the cruel edge reality had imposed on his world, 'I could go on to complete the whole island. It isn't like it was before: we've got maps, knowledge of the terrain . . . The other island would be child's play after that. I can make them so perfect nobody'd notice the difference. Can you imagine? We could open a Disney-style Malvinas World. And when they get started on the Malvinas war films, then they'll come knocking, you'll see.'

He looked at me with wide eyes and trembling smile, begging me not to destroy the dream in two words, perhaps hoping that after my visit I'd persuade the others of the need to wait as long as it would take. I imagine that at some stage, out of sheer desperation, he considered using the old ruse of undoing at night what he'd built during the day, but he must have realised how useless that would prove: it wasn't us he wanted to cheat, but time itself. The town, which had lasted just seventy-four days, would attain eternal life through him, and I was standing before someone who'd found a purpose in life and given himself to it body and soul, to the exclusion of all else, rejecting other realities as illusory, deaf to any voices but the ones that reached him from the shores of his promised land. It made me envious and I decided to get my own back.

'If you ask me, it's done,' I said.

He fell back on the creator's stock excuse.

'Maybe for you. You see it from the outside, you only go by appearances. But only I can tell when it's really finished.'

'And what will you do when we stop sending you funds?'

His face looked like someone had just twisted his arm, and his eyes filled with tears.

'You too, Felipe . . .?'

'You know there are people who've gone hungry to support you over this. But the idea was always to use it to plan the recovery. You're perverting a collective project for purely personal ends.'

It was as easy and risk-free as making a child suffer.

'How can you say that, Felipe?' he said tearfully. 'Look at us standing here together,' he said, pointing at the barricade of old tyres and the blue-and-white house where we'd sometimes had to stand guard. Alongside Ignacio and myself were Sergio and Tomás, and we were eating something apparently and drinking maté all together, chatting and having a good time, hoping upon hope that the conversation would never end, as if we knew what was in store for us. 'They just want to scare us. You'll see, everything'll sort itself out without a shot being fired,' Tomás would repeat to us, world without end, like a mantra against the first screams falling from the sky, and we'd nod, confident that the mere repetition of sounds would be enough to stop time and make his words come true.

'The tyres are good. How did you make them?'

He smiled proudly, wiping away a tear on his sleeve.

'Polo mints and dirty fingers. And the best thing is you don't need glue.'

'Another display of Argentinian ingenuity,' I acknowledged. 'But you're straying from the facts,' I said, pointing at myself. 'I was locked away with the radio all the time. They had me translating the BBC all day.'

'What do you want me to do, put you inside where no one can see you? There's no pleasing you bastards. Ramiro's already driven me bonkers about putting a 12.7mm machine gun on Enriqueta, when he never actually set foot out of town or ever carried more than a twisted old FAL. Look, there he is, otherwise I'd have had to give him the money back. Ah well, I've no objections. Now at last we get to choose. That's why I put us all together, Felipe. Even if you get annoyed with me and don't want to see me anymore, here at least we'll go on being friends forever,' he said, and smiled in such a way that I couldn't help being moved.

'Actually, it looks great,' I admitted, won over to his cause once again. 'I'll see if I can talk the lads into giving you an extension. It can't be forever, mind,' I warned him, but I think he only heard the first half. He was so desperate that every day gained savoured of eternity.

I hung around a long time, locating the vague and disembodied memories of ten years ago in the model's network of precise distances and ratios, asking questions, recording details. I took with me a pile of books and magazines, staggering under their weight, and, at the top of the stairs, before I disappeared into the night with my burden, Ignacio, showing he *had* been listening till the end, shouted to me from below.

'If you can't persuade them,' he said to me, 'I've got another message for them.'

'What?' I shouted.

'Tell them I shall defend my Islands whatever the cost may be. Tell them I shall never surrender.'

Chapter 3

THE MALVINAS STRIKE BACK

There was good news when I got home. Kevin's game had arrived and, in my eagerness to try it out and see if it was any good, I dumped all Ignacio's magazines and books on the floor and, bypassing the toilet, went and sat at the keyboard, still wearing my jacket, the last traces of alcohol neutralised by the onrush of adrenaline coursing through my veins.

The first few screens brought a knot of sheer pleasure to my throat, and I had to swallow hard several times before I got used to it. The game covered all the options of modern warfare, from the two World Wars and a hypothetical nuclear holocaust to the Gulf War – the real star I suppose, having been a war game before being an actual war. The most prestigious wars came ready-to-play: all you had to do was pick one from the menu, and away you went; but that wasn't the best thing about the game. You could, for example, invent new wars – Argentina and the United States v England, say – selecting landscapes, uniforms and armaments from an apparently inexhaustible catalogue; or you could – and this nearly blew me away – change the rules of wars already fought: give the Bomb to the Germans, for example, or nuclear submarines to Argentina. I gave the catalogue of ready-made wars a quick glance: WWI, WWII, Korean, Seven Days, Vietnam, hypothetical invasion of Cuba, Global Nuclear Apocalypse, Nicaragua, Panama, the Gulf . . . The South Atlantic War wasn't even named. The same with the armies: the only Latin Americans featured were the Cubans and the Sandinistas (an interchangeable option, with the same little bearded soldiers for both). There was nothing for it but to simulate our own by combining chunks of major wars, but before starting, I decided to try to get the hang of one from the menu.

Desert Storm. Just scrolling through the list of armaments and coordinating the main armies (I searched for the two frigates that Argentina sent to the Allies, but to no avail – the bloody ingrates) took me half an hour, but, once I had everything ready, it only took me a few minutes to bury the Iraqi cities in the desert sands. It was fun at first, then it just got monotonous: back to the old munch-munch Pacman routine; if you were lucky, a rogue Scud would pop up every now and then and be brought down by Patriots before you realised, or there'd be a building full of Kuwaitis to skirt around; the first one took me by surprise and I left no one standing, and the screen flashed up this banner: 'Don't be fooled by the sheets on their heads! They were your allies, Asshole! Wake up and watch out for the little flags!' Only after several screens did the high command give me the go-ahead to launch a ground assault, and for the first time I made face-to-face contact with the enemy—at least for a few seconds, before burying them alive in their trenches with bulldozers that trundled back and forth like buggies on a day out at the beach.

'We were right to choose prayer-time. They were all facing towards Mecca.'

'Just look at that line of asses.'

'Don't forget the contraceptive, Mike. You know what these Mohammedans are like.'

With all those rifles and helmets and feet poking out of the landscape it reminded me of a sandpit in the local square after the kids have stopped playing soldiers and left half of them behind. I was shocked by the lack of sporting spirit, but you couldn't deny it was practical: at least the Iraqi prisoners didn't have to break their backs digging, the way we'd had to. I felt a little envious: just a few years later the first virtual war in history had been waiting for me and all I'd got were the trenches of 1914. On the other hand, I recalled in consolation, if virtual war had been possible in '82, it would only have been virtual for the English: we'd have been landed with fighting on the side of reality – as usual.

So for the land battles I went for WWI, with its endless mud-filled trenches and fixed-bayonet infantry charges. I modernised the armaments a bit, of course, taking ours from the WWII menu and England's from the Gulf War. I chose a landscape from the Russian front in '44: there wasn't so much snow and the terrain did fairly well; but the soldiers were wrapped too warm to pass for Argentinians. The Nicaraguans and Cubans on the other hand were just too summery-looking, many of them having Havanas and parrots on their shoulders – not to mention the beards. I searched and searched but in the end all I could come up with were Iraqis: they did very nicely, with their swarthy faces and their mid-season uniforms. I gave them a bit of a shake to get the sand off and they were ready for combat. All I needed now was our ships, but it was a doddle to download them from the WWII files, and, strangely moved, I keyed in the date – 1st April 1982 – and launched the invasion of the Islands. It must have been around nine at night.

There's no way video games will ever become a record of past events; it's the skill of the player that defines what happens on-screen. But that ability can be manipulated: any game can be programmed so that any player, even the best, inevitably loses; by the same token, it can be 'set up' so that any tosser with minimal reflexes and intelligence will always beat it. But the final outcome aside, the path taken to achieve it depends on the individual: the storyline's always different depending on the player. I had to shake some life into the inert corpse of history, to twist its arm without making it scream, to show it some respect without letting its fat arse park itself on my freedom of movement. In the first task I was helped by all those veterans who, like Sergio, would be forever happy with an outcome quite out of kilter with our notions of what ought to have been; in the second, by the fact that freedom and variety in games are more illusory than they seem. The stories that emerge from them aren't really created; they all pre-exist in the computer, and the players are nothing more than pieces in the mechanism whereby the game actualises a handful of the few perfect stories it comprises.

Only one thing was certain: you couldn't rely much on Verraco: he was even worse at war games on computers than the other kind, so I picked one of the simplest levels for him and got ready to launch Operation Rosario

On 1st April the Class 42 destroyer *Santísima Trinidad*, with Verraco on board – a poetic licence to indulge the customer, as he had in fact arrived by plane on the 16th – anchored a mile off the coast of Isla Soledad and successfully landed ninety-two amphibious commandos in rubber dinghies. I scanned a map of the airport and town from one of Ignacio's magazines so that Verraco could lead his men to the marines' barracks in Moody Brook without getting lost. I got it almost perfect. Drawing maps was what I'd most liked doing at primary school: once, in year six, I'd had to make a wall chart of the Islands out of cardboard and the teacher had given me ten out of ten. Her name was Mónica, and my willie started twitching in my shorts when she leaned over the map to stamp my mark in my book and her tits almost brushed the Islands: perhaps the origin of my erotic fixation with them.

Next up was the *Cabo San Antonio* tank transport, which, escorted by an Λ69-type Drummond frigate, spewed from its full belly twenty-one FMC amtracs packed with our marine infantry. The heavily armoured amphibious tanks drove up onto the beach, some heading straight for the airport, others for the town, where there was more action, and I chucked in a shootout between our tanks and the Royal Marines hidden along the access road. In the end Verraco's tactical ability, the numerical superiority of his men and my uneven allocation of fire power had the marines turning tail and the Argentinian forces pouring in to occupy the town. This was where the problems began, because in my eagerness to get started I'd forgotten to give them one to occupy.

'Cold, isn't it.'

'I didn't know you reached Kuwait by boat.'

'Look, look. Midget nuns. Let's rape 'em.'

My Iraqis were walking about in a daze, roving over the open ground like wind-up toys, shooting at the radioactive, snow-dusted Russian weeds. Checking the menu I found one

that looked like it might do: a Norwegian town on a fiord, awaiting the coming of the Germans. But I wasn't going to get off
that lightly. Almost every one of us, Verraco included, knew the
town by heart and wouldn't have a crummy substitute palmed
off on him. I spread out the maps, photos and magazines around
me and, mouse in hand, began touching up, erasing houses till
I had the right number, shunting the public buildings around,
removing the trees from the outskirts, carefully redrawing the
outline of the seafront avenue. I didn't fall into the temptation,
though, of perfecting the reproduction ad infinitum the way
Ignacio did; there was no need to, because in this version of
the story the town was going to remain ours. And besides, now
that 1st May marked the start, not of the loss of the Islands, but
of their ultimate recovery, I wanted to get to it as soon as possible, to beat time itself, not by stopping it but by outrunning
it. Once the barracks and town were ours, the game flashed
up a Norwegian church – whose spire I'd blown away to make
it look like the Governor's house – which was instantly surrounded by the second group of amphibious commandos led
by Captain Héctor P. Verraco, who riddled it with bullets until
the one hundred English marines hidden inside surrendered.
I was tempted to send the lot of them to their deaths – Verraco
wouldn't have given it a second's thought – but in the actual
invasion the order had been 'not to cause unnecessary casual-
ties among the enemy' and I felt that by doubling the number
of defeated defenders I'd given him enough satisfaction for one
day. With the surrender of the English Governor to Captain
Verraco (why not? the game was meant to be an all-you-can-eat
buffet for him after all) the recovery of the Islands was complete: with the first light of day the Argentinian flag was once

again waving against the pure blue sky of the Islands for the first time in almost one hundred and fifty years. I left it fluttering there and had a smoke while I checked back over the work so far. It looked so good it even surprised me: no veteran would be able to resist it. And what's more, it was turning out to be unexpectedly realistic, even in the details – apart from one or two off-notes like the sabre-twirling Iraqis, the flags with Saddam's face on them and a Kuwaiti palm tree I'd overlooked and had to chop down. I wondered then if the Iraqis really were the way they'd looked on CNN: hordes of fanatical fundamentalists hell-bent on dying for Allah and Saddam. After all, we Argentinians had shouted and grimaced in the square and burned flags, the whole damned circus; beyond our own borders we must have looked very fierce. And the faces of the Iraqi prisoners after the lightning defeat looked quite a lot like our own: slightly confused, dirty, worn out, unsure of what they were doing there and relieved to have been beaten so quickly.

My enthusiasm was blunted slightly when I checked the time: at this rate it would take me days to write the war all the way to the end, and Sr Tamerlán might start getting impatient. So I threw in a map showing how the Task Force reached the Islands and got down to the game in earnest.

The real game begins in the small hours of 1st May, when a Vulcan bomber, flying non-stop at an altitude of 10,000 feet from the British base on Ascension Island, 4,000 miles from the Malvinas, approaches its target, the airport at Puerto Argentino, and unleashes its 24,000 pound bomb load at quarter-of-a-second intervals. But this treacherous opening to the hostilities doesn't catch the ever-vigilant Argentinian defences off guard: locating the aggressor on their AN/TPS-44 tactical surveillance radar screen on Colina del Zapador, they launch a swarm of English-made Tigercat surface-to-air missiles (a taste of their own medicine) with a range of 4,800 metres and optical guidance, and another swarm of Franco-German-made all-weather Roland missiles, range 6,000 metres, with optical or radar guidance (both luckily available on the game's armaments menu), supported by the two or three 35mm Œrlikon cannon commanded by the two radar units of the Swiss-made Skyguard digital fire control. Even wearing baseball mitts Verraco couldn't fail to hit the target. In the two or three trial runs I played the doomed Vulcan was, in a matter of seconds, flying through a hail of popping popcorn and, after reeling from the force of the impacts for a couple of seconds, it nose-dived towards the lower edge of the screen like a duck downed by a shotgun; and, as foreordained, the first action of the war concluded with victory for the Argentinians and humiliation for the English. But they don't learn their lesson and, their judgement clouded by frustration, they make a second attempt: at first light, eighteen British Aerospace Sea Harrier VTOL fighters, with a range of 400 km and a top speed of 1,160 kph, equipped with 30mm cannon, machine guns and American-made air-to-air AIM-9L Sidewinder missiles, take to the air from the aircraft carriers, twelve from the *Invincible* and eight from the *Hermes*, nine of them attacking the airport at Puerto Argentino and three, the airbase at Goose Green. The airport's air defences eventually lay waste to them all, although the speed and frequency of the planes on the screen would make it impossible for a player to stop some of them dropping their bombs and causing superficial damage to the airport and its surroundings, which in any case would be erased by the following screen. Rather than out of a desire for verisimilitude (in a video game?!), I did this so as not to detract from the game's excitement: nothing is more boring than winning effortlessly; small defeats have to be dosed out here and there to spice up the otherwise bland taste of victory. The three at Goose Green have no better luck: alerted to their advance (you could open a window in the top right-hand corner of the game and activate a radar screen), a squadron of Pucarás takes off from the bumpy grass runway. This Argentinian-built tactical attack and support aircraft was the biggest surprise of the war for the English: equipped with two 20mm HS-804 cannon with 260 shells, and four 7.62mm Browning cannon with 900 shells, and a capacity to carry up to 1,500 kg of bombs under the wings, despite its turboprop engines and maximum speed of 520 kph (not even half the speed of the enemy planes) its excellent manoeuvrability and the intrepidness of its young pilots enable it to fight the ultra-technologised Sea Harriers on an equal footing and defeat them. Like nimble bumblebees they buzz around the heavy enemy hawks, which, flown by automata relying on last-generation computers, radar and missiles, can do nothing to stop the underrated little Spic planes (actually German Stukas from WWII – *you* try finding a Pucará on the menu; they didn't look a bit alike, but with what Verraco knew about planes . . .) The English are soon laughing on the other side of their faces: the Pucarás, which from that day forth they were forced to christen 'the invisible ones' out of implicit admiration, come and go as if by magic: their simple weapons are more potent than the ultra-sophisticated technology, and one by one the planes that had been the pride of NATO come crashing to the ground. But even this heroic feat is too paltry for the plucky little gaucho planes' international baptism of fire (the only previous service they'd seen was against land-based guerrillas in the Tucumán jungle). On its own initiative, without even landing to refuel, one of them pulls off one of the greatest feats of the war: flying north-east, two metres above sea level and invisible to the radar, its props slicing the crests of the waves, it approaches the aircraft carrier *Hermes*, 28,000 tonnes, 1,350 crew, carrying twelve Sea Harriers, eighteen Sea King helicopters and Lynx anti-submarine helicopters, and releases its bombs into the side of the gigantic ship. Then, taking advantage of the helpless plight of the marines rushing around desperately trying to control the blaze and of the Sea Harriers crashing into each other as they struggle to take off and save themselves, it returns and strafes the deck with its cannon and machine guns, killing, among others, the Commander-in-Chief of the English forces, Rear Admiral Sandy Woodward himself. Pouring smoke, the disabled *Hermes* sails away, while, decked in glory, the heroic Pucará returns to its base or crashes into the sea, machine-gunned in revenge by the surviving Harriers, depending on the skill of Verraco or his opponent. (Verraco had the choice of playing the computer or another player, and I could just picture his subordinates swearing under their breath every time he came out with 'Gómez, I need you for a moment,' and they just knew from his tone of voice that it was their turn to be the English again.) It took me another half an hour to finish the first screen: dogfights between Harriers and our planes, naval bombardments of Puerto Argentino, air attacks on English ships . . . By digital nightfall the English had lost a quarter of their fleet, half their helicopters and all their aircraft, and if it weren't for the automatic renewal that the next screens would bring, they'd have had to abandon the war that day and swim back to the North Atlantic with their tails between their legs.

The next screen (I didn't even bother to pee, I was so into it) would make Verraco the Commander of the *Belgrano*, a 10,650-tonne cruiser equipped with Sea Cat missiles and fifteen 15.6˝ cannon with a range of thirteen miles, and a crew of 1,093 men, escorted by two destroyers, the *Piedra Blanca* and the *Hipólito Bouchard*, both equipped with Exocet surface-to-air missiles with a range of twenty miles. For all three I used American ships from WWII, only switching flags and names (the cruiser had in fact fought the Japanese under the name 'Phœnix'). At the first levels of the game Verraco would need only one or two flicks of the joystick executed with the reflexes of someone who'd just rolled up after a Sunday barbecue and a flagon of red in order to dodge the Mark 8 torpedoes that the 4,900-tonne, 103-crew English nuclear submarine *Conqueror* was firing at him. Then all three ships sprayed it with Hedgehog depth charges (so many that on-screen it looked like a peppered sausage) and I imported a little mushroom cloud from Global Nuclear Apocalypse to mark the moment when *Conqueror* exploded like a toad. Once I've finished with all this, I thought contentedly, I'll have to make copies and send them to my friends. This one of the *Belgrano*, for example, would cause a sensation: I knew at least two or three survivors willing to sell their wife and kids for the chance to get their own back on the English sub. And, while I was at it, I threw in a gun-slinging torpedo duel between the *San Luis* and some English submarine or other, to give the only Argentinian sub a chance it never had in the war.

When you're plugged into the computer, you sometimes

hope you can match their staying power: computers never lose their glow, their reflexes or their operating speed, never start making mistakes. But, sooner or later, we biological organisms need to rest. We run down so fast . . . I'd started four hours earlier and I could already feel the first waves of fatigue behind my eyes, and my skull was beginning to reverberate like the inside of a bell. I tried not to take any notice and to concentrate on all I still had to do: I'd only just completed the first days of the war.

The third screen ought to have been a doddle, as I hardly had to alter any of the original outcomes; but I always find it easier to invent than to copy, maybe because the unpredictability of the video game is better suited to random outcomes and the open possibilities of the imagination than to reproducing the frozen past. Or maybe it's just me. That 4th May Verraco had to sink the 4,100-tonne, 268-crew destroyer HMS *Sheffield*, equipped with Sea Dart missiles with a range of forty miles, sailing peacefully south-east of the Islands accompanied by the destroyers *Coventry* and *Glasgow*, unaware that a Neptune reconnaissance plane had spotted them and was transmitting the information to the Río Grande base, from where two of the Argentinian Air Force's five Dassault-Breguet Super Étendard strike fighters would eventually take off. Flying at a speed of 1,200 kph, with a range of 600 km (they had to be refuelled in mid-air via a Lockheed C-130 Hercules), they remained within the radars' dead zone before releasing the Exocet AM39 air-launched missiles they were carrying. I gave the *Sheffield* no chance to save itself; do what it might, one of the missiles would inevitably snap it in two like a baguette and send it to the bottom. I couldn't run the risk of the most optimistic day of the war being ruined by a piece of clumsiness from Verraco (he, of course, would put it down to his innate skill: 'Look, look, I never cock it up, I sink it every time – Yes!'). I completed that day made to the measure of our dreams with an attack by Sea Harriers on the airbase at Goose Green, from which, aiming the 35mm Œrlikon anti-aircraft batteries with average accuracy, it was possible to shoot them down in threes with zero risk, and for the rest of the screen I simply reproduced the outstanding action of the next two weeks, while giving Verraco enough lee-way to improve on the results: so the *Narwhal* manages to down the two Sea Harriers and the marine-packed Sea King helicop-ter that attack it; the eighteen Skyhawks that leave San Julián manage to sink the *Broadsword* and the *Coventry*; in the only na-val surface battle of the whole war, in the San Carlos Strait, the freighter *Isla de los Estados* sinks the 3,250-tonne frigate *Alacrity*, equipped with MM38 Exocet and SAM Sea Cat missiles, torpedo launchers, a 115mm cannon and a Sea Lynx helicopter; squad-ron after squadron of Skyhawks attack the destroyers *Glasgow* and *Brilliant*, putting them out of action . . .

I leaned back in my swivel chair, laced my fingers together and pushed till I made them crack, then rubbed my closed eyes with my fists. Tiring work this, reinventing a war. My swollen bladder pissing just a dribble, my forehead pressing on the back of the hand that held a cigarette, against the cold surface of the tiles, I took to imagining that the cardboard match bobbing in the bowl below was an English ship foundering on the rough, yellow sea, and pitilessly directed the yellow stream at it, telling myself 'If I sink it, everything will turn out exactly as I planned'; but the little fucker stayed afloat. It was almost two in the morning and the smoke from my cigarette reminded me once again of the emptiness in the pit of my stomach; I hadn't eaten anything since the peanuts and crisps at the bar. I'd become so immersed in cyberspace that I believed its electronic stimuli were the only sustenance I needed; it was inconceivable to interrupt my trance and attend to the demands of the flesh. Wrong decision again: the smell of too many fags crushed against the aluminium of the ashtray, the smoke rising from my lungs to my brain, brought on first dizziness, then breathlessness, then nausea. It often happens when I'm nervous, it's late and I'm alone, and I've smoked too many cigarettes on an empty stomach. I went to the fridge and took several gulps of ice-cold water, then opened a window and inhaled lungfuls of cold, damp air. I needed to go and lie down until it went, but I couldn't afford to; so I stood there, clinging to the window, feeling the pin-pricks of cold sweat on my face, forcing myself to inhale and exhale until the nausea backed up down my throat to my chest, my stomach, and further down, where it couldn't bother me any more. The big moment has come, I told myself, returning to my chair and sighing in contented resignation; you don't have to put up with it any more: the English are about to land and you can't be there to greet them in such a state of weakness – if not for yourself, at least do it for your country. Would that all the sacrifices it demands of us were as agreeable as this one, I purred to myself as I took everything I needed out of the drawer. For luck I combed a line on the map of Puerto Argentino to exactly the length and breadth of the airport runway and, pretending my nose was a Pucará landing on it, railed it in one. 'Now, my English friends,' I said to myself, my nose dribbling with delight, the white fire fizzing through my nerves like a powder trail, 'bring on the little prince, come and get us.'

That 21st May is a storm of steel: 3,000 marines, from 40 and 45 Commando, and 2 and 3 Para, try to land and establish a beachhead in the San Carlos area at the far north of the strait, but they weren't expecting a detachment of just sixty Argentinians to fight to the last man in the surrounding hills. It was just like the movies: Rambo mowing down several enemy platoons single-handed, each one approaching over the growing pile of corpses with a 'Whassup man?' and taking a string of bullets in the chest. With the first thousand marines out of the way, the screen switches to the ships hemmed into the narrow waters of the channel, at the mercy of the Argentinian planes, who don't need to be asked twice: successive waves of IAI Daggers (the Israeli version of the Mirage) and US-built Douglas A-4 Skyhawk fighter-bombers attack the big ships, which, unable to manœuvre without crashing into each other, start blowing up and sinking one by one: in the front line the frigates, *Ardent*, *Broadsword*, *Brilliant*, *Argonaut* and *Alacrity*; then the cruiser *Antrim*, and the frigates *Yarmouth* and *Plymouth*, the landing platform dock craft *Fearless* and *Intrepid*, and the 44,807-tonne troop transport *Canberra*. Several Sea Harriers (maximum twenty) and Sea King and Gazelle helicopters (maximum fifteen) are lost by the English in the aptly nicknamed 'Bomb Alley', and their ground forces, without any provisions or armaments other than what they're carrying on their backs, are cut off by the Argentinian troops, who, arriving in ever greater numbers from Puerto Argentino and Puerto Howard, advance on them and drive them back into the sea. An act of suicide or desperation, the English landing has failed and once again they've lost half their fleet. Now things were really hotting up, and I combed another line on the edge of the keyboard and railed it through a fake hundred. I felt like having some fun and devoted the next screen to dogfights, probably the best thing in the game. I set the target as two ships: the destroyer *Coventry*, equipped with Sea Cat and Sea Dart missiles and 115mm and 20mm cannon, and the frigate *Broadsword*, armed with Sea Wolf, Exocet MM38 and 40-mm cannon; and around them, operating from the various aircraft carriers, the feared Harriers and Sea Harriers. Then I selected a gaming option that, instead of showing the planes on-screen, put me inside the cockpit, as in a flight simulator, and the enemy in front or behind, depending on luck. I patrol the area in my Mach 2.2 supersonic Mirage until I detect an enemy ship and prepare to attack: I easily dodge a Sea Dart but, before I get within range, the radar warns me of a Harrier behind me and I have to accelerate and climb to lose it (the higher the altitude, the greater the difference in speeds). Once I'm sure I've done it, I make a fresh approach and this time the Harrier appears in front and the dots of light from my cannon converge on his tail until smoke starts billowing out of it, and I finish him off with a nonchalant Sidewinder (the pilot ejects and is lost in the sea). But two more Harriers have taken his place (double drat!): one of them I foil by forcing him to fly so low that he eventually crashes into the waves, and the other, on picking me up behind him, tries the dirty trick of viffing (climbing vertically in mid-flight and decelerating, letting me zoom past below to get me in his sights and waste me at his leisure with his two missiles). But I manage to elude him by going into a corkscrew spin and, to make the most of the effect, I do the last thing he expects: I make a U-turn and fly *at* him, head-on. Without missiles, his machine guns aren't up to much and my other Sidewinder puts him out of his confusion, so I can just drop altitude and release my bombs on the *Coventry*, which sinks in seconds flat. Then I jump to the cockpit of a Super Étendard, from which, after a complex approach to elude the radar, I manage to stick an Exocet into the troop carrier *Atlantic Conveyor*, equipped to serve as a third aircraft carrier, which, taking to the bottom three giant Chinook and six Wessex helicopters, tents, gear and portable runways, caused the English the biggest logistical setback of the war and delayed the attacks on Darwin and Puerto Argentino for several days. There were two of the original five Exocets left (I hadn't called up any more, otherwise Verraco would even have launched them at the rubber dinghies) and I brought forward the attack on the aircraft carrier *Invincible*, so I could get it in the same screen. I had to get this one just right: it's still the most controversial of the war (like a tennis match, each opponent keeps banging on about whether it was 'In' or 'Out' and neither is prepared to back down). Verraco himself was obsessed with the subject: in his wallet, alongside the photo of his wife and kids, he carried 'a secret photo the English never disclosed' showing the proud ship listing to port and almost disabled. Hundreds of times he'd shown it to me: a pewter sea, out of which pokes the tip of a table, and a cloud of grey ectoplasm shrouding the sky; but if anyone took it into their head to argue with him, he'd go blue in the face, his veins bulging, and he'd threaten them with council of war and court martial, even if they were civilians. So anyway, two Super Étendards and four Skyhawks pounce on it, and one of the Exocets breaches the hull amidships and the Skyhawks stick their 500-pound bombs into the hole, putting *Invincible* out of action and, while we're at it, sinking it, just to prove that fiction can even outdo imagination.

With annoyance I noticed my head was starting to ache and immediately felt the first rush of panic. No one who has never suffered headaches like mine can understand the sheer terror I have of them, and the hatred. Normal headaches only sink their teeth and claws into the soft dough of the brain, but mine have an iron-tipped tool with which they dig, rake and plough, working the furrows up and down, sowing pain. It won't let me finish, I hissed through clenched teeth, it won't let me finish. I can take a bit more and it'll go away, but it always comes back with a vengeance after that, again and again . . . Knowing it was futile, I grabbed two aspirins from the bathroom cabinet and let them dissolve under my tongue, savouring them slowly like mints, pulling a face every time the bitter juice ran down my throat. The most sensible thing, I thought as I massaged my forehead, was to call it a day, have something to eat, grab a few hours' kip and carry on tomorrow; with any luck it wouldn't be too late and I could keep it at bay. But we're at war, and in wartime you can't choose when to call it a day. It must have been about four in the morning, the ideal time for the English parachutists to advance in their little red berets along the isthmus towards Darwin, where they were soon trading shots with the Argentinian forces, treading on mines and strafing each other with cannon and rockets and grenades. Bleep! Bleep! Bleep! Almost two hours they spent annihilating each other in the seeling darkness, in the angry, gloomy flashes worn by the night on my computer screen. I'd always been amazed how easily people are killed in films: bang and you're dead, bang and you're dead . . . The video game has perfected this: people don't even die; they just go out, no screaming, no lingering agony or spilled guts, no blame or grief or disgust.

This was what I wanted to avoid, I thought, as the pain howled and whistled furiously round the walls of my skull. The game had started out as a brilliant solution to the problem of how to get into the SIDE and get my hands on the files Tamerlán wanted, a ruse so simple, so clever, so *safe*, that I should have been toasted and slapped on the back with shouts of 'Eureka!' and references to the Gordian Knot and Columbus's Egg. Surely there was some other way into the SIDE that wasn't through the Islands. I should have known when to stop before it was too late, to backtrack if need be. Not this suicidal forced march, this blind headlong rush, this charge through the minefield in the dark.

But it was too late now and I had to go on regardless. Humming 'Popeye the Sailorman' to myself, one eye closed from the irremovable pain, I combed a long line of all the charlie I had left on the mirror and launched it into my brain. That did the trick. Two Pucarás appear buzzing over the line of hills and release their napalm bombs on the terrified English; the anti-aircraft batteries lower their guns and begin to fire level with the ground, putting the fear of God into the enemy with the straightness of their aim; the Argentinian defenders cornered in the school building pluck up their courage and, transfigured by the white spinach, manage to drive back their attackers and push forward. The order to counter-attack sent that noon from Puerto Argentino turns out to be superfluous: the English beat a hasty retreat. The fighting lasts the rest of the day, and, while they retrace their steps to the beachhead, our Skyhawks and Daggers and Mirages annihilate the waiting ships, cutting off their retreat: when their men realise, some leap off the rocks and drown in the freezing water, others crowd together in the landing craft shuttling back and forth across the empty sea in search of the ships that are no more, like dogs that have lost their owners, until some compassionate missile puts them out of their misery; most surrender without a fight. We battle all day, without a break, without sleep, without anything to eat, but it's worth it. I don't remember getting up to go to the toilet or taking my hands off the keyboard or the mouse other than to scrape together – so long ago – the last crumbs of charlie stuck to the silver foil. My headache, increasing geometrically with every postponement, was now roaring like falling bombs. It must have been the hunger, too, but I couldn't face a thing. Leaving the battlefield, unnoticed by the cheering victors, I groped my way to the toilet to splash some cold water on my head, but when I tried to turn on the tap I discovered it was out of reach, hidden behind a wall of ceramic and pipes. Without knowing how long I'd been on the floor – I could hardly feel my cheek, ice-cold against the wet tiles – I dragged myself to the toilet bowl and tried to throw up. Nothing, just a deep retching that tore through my guts and pumped blood more painfully to the throbbing, swollen mass of my brain. Chewing a little toothpaste with chattering teeth, I wandered about the room, my wet hands on my forehead, praying for an Englishman to appear soon and put me out of my misery. They said the Gurkhas would remove your head with a single chop. I found the blister of Migraleve, almost empty. I couldn't remember having taken the rest, but I finished it just in case, swallowing the two pills with water and Reliveran. The liquid made me shake with cold and my nose was running; blowing it barely eased the shooting pain, the pain of a steel arrow cracking the bone between your eyes that only cocaine can bring on. I caught sight of my reflection in the coke-streaked mirror, blurred and scored by fingers of saliva, chopped into planes of pain: one eye higher than the other, nose in profile, mouth crooked. I ordered myself back to the keyboard and obeyed, whimpering softly, trying to silence the insistent voice that kept repeating, 'Why do you do this to yourself? Why do you subject yourself to it?' A pain in my chest – one of astonishment at what I was capable of forcing on myself – tried to garrotte me but I fought it off. Pain is a luxury I can't afford with all that's at stake. I have to finish. I could smell victory, so close . . .

I sat down with a sigh and moved my fingers towards the keyboard, but, numb from the coke and endless hours of use, they landed on the keys like iron gloves, hitting several at once and messing everything up. Then I was in the kitchen, pouring a bottle of ice-cold water over one hand then the other, feeling some relief after the pin-pricks of pain, thinking about the leftovers of the forgotten Balcarce pudding I'd caught a glimpse of when I'd opened the fridge. Something sweet like that might do it, although, to keep the waves of nausea at bay, I tried not to think too much about it. Closing my eyes, holding my breath, I lifted it out of its box using my whole hand as a spoon, and stuffed it in my mouth. I couldn't swallow it: when I chewed it the pastry, rather than decreasing, grew and grew, churning about inside my mouth like cement in a mixer. The meringue and caramel turned to glue at the back of my throat, and the first retchings began; but I was determined not to let it out. Everything in the kitchen conspired to make me think of food and, gritting my teeth against the spasms in my throat, I went back to the living room and fell to my knees on Ignacio's magazines. I eventually managed to swallow and no sooner did I feel the pudding hit my stomach like a trowelful of fresh cement than I made the mistake of opening my mouth to take in some air and it all flew out in two long spurts all over the open magazines. I looked at them, first in surprise, then indignation. Furious, I stuffed my hand with the bits of pudding still on it into my mouth and sucked it down to the wrist, then used it to scoop up the semi-liquid paste off the floor and magazines, and after every scoop I stuck my hand back in my mouth and sucked it clean. It wasn't that bad and was actually easier to swallow, but my body betrayed me once more: without so much as a retch, a reflex of my stomach expelled it again. I began to moan, loudly, because it was now too watery to scoop up with my hand, so, on all fours, I sucked it up directly off the floor, the pain kicking and screaming every time I lowered my head, like a madman in a padded cell, and, clamping my hand over my mouth, I grabbed a roll of 4cm silver duct tape from the drawer. Gripped once again by despair as I couldn't use my other hand or my teeth to cut it, I tugged at it until I managed to pull off a twisted piece and sellotape my mouth shut. Now, I said to the contents of my mouth (mentally, of course), you're going to stay put, and, when a fresh retch filled my mouth, I swallowed again, and again, until I doubled up on the floor, exhausted, my cheek resting on the vomit-spattered magazines, and fell asleep on the map of the Islands.

The dream I had was slow, mysterious, silent, like a film: just a noiseless, floating travelling shot of soldiers on hilltops, as if taken from a slow-passing helicopter and projected without sound. Graceful and erect, they were all standing in the mouths of their caves to watch it fly past, leaning gently on their rifles and machine guns like Zulus on their spears, looking impassively on, their sunken-eyed faces almost invisible under their beards and expressing nothing more than a mildly irked interest like that sometimes shown by lions for the camera in wild-life documentaries. The hillsides were steep, far steeper than my memory had painted them, vertical like the towers of a castle, the highest stone needles wreathed in wisps of fog that sometimes hid them and their perching sentinels from view. Looking more carefully, it was easy to make out the ones that had had lighter complexions and eyes, and you could still make out on some uniforms the olive green or the mottling of camouflage that had once served to differentiate them. It wasn't difficult to understand then: the soldiers were an admixture of Argentinians and English, caressed by the hand of time till they'd become almost indistinguishable, and if the certainty of being the true owners of the land emanated from them like an aura, distinguishing them as the men that no army could drive out, it was because on those peaks, lit by the last ray of sunlight stretching over the shadow of the rising and falling plains, dwelt only the spirits of the dead.

I awoke with a start in that dread chasm at the centre of the night, as if, in the vast silence, someone had shaken me to warn me of imminent danger. I should have been so lucky: I was alone. The rest of the world had disappeared, swallowed by the silence and the dark. I got up, my heart revving feverishly, rather than beating, on a frequency of its own that had nothing to do with the rest of the body. I noted with infinite gratitude that my headache had receded, though I knew it was still crouching among the furniture, in the corners of the room, where the light didn't reach, biding its time. Carefully, so as not to get myself any dirtier than I already had, I took

93

off my sweatshirt and tank-top, screwed them into a ball and threw them onto the plastic crate from the laundry. Shivering with cold until the water ran hot, I soaped and rinsed my face, hair and arms, right up to my shoulders, several times, without being altogether successful in getting rid of the smell, until a glance at the mirror showed me I still had the duct tape stuck over my mouth and that the smell was coming from within. I don't know how many times I brushed my teeth, chewing the toothpaste and swallowing it as well. I walked around the house turning all the lights on, breathing deeply with difficulty, kicking the magazines strewn across the floor. I made myself a large cup of milky coffee in the kitchen and drank it with bay biscuits, dunking them bit by bit to soften them up and swallowing them with difficulty, as if learning anew. I looked out onto the patio, through the half-open window: an overcast night, a sky of melted wax, a thin film of damp spread over everything, as if the noisy breath of the building – pipes, bed-springs, a dog growling in its sleep, an old man coughing, the hum of my computers, a telephone ringing in an empty apartment – were circulating through its rooms and corridors, and condensing on its walls, flowerpots, tiles, windows, doors . . . Further afield the growling and snorting and chewing of broken glass of a busy dustcart, and from the motorway the purring of engines and the displaced whistle of air and whisper of tyres on the wet tarmac. How long had I been in here? Was this the first night or the second? I looked for my cigarettes, but the packet was empty. I couldn't remember smoking the last one. What a pleasure it would be now to grab wallet and keys, wrap myself in my coat and walk to the Shell station on Avenida Independencia, clicking my heels on the flagstones, ordering a jumbo hot dog and chatting with the manager for a while, he'll listen to anyone at that time of night to stop himself falling asleep . . .

'If you go out now,' I answered myself sharply, to drag myself away from the crack through which the night air burst into my coke-ravaged nose, 'you won't be able to go back. If you've got this far,' I told myself, resorting to the most idiotic, the most criminal of excuses, 'you're better off finishing at all costs, rather than giving up and losing everything you've done. Just a little bit more,' I murmured as I dragged myself back to the screen, which had been waiting trustingly all this time, knowing I had no choice but to return. Where was I to go in any case? The English had me surrounded. They'd advanced on Puerto Argentino on different fronts: 3 Para and 45 Commando had crossed the whole island on foot from San Carlos; 42 Commando and 2 Para had travelled by helicopter as far as Monte Kent, from which they could see their final objective, sharp and clear as if on a model, incredibly close: the town lay at their feet. The ones that had had the worst of it were the Scots and Welsh Guards, who had arrived with the Gurkhas from the south in two ships: the *Sir Galahad* and the *Sir Tristram*. Daylight and the Argentinian planes (I sent in six odd Skyhawks so as not to waste time looking them up) caught them on manœuvres in a lost cove, isolated and with no air cover: almost fifty were horribly burned to death before they set foot on land. With varying degrees of luck, they completed the cordon and by the night of 11th June they were ready to strike. Almost 9,000 of us were waiting on the other side with three 155mm cannon, forty-two 105mm cannon, anti-aircraft batteries, mortars, machine guns, FALs, FAPs . . . The Navy had withdrawn all ships to the mainland, the Air Force, all planes and helicopters: now it was up to the Army to manage by itself. Puerto Argentino was like the village in *Asterix the Gaul*: 'The Malvinas are entirely occupied by the English. Well, not entirely . . . One small village of indomitable gauchos . . .' All we lacked was the magic potion.

The English start with Monte Longdon, defended by B Company of R7, a platoon of Mechanised Engineers Company 10 and a few marines with 12.7mm machine guns (no need to look that up in a book). 3 Para attack during the night after an intense bombardment to 'soften up' the Argentinian defensive positions, but this time the RASIT land surveillance radar is operational and the English are caught out in the open by the Argentinian fire, which, with the protection and height afforded by the hills, picks off the various companies one by one. I couldn't remember how I'd installed the surrender and prisoner-taking options before, and I didn't feel like going back to check, so Verraco was just going to have to kill them all, which, knowing him, wouldn't bother him in the least; after all, this had been *his* battle, and he wouldn't want the slightest bit of realism to interfere with a revenge fantasy he'd been nursing with maternal devotion day after day for ten whole years. Longdon had been the toughest battle of the war – although our mates at Goose Green also claimed that dubious privilege – and, despite being the one I knew best, the effort of including it in the game once again left me exhausted. I was dying to get some rest, but there was no time: 45 Commando of the Royal Marines are already advancing on the Cerro Dos Hermanas, which awaits them defended by some three hundred men from C Company of R4 and B Company of R6. Calmly, leisurely, the Correntinos use the English for target practice as if they were caiman or capybara, and celebrate the next morning with maté and a chamamé knees-up. Before dawn Verraco would still be contriving to tempt 42 Commando into a reckless assault on Monte Enriqueta, letting them advance to a pre-set point, after which 300 soldiers would emerge, armed to the teeth, from the very bowels of the earth, and the English would fly like fresh-mown grass. Here ends the first night of fighting.

The second, which included the assault on the inner ring of hills surrounding the town, was far simpler. The Scots Guards – green about the ears compared to the marines – found themselves up against the marine infantry from R5 on Monte Tumbledown, and to save time I copied the battle of Dos Hermanas (as long as he was winning Verraco wouldn't spot the ruse) and for Wireless I copied a few sequences from Longdon, which had also been attacked by paras and defended by R7. Then I spent about fifteen minutes weighing up the pros and cons of inventing the battle of Monte William, because I couldn't take any more. But I could just picture Verraco: 'What, Félix? You make me a video game of the war and don't put any Gurkhas in it?' The number of times I must have heard him say 'I'd like to see those kukris take on our Correntino machetes,' but as there was no gaucho duel option on the menu and the neurons in my brain had long since fried their last synapse, I rifled through the pile of floppies until I found a Ninja Turtles game I'd copied for a neighbour's kid and threw in a couple of sequences from that: the Japanese did pretty well for the Gurkhas, despite the samurai sabres, and the Ninja Turtles looked more human than we did after two months in the trenches. So we won the battle with sticks and karate kicks and, though it was all quite ludicrous and at any other time would have had me in stitches, I now found it rather sad: my own jokes were depressing me. The Gurhkas were the ace up the enemy's sleeve and, once they were defeated, their fate was sealed. But maddened by the inconceivable defeat of the men and arms of NATO at the hands of an army of spear-toting natives, they attempt one last counter-attack and a group of officers orders their last, exhausted and demoralised troops to make a suicide attack on Colina del Zapador, a gently sloping hill two kilometres from Puerto Argentino: the few survivors of 45 Commando and the Welsh Guards that hadn't been consumed on the *Sir Galahad* stumble like zombies into the fire power of our marine infantry, and if a few escape with their lives, it's because, at about 1300 hours on 14th June 1982, the English High Command, finally understanding the desperate nature of their position, run up the white flags over San Carlos, Goose Green and Kent, and at 2100 hours the same day Major General Jeremy Moore *unconditionally* surrenders – this time without crossings-out – to the Commander-in-Chief of the Argentinian forces, General Héctor P. Verraco. The remains of the fleet, mainly transport and supply ships, had turned tail several days earlier, leaving the landed troops to their fates. The few surviving soldiers and officers (to a man, they all had to leave the Islands as prisoners on Argentinian ships, there being no honourable retreat option on the menu) are taken to Buenos Aires to be paraded at the victory celebrations and then rounded up like cattle onto a Buquebus and ferried over the river to Montevideo.

The Argentinian ships, on the other hand, enter the southern ports sounding their sirens and laden with victorious soldiers, and what wild delight there is in the population, who come out to welcome them as a single man and carry them through the streets on their shoulders. Young girls hurl flowers at their feet and slip scraps of paper with telephone numbers into their palms; mothers lift their children to watch them pass and fill their arms with food; fathers crack open bottles of wine and raise their glasses to them in the middle of the street. They advance in a cloud of blue-and-white flags and ribbons and confetti that rain down from on high as if the very stands of heaven were celebrating too. An airlift on an unprecedented scale is organised to take them to their homes as soon as possible and, a few hours after the last shot was fired, they're eating ravioli or barbecued ribs, kissing their girlfriends, playing with the dog, and the celebrations in every neighbourhood last till dawn. The houses of ex-combatants can be recognised by the queues of neighbours eager to congratulate them, which start at their open doors and stretch round the whole block. Special charter flights are hired to whisk to the Islands the relatives of those privileged enough to stay behind and look after this new corner of the Fatherland, just so that their fathers and grandfathers and brothers can walk with them hand in hand through the lands and under the skies for which they'd been willing to part with each other for ever. And they walk together late into the night, oblivious to the cold, in groups of two, three, six or seven, some with their children in their arms, pointing to things they'll never forget: 'That hole was made by an English missile; this is the Governor's house, the scene of the first skirmishes; we took enemy prisoners to the port along this avenue; this is a Kelper, Señor Jones. Don't be afraid; he's Argentinian now, like us. Keep them for after dinner and say thank you to Señor Jones.' Meanwhile, back on the mainland, lists of ex-combatants benefiting from special employment schemes, housing plans and scholarships start being published in the first week after the victory, not to mention pensions for the war-disabled and the families of those who laid down their lives for the Fatherland, which have been declared a national priority. A few days later a procession is organised, a Roman triumph in honour of the liberator of the Malvinas and brand-new president of the Argentinian people, General Héctor P. Verraco. Standing atop an Islands-shaped carnival float pulled by assorted paras, commandos, Scots Guards, Welsh Guards and Gurkhas held hostage, Verraco parades up the Avenida 9 de Julio, followed by the victorious troops and an impressive cortège of jeeps, lorries, tanks, missile launchers and anti-aircraft batteries, while wave after wave of Mirages, Skyhawks, Daggers and Pucarás, and captured Harriers, skim the tops of the buildings, merging their wide, white contrails, which, flanked on either side by the blue of the sky, form a huge patriotic flag that wraps the city in its folds. Awaiting him at the monumental victory temple erected in record time at the junction of Avenida Libertador is the Pope, who has prolonged his visit to Argentina especially (Verraco had better not look too closely because, finding no Popes on the menu, I'd had to make do with an Ayatollah), with a laurel wreath in his hands, which, with due respect, the Argentinian general takes from him and lays over his temples himself.

I decided to close the game with an image of Puerto Argentino exactly as it would look today, ten years after the victory. I did this by scanning some photos of Ushuaia, the most similar-looking Argentinian city I could find, and combining them with the landscape of the bay and hills surrounding the

Islands' capital, thus turning it into a city of high-rise buildings and newsboys touting *Clarín*, *La Nación*, *La Prensa* and *La
Gaceta de Malvinas*; of people buying Particulares or Chocolinas
at the kiosks, or tucking into prime rib and chips or gnocchi or
milanesas and quaffing Quilmes in the pizza parlours at lunchtime; of record shops from which blared the voices of Sandro
and Charly García; of bars where, on Monday mornings, over
their coffee and medialunas, people discuss Racing v San
Lorenzo, or the possibilities of their local team being promoted
to the first division; of children in white pinafores on their way
to school and high-school children from the mainland on their
school-leavers' trips buying the local chocolate while they wait
for the coach to take them skiing on Monte Longdon or out
clubbing in Moody Brook; of colectivos unloading their passengers at street corners and mothers discussing Mirtha Legrand's
latest chat show at the hairdresser's. It was mid-morning, and
the noises of the city, which I'd thought were from the streets
of Puerto Argentino, were coming from outside my apartment
windows. We did it, I thought, closing my eyes and listening to
the disc purring as it recorded the finished version of the game.
We won.

The second part of the plan was pretty simple. There were
two possibilities, depending on how things panned out: a) once
inside the SIDE, I'd search for the list of witnesses while I was
installing the game on the computer, copy it and leave Verraco
eternally playing at defeating the English in his Land of Oz at
the end of history; or b) once inside the SIDE, I *wouldn't* be able
to find the list of witnesses, so I'd install the video game, leave
Verraco playing, et cetera, et cetera . . . Only this time, while Verraco was picking off Sea Harriers the way he must have picked

off pigeons with his first air rifle as a kid, a search program, curled up like a worm in the secret entrails of the game, would scan all the computers in the circuit one by one until it found what it was looking for, sink its pirate hooks into it and wrap it in its coils until I could come back for it. And because I needed a good excuse to get back into the SIDE to retrieve it, we move on to plan c): once its work was complete, the worm would send the program a signal to activate a virus in the vulnerable digital blood of Verraco's game: Falklands 140682.

At first I'd thought of a virus that completely reversed the results of the game, swinging it in favour of a total English victory, just as I'd first marshalled all the advantages to our side. But then – less out of mercy than strategy – I decided to make the rare Argentinian victories immune to the virus: Verraco's nightmare was that the game would tell the truth, not that it would lie, and if he failed on 2nd April or the *Sheffield* escaped, he'd feel cheated, more furious at me than humiliated by reality, which was where I really wanted him. So I limited the action of the virus to sequences whose outcomes I'd crudely rigged for an Argentinian victory. So the landing, for example, would be immune to the virus, unaltered, with the additional advantage that Verraco would be beside himself with coke-fuelled triumphalism when, on 1st May, the Vulcan slid through the night sky of Puerto Argentino, as invisible as the new moon, and left the airport useless for the duration, to any planes other than the rugged Hercules transport aircraft; and then, at first light, the Sea Harriers bombed the airport again – with a bit of luck the anti-aircraft defences might shoot down a couple at most – and the base at Goose Green, where they trashed the useless Pucarás on the ground – including the one that would never get off the ground to attack the 28,700 tonne aircraft carrier *Hermes*, et cetera. Luckily, I didn't have to redo everything: the virus only speeded up the actions and reaction times of the English, and, save for the odd occasion, Verraco was always destined to lose. When he realised that the Skyhawks, Daggers or Mirages were no match for the Sea Harriers (our planes didn't win a single dog-fight in the whole fucking war!), he'd begin to crack, and things would only get worse on the next screen, when *Conqueror* sank the *Belgrano* along with a third of its crew, while our only submarine, the *San Luis*, would manage to torpedo nothing more dangerous than a whale. The Exocet would give him a breather, but wouldn't be enough to dispel the black cloud of the past gathering over his head. Because sinking the *Sheffield* also entailed that the *Narwal* could do little to halt the strafing of the Sea Harriers; that, of the crew of the freighter *Isla de los Estados*, only two would survive the attack by the ultra-equipped frigate *Alacrity*; that too many Skyhawks and their pilots would be lost just to put the destroyer *Glasgow* out of action; that on D-Day (how the victors love to repeat history) the English would land without too much trouble, just one frigate destroyed and two hit at the expense of ten of our Daggers and Skyhawks; and, although over the next few days we'd sink the *Antelope* and, on 25th May – our last schoolboy day of glory in the war – the *Coventry* and the all-important supply ship *Atlantic Conveyor* with another Exocet, the English were already established on the Islands, and three days later would take Darwin and Goose Green, cutting through us like a mower through a garden full of toads squatting in the grass. And the aircraft carrier *Invincible* would escape the Exocet that Argentina's powerful desire and feeble destiny had in store for it, and in the days that followed the enemy troops would sight Puerto Argentino for the first time, surround our defences with their artillery and begin to pound us relentlessly in preparation for the final assault. It would all happen so fast that Verraco would relive every minute of those seventy-four days in one or two hours of game-time, the way they say a drowning man relives his whole life dissolved in the water filling his lungs. Longdon, Enriqueta, Dos Hermanas, Wireless, Tumbledown: repeating history without improving it, the virus would eat away his dreams one by one, leaving his fantasies as poor as his memories, snatching defeat from the jaws of defeat.

Chapter 4
SIDE SHOPPING MALL

The new building of the State Intelligence Secretariat lies in the bowels of the recently opened shopping mall at the junction of Avenida Córdoba and Calle Paraguay, and bears the same relationship to it as the tunnels of an ants' nest do to the mound above – in this case a solid concrete sandstone-coated cube with no communication to the outside world other than two large entrances, around which the ants swirled in a strange inversion of nature: entering empty-handed and emerging fully laden. Pushing my way through – only a couple of them directed curious glances at my combat uniform – I made for a restricted-access lift that plunged like a lead weight into the depths of the building past all three floors of car park before depositing me in the officially non-existent fourth basement, the first of the descending series that bored into the foundations of the city. I came out into a narrow passageway bathed in the cold, familiar glare of fluorescent lights; on the day of its inauguration, I remember, it was as wide as an ordinary city street, but, in no time at all, an obstinate scale of divisions and partitions had narrowed it to such an extent that in several places you had to edge your way through. The uncommon degree of horror vacui that possesses the Argentinian civil service never ceases to amaze me: two days after moving their dossiers and lever-arch files and yellowing snake plants in plastic pots into the new building they were already drafting the first memorandum to request a division, starting by slicing every room in two widthwise, then lengthwise, putting up ever-shorter fluorescent tubes; then, wielding their formica, plywood and hardboard like broadswords, they advanced on the corridors, waiting rooms and halls, the most daring of them building kiosks in the middle of nowhere, which immediately began to secrete their own divisions, eventually merging with other nodes of growth, the way the separate parts of a coral atoll gradually coalesce. I'd been to Verraco's section on several occasions before, but I could never follow the same route twice, because the building mutated and transformed like a living organism, faster than my sporadic visits would allow me to revise my mental map, and I had to make several detours before I eventually found it.

The 'Argentina's by 2000' Division occupied a sort of enormous, brightly lit cave, where more than twenty people, impelled by the eight-year deadline, were feverishly working – or pretending to – on a variety of plans to regain the Islands. Between these walls, painted that government-issue canary yellow that, even fresh, looks thirty years old, on this synthetic, mustard-coloured carpet pocked with small black craters from cigarette ends, and studded here and there with smooth patches of greying chewing gum, under the mind-numbingly lethargic light in which several outdoor plants were doing their unenthusiastic best to survive, on the sturdy wrought-iron desks upholstered in liver-brown PVC that stood like colossi supporting the unstable accumulation of folders, minutes, memoranda, reports, correspondence, magazines, leaflets, circulars and press releases that, like the walls of a gorge, displayed the different geological eras of official activity, had been devised some of the most brilliant alternatives to the second and final military occupation of the Islands, which for now didn't look very likely. Among other things, Verraco's people had laid plans to kidnap Prince Charles and Lady Di, and demand a ransom of one island each (they had to cancel when they found out about their imminent divorce in *Hello!*), to subsidise the IRA for terrorist attacks on the Islands, to play England for them at Wembley ... The main problem was the obduracy of the Islanders, with whom Verraco was obsessed. 'I told Menéndez when we were there,' he'd repeat to whoever would listen, and didn't bat an eyelid when imagining a lowly captain giving it straight to a brigadier in the middle of wartime: 'Let's sort out the Kelpers the Argentinian way: leave one of them standing and he'll start kicking up a fuss about the Islands being his. But no, the bloody fool took it into his head to protect them like some endangered species, pandas or dogos or whatever, next thing you know he'd be sticking 'Save The Kelpers' stickers all over the Island. And now those 1,500 bastards spitting on the barbecue of 30,000,000, ten times as rich as before the war, and it's all thanks to us – we ended up doing them a favour.'

I'd wondered about that more than once myself: why in the whole war the very same milicos, who had, in their own back yard, perpetrated all the atrocities in the world catalogue and added a few new ones of their own devising, hadn't committed a single one against the native Islanders. Presumably, they were tending to their international image, but it just didn't add up – too rational. Maybe it was just that, if you're going to commit atrocities, you need to see the other as an inferior, and the Kelpers were too White, Aryan and Anglo-Saxon for the Argentinian milicos to dare trample on them. Resigning himself to political negotiation, Verraco had succeeded in interesting the Foreign Ministry in a purchase-and-sale plan: a million dollars for every Kelper in return for their acceptance of Argentinian sovereignty. The scheme was quite advanced when word filtered through to the ex-combatant centres, who organised a demonstration with the slogan 'The Blood We Shed Is Not For Sale', which Verraco himself took part in so as not to be caught with his pants down. 'Now it'll be another eight years and we'll be back to square one, and in the meantime the bastard Kelpers will be fucking like rabbits to increase their worth, while we end up spending ten billion instead of one and a half.'

The English, on the other hand, he got on much better with: it wasn't the first time he'd negotiated with them. He'd begun as soon as the war was over, when the victors returned 4,700 prisoners to the mainland on the *Canberra* and Verraco managed to sneak a lift: when he saw the English at the dock separating the officers from the winding lines of prisoners to keep them on the Islands, he'd got hold of a conscript with a bandaged eye and, taking him to one side, made him remove his coat and jacket and bandage, and swap them for his officer's uniform, and barged his way back into the line. When the others started yelling, 'Oy, you bloody queue-jumper,' he lifted the patch and hissed furiously, 'I'm a commando, you bloody fools; we're going to take this boat and restart the war.' Once he was on board, he discovered that all the deluxe cabins were taken and he'd be sent to sleep on the ballroom carpet, but remembering that when it came to sleeping arrangements he was still an officer, he decided to slip off in search of a cabin.

Tomás, 'El Gordo' Tomás, had just undressed for the first time in two months and, standing barefoot on the miraculously hot floor of the bathroom, was doing his best to recognise the skinny guy staring back at him in the mirror: hair matted in rat's tails, the sunken hollows of his face covered by the undergrowth of patchy beard, an enormous head floating above a puny body with skinny little child's arms and washboard ribs. Twenty kilos lighter, ten years older. Confused, thinking it was someone else in the mirror, he turned round and only found the half-open door, the silence of the cabin, Sergio's feet; Sergio had been lying there in full combat gear for six hours staring at the ceiling without standing up or changing position since they'd arrived. The blissful rush of the hot rain made him forget everything: he was back at home getting ready for Saturday night and, when a knock came at the door, he almost shouted 'Sod off, Tits. I'll be out in a minute' at his sister. Stepping back into his identity as a POW, he wrapped himself in a towel – spongy, white, unimaginable – and went out to see who it was; Sergio hadn't taken his eyes off the ceiling in spite of the hail of knocking. Whirling in came Verraco, the Tasmanian Devil incarnate. 'You fucking queers!' he yelled. 'These are the soldiers of the Argentinian Army? Your comrades-in-arms died in the trenches and you're perfuming yourself like a cheap slut! What's wrong with you, tarting yourself up like that? Got a date with a nice little English, have we? That why they gave you this cabin, is it? Get out of my sight, before I ...'

In spite of the uniform, Tomás realised he was an officer

and was about to obey the order automatically when something occurred to him:

'Hang on. Shouldn't you still be on the Islands?'

Verraco lowered his voice, his weasel's eyes darting everywhere.

'Shhh. This is a secret mission. We're going to take this ship and recapture the Islands. I'm the operation's Commander-in-Chief and I need this cabin as a base,' he said, eyeing the thick beige carpet that Tomás was standing on in his bare feet, and Sergio, without taking his eyes off the ceiling for a second or moving his lips any more than was necessary, said:

'Get out.'

I don't remember exactly what Verraco's reply was; something about a court martial I suppose, because Sergio uncoiled like a spring – a spring it had taken him six hours, or sixty days, to wind up – and in a flash was pounding his knee into Verraco's groin, bashing his head in with the cupboard door and then dragging him out into the corridor by the hair, screaming at him wildly 'Get out! Get out of my fucking room! Get out of my room!' It took three English to grab him and give him a shot to calm him down, and Verraco wound up with five stitches in the head (which he later claimed to be war wounds). Luckily for Sergio, it all happened so fast that Verraco didn't get a proper look at his face.

Ignacio watched him trudge back to the tea- and tobacco-coloured lozenges of the ballroom carpet, limping and bowed, but undaunted: rather than ask permission, he started kicking the slumped conscripts, waking them from their first deep, dry, sheltered sleep in sixty days (the ship's coffee had come with something more than milk in it), braying for them to let him through, 'Fucking dogs, the holiday'll soon be over for you lot,' and if a guard hadn't intervened, half-doped as they were, they'd have thrown him overboard. Then he started shouting for someone who could speak English and, when he found him (some kid from Hurlingham that Ignacio had been talking to), he ordered him to act as interpreter and parley with the enemy. When the kid got back (without Verraco, the English finally realising they had to keep him in a safe place till journey's end), he told Ignacio what he'd begun to translate, as far as modesty allowed: Verraco was apparently convinced that the surrender authorised the English to enter Buenos Aires and wanted to offer the friendly troops his services for whatever they might need. 'I shall be your guide in Argentina,' he made him translate to the English sergeant, who squinted at him befuddled. 'I take you to the best grills and cabarets, *Argentine meat*, best in the world. You think you had enough of Argentine bombshells in this war? Wait till you see the ones we have back home,' he said, obsequiously winking the eye that Sergio hadn't shut for him, and, when he saw the Saxon's indifferent expression, he turned to his interpreter and said, 'Did you translate it right? Did you? Did he get that bit about the birds?' But his insistence on the bombshells must have been his downfall, because the sergeant collared Verraco by his ear and frog-marched him off for interrogation.

I saluted a succession of familiar faces and asked them where he was. 'He'll be right here,' they told me. 'He was expecting you; he does nothing but talk about this video game. You brought it, didn't you? Siddown, siddown. Want some coffee?'

They were watching a video entitled *You Choose*, designed to seduce the Kelpers into accepting Argentinian sovereignty.

The bit I saw alternated images of local tourist spots like the Iguazú Falls, the Rambla and its sea-lions in January ('Mar del Plata: Happy City' read the subtitles), the Casa de Tucumán and San Carlos de Bariloche, interspersed with grey shots of the Liverpool Docks, the stony beaches of Brighton, abandoned coal mines in Newcastle and the slums of the East End under a winter fog. Next, exaggeratedly carefree, blonde-haired Argentinian families shopping in a mall, visiting the zoo, buying balloons for children in squares . . . against a multi-racial mass of squatters shooting up among piles of garbage, teeming Pakistani, Caribbean or Arabic quarters, punk parties where shorn teenage girls with tits poking through the holes in their corsets inserted tongues pierced like shower curtains into the ears of swastika-skulled skinheads ('This could be your daughter,' read the subtitle). A mellifluous radio voice crooned seductively: 'Argentina, land of promise . . . where natural beauties by the hand of man have achieved at all harmony . . . the better country of the world can be yours . . .'

I approached the desk of Mr George Turner, the Kelper they kept as a consultant. On 2nd April the troops entering Stanley had found him waving a solitary little light-blue-and-white flag, and from then on he'd become the spokesperson for the conciliatory position. His attempts at rapprochement with the Argentinian authorities over those two months and a half hadn't exactly paid off, unless you count being kicked out as a collaborator after the defeat. After bobbing along on the seas of exile, he eventually landed up in this dark cellar, where his first-hand knowledge of the geographic, demographic and economic ins-and-outs of the Islands had at first been deemed of prime importance. 'If we'd had a man like this around when we planned the campaign in '82,' Verraco had announced with one arm around his shoulder, 'things would have turned out very differently.' The initial enthusiasm soon gave way to mere interest, then tolerance, and finally exasperation and ostracism. Turner knew practically everything about the Islands, but after the first two months there wasn't much else to tell, and he inevitably began to fall into repetition, exaggeration and irrelevant anecdote. He became more of an anachronism with every passing year, and, little by little, his information and opinions acquired that sickly sepia tone that advertises how far the political has become the merely historical. George, however, hadn't stopped dreaming, and few people defended the idea of recapture by any possible means the way he did: it was his only ticket back to the Islands. Macerating in Argentinian Scotch from breakfast time, his nostalgia would grow with the passing hours, until afternoon found him hugging the empty bottle, making a vaguely masturbatory movement with his hands that no one understood, until a passing native Patagonian from Chubut identified it as the action of shearing sheep, and they frequently had to take him back up to the surface and hail a taxi at the mall's exit to whisk him off to his bedsit in Constitución. He hadn't seen me for two years but greeted me effusively all the same: ever since my departure he hadn't had a chance to hold such fluent conversations in his native English, and – lying through my teeth – I told him he was looking well, though, after such prolonged confinement away from his natural habitat, he was deteriorating like a zoo animal: the once rosy red chops now pallid and bony, the vigorous, blonde hair now thatching his head with dimmed and dull tufts of dead straw. He poured me a half-glass from the almost empty bottle and started spouting drivel in his native tongue:

'You might find it difficult to imagine now, my Argie friend' – that's what he called us – 'but in my day the Islands were one of the quietest, most peaceful places to live on earth. Before the war it was all peace and friendship: life may sometimes have been boring, but it was simple. Our time was divided equally between work, looking after the vegetable patch and healthy recreation with family and neighbours: cutting and drying the peat, playing darts in the pub, going to the cinema in the church or having dinner at a friend's house. True, there *was* a shortage of women and more than one suitor left the dance floor with a handful of teeth for not having respected the dance cards, and it wasn't uncommon for us, well into the fifth pint, to burst into the ladies and grab a handful of whatever was on offer, but sometimes young English misses would come over with temporary contracts, and then we had a right old time, us Stanley lads did, trailing down the street after them like dogs on heat. I remember one,' he said smiling glassily, a dribble of saliva trickling from the corner of his slack lips, 'a secretary of the Falkland Islands Company, who used to go bathing in the sea off the company dock in summer. But the interesting thing was that she did it in her birthday suit,' he said, winking a tearful eye at me, 'and at that time of day – noon – all work in town would stop and the neighbouring piers were in danger of collapsing under the weight of the spectators. Until the local women, guided by our invaluable pastor, the Reverend Angus Mothbite, decided to put an end to the spectacle by removing the pier's ladder while the unprejudiced and unprepared young woman waved her arms about vigorously in the icy waters of the bay. Her teeth were still chattering a week later when she boarded the plane. By the way,' he went on, 'did I tell you the one about the "nice girl" who serviced twenty men in one night? Before the war, the men used to get back from the shearing a little . . . "charged up", if you get my drift,' and he made an obscene gesture I couldn't help nodding to. 'It reminds me of a joke my friend Stephen "Hogpen" Bullock used to tell: why are pansies more sensitive to the solitude of country life?' Then, without waiting for a reply from my already cramped smile of friendly interrogation, he said, 'Because it's always easier to bugger a ram than get buggered by one,' he exploded, spraying Scotch like a harpooned whale spouting, and immediately pulling himself together: 'Now that's something you *never* saw among us; our community was safe from the moral corruption that afflicts the rest of the world. No homosexuals, no drug addicts, no communists (we used to carefully question every Polack who tried to desert to make sure they weren't double agents), and – as you'll have confirmed during your I hope pleasant stay in our midst – no colonial races. A few English tourists used to come and visit, not to discover the exoticism of the southern seas, but to regain the taste and smell of the England of their grandparents, now irretrievably lost. Anyway, to get back to our story, there are thirty men in the queue, and the one who goes first, well-known in the Islands for his virility, goes to the back of the queue and at dawn, when it's his turn again, the girl turns him away in a huff: "What do you think I am? A whore?"' he concluded and went as red as a pillar box with laughter. 'I remember you as a polite, cultured young man, different from the insensitive rabble I'm surrounded by, which is why I'm trusting you with these vignettes of idyllic life in the Falklands . . .' (the Islands' old name used to slip out whenever he got sloshed). 'Right now I'd be in the pub with friends, reminiscing about last year's February celebrations. Have I told you about the February festivities, dear boy?' he asked, the words floating in the aspic of his voice, and it was no use telling him he had – several times and in a wealth of detail. 'The February celebrations are held at the end of the shearing and last for a week, and the farms fill with guests sleeping ten or twenty to a room. No coincidence then that most of us Islanders are born in November! The preparations get under way six weeks beforehand: the women make their preserves and puddings, and the men train their animals. We have country horse-races, sheepdog trials, tests of horsemanship, bull-riding, sack races, pillow fights . . . and the women have to catch a cock! They yomp in from the four corners of the camp to take part. And the dances! Every night there's fox-trotting, waltzing, barn-dancing . . . even pop music performed by our local Beatles group: Agatha Kristie.' ('Just as well we lost,' a passing orderly whispered to me and immediately dodged the rubber I shot at him.) 'Ah, the last one I went to,' he said, resting a hand on my shoulder so as not to fall over. 'One of them got up on the dinner table, like that hippie film they sometimes show on cable – have you seen it? – and started dancing, and we had to whack him in the shins with a leg of roast lamb to get him down. And in the middle of the Scotch dancing someone let this huge pig loose on the dance floor! You should have seen the women's faces! Terrified, the pig crapped all over the floor and people kept slipping and falling in the shit! Mrs Merryweather broke her hip and we've been calling her "the lame sow" ever since! Died recently she did,' he said, downing another glass of

Scotch to replenish his tear ducts. 'If there's one thing that's never been lacking in our Islands, it's good, clean fun,' he went on and started giving me a detailed account of Friday nights on the town, '. . . five men to each woman, sometimes not even that, and then we'd end up dancing with each other . . .'

I was saved by Verraco, who whirled in shouting at me without saying hello. 'What are you up to! You haven't installed it yet? They're all waiting.' I said goodbye to George, who in his drunken stupor had perhaps mistaken my hand for one of the Islands and wouldn't let go, and stepped out into the corridor. An unmistakable, welcoming, almost homely aroma filtered under the door of my old office, and in my enthusiasm I knocked loudly, without noticing that the old wooden door had been replaced by a press-board one, into which my knuckles sank, making a dent, at the bottom of which a fine crack appeared, and in my attempts to grout it with saliva my finger went through to the other side; but before I could pull it out again, I felt someone grab it and cried out, backing my arm up with such force that it took the skewered door with it. 'I've got him! I've got the spy!' screeched an indignant voice from the other side, without letting go or showing itself, the door still suspended between the two of us. I tried to circle round him, but that only made him turn too and we'd started to get dizzy when, with a shove, I managed to pop the door back into its frame, this time with me on the inside and my dancing partner on the outside. While I was holding the fort against the battering of his fists, I checked out the alterations they'd made: it was narrower owing to a new partition, and a lot of the old computers had been replaced, but something intangible preserved its identity. The smell probably, I thought, as I scanned the place until I spotted a wisp of smoke and let go of the door to open a drawer which, as if it had been holding its breath, exhaled a blast of white fumes. Catapulted forwards, a gangling nerd burst into the room and trained his bright, glassy eyes and chinless jaw on me, and shouted at me in that shrill and brittle voice affected by young men who've been given too much authority:

'You haven't touched anything, have you?'

I pulled furiously on the spliff to breathe life into its embers. Then I held it aloft.

'This.'

'You from narcotics, are you? What section?'

'I'm from the outside.'

He brushed aside a greasy cowlick that had got in the way of his disbelief. He looked as if he'd just woken up from a nap in a tin of sardines.

'Outside? Are you pulling my leg?'

'Can't. No hands free,' I said, puffing merrily away. 'Verraco sent me.'

His face changed the second he heard the name; even his hair suddenly perked up as in a before-and-after shampoo ad.

'But then you must be . . . Forgive me, Master, I didn't recognise you, come in and sit down. Félix, Felipe Félix, my God.' He offered me a seat, another joint, a right hand with long, serrated, black-rimmed nails. 'You don't know how often I've imagined this moment . . .'

'And who are you?'

'Your disciple.'

'Didn't know I had any.'

'I applied for this job so I could study your designs in

depth. I tried to follow in your footsteps, you know. If you've got time, I'd like to show you some improvements I've made, I mean changes . . . I always wanted to be like you.'

'I didn't.'

He eased the tension floating in the air with conciliatory gestures of his long, fine fingers, flat-tipped like spatulas, adapted to the computer keys the way bats' fingers are adapted to flight or seals' to swimming.

'I know, I know. I don't belong here either. This is just a temporary thing. So I can be close to them,' he said, caressing the nearest computer. 'That's the price, isn't it? Did you bring the game? I'm dying to try it out.'

I nodded wordlessly, as I was holding my breath. I needed a more relaxed working atmosphere to perform the task in hand and, as the one outside wasn't looking very favourable, I'd just have to create it inside. The rough edges of reality were soon mellowed by the smoke, becoming as soft and malleable as a dunked bay biscuit.

'Why did they isolate the network?' I asked him.

'Look,' he apologised, 'it's nothing to do with you. I know your defences were extremely secure, but paranoïa's an endemic disease around here you know. And since they don't know the first thing about computers . . . Every time they pressed the wrong key and the screen vanished, they started screaming "Digital subversion! Computer anarchism!" It was better I swear, you were breathing shit, it was unbearable.'

'I know. Why do you think I left?'

'Anyway, it's a logical inevitability. Paranoïa, I mean. You know. If the intelligence service exists to keep an eye on *everybody*, it has to incorporate another service to keep an eye on the first one, then a third, and a fourth . . . A classic infinite regress. That's how you formulated it, isn't it?'

'More or less. I wanted to show them that an intelligence service that works properly is a logical impossibility. Just to wind them up.'

'But you were right! Your predictions were right! That's why the SIDE only investigates itself now. The idea being that you can only solve the crimes you commit yourself. It simplifies everything. They've even decided to start with the solution and plan the crime backwards.'

I looked uneasily around me, then at the garrulous nerd, with an annoyance that masked the beginnings of fear. The dope had begun to kick in. I should have thought about this before taking the first toke.

'Aren't they listening to us?'

'Of course they are.'

'So how come you're telling me all this?'

He'd just taken another synthetic cherry drop out of its sticky cellophane wrapper (his third: he apparently survived exclusively on them) and wiped his fingers on his pants before answering in sugary tones:

'The only thing secrets produce is more curiosity. But, if we tell them all . . . We conducted tests. We tied the subjects to a chair and revealed the most horrifying state secrets to them one after another. You know how long the subject with the most staying power lasted? Two hours. After that it was like he was listening to the sea. You asked him to repeat things for you and he'd start mumbling nonsense. Information is the new opium of the people.' He let out a laugh of insincere humility. 'But anyway, you know all about that better than I do.'

Although theoretical digressions can normally grip me for hours, especially when I'm stoned, something was beginning to bother me: the eager looks of approval as he repeated my pedantic theories of yesteryear, the mixture of adulation and arrogance, the dreadful brotherhood he was yoking me into. It wasn't his fault; it was just that it bothered me to see myself reflected in such a deformed mirror. What was I going to do if he decided to stick around? It was vital for me to work alone if I was going to avoid discovery.

'Look, the way I see it, the SIDE's an anarchist utopia in reverse. An organisation without leaders where nobody's free. Nothing like the tower, is it.'

I have to admit that the combination of the dope and his inane prattle had made me drop my guard, but if he was testing my reaction, he can't have seen much more change in my expression than a statue's when a bird shits on its head.

'You mean the Tower of the English in Retiro?' I asked, with wide-open innocent Tweety Pie eyes.

He laughed. For a moment I thought he had a keyboard in his mouth, but it was just his stained teeth.

'Come on. You know which! The Tamerlán Tower! An antiquated design. So rigid, compared to ours. Its function is to make people feel permanently watched over, even if they aren't. Here it's the other way round.'

Waves of relief ran up my thighs. It was just another theoretical question.

'It's the master's eye that fattens the beast . . .' I muttered, without a clue what I meant by it.

'It can't see into these tunnels. It's we servants who keep an eye on the masters here. We complement each other. We're the moat around the castle. And they,' he said with a slight bow towards the almighty computers, 'are the higher authority on which the whole human sphere depends. Plato was right after all. In there live the Ideas and we are the new philosophers governing the Republic, because they'll only speak to us.' He drew closer until his voice became a complicitous whisper in my ear. Bad breath and all. He raised one of his E.T. fingers: 'We hold the power of the key. Now you know who's running the show here. One day we'll even be able to do without the agents, and a handful of us hackers spying on each other's computers will be able to cope with all the work. Soon there'll *only* be simulations, virtual wars. An exact copy makes the original unnecessary.'

'Try dropping a colour photocopy of a blotter and see if you flip,' I muttered.

He smiled. He'd been provoking me.

'I know. Your generation still believes in all that stuff about extending human capabilities. But look at them. Isn't it us who are extending them?' he said, patting one as if it were a thoroughbred. 'The human mind's an imperfect machine. Some day they'll replace us completely.'

Instead of answering him I went to the nearest keyboard and typed in a simple instruction. Immediately the ordered columns, lines and graphs on all the monitors shattered like so many reflections on a still lake into which someone just threw a stone, and one by one the screens died into a series of windows open to a starless night sky. From the neighbouring rooms came shouts, wails, swearwords, anguished cries for help. The nerd's face had gone a delicate shade of matt grey like the plastic of the computers, as if, chameleon-like, he wanted to blend into them.

'What have you done . . . ? All the . . . systems are down. What have you done?' he stammered.

'The paradox of the hanged man. Haven't you read *Don Quixote?*'

'No, what's that got to do with it . . . ?'

'You should read it.'

'Paper hurts my eyes. You'd better fix this, Félix, or I'm a dead man.'

'You're the governor of an island. On the island there's a river; over the river there's a bridge; at the end of the bridge there's a gallows. Everyone who wants to pass that way has to say where they're going: if they tell the truth, they're free to go on their way; if they lie, they're hanged from the gallows. The system works admirably until one day a man arrives who says he's come to be hanged on that very gallows. See where it's going? If they decide to hang him, he was telling the truth and doesn't deserve to die; if he doesn't die, he was lying and they're obliged to hang him. What would you do in their place?'

Six telephones started ringing at once. The nerd stretched out his hand, wondering which one to grab, like some new variation on Russian roulette. He let them ring.

'What did you input that into the computer for? You've driven it mad. Computers can't solve logical paradoxes.'

'Because they're perfect. So, what would you do?'

'Nothing, you can't do anything. The problem has no solution, I've already told you!'

'Sancho found one. You know what he decided?'

'No!'

'That he should live. When justice is in doubt, it's better

to opt for mercy. The only way to solve a paradox: skip a level. From logic to ethics. Isn't it brilliant?'

Just then Verraco whirled in like a miniature twister.

'What are you up to, you dickh— Oh, Félix, it's you. I should've known. Have you installed the game for me? What the fuck is going on?'

'Slight glitch. We're sorting it out, but we have a problem and we need your opinion. Imagine you're the governor of an island . . .'

'If they'd made me governor instead of Menéndez, I still would be, I can assure you.'

'That's right. You're the governor of the Malvinas. You put a gallows on the Moody Brook bridge . . .' I told him the rest. When I'd finished, he stood there staring at me.

'So?'

'So what would you do?'

'Hang him for being such a smart alec. Where's all this leading?'

I looked at the nerd with raised eyebrows.

'Now do you understand why we're irreplaceable?'

* * *

With the nerd out of action and banished to some obscure tunnel of the anthill, I sat, fingers itching, in front of the keyboard's array of smooth nipples and, with the adrenaline rushing through my veins, I began to run through the files where the secret lives of everyone in Argentina worth knowing anything about flickered in the crackling fire of ones and zeros. My successor had changed the codes and cancelled several shortcuts I'd left for myself, but he hadn't detected them all. You're pretty good, kiddo, but you're no match for the Master, I crooned mentally to him as, in a few keystrokes, I reached the files on Tamerlán and his sons. While I was copying them onto floppies, which the machine dropped one by one into my hand like an obedient dog, I checked, just in case, to see if the file I was looking for was among them. Apparently not: they only went up to 1991; all the files on this year had to be somewhere else. It took me another ten minutes to find out where. The file name was C/TAMERL.592. It was impregnable; hacking into it and dodging the alarms manually could take me hours. Time for the Falklands 140682 worm to work its magic.

* * *

Back at home, I bunged the floppies in the computer and grabbed the receiver to call Verraco. I'd left him playing, drooling with joy, yelling 'Gotcha! Gotcha! I'll show you, you bastards!', the veins in his neck bulging with the strain, belching out hoarse cries of victory every time he sank a ship or shot down an enemy plane. He'd forgotten all about the outside world and its inhabitants; his only reality, that screen glowing with colours so much brighter than the drab hues of nature. 'Verraco is back! Nobody believed me, but, here he is!' he yelled, wrenching the joystick back and forth in his clenched fists. Rarely had I seen a happiness purer than that which steadily invaded the screwed-up face of this old, moustachioed child as one by one he recovered the positions he'd lost ten years ago. He'd entered an ideal world of repetition without boredom, of surprises without nasty shocks, outside all time but the one created by the temporary obstacles the computer put in his way; without changeovers, without stopovers, without a military career, he could jump from the option 'Rambo Single-Handed v The World', mowing down, immortal, twenty divisions of the English army with a single machine gun, to the no less illusory 'General Controlling Every Step of the War like a Game of Chess', the two polar, yet complementary, opposites of every dyed-in-the-wool soldier's fantasies.

'So? How's it hanging?' I said to him when he picked up.

'We're winning!' crowed his jubilant voice at the other end, and he hung up without further ado. Better that way. While I waited for the virus to take effect, I had time to quietly read through Tamerlán's record and find out a couple of things that had intrigued me.

The Tamerláns had arrived in Argentina just after the end of the war, but there were no records prior to 1955; some far-sighted employee, perhaps paid off by Wolf Tamerlán suddenly coy about his former proximity to President Perón, probably burned them, along with the stacks of portraits of the now-deposed 'fugitive Tyrant' and Evita that in those days hung on every wall. Then, patiently, over the years, his conscientious successors had gradually filled in the gaps with newspaper and magazine cuttings and assorted documents that patched together an official, somewhat sweetened version of Wolf Tamerlán and his son Fausto's first ten years in Argentina. In one interview from 1973, for example, appeared a photo of a forty-something Fausto inaugurating a working-class housing complex, grinning in his brand-new leather jacket and sharing the V-for-victory with all around him. 'The Day I Came To This Country, I Was Already A Peronist,' bragged one headline, and then went on: 'We disembarked at the port alone, my father and I, down a gangway left by the sailors in their haste, before we lost sight of them. There was no one there to welcome us, no one in all the endless empty port, and we trudged for blocks without running into a soul, dragging our only suitcase behind us. We didn't even know what direction the city lay in. But it was a sunny day and, in my childish innocence, I marvelled at the fact that we were sweating in our shirtsleeves in mid-October and that the branches of the trees were so full of leaves. We walked for two hours: the bars, the shops, the houses . . . everything was closed; there wasn't even any traffic. We were used to seeing devastated cities as dead as the landscape of the moon; but this – an entire city, with all its flowers and the singing of the birds, and devoid of people – this scared me more than anything I'd seen in the war. Reaching a broad avenue, we heard a distant roar drawing nearer, and the flagstones began to shake beneath our feet as if a stampede of thousands of animals (no offence) were headed in our direction. Curious, we quickened our pace towards the corner from where the tremors seemed to be coming and, when we got there, we were swept up by a torrent. Like a river bursting dam after dam, the fervent, pulsing human tide dragged us with it. Struggling just to stay together, we let ourselves be carried along until it flowed into a large square, a sea of dark brown heads dancing before the great pink reef that held back the pounding of its heavy swell. Tired from our trek and sore from the trampling, we took off our shoes and, as we had done so often in Rome, sank our feet into the balmy cool of a fountain. [*He smiles.*] Delighted at our daring, pointing at us and shouting "The Gringos! Look at the Gringos!" dozens of sweating workers imitated us, and soon the fountain was filled with their laughter and splashing. My ears still ring with the sound rising up from that human swell, like a seashell that is always with me; and without knowing its meaning – without even knowing if it was a complaint or an insult or an expression of popular jubilation – we joined in with the chorus of this people that had taken us to their bosom. With difficulty at first, then with enthusiasm and finally with genuine fervour, struggling with our guttural rs, like babes astonishing their parents, we pronounced the first word of this new language that would change our lives for ever: "Perón! Perón! Perón!" It was 17th October 1945.'

The next two decades, on the other hand, were so detailed it made you yawn and I flicked through them, taking the odd peck at the tastiest titbits. The smoke hadn't yet lifted on the bombardments and executions of '55 when old Daddy Wolf, arrested pre-emptively for his real or feigned sympathies with the fugitive Tyrant, began to do business with his captors, who were dazzled by the former officer's background and, grateful for the juicy cuts that came with each public work they threw at his feet, they also decided to turn a blind eye to the arrest warrants taken out by the police forces of six European countries intent on discovering the fate of certain golden rings Herr Tamerlán had managed to grab while riding the merry-go-round of the war. He had enough time left to see his son graduate as an engineer and buy him his first estancia as a wedding present for marrying the surname furnished by a rather mouldy representative of the local aristocracy, Remedios Prado Agote; but not enough to meet his first grandson, Fausto Tamerlán II, born two months after his grandfather's plane nose-dived into the Misiones jungle not far from the Brazilian border.

It was Konrad Fuchs, Wolf's partner in the construction business, who arrived in Argentina in late '46 at his former boss's invitation, who should have been on that plane, but he'd made his excuses the day before, blaming an infection, and people were amazed at his miraculous escape, which didn't, for all that, leave him in legal control of the company: he and the son of his late partner both came to be equal majority shareholders, so that neither would hold sway over the other; but the truth was that Fausto, until that moment – his twenty-fifth birthday – had done little more than chase after young boys once he'd given his father the heir he demanded, and the practical, day-to-day running of the company passed to Fuchs. Fuchs & Tamerlán plc moved beyond the restricted field of civil construction and property speculation, buying and selling land and even whole towns, obtaining monstrous public contracts as a front for German holding companies, and on into public works on a grand scale such as the El Chocón Dam. Seeing that the company gravy train was whistling past and threatening to leave him standing at the station counting the small change, Fausto caught hold of the tail-end carriage and little by little, each step taking years, he moved up through the freight compartment, third class, second class, first class and pullman until he was standing at the engine driver's side. From the locomotive, a new twist in the convoluted braid of Argentina's destiny – which by now resembled a DNA chain – could be seen in the tracks ahead. Sensing his time had come at last, Fausto pointed out the imminent danger and, when his partner stuck his head out to see what it was, he pushed him out of the train.

The opening pages of Fuchs' catalogue of woes were laced

with the clichés of the day: kidnapped by Montoneros outside his house in front of his wife and kiddies, who were coming out to wave him goodbye, he withstood two months' captivity before showing up at the door of the company, located in those days in a building on Paseo Colón, with a bullet in his head and a placard round his neck listing the charges for which he'd been tried and found guilty, but omitting the main one, which was not coming up with the ransom money in time. Fuchs' wife was ruined in the attempt, selling off at bargain-basement prices all the properties, company assets and so on that weren't tied up, mainly to her husband's partner, who, after extremely careful calculations no doubt, did everything in his power to round up just enough to fall short of the required amount. But the really juicy part was yet to come. One of the Montoneros captured a few days after the 'investigation' confessed (it never ceases to amaze me how these written transcriptions of torture sessions read like people chatting in comfy chairs, smoking pipes): 'He handed him to us on a plate, with a detailed list of all his comings and goings, weapons, bodyguards, et cetera. He saved us all the groundwork; months it can take sometimes. That's why we fell for it, and also because he promised us he was worth more than he looked. "He's very clever," he assured us, "he'll try and convince you it's too much. But you stand your ground and don't ask for less than five, lads. Any trouble, I'll cover the difference. And remember: ever onwards to victory." We tried Fuchs on three occasions just to kill the time, but it was no use. We had to execute him after Tamerlán appeared on TV saying he'd already delivered the money to us – you all saw it; the fucker even had the nerve to look straight into the camera and send us a message: "We all want a better country.

But this isn't the way. Think, boys . . . before it's too late." He grabbed the company and the cash in one fell swoop. Tamerlán fucked us all.'

I looked up from my monitor at the ceiling. I could picture him clearly now, even better than when he'd told me himself, on the building's terrace roof – the traffic on Paseo Colón, the red night sky of Buenos Aires, the distant river – raising his chalice to heaven and drinking a toast with the Only One who, for the time being, still stood above him, gulping down the gold nuggets in the stream of sparkling liquid: choicest blood and flesh, only for the elect. Yes, the Tamerlán I knew had been born that night, or rather conceived. No sooner had I returned to the ordered stars of the digital night than I corrected myself, for the next paragraph of the Montonero's confession pointed to a more decisive nativity in this garbled astral chart: 'So two months later we decided to hold him to a strict reckoning . . .', and I scrolled down several pages to find out what he was talking about – though it wasn't hard to guess.

The Montoneros had motives to burn: apart from setting them up – thereby merely bowing to the new star of the times – and having the militants who dished out leaflets on his building sites and used to come and go as they pleased beaten up and kicked out, to add insult to injury, he became close friends with the arch-villain of the day, Perón's right hand and founder of the Argentine Anticommunist Alliance – the infamous Triple A – José 'The Wizard' López Rega. It all started with the Altar of the Fatherland, a kind of Roman Forum mega-development where all Argentina's national heroes from San Martín to Perón would be buried. For the sake of securing the contracts, it seems that Tamerlán even took part in secret rituals to bless the works, sacrificing yellow hens at midnight and sambaing, maracas in hand, with The Wizard and some phony Brazilian *pai-de-santo* on the hills of rubble, which was as far as the project ever got. But I suppose Tamerlán never bothered much about his kidnappers' real and quite understandable motives; they must have appeared to him merely as the instrument of a higher wrath that used them to make him atone for his treatment of Fuchs. If such an egocentric as Tamerlán – the term is too small for him: let's call him a *geo*centric – comes to believe that the machinery of the universe is driven by moral laws, he must then have thought that a large part of that machinery was set in motion to punish his crime in the worst possible way, with a refined cruelty for which no random chain of events could be held responsible. Being blown up in your car or machine-gunned or kidnapped was just one of those risks you learned to live with in those days, but for the Judas to be his own son, his heir made by him in his own image, was as if he'd been stabbed by his own reflection in the mirror. He had nine months to reflect on the matter, nine months underground in a damp cell, where there was neither light not air, nor any sound other than curt voices muffled by hoods. One of those voices, to which he couldn't, until much later, put a face other than the blurred, Protean one his imagination had given it, informed him that it had been his son who'd turned him in; although, from what the boy would claim when questioned, it was a female classmate from the Buenos Aires National School who'd milked him for semen and information in equal measure, and, if he'd ended up taking part in meetings and sit-ins and *Anti-Dühring* study groups, it was out of love and the landslide of class guilt that his more radicalised schoolmates had landed him with. The voice that now sprinkled the spores of doubt daily in the father's ear, spores that in the hours of interminable darkness proliferated in his mind like toadstools until they made him picture his son's face beneath any of the hoods that had dragged him from the men's sauna where he was ambushed to the waiting car – the same voice that behind his comrades' backs would negotiate the prisoner's ransom with Army Intelligence, was that of a young man who served in the armed organisation under the nickname 'Chirolita' and studied at the Faculty of Medicine under the name Alfredo Canal. It's difficult to say for sure exactly how far his intervention affected the course of events; but the truth was that when, on a day like any other (the very concept of 'day' must have been wiped out in the private calendar that reigned inside the hole; by the outside world's it was mid-April 1976), shots and explosions rang out, and a pair of rough hands dragged up into the blinding light a very different man from the one who had made the descent, the soon-to-graduate Dr Canal had already laid the foundations for his new career as the Rasputin of the afflicted family of builders.

The life-saving hands in question belonged to an army officer active in the task groups that had waged the first battles of the Dirty War: his name, Arturo Cuervo, rang a bell from somewhere, probably Malvinas; I made a mental note to check up on him later on. Shared experience sometimes creates deep bonds between the most dissimilar of people, all the more so between the son of a German officer and this enthusiast schooled in the same ideals. Through him Tamerlán cemented his ties to the upper echelons of the military, but if in his dealings with them he was little different from the other big businessmen who promoted and supported the coup, it was his more intimate, engaged relationship with Captain Cuervo that set him apart. The visiting hours left little room to suspect humanitarian motives: 'Olimpo Garage, 25/7/76, 23.45 to 06.15; Banfield Hole, 01/11/76, 00.45 to 05.15; Orletti Motors, 09/3/77, 02.30 to 08.55; Olimpo Garage, 10/7/77, 00.00 to 08.30 . . .' There were no details of what he did in his nocturnal descents to these discreet concentration camps spread over the length and breadth of the city, whether he was content to look on at what Cuervo and his henchmen were doing or whether he'd sometimes be allowed to join in; whether on trying his hand he limited himself to those responsible for his captivity or whether, in the event, he wasn't picky; either way, the face that came out of those pits of pure pain with the first light of day can't have been a very pretty sight. What was it – aside from his self-professed contempt for those colleagues who let the military go about their dirty work with impunity while they kept their own noses clean – that ate into him and made him return to the nocturnal depths again and again, with Cuervo as his Virgil? Was it perhaps that a delicate equilibrium resulted from the balance of his diurnal and nocturnal activities, the latter maybe fulfilling for him the same function as did weekends in some Club Med for his less imaginative colleagues? What is certain is that Tamerlán and his empire reached their peaks of splendour in those years: the two peaks of the towers to be specific, which he started building shortly after his release. Four years he took to erect that mountain of light in the sky, gestated during his nine months underground; but clearly some secret taste for the more tempting regions of the night had seeped into his blood for ever, because, for all the days spent in the lucidity of the heights, every now and again he had one of those nights when fear and pain were darkly sought, like a fever taking hold of his entire organism.

There seemed to have been a reconciliation of sorts between father and son before the opening, attended by the top brass, and at around the same time there was a cooling in the relationship between Tamerlán Snr and now 'Major' Arturo Cuervo: the latter, apparently unsuccessful in his attempts to convince the former that the best property deal in Argentina since the Conquest of the Desert was to invest in the future of – I knew it! I just knew we'd get there sooner or later! – the Islands. Tamerlán's son, who'd just arrived from Austria and found himself doing his belated military service under Cuervo's protective wing, also had something to do with Malvinas, but, before I could find out exactly what, the telephone made me jump, as if it had screamed rather than rung. At the other end Verraco's voice was trembling. I could hear the tears in his choking voice.

'The English have won! They're entering Puerto Argentino!'

I calmed him down as best I could: 'Listen, you can't win them all; let's try not to give in to triumphalism, Commander Sir; remember we promised not to make the same mistakes the second time around.' I gave him a few practical tips and persuaded him to try again. His call had made me anxious and I couldn't go on reading, so I stuck some leftover takeaway milanesa and chips in the microwave and gobbled them down while I waited for him to call back. It was no more than an hour before I had the exquisite pleasure of hearing the broken voice of my former Commander when he rang back.

'They're sailing on Buenos Aires! I can't stop them!'

'I'm on my way,' I told him, and hung up.

With reddened eyes Verraco leaped up when he saw me come in. The English flag was waving from the Obelisk. It was an unnecessarily cruel touch, I admit, but one I just hadn't been able to resist.

'What happened?' I said to him, feigning intense curiosity.

'I don't know, we were undefeated, then suddenly . . .' He shook the joystick, which had cracked from the effort and now hung limply from its wires. 'This piece of crap kept getting stuck and my shots kept going wide and the game kept getting faster and faster . . . Did you really understand what I asked you for?' He smiled, forcedly, aware that the others were watching us. 'It's not as if everything had to be a pushover for us, but hey . . . you could at least have warned me; how embarrassing, my subordinates are going to think their chief . . .' He lowered his voice and whispered in my ear: 'Isn't there some way we can sort it out?'

'I made it as easy as I could,' I said in whisper loud enough for everyone to hear. 'I can't understand how the English could have won.'

Stifled giggles were heard and Verraco scoured the room with furious glances.

'I'll have to check all the software. It'll take time.'

Verraco had remained standing there at the side of the screen as if it were an X-ray and I the doctor drawing in my breath before hitting him with 'It's cancer.'

'A *long* time.'

Once I was sure no one could spy on me over my shoulder, I clicked my fingers over the keys to whistle for my tracer program and up it popped, obediently wagging its tail, with César Tamerlán's file in its mouth. It was all here: his statements, those of the witnesses, blurred photographs of the broken window and dented lawn, with selected pixels highlighting the dead man's outline and, at the end, the sacred scroll, valued at one hundred thousand dollars, with names, addresses, phone numbers, IDs and all the information Tamerlán needed to bribe the witnesses effectively. Victory, victory! I exclaimed to myself, closing my eyes and thanking the infinite heaven of cyberspace that had rained this manna on me. While I copied everything onto a floppy, I killed the virus so that, from now on, Verraco could suck on his new dummy hitch-free. I copied not only the SIDE file, but the Federal Police file too, and made back-ups of both just in case. A hundred thousand dollars. Piece of cake.

Chapter 5

THE FREEDOM EQUATION

1   Margaret Hilda Thatcher
2   Leopoldo Fortunato Galtieri
3   Liverpool FC
4   CA Boca Juniors
5   Sir Winston Churchill
6   Juan Domingo Perón
7   Carlos Menem
8   John Major
9   William Shakespeare
10   Jorge Luis Borges
11   Jeremy Moore
12   Mario Benjamín Menéndez
13   Che Guevara
14   Sid Vicious
15   John Lennon
16   Carlos Gardel
17   Evita
19   Lady Di
19   Pucará
20   Sea Harrier

21 San Martín
22 Nelson
23 Paul 'Gazza' Gascoigne
24 Diego Armando Maradona
25 Nicanor Costa Méndez

'The wound in your head seems to have affected you in a highly original way, Sr Félix. In all the literature on the subject I can't remember a single case like yours.'

'I swear to you, the names were there last night,' I said, unable to prise my terrified eyes away from the screen.

'Perhaps your computer's the one that needs the treatment then.'

Fingers trembling, I dived to the deeps of my files. I'd brought something else with me from the SIDE: a sneaky little program. I displayed it on the screen.

'Here it is,' I said.

'What.'

'A vampire.'

'Expand please.'

'A program that activates itself at night. A species of virus. This is what's replaced the real names on the list with these ridiculous ones.'

'How did it get in there?'

I reread the list to confirm my initial suspicions. The nerd's revenge, for sure.

'You see all the names referring to Malvinas? It has nothing to do with you people; it's personal. My replacement at the SIDE: my disciple.'

'Is that how they all remember you?'

'Never heard of Judas? Brutus? Jung?'

'Yes. But I'd rather hear how you mean to fix this.'

I went back to the files and scrolled through them while he watched.

'Look: nothing else has been touched – statements, addresses, documents, phone numbers . . . all real. I expect you've already got some of the names – the real names, I mean. And for the others, all you have to do is phone and ask . . .'

I didn't even find myself convincing. I looked skywards to avoid my reflection. Through the skylights, the grey clouds of the winter evening swirled past. I watched the pensive Canal out of the corner of my eye as he tapped his kneecap with one of the floppy disks, making his leg twitch almost imperceptibly every so often. In the end he sighed and, signalling to me to stand up, he led the way to the mirror that connected with Sr Tamerlán's office, which, instead of dissolving magically like last time, remained fixed and frozen, taking sadistic glee in conspiring with its neighbours to reflect my thousand faces of a dog that's just wet the carpet. The psychoanalyst touched the glass with his fingers, paused for a moment, then removed them.

'We'll have to wait. Sr Tamerlán's lobbying support.'

Five interminable minutes went by before the door opened and our reflections disappeared in the stream of air as in the choppy waters of a lake. Even before my eyes registered it, Tamerlán's presence announced itself with an unmistakable bellow.

'You're hopeless! Hopeless! A poxy little law to get that fucking reserve off my back and you can't get it passed! You should have twisted the president's arm to sign a decree then! Why do you think I *put* you in Congress? The ecologists are going to eat me alive now!'

When I went inside, I could see them. There was a stout-ish, balding man with a skimpy little beard sheltering under the desk, trying to nestle deep into the tangle of computer wires like a wounded animal in the undergrowth while Tamer-lán ran round the desk dealing out kicks and taking swipes at him with his riding-crop whenever he got the chance. The congressman was very well dressed, in an Italian-cut silk suit of a shiny, metallic blue like the sides of a swordfish; Tamerlán sported black shorts, red satin vest and unlaced white boxing shoes. A punchball that hung from the ceiling partially justi-fied his outfit. He stuck his hand in and managed to grab the congressman by one foot and pull, while his prey clung to the wires and squealed. When he had him within range, he let fly a kick to his buttocks, which wobbled like a waterbed under the silken trousers.

'Pah! Silicone!' roared Tamerlán, kicking him again to check. 'Instead of pulling his finger out and getting my law passed, his lordship decides to spend his time and my money getting his cute little arse lifted!' he said, and noticed me. Mo-mentarily forgetting his prey, he put down the riding-crop and advanced on me, smiling and holding out his right hand.

'He's failed, Sr Tamerlán.'

The doctor could at least have given me the chance to shake it. Tamerlán's face became as hard and expressionless as a cliff face.

'What do you mean?' His booming voice sounded like he was gargling with rocks.

Canal held out a printed copy of the list. Tamerlán read it down to the last name.

'What the fuck is this!'

Canal explained succinctly; Tamerlán eyed me grimly.

'Damn it, Félix! You too?' He turned to his analyst. 'And all I can do is take it out on this guy,' he said, grinding his heel into one of the congressman's hands as he tried to crawl away. He howled with the pain and took refuge under the desk again, where he set about licking his injured hand.

'Why not me?' I said defiantly. 'I thought you were the superman. So?'

'Precisely,' he answered.

'The abject personality . . .' began the analyst.

'Be quiet; I can explain myself,' Tamerlán interrupted him. 'You see that guy?' he asked me. 'Look.'

Hopping on one foot, he took off his other boot and hurled it across the room, where it bounced off the glass; it had barely landed on the carpet before the congressman had scampered to fetch it and carry it proudly back in his mouth. Tamerlán, after tugging it about in play for a bit, took it off him and dried the slobbered leather on his pet's silk tie, who pranced excitedly around him, eager to repeat the game. Tamerlán put the shoe on and kicked him out of the way.

'Do you see him suffering? Do you see him looking at me with hatred? Humiliation has to be desired to be deserved. You aren't cut out for it, Sr Félix.' He gave me the once-over like a judge at a cattle show and wrote me off. 'Fodder for professional thugs, that's all you are. Nothing of interest to me. Check against what we have, Canal, and see what can be salvaged.'

The analyst went over to one of the computers and inserted the floppy disk. Tamerlán, meanwhile, had gone across to his desk (the congressman trying to inch closer, unnoticed, to lick the tip of his shoes) where he poured himself a glass of water from a brim-full cut-glass decanter. He paced about the room, drinking thirstily, gnawing on the handle of his riding-crop between swigs.

'Doesn't coke make you thirsty?'

He was trying to be friendly, entertaining me with a little light conversation.

'Very. Acid's worse.'

'Definitely.'

There was an awkward silence. Neither of us knew how to go on. He was the one who broke it, naturally.

'What did you think about what happened the other day?'

'You're referring to . . .'

'. . . to me buggering my son, that's right. We're both grown-ups; I think we can discuss these things like adults. Fortunately, there's no censorship in this country any more. I swear to you, the military sometimes . . . They're like those unwanted dinner guests you invite out of a sense of obligation, who stay till three in the morning, drinking your whisky and boring the pants off you, convinced you're having as wonderful a time as they are. The things we have to put up with. And I was brought up by one, mind. I'm not saying they haven't made a contribution,' he added, correcting himself slightly, like a helmsman shifting course with an imperceptible movement, perhaps in the belief that, as a former soldier, I might take offence. 'A keen observer can learn from his dog. We learned from the military not to be afraid, to bare our teeth – to bite. The politicians had us too used to negotiating. Haven't you finished yet, Sr Canal?' he asked impatiently.

'No.'

'No. Idiot!' he muttered, landing the congressman a kick in his unprotected left kidney. 'Where was I? Ah, yes. Fathers and sons. The father's influence over the son. Let's take another example. Yourself. Just look at you. I'm sure your father did far worse things to you.'

'I'm the son of a single mother.'

'Don't you see? Beating about the bush only creates traumas. A frank and open attitude, on the other hand, may cause annoyance early on, but never confusion. And in the long run they're grateful to you. Isn't that right, Sr Canal?'

Canal made no answer, in deference to that time-honoured mania of psychoanalysts for playing tennis without a ball. It made no difference; Tamerlán was unstoppable.

'I firmly believe parents shouldn't be afraid of acknowledging their sexuality before their children,' he proclaimed. 'Look, Sr Félix, I'm the first to admit that everyone's entitled to express their opinion about the problems afflicting the world. But only mine is right. The great evil of our age, Sr Félix, is hypocrisy.'

His voice had slid gradually toward the same rapt and dreamy tone that had preceded his last great act of sheer terror. I looked around me in alarm: his son's office was empty; on the floor below a young girl wept with frustration in front of a computer screen; in the other visible offices Tamerlán's employees were going about their business – or rather, his; finally I spotted the congressman under the desk, massaging his booted kidney, and breathed a sigh of relief. If he comes over like that again, I thought to myself, I know which of us is more likely to be the object of his devotions.

But my confidence soon wilted when Tamerlán walked

towards me and, linking his arm in mine, escorted me around the resonant floor of his office.

'You work for me, Sr Félix, but perhaps you haven't quite understood what it is you're working *for*. It's of the utmost importance that you and I understand each other over this, Sr Félix. You'll see. Everything that's worth anything in this world – art, science, culture: civilisation, in short – has been built by us.'

'Us?'

'No. Us. Look at the communists. Keeping a community of equal men going, handing out food to everyone, reducing wars to a minimum – easiest thing in the world. Without us, Man today would still be much the same as he was two hundred thousand years ago. *We* introduced inequality, and inequality is the engine of change. Without *us*, progress and civilisation simply wouldn't have existed. And what *is* civilisation you may ask me.'

'What is civilisation?' I asked, not because I had the slightest interest, but because I knew that Tamerlán needed an echo to talk to.

'Civilisation is control – controlling others primarily; but, to do that, we have to control ourselves. If the rider runs wild, how can the horse be tamed? We've fallen into the trap, Sr Félix: the civilisation we have created has led us to a dead end. If our control over others is to increase mathematically, our self-control has to increase geometrically. And every so often, in fairly regular cycles I daresay, our strength turns against us, restrains us like a straitjacket and, unable to bear it, we let ourselves go, and then everything goes with us. Every time we stage a revolution to rid ourselves of the unjust shackles

imposed on us by society and try to relax for a change, to loos-
en up a bit – to indulge in a little harmless *decadence* for God's
sake! – our enemies seize their chance and, to contain them,
our iron fist closes even tighter than before. And then they accuse us – us of all people – as if they weren't the ones forcing us
to take such extreme measures.'

For a moment I thought of patting him on the back to
console him but, as my left arm was still linked in his, trying it
with my right would be the spastic act of a contortionist.

'On behalf of all of us I'd like to apologise . . .'

'Not you lot! I'm not interested in the middle class! You're
subject to our authority, just like the poor, and at the same
time your norms of self-control are almost as rigid as ours
and certainly far more boring. No. Consider the poor. When
they eat, for example. What lightness. What swing. With our
kind, the act of eating is *heavy*. They, on the other hand . . . serve
everything on the same plate, even dessert; they eat with their
fingers; they tell dirty jokes to revolt their table companions
and laugh with their mouths full; they talk about excreta, sex,
disease and death, pick their rotten teeth and fart and belch
and puke on the table, which is only cleared when the owner of
the house and his brother-in-law, pissed on adulterated plonk,
attack each other – one with a fork, the other with a broken
bottle – and half the family lands up in hospital. At home two
cousins take advantage of the grown-ups' absence to fuck on
the backyard table while their little brothers and sisters watch
and clap without knowing why. The sunlight through the
lusty vine traces filigrees on their skins; the bursting grapes
drip their honey, the cicadas drone their song . . . How can *we*
the rich eat all stiff and straight-laced as if someone had stuck

the proverbial poker up our arse while *they* the poor laze about with their legs open, having a whale of a time? Table manners! Want to know what *good table manners* are? I would sometimes come home after a business lunch, or worse still, an *intimate* dinner party with friends, where I'd eaten *politely* – as if it were possible to tear something apart with your teeth *politely*, digest *politely*, turn dead animals and mutilated plants into shit *politely* – I'd get back from forcing down a *distinguished* dish, in a *distinguished* restaurant, with *distinguished* diners – a drove of sluts and queens trying to hide the fact they're no better than pigs snuffling about in the sty – and shut myself in the kitchen and eat flour by the handful straight from the packet – flour – choking on the dust that got into my nose and lungs, retching till I managed to turn it into a paste and swallow it, and only then – only then – would I feel something akin to the joys of the gourmet. No pauper, for all their complaining, has ever had to go through what we go through day after day. They may be in chains, but on the inside they're free. Ours is the opposite situation. Especially here in the city. Now, in the countryside . . .' He inhaled deeply as if drawing in the combined fragrance of alfalfa and camomile. 'Ah, the countryside. In the country you can still go into a peasant's shack and shag the wife and all the daughters, in descending order of age – even the little boys if that's your thing. Try doing that in a humble but dignified working class home and see how far you get. If they don't lynch you there and then, you'll have the delegates in your office the next day and a strike on your hands. Don't think I don't appreciate resistance to authority, mind you. The unimaginative members of my class who want to break the will of the people once and for all are like that dove of Kant's that thought it could fly better without the resistance of the air. No, the working class keep you – how can I put it? – in train-ing. But everything's more relaxed in the country, of course. It's even better in Mexico or Peru: they still have Indians. I tell you, we made a big mistake here, exterminating them. Our greedy grandparents left nothing for us. Their only legacy to us was work, work, work. When do we play, I ask you? Where is our garden of earthly delights? Where do we go when the bell rings for break? If eliminating feudalism in Europe was a regrettable practical necessity, the rest of the world still offered innumer-able opportunities to give your animal strength free rein and to wallow in the sweetest quagmire of all: subjugated human flesh; and the best thing is, it comes guilt-free. Remember what Nietzsche says about conscience? "It is the instinct of cruelty, which turns inwards once it is unable to discharge itself out-wardly." After the Great War, Germany had her playground in the colonies taken from her and was eventually forced to do it in Europe. That was her great sin: doing it to the Europeans. If you keep the dog cooped up all day, it ends up doing it on the carpet. But is that the dog's fault? The truth, Sr Félix – that diamond truth, pure and hard and brilliant, that generation after generation tries to besmirch so they won't be blinded by its light – is that one's freedom begins where another's ends. The times I've tried to explain it to my son, and yet . . .'

That must have been why he'd decided to pour his heart out to me: his hundred thousand, along with an incomplete list of names, had bought him this docile rubber doll to soothe the ardours of his mind.

'I have to admit, I didn't learn it from my father, but from him,' he said, nodding in the direction of some ghostly presence and laughing indulgently. 'Better than he himself could ever have imagined.'

'Who?' I asked.

'*Him*,' he repeated, letting go of my arm to approach and point – there was no mistaking where this time – at the turd that rested in its acrylic sarcophagus like a mummy and its trove. 'The late Mr Fuchs. We *need* our utopia, more, far more than the poor do. They're happy to endure from day to day, whereas we always have to move forward. Our critics should realise, at least momentarily, the *energy* it takes to keep yourself at the top, never mind to keep going onwards and upwards . . . It's easy to criticise from down there on the plain. From up here things look different. Can't you feel it?'

'Definitely.'

'When we stop, when our sole aim in life is to *preserve* what we have instead of moving forwards, we begin at that very instant, imperceptibly, to move backwards. We need a higher goal, we need new frontiers, for the coming new millennium. We all need an ideal, we all need a reason to live. Have you read Eva Perón?'

'I didn't think that was your kind of bedside reading.'

'Who do you think I read? Donald Trump? Give me some credit, Sr Félix. I'd like to think that all you've found out about me has been of some use to you.'

I pulled the face of a cat that's eaten the canary and just burped two yellow feathers. Tamerlán rejected my feigned surprise with a flick of his hand.

'It was obvious. You could never have resisted the temptation. You're as addicted to information as I am to money: each is an end in itself for us. But if you think you know everything about me, you're wrong. Neither you nor anyone else could know I met the woman personally. I was all of fifteen, but I held out my hand like a proper little gentleman, and she patted my head and gave me a kiss on the cheek. A little later on I asked to be excused and went to the bathroom for a wank. One of the few women who's ever had that effect on me. My father and Perón, meanwhile, were walking in the garden swapping stories of the military life. When the Montoneros included the demand to place a bust of Evita in every office of the company as a condition for my release, they never imagined such a gesture would be more meaningful for me than it ever was for them. Remember, Canal? What a comedown for you people, eh?'

'I remember clearly,' answered the transistorised voice, immersed in its examination of the screen. They spoke to each other matily like old friends, like partners in crime.

'As you may be aware, Canal was one of my guards: university student impatient to see some action, you know the story. Students in the United States are set minor business deals from the first years of their degree so they can find release; here in Argentina they became guerrillas. We came to understand each other very well over those nine months and have been inseparable ever since. He was the one who told the police of my whereabouts, which is why he's here now, chatting to us instead of to the catfish at the bottom of the river. Remember how we laughed about the busts. Here, I still keep the one they put in my old office – a souvenir.

He walked over to a cupboard and came back bearing a plaster bust of Evita in his arms, like a birthday cake, yellowing and stained by the passing of time, with a Mona Lisa smile and blank, blind eyes fixed on eternity. He put it down on the floor by the desk, next to the congressman, who'd nodded off and now awoke from his nap and cautiously sniffed the new object like a curious cat. Tamerlán looked at him severely.

'So?'

Understanding, the congressman raised his head, obediently pulled down his fly and, cocking his leg, urinated at length on the plaster head, instantly darkening the taut hair and tight bun, while Tamerlán gazed at her admiringly with arms folded.

'What a woman! Shame she wasn't a man. We'd have a different country by now. Ah well,' he said, speaking directly to her, 'don't give me that look. Pigeons would be worse.' Then to the congressman: 'That's right: mark your territory properly; you don't want other dogs taking your place.'

'Is he a Peronist?' I asked, referring to the congressman, who was now sniffing at what he'd just done.

'Of course. What fun would it be if he wasn't?'

'And he does everything you tell him?'

'He's mine; I bought him. Cost me a pretty penny, I can tell you. A friend of mine once got landed with a fake congressman he bought on the cheap. This one's the genuine article, elected by the people. But that's no guarantee nowadays. *Ecce signum.* And who can I complain to now? That's one of the many disadvantages of democracy. What I'm about to tell you may sound reactionary, but I believe we should bring back the restricted ballot.'

We watched him in silence as he turned round and round on the floor, and curled up again.

'Doesn't say much, does he.'

'You should hear him in Congress.'

'And does he cost a lot to keep?'

'Not really. He doesn't consume much. He does pretty well on his congressman's allowance: car, pocket money every month and that's it. I buy him a treat though from time to time, when he behaves.'

As if by magic, a piece of folded foil had appeared between his fore- and middle finger and, opening it, he emptied the contents onto the glass of the desk. There was almost two grams. The congressman leaped up on all fours, his shiny nose scenting the cocaine as soon as it made contact with the air and, with a multiple reflex that would have delighted a convention of Pavlovians, his nostrils dilated monstrously, his eyes popped out of his head and two frothy cascades of saliva began to pour from the corners of his mouth. While Tamerlán combed out four lines as wide as those of a zebra-crossing, the congressman attacked from below, squashing his hands and face grotesquely against the glass and licking with his long, red tongue the stardust that stretched above him as vast and distant as the Milky Way, less than a centimetre from his ravening membranes.

'So we're awake now, are we? We'd be ready to do anything now, would we? Too late! You should have remembered before!' Tamerlán tortured him by taking an exaggerated length of time to measure out the four avenues and shunt a few grains around to balance them up, while the congressman huffed and puffed under the glass like a seal trying to come up for air under a thick layer of ice.

'One, two, three . . .' I counted to myself, trying to conceal my own excitement. And it was real: standing beside his masterpiece, Tamerlán held out his arm and palm, inviting me to come over, while his other hand held out a tightly rolled banknote. Gingerly, I took it from his fingers and snorted the lot; the kick from the coke under my left eye made me recoil. Never in my life had I done so much in one line. As the psychoanalyst, his brooding brow contracted in almost human ill humour, approached to receive another rolled banknote, I unrolled mine. It was a hundred dollars, and I offered it to Tamerlán.

'Never use someone else's straw, Sr Félix. This is the age of AIDS. And never use the same straw twice. It's bad luck. Keep it and spend it.'

Meanwhile the psychoanalyst inhaled his line: precisely half up his left nostril covering his right with his forefinger, the other half up his right nostril covering his left with his other forefinger. Like a clockwork toy just wound up he went buzzing back to his post, pocketing the note, unrolled and folded into four in the inside pocket of his jacket.

Tamerlán approached now (obviously the congressman was last in line), but, instead of one note, he was carrying two, one in each nostril, and was smiling with his two fancy-dress fangs, the very embodiment of the capitalist bloodsucker.

'Never seen this one?' he asked me. 'The Transylvanian Double Whammy. Watch.'

In front of the desperate congressman, who was wriggling and pulling faces, his dribbling muzzle pressed against the glass, Tamerlán leaned on the desk and, placing a straw at the start of either runway, snorted two lines at the same speed without leaving a crumb. Exaggerating his nasal intakes of breath, he stood there, arms akimbo, watching the whimpering figure at his feet.

'What a sorry sight. Human dignity is just another commodity these days. If they were all like him, our efforts would be wasted, like those of a genius reigning over a tribe of idiots. All a mite embarrassing, isn't it.'

'As my grandfather used to say,' I broke in, emboldened by my racing pulse, my heart using my ribcage as a punchbag, 'there are people who think if they eat shit they'll shit chicken chasseur.'

'Nice. Anyway. Where was I? I think a great deal more clearly now. Now, Canal, let's see if you can sort this mess out!' The psychoanalyst didn't answer, his fingers a blur over the keyboard, like the legs of a spider when an insect is trapped in the web, spinning it round and round, wrapping it in its silken shroud. 'Ah. I love land, money and cocaine, because they have no limits. But time . . .' he said, darkening his voice and addressing the sombre river that rippled in small crests in the wind, which blew stronger and stronger from the south-east, '. . . time is my worst enemy. Time has slapped me in the face and thrown down its gauntlet,' he said, screwing up his face to deepen the wrinkles, 'and I've decided to take it up. That's why my son's so important, Sr Félix. He's the last weapon I have to meet that challenge. We're almost there; I can see our goal, so glitteringly clear . . . A century or two at the most and we'll see our dream realised. We've solved the equation of money by creating poverty for others to produce wealth for ourselves. But we haven't solved the equation of freedom. We haven't yet found a way to control others without controlling ourselves. As a class we've had to subject ourselves to the most rigorous norms of self-control that have ever existed, and all in order to get rich. Now that we have what we want, we should begin the struggle for our freedom. But our undoing is our ambition for more money, which necessarily entails having more paupers and more perfect systems of

control. We have to discover the most efficient way . . . of imposing our freedom on the rest of the world. Freeing ourselves from
these golden shackles that choke us.'

'So you can shackle others with them,' I broke in.

'You're getting the idea. Having more strength hasn't
made us freer; just the contrary. There's the rub, the riddle, the
equation reduced to its simplest form. If I manage to solve it, if
I manage to solve the perverse equation of control and make
it equal that of money, so that our freedom increases in direct
proportion to the slavery of others, then my life will not have
been in vain. That's where the Third Foundation comes in: a
city of the future ruled by free men!'

He was a torrent now, an avalanche of pure white snow
roaring down from the summit of a high peak, devouring
everything in its path; I had to ski with him to avoid being
buried alive.

'Like everyone else, you must have heard of conspiracies,
secret lodges, invisible hands ruling the world from the shadows. It's a vile calumny. *We live in the light.*'

A tear had opened in the thick covering of winter clouds
and, through it, the last of the evening sun cast a divine beam
that fell directly on the erect figure of Tamerlán: arms extended, eyes lost in an expression of complete beatitude. His shadow
shot across the floor and on reaching the window carried on,
projecting itself out and over the city to the horizon.

'In the last two hundred years they have managed to
make us feel guilty about our strength and wealth, ashamed
of flaunting it, the way they used to beg us to in the olden days.
That stage is drawing to a close. We no longer have an enemy
out there to confront and the time has come once again to

exercise our dominion from up here, in the heights,' he said, so vehemently that, for an instant, he created the illusion that we were floating above the world in an Olympus of pure light, erected only by the magic of his words. 'Transparency – *absolute* transparency such as exists up here – is the least of my aspirations. We have to be equal to the times, to understand that the danger has passed and we can come out, stop skulking and *show ourselves* the way we did in the past. The bourgeoisie was a transitional stage, a five-hundred-year Leopardist rodeo, after which we can go back – this time perfectly and for ever – to what deep down we never stopped being: feudal. Everything must come to light.'

'Ethic cleansing you might say,' I contributed.

'Don't be stupid: you're on coke, not dope. It's precisely the opposite. We have to lead again, this time without being manacled by all this legalistic bureaucracy. Haven't you noticed? People generally defend lies far more fiercely than truth. We expend so much energy *concealing* what we do that we have barely any left to spare. Who are we concealing ourselves *from*? From public opinion? We *are* public opinion. From the people? They'd be *happy* to see us act openly: they'd admire and love us for it. I daresay ninety per cent of their animosity towards us stems from the feeling we're concealing something from them. And they're right. That's why we need to draw back the veil from their eyes so they can see us for what we are. The wall that fell three years ago was the wall of our shame. Once again we could walk naked through our paradise, without need of that annoying fig leaf that rampant Marxism had forced us to wear. The brutalised masses of the East crossed the rubble without understanding and roamed the streets of the other side as men

and women possessed, their heads swimming with the glare
of the neon, their muzzles pressed to the windows, with their
indifferent displays of electrical appliances and prostitutes. Do
you know the first thing East Berliners bought in West Berlin?
Cars, televisions, Coca-Cola? No. Bananas. Years of spying on us
through the keyhole hadn't prepared them for such obscene ex-
hibitionism. And, shaking them in their faces, we could finally
tell the proles on our side: "Look, look, here are your heroes,
these dopey, gawping simpletons who slobber and wet themselves over the spectacle of our naked potency. Look how they
come to suck, these brave new men. And you come to papa too,
or by the time you wake up your admired comrades will have
drunk it all and there won't be a drop left. The vacancies, my
dear boys, are far more limited than before, and if you think
you're out for a stroll, think again. I'd get galloping if I were
you." You know, Sr Félix, after so many years of misunderstand-
ings, what a pleasant surprise it was to confirm they'd never
actually stopped loving us? They were waiting behind the wall
like Romeos on heat. That's why I'm on this crusade for absolute sincerity. Despite spending most of my life in this country,
Sr Félix, I can never get used to seeing how people are deceived
here; believe me, I'd reveal everything tomorrow: we've wasted
too much time already. I have a book half-finished. It's called
The Entrepreneur, Or the Emancipation of the Upper Classes. If only I
could wash my hands of this whole mess and devote my time
exclusively to finishing it . . . I know I have to do it myself. There
are no bards left to sing the feats of kings. Nowadays the great
inspire no one but the writers of Yankee soaps. Strength has
been so dehumanised that only weakness looks human. Who
wants to sing the exploits of a plc? If some ambitious hack

decided to tell this story, he'd probably choose *your* version, Félix, over mine. Get the picture? My triumphs as seen through the filter of your defeats, not the other way round.'

He'd walked over to a chair, from the back of which he picked up a short silk robe and proceeded to wrap himself in it, and pace up and down in the grave pose of a Renaissance sage.

'Canal will point you in the direction of the unconscious. He says I've a way to go before it can manifest itself. *Manifest itself!* Sometimes he sounds like a spiritist. I don't know. That's another of the paradoxes that make me feel uncomfortable. In order to do the most desirable things you have to lose your consciousness (or conscience; I never could tell them apart) and regain it to enjoy them. Conscious, unconscious . . . When I think about it, I feel so bad that I seek solace in cocaine and alcohol, the only combination that reconciles the best of both states. Care for some more?'

I shook my head because the last snort had closed my throat so much that I was having difficulty speaking. He took another paper envelope from the pocket of his robe and, opening it, sank his nose directly into it.

'Didn't you have a heart attack once?' I managed to croak.

'Yes, but that was after five grams. I look after myself now,' he answered, nodding in thanks for my concern. 'Ah. What cold. What clarity,' he exclaimed, the tip of his nose as white as a snow-capped peak. 'Clarity and altitude go together,' he said, approaching a console on his desk and pressing a button. All the windows overlooking the river opened and the icy breath of the south-easterly swept into the room, scattering his papers and making his robe flap like a flag.

'You realise, Félix,' he crooned in delight, closing his eyes to the wind like an adventurous captain standing on the prow of his ship, 'they were wrong. It isn't the artists, it isn't the lunatics, it isn't the revolutionaries. It's us. The only ones who dare to confront society and shake it out of its inertia, who wrest from the instrument the notes that nobody thought lay in it, in pursuit of the unattainable melody that's always a little further on, almost touching it with our hands . . .'

'Sr Tamerlán!'

Canal had spoken. We both ran to his side because no one could remember how to walk any more.

'So? Do you have them?' Tamerlán asked anxiously.

'Cross-referencing our data with the SIDE's I got three more. That makes fifteen. We're still ten short.'

'That's what you interrupted me at the best part for? I was scaling such heights . . .'

'There's nothing else to do at this end. The hacker,' he said as if I wasn't there, 'has only contributed three names. At a hundred thousand each, that's . . .'

I interrupted before I heard the embarrassing result of his calculation.

'You only had some names and the most basic data before; now you have what each one knows, or at least declared, as well. And you have their complete records, which may be useful if you want to put the squeeze on them,' I insisted, making an effort not to sound like a street vendor on a packed bus extolling the virtues of a set of Chinese needles with a threader thrown in. 'Why don't we go through the back-ups one more time?'

Canal offered me his seat and I gave them a quick look only

to discover that not one of the original names had survived. The nerd had been more than thorough: he hadn't wanted to play a joke on me, but to fuck up my work. My mind went blank for a few seconds, my eyes fixed on the name Prince Charles.

'There's something funny here,' I said.

'Another joke from your friend?' Tamerlán inquired.

'Maybe, but I don't think so. Why would he only add a name to the Federal Police back-up file? And it comes with a statement too. He didn't have time to write that himself. No, this is something else.'

'Spit it out, Félix, I'm not on opium,' Tamerlán urged me, manically wiping his nostrils with the back of his hand as they leaked like a dripping tap. 'What do you mean?'

'There's a twenty-sixth witness. The police or the SIDE erased him or her from the final copies, but they've been overlooked in this draft.' I keyed in 'search 26' and the screen changed, the cursor blinking under the number searched. 'Here it is. "Twenty-six persons." I was right.'

'Your evidence, Sr Félix,' Dr Canal intervened with exaggerated calm, even for him, 'is not very persuasive. Not to mention the fact that this would increase the figure of your failure by one witness. Your faithful disciple no doubt forgot to . . .'

I let him prattle on while I went back to the main SIDE file and keyed in another search command. At the fifth attempt I found what I was looking for.

'Eureka!' I yelled. 'Got him! There were twenty-six of them and here's the proof.'

'What proof?' said Tamerlán, virtually climbing into the screen.

'In this witness's statement. See where it says "I left my

160

house at 6.00 p.m. and took the 125, which dropped me at the port at 7.00 p.m. . . . " You don't notice anything?'

'He took a bus. So? I've already told you they were nobodies.'

'Tell me the route of the 125.'

'Listen, Félix. Don't try and be funny. I haven't taken a bus since I was eighteen. You tell him, Canal, you who know everything.'

'I can't.'

'Come on, be a good fellow, let's play along with the lad.'

'I can't, Sr Tamerlán. The 125 doesn't exist.'

'Go on, tell him,' I interrupted enthusiastically, 'tell him which bus runs from La Matanza to the port.'

'The 126, obviously,' he snarled. 'But you still haven't convinced me.'

'What about this? "Benjamín Menéndez" works at the Cangallo, I mean Perón branch of the Boston Bank. Look at the phone number: 325-8425.'

'What's wrong with that?'

'It should be 326.'

'You know the phone book by heart, do you?' he retorted, trying to disguise his annoyance with sarcasm.

'I scammed them once.'

He knew he was defeated and, turning his back on me, went and looked out of the window.

'Have you two been rehearsing this?' Tamerlán asked bad-temperedly. 'Maybe you should try and explain.'

'It's simple,' I said. 'Whoever made the change ordered the program to put "25" wherever it said "26". But they forgot to specify that that was valid only for *isolated* sequences. The program recognised the "26" in the "126" and turned it into

"125". Same thing with the phone number. Result: a bus that doesn't exist and a witness at large somewhere, who, for some reason, someone at the SIDE has taken the trouble to erase all trace of from their computers . . .'

I felt radiant, like a schoolboy on a TV quiz show who just got the last question right and won a trip to Bariloche for his class. Tamerlán too was looking at me with poorly disguised satisfaction.

'Sr Félix, you've managed, however fleetingly, to renew my wilting confidence in your abilities. I'll give you another chance. Now get me the real names of the missing witnesses, including your mysterious phantom.'

'I don't think I can get back into the SIDE,' I began.

'You'll have to do it door to door then. You have the addresses there.'

'Computers are my thing; people are too complicated. Isn't there anyone suitable on your staff who . . .?'

'They'll be working in parallel, you can be sure of that. If, between you, you get what I need, I pledge to pay you the agreed sum. But if you don't try, and they don't succeed, you'll have to return every red cent.'

It was a convincing argument: I'd already spent quite a few.

'There's something I'm going to need,' I said. 'The logical place to start is over there.' I pointed at the opposite floor of the neighbouring tower, where some workers in overalls were standing on ladders taking measurements of the windows. 'The pyramid sales people: I'll need some background on them and a contact to get in.'

Tamerlán went over to his desk, where he selected an

option by tapping the screen with his forefinger. His voice was captured by hidden microphones: 'Marroné!' he shouted. A woman's voice answered. I could see her: a ruined blonde appeared simultaneously on a monitor and beneath our feet in one of the offices on the floor below.

'He's not here, Sr Tamerlán.'

'I know, I can't see him. Where the fuck is he?'

'In the bathroom, Sr Tamerlán.'

'Again?' he exclaimed in disbelief. 'Get him out or I'll light it up so everyone can watch him taking a dump. Have him prepare all the information we have on Surprises.' He looked at me inquiringly. 'Would you like it printed or on a floppy?'

'You can send it by e-mail,' I said. 'My address is . . .'

I said it aloud; the secretary made a note. Meanwhile, Tamerlán picked up the two empty wraps melancholically and tossed them under his desk in front of the congressman's snout, who pounced on them, snuffling and grunting like a truffle pig, and hoovered up the leftovers with a series of obscene snorts, chewing them like gum to extract every last crumb after his nose had performed the impossible.

'Marroné will give you another ten per cent of your money and make the relevant contacts for you. You have two days. Make the most of them.'

He said nothing else. Still scowling, the psychoanalyst escorted me to the lift.

* * *

Marroné's secretary, a peroxide blonde in a tailored suit with pencil skirt, came out of her boss's office for the second time and again asked me to wait please. The third time, she came out wringing her hands, all contrition, her sculpted nails lacerating her palms, her incisors dark with lipstick from biting her lip, a tear of irate frustration welling up thick with mascara under her oval mirrorshades. She didn't know what to say and, balancing on her heels as if walking a tightrope suspended above the void, she disappeared behind the mirror without noticing I was following her.

On Marroné's desk three phones were ringing, a fax machine beeping and an intercom demanding his presence at the top of its voice. The secretary, her ear pressed to the frosted glass, knocked insistently on a side door.

'Sr Marroné . . . Sr Marroné . . . Please, your appointments are waiting for you.'

She'd wait a few seconds, then try again, quite undermining her warnings with her entreaties, and vice versa.

'Sr Marroné . . . the red line's ringing. Sr Tamerlán will be sending someone from security any second now to see what's going on. I think I can hear the lift coming down. If you come out now, there may still be a chance to stop him, Sr Marroné. But if he comes down and finds you in there . . .'

Her knuckles rapped continuously and monotonously, and her breath misted the glass as she spoke. From the other side came a solid, palpable silence, a silence you could feel in the pit of your stomach like a heavy meal.

'Sr Marroné. I know you're in there. I can see you sitting down. That excuse about the colic won't work again. Sr Marroné . . .'

My first impression was that two or three racehorses had been locked in the executive bathroom and that, dazed by the long wait and the desperate tap-tap-tap, they'd hallucinated the starting signal and started running round in circles in the locked stalls. The fragile door bulged outwards from the rattling and a howl, inhuman in its animal pain, streamed through the open cracks, making the hair stand up on the back of my neck. The frosted glass cracked cross-wise then shattered, opening a gash in the secretary's tapping hand, which recoiled as if she'd grabbed a spider while absent-mindedly fiddling with the paperclips in her drawer. Finally the door imploded with a sharp tug and in the doorway stood Marroné, framed by tousled hair, tie unknotted and a prodigious spiral of toilet paper that began at the almost empty roll in its holder, wrapped itself several times round his body and plunged up the tightly clenched crack of his arse.

'Stop iiiit! I can't stand it any more! You won't let me sleep, you won't let me eat, you won't let me screw, and now you won't let me shit! I can't shit in five minutes, I can't shit to schedule! I'm constipated! I'm filling up with shit and you won't even give me five minutes to get rid of it! I can't stand it any more, I can't bear this life! I want to read Proust! I want to read Proust!'

He'd thrown himself to the floor, wrapped in the string of toilet paper like a badly wound turban, and begun to sob, his forehead and knees sunk into the thick beige carpet; the secretary, sucking her blood-drenched hand and looking down on him with that curiosity-free contempt that only years of conjugal or professional cohabitation can impart, gestured to me.

'Let's go before he starts singing "The Bear". That's the part I can never stand.'

Through the glass I watched her return to reception and

take some alcohol and cotton wool from a cabinet to clean her wound. I followed her in, closing the door behind me on the now quieter figure of Marroné, whose laboured sobbing was almost imperceptibly becoming a continuous and melodious murmur:

> I used to live happily in the forest
> I'd walk and walk forever and a day
> I was king of morning, afternoon and evening,
> Stretching out at night to rest I'd lay . . .

Marroné's secretary turned round before I reached her, and held out her open, alcohol-drenched hand.

'Ow! It's killing me! Blow on it, for God's sake, blow on it!'

I took hold of her two open fingers and obeyed. She closed her eyes and smiled, sighing with relief. It was funny, but in a few minutes her boss's little sketch had created a kind of intimacy between us. I tried to kiss her wound when I'd finished, but she pulled her hand away and slid it between my fingers, less out of rejection than as an invitation to follow.

'Fancy a coffee?'

Standing beside the electric coffee-maker, she lit a cigarette and, without turning round, stretched out her arm at a right angle to her body and held out the packet. I took one. In the invisible room next door the murmuring continued:

> But one day the men came with their cages
> Locked me up and took me off to the city
> They taught me pirouettes there in the circus
> And so I lost my precious liberty . . .

'Does it get any worse than this?'

She shrugged. She exhaled. She climbed down from the torture of her high heels to bring over two coffees and we sat down on the appointments side of the desk.

'It's difficult to hate your boss when what you see when you look at his office is your own face.'

'Have you worked here very . . . ?'

She nodded. She scratched one thigh, the clean crackling of her nail on the invisible mesh of her nylon bringing the first spasm of lubricant to the tip of my prick.

'You must have seen a lot.'

She cast me a wan smile, accompanying it with a gesture that took in our reflections in the side walls and ceiling, and the visible parts of the corridors and floors below us.

'Seeing . . . not seeing . . . imagining. Differences are lost up here. Here's one for you. There was one manager who got fired and had the gall to ask for an audience with Sr Tamerlán, who kept him standing outside his office for hours on end suffering everyone's mocking looks and smug smiles as they came and went; Sr Tamerlán kept up a constant stream of traffic just to humiliate him, and called in lower- and lower-ranking staff – of a certain breed, shall we say? – just to see how long he'd last. He'd come to the door, for example, to personally shower greetings on the head sanitation engineer, slapping him on the back and showing him in. "That's what we need here: people to take the shit out," he said, and stared in the direction of the waiting man who, beside himself, eventually pulled out a gun and pointed it at the mirror, no doubt hoping to smash it with the first shot and hit Sr Tamerlán with the second. The two shots rang out, the mirror shattered and the manager dropped dead. Sr Tamerlán's bodyguard, Dr Canal – oh, you know him

– had been quietly watching everything from inside and had fired before the second shot – although the manager must have died thinking that he and his reflection had iced each other. They installed the metal detector after that.'

'You can tell me the next one sitting here,' I said, patting my lap.

'Remind me to sign the cheque for you before you leave. Sr Tamerlán said ten thousand. Will that do?' she asked as she straddled my lap cowboy-style, resting her elbows on my shoulders to brush her lips on mine, as light as a feather, then shoving her tongue all the way down to my œsophagus. I'd felt nothing like it since my tonsillectomy.

'I've been to so many places,' she said, 'but I might as well have been nowhere: because I've never been to the only one that matters.'

For some reason I puckered slightly.

'Where?' I asked.

'There,' she said, pulling her hand out of my fly to point. 'Up there. Where you went on the first day.'

There was a new twinkle in her eyes as if she'd just spent the whole night looking at the stars and now had them imprinted on her retinas forever.

'Tell me about him,' her feverish breath pleaded in my ear.

I obeyed. Despite my neutral and factual tone, my account of Sr Tamerlán's habits had more effect on her than all the obscene nothings I'd ever poured in the ears of womankind. Her hips began to sway, independent of her will; her hands worked my prick like a bicycle pump; her tongue sought out the hollow of my sternum and punctured it like a tin opener. Not to be outdone I sent one hand outside her clothes to her buttocks and the other inside to her tits. But it all felt rather mechanical, as if I was doing it out of, well, politeness.

'I'm not comfortable,' I told her. 'I feel watched.'

'Do you?' she said with delight, rolling her eyes upwards until only the whites were showing. 'Do you?'

'Isn't there somewhere more private?'

'Oh, all right. But promise you'll carry on telling me. Let's see if there's any room in the Ladies. If he wants to, Sr Tamerlán can light them up and make them see-through, but he rarely bothers. When he does, though, he always takes you by surprise.'

She'd stepped out into the corridor without bothering to straighten her tousled hair or ruffled clothing. I followed her to the toilets. She went in first, with a squeeze of my crotch to bid me a temporary farewell.

'Come on,' she shouted to me from inside.

I looked round for her, scanning the row of cubicles, all identical except one.

'Here, in the handicapped loo. There's more room. Come in, I want to show you something.'

I opened the door. She was waiting for me astride the toilet, her hour-glass jacket tight around her waist, her black stockings around her thighs and, between them, nothing but her hands: one in front and the other round back, her fingers interlaced between her legs, except her right forefinger and left ring-finger, with which she was masturbating simultaneously fore and aft.

'Come in here,' she panted.

'In where?'

'In my mouth. Oh, no; I need that to talk. Carry on.'

I'd got to the bit about the congressman when, with a double pop, she took her hands from their places and held them out to me.

'Right, now, come here. I'll take you wherever you want to go,' she offered, and I nearly said I just wanna go home, when a sound like a car alarm came over the loudspeakers.

'It's him, it's him,' she screeched, slamming her legs shut and, lifting up my prick on her way out like a barrier at a level crossing, ran outside into the corridor. Thinking she might need them later, I picked up her skirt and knickers from the floor.

I found her sitting on her desk, her legs wide open, with a foot on either chair. In her right hand she held a banana-shaped phone.

'It's Sr Tamerlán,' she said, her eyes ablaze. 'He wants a word with you. Try and keep him on the line as long as you can, please.'

I nodded and stretched out a hand to take the receiver, but, instead of obliging, she stuffed three quarters of it into her cunt, leaving only the mouthpiece outside.

'What are you waiting for? Start talking.'

Trying not to get my nose wet, I spoke into the only part of the phone that was still visible.

'Sr Tamerlán . . . Félix speaking.'

'I was forgetting something,' Tamerlán's sonorous voice sounded bubbly and muffled, but the powerful vibrations radiating over the receiver shook the secretary's body into shudders and spasms; I could barely hear him because her belly dancing was making it hard for me to keep my ear pressed to the phone. I got hold of the receiver and pulled and, before she sank it back

170

into the depths of her body, I managed to hear 'Another job for you when you've finished this one.' I shouted back that that was fine, without much hope of asking what it entailed, and, when the secretary realised from my tone of voice that he was about to hang up, she hissed furiously:

'You can't finish so soon! Don't leave me like this!'

I did what I could to keep Sr Tamerlán on the line, but all I could make out was the occasional word of his bursting towards the surface like a bubble. Right at the last, when I was shouting and the secretary had opened her legs as wide as they could go to receive the full impact of the volume bursting into her whole body, I heard his parting words:

'And tell that bitch to let go of the receiver, or I'll have her sealed with tar like a pothole.'

* * *

I was surprised at how solid the ground of the port felt under the soles of my trainers, the dull crunch of sand on the roadway, the green blasts of grass growing in the joins where the tar had come out. I crossed the avenue of the Costanera, whose only traffic was a surplus of last autumn's brown leaves stirred up by the wind in the vain hope of finding something of interest, and reached the wall, whose broad back contained the batterings of the river and stopped it pouring into the city. I rested my palms on the cold granite, pressing my fly against the stone edge and raising my feet in the air, and balanced there, watching five wet cormorants standing on five dark piles, between which plastic bottles and eddies of dull sediment bobbed and swirled. I jumped backwards, pushing myself off with my arms, and made a perfect landing on my heels. The rough pattern of the stone was impressed into my palms, which tingled for a few minutes as I walked along the wall. It was that time of day when the Costanera receives its pariahs, dragged by the wind to the edges of the city: couples so down-in-the-mouth that they don't mind parading the last vestiges of their love in this forgotten corner; office workers running out of excuses to delay their journeys home; anglers stiff with cold standing amid piles of inedible yellow catfish twitching their last in the dust; a Tamerlán & Sons employee who can at last take off his glasses, rub the bridge of his nose with two tired fingers and ask if they're biting without worrying about the answer; a lorry driver headed south, sipping maté high up in his cab and staring vacantly at the river; three kids with little home-made packets of sweets no one wanted to buy from them, walking along the edge of the broad wall and playing at pushing each other into the water; two firemen in blue staring at the horizon in silence from their red engine parked on the green grass . . . I watched them all as I passed, and they watched me.

I ordered a milanesa sandwich at a choripán stall, and a Coke to mitigate the effects of the coke. I had trouble swallowing at first, but after a few mouthfuls I realised I was starving, and the Coke sent my throat into spasms of delight. The simple pleasures of the poor, I thought, as I stamped to restore a little warmth to the soles of my feet. A small, white, woolly dog had been curled up on the floor amid the tables, uncleared since midday; it started when the wind blew some serviettes onto it. I gave it a hard crust of milanesa as a consolation and left it chewing and watching me out of the corner of its eye to see if there was any more.

Past a long, slender stone breakwater, as straight as a line drawn with a ruler on the surface of the river, the Ecological Reserve began. I got up onto the wall and walked beside the wire fence for a few blocks, till I found a gap and squeezed through it, plunging into the interlocking embankments that lined the lagoons and swamps carpeted with water hyacinths and, losing all sense of direction, I felt as if I'd left the city five centuries behind. I made for the open river, skirting the shores of a large lagoon from which I was watched with supreme indifference by a brace of orange-toothed coypus. I stopped a couple of times to take in the view: black-necked swans sailing in silence on the clearest of waters; a motionless heron scrutinising the surface of the water with the intensity of an old watchmaker; a lily-trotter delicately treading on each floating pad and hopping onto the next when the water began to wet its slender, yellow toes. I thought of Tamerlán's bulldozers and how they'd eventually reach here too, burying the nests of coots and lapwings and swans under avalanches of rubbish and rubble and earth, tearing up the young ceibo and willow groves, filling in all the lagoons, save the odd one, which, dredged and purged, would be left to adorn the golf course. There were already several 'upgraded' sectors in the Reserve and I had to cross one before I reached the river: a flat, dead, brown expanse, where the only sound was the snapping of the wind in the blue-and-white-striped polythene bags caught in the still-living branches that protruded bent and broken from the labyrinth of caterpillar tracks.

Balancing on pebble-incrusted concrete slabs piled in disorderly fashion by the force of storms, and leaping pools of grey crabs that scattered as I passed, I reached the water's edge.

It was low tide and the rubbish glistened, covered in a brown sludge where the water had retreated. I skimmed half a dozen stones, most of them tiles or bits of hollow brick polished by the water, pulling off a fiver at my fourth attempt, and turned towards the city.

Only the city's tallest tower blocks poked out above the foliage, their summits lit by the last rays of sun as the shadows spread across the plain. They looked implausible from the swamp, riding mirage-like over the undulating scrubland, fantastical towers of ice that would vanish into the sky if I approached them; and taller and nearer than any of them, the last light of the evening shining through the central fissure like the white of an eye between half-closed lids, Tamerlán's twins towered above them all. Facing the city, legs akimbo, I got out my prick and pissed long and hard into a puddle, and then, inevitably, tried to have a wank. I didn't get very far: the cocaine, the fatigue, the icy wind blowing between my legs, did little to encourage my stuttering erection, and the image of the blonde secretary, which I'd managed to conjure up, wet and panting before my eager eyes, gradually faded until, through it, I could see the lights of the two towers shining against the dismal sky. When the tip of my prick no longer emerged from its sheath of clenched fist, I realised I'd failed again.

Two or three choripán stalls had lit their hurricane lamps and, navigating by their greenish-white glare, I left the Reserve and walked along the Costanera in the direction of the silver tower.

Chapter 6

SPANISH SURPRISE

'We started out with a small jacket workshop in the late seventies. Me and my partner did the lot: bought the leather, cut the leather, worked the sewing machine and did the distribution, mainly to workers wanting to flaunt their new socio-economic status. We sewed labels into the lining over the pockets saying "Made exclusively on the premises. No workers were exploited in the tailoring of this jacket." Of course, in those days, we hadn't made the discovery of importing them from Bolivia and Peru,' he said, weighing me up out of the corner of his eye to see if a complicitous wink was in order, and, not knowing what to make of my features collapsing with exhaustion, he saved it for a more auspicious moment. 'The first time we went bust was in '75, but, thanks to a timely inheritance from my in-laws, we were back in the ring two years later, this time with a menswear shop: affordable suits and shirts for ambitious office workers and small businessmen. We still have some in stock,' he added enticingly, shaking the tip of his outrageous red and green tie like his prick after a piss. Its impact on my retina was like staring at the sun, so that, whenever my eyes strayed to the vast, white expanse of the fat man's shirt, they saw a series

of identical, negative ghost-images, like dancing girls in a chorus line – mercifully somewhat fainter than the original. 'You
wouldn't be interested in . . .?' He read the no in my eyes and
went on. 'The current government shook us out of the provincial slumber most of us small and medium-sized businessmen
in this country were wallowing in, resting on our crumpled
laurels until they were swept away by the start of imports, and
we were washed up on the hard-but-healthy shores of fair com-
petition. We applied for massive loans to modernise the factory
so that we could compete with imported clothing on an equal
footing and bring it to its knees. But by the time we were ready
to do battle, the floodgates of customs had opened wide and
the torrent buried us. We got through the worst by burning
down a couple of warehouses and claiming the insurance, but
we've still got a full one left. The day after that we switched to
importing coat-hangers. You understand? Coat-hangers. Coat-
hangers are easy to manufacture, materially pure, adapted
to all tastes and never go out of fashion. You buy coat-hangers
there, and you sell them here. Light. Simple. Coat-hangers.'

For the clothes you don't make any more, my numbed
mind absurdly spelt out. Then I said:

'What about Surprise?'

'Ah. That's the other secret of success: diversification.
"Never put all your eggs in one basket," as the English say. We
found the company motto irresistible,' he said. That habit of
his of always speaking in the plural, as if he were two people
rather than one, was beginning to fray my neurons. Maybe he
is, I thought looking hard at him; maybe he's phagocytised his
wife like an amœba. 'You don't *need* money to *make* money: in
Surprise your friends are your capital.'

We'd reached Fatty's office, which he unlocked with his own key, pushing the door open enough to edge his hefty bulk through. Inside, all four walls were lined from floor to ceiling with closed boxes of varying sizes bearing the words 'Christopher Products' (a few more in the doorway and the fat man would be walled up like the character in that Poe story); the only thing offering any contact with the outside world was a television screen embedded in the great wall of cardboard. He pushed aside a few more boxes on the top of his desk, and a snarl of tangled coat-hangers, to make some room and invited me to take a seat. I did; on *his* side of the desk, in the reclining swivel chair with armrests that looked like just the place for my level-3 coma. Making a visible effort to force his indignation back to the depths of his immensity, he sat down smiling on one of the straight-backed chairs meant for his evidently rare visitors, his ample arse spilling over the seat on three of the four sides. He rested his dainty hands on his belly, interlacing his fingers so that they wouldn't fall to the sides under their own weight, and ratcheted his smile up a notch, his conscientiously pruned beard framing it in a halo of dependability.

'Sr Marroné has informed me that Sr Tamerlán expects from me full and unstinting collaboration with you,' he said, running out of breath a couple of times with the artfulness of his syntax. I took a cigarette from its box without offering him one, tapped the filter a couple of times on the glass of the desk, lit it, inhaled, exhaled, and said:

'What's this Surprise thing? Tell me about it.'

The beam on his face showed that he'd clearly been dying to, fearing I might not give him the chance. It's been a long day, I thought.

'Surprise is the company of the future,' he began, pausing dramatically. My eyes must have reflected as much emotion as those of a deep-frozen cod. He smiled to show he understood my scepticism and went on: 'Surprise isn't bound to any physical space: its headquarters can be your house, your favourite bar or, as in my case, your private office.'

'Street vendors' processed the chips in my brain.

'Surprise doesn't force you to stick to a rigid, unnatural timetable, or to adjust your own and your family's lives to a set salary that's never enough to make ends meet. In Surprise you *choose* the salary you want to collect every month. It's the salary that adapts to you and not the other way around. A Copernican revolution, what!'

'I've worked on a commission basis as well,' I muttered with displeasure.

He raised a plump finger of admonition in the air and wagged it like a metronome, his lips pursed:

'In Surprise nobody works for anybody: there are no employees, only partners. In Surprise, for the first time, the golden dream and the president's promise to the Argentinian people have been realised: to turn the proletariat into the proprietariat. You'll have understood immediately, as someone so clearly intelligent, that such an achievement fully fulfils the utopian aspirations we hold most dear, and which we pursued in the wrong direction when we were young. We wanted to turn the proprietariat into the proletariat, when it was the other way round. Our president stood reality on its feet, the way Columbus did with his egg. That's why we've christened our new line of cosmetics "Christopher". Hard to find a better name to symbolise our ideal: Christopher Columbus, the gravedigger of feudalism, the discoverer of new worlds. Surprise has successfully dismantled the antiquated hierarchy that had stuck like a suckerfish to the plainly egalitarian and democratic dynamic of the marketplace. There are no more relics of feudalism in Surprise: no lords and vassals, no masters and servants, no bosses and employees. Only partners. Friends,' he finished, invitingly modulating the last word. I didn't say anything.

'Explain to me how it works, this "friends" thing.'

'You only need to invest one thousand dollars to join our chain of friendship, a tiny sum when you think of your returns. Minimum earnings of ten thousand dollars guaranteed in your first year alone! Friends! Well-being for you and your family! Self-confidence! In exchange for that initial sum you receive your first batch of products from our exclusive line.'

Like someone displaying the crown jewels, he opened one of the cardboard boxes to demonstrate the Christopher product line to me. My expectations weren't high, but I still found it hard to believe that such an edifice (at least a hundred people turned up on the top floor of the most exclusive tower block in Buenos Aires for every meeting) was built on just a few pots of face cream and other cheap cosmetics packed in little pastel-coloured boxes with gold lettering, and a line of chains, bracelets, earrings and watches, barely more presentable than the one Fatty was wearing for lack of contact with human skin. There must be something more to it, I thought to myself. All that cash has to come from somewhere.

'That will make you a retail partner of our company,' Fatty was saying in the meantime. 'You'll be entitled to discounts and purchase orders in restaurants and shops throughout the country. Once you've sold four lots, with a twenty-five per cent mark-up on your sales, and recruited four new friends to Surprise, or by investing two thousand up front, you'll be promoted to wholesale partner, and can charge a forty-five per cent mark-up, plus fifteen per cent of your friends' sales. By improving your sales, bringing in more friends or paying four thousand dollars at the start, you gain access to the category of business partner, and can charge fifty per cent on your sales, ten per cent on those of your wholesaler friends, twenty-five per cent on your retailer . . .'

I started doing the sums. The levels of the pyramid grew in a geometric sequence: one, two, four, eight, sixteen . . . With percentages like those, the first one made his money when the sixteen members on the fifth level paid up, the two guys on the next level with the thirty-two members of the sixth . . . If, for example, I entered with those thirty-two, I'd only collect what was mine once 1,024 partners had joined. Of course, I wasn't counting the percentage on sales, because the idea that anyone could buy those knick-knacks in the numbers needed to rack up a profit was more sad than funny. So that was the secret: the ones higher up took the money from the stooges below, and the stooges below only stood a chance of getting back what they'd lost (and, in exceptional circumstances, of making a profit) if they found more mugs – a lot more – willing to lose money further down the line. I suppose the majority joined in good faith, and only once they were on the inside did they realise their so-called friends had shafted them to save their own skin. At that moment you had two options: get out and stick the bracelets and pendants up your arse (lubricated with the face cream), or stay in and hang on tooth and nail, praying the pyramid wouldn't collapse before it was your turn to collect. And if you wanted to stay in, you had to invest more cash (which you didn't have) or recruit more friends, because you sure as hell weren't going to sell anything: or to put it another way, shaft *them* the way *you*'d been shafted. At any rate, you only stood a chance if you came in at the highest levels; after the sixth or seventh, practically speaking, you didn't stand a chance, and any further down all the adults in the country would have to join Surprise to bail you out. So this was the secret of the enormous profits: what was being traded at Surprise wasn't costume jewellery and cheap cosmetics; it was people.

'One meeting, once a week,' I said, thinking aloud. 'Same time, same place,' I went on, waiting for him to corroborate. 'How long have they been held in this tower?'

'Four months. I made the arrangements with Tamerlán & Sons . . .'

It is possible, I thought to myself, mentally muting Fatty to think properly, that Tamerlán's right: that his son did commit the crime that night, at that time, at that window, precisely because he knew there'd be witnesses. What the fuck's going on here, I thought. What am I getting myself into?

'Tell me about that night.'

He'd obviously been expecting the question since we met, and most of his verbal incontinence had been meant to delay it.

'What night?'

I put my feet on his desk and reclined as far as the chair would let me. It groaned when it reached full stretch.

'Exactly one week ago at the Surprise meeting, you all saw a man being murdered by Sr Tamerlán's son.'

'Not me,' Fatty hastily covered his wide back. Tamerlán was right, I thought. This is going to be cheap and easy.

'Listen to me. I know everything. I work for Sr Tamerlán.'

'You can tell him what I told the police then. I didn't see anything. Nobody saw anything. People think they see things. Always think the worst. A man fell, true. An unfortunate accident. Cleaning firms will sometimes send temps, people with no references. While cleaning, the man finds a bottle of imported Scotch. He's tempted. He tries a sip. He's never tasted anything like it. Nectar of the gods. He puts the bottle down in amazement. Was that taste real? He decides to take another sip to check. You finish the story. And yet, what's the first thing people deduce when they see him fall? He was pushed. And all because a man stretched an arm out to him through a broken window. How do they know he wasn't trying to help him? A man with everything going for him risked his precious life to save a perfectly worthless life. And that's how they repay him. The mean-minded never acknowledge altruism in others. They bring everything down to their level, the only one they can understand.'

'Do you need me to spell it out to you?'

'What?' he asked in a tiny voice. His tie hung flaccidly over his defeated paunch like the tongue of a panting dog on a hot day. Discreet pearls of oily sweat beaded his brow.

'You owe Sr Tamerlán four months' rent. And all your capital is tied up in this company of the future, so for the time being your present looks pretty grim.'

That put an end to the fat man's forced joviality. Big men eager to please are generally a pushover. It never comes naturally to them; they sweat a lot and wrestle with their obsequiousness like a belt with no more holes. Little men, on the other hand, play it cool: their fawning's second nature to them.

'The meetings are held on the top floor of the tower. The one right opposite Sr Tamerlán's office. There were fewer guests than usual that day – a quarter as many – because there was a match on.'

'I remember: Boca v San Lorenzo. The Crows bit the dust yet again.'

'A shame, because the main speaker was one of the founders of the company, whom we'd flown over from Madrid specially for the event. You know, with the 5C celebrations, the Mother Country is promoting a much more aggressive policy of expansion and joint ventures. Europe once again has eyes for America.'

Yes, five hundred years later they're coming back to see if there's anything left, I thought.

'Tell me about that night,' I said.

'Perhaps you'd rather watch it on video.'

What video!? screamed my brain, but fortunately my teeth snapped shut with an audible mental click on the question before it managed to escape. 'Naturally,' I answered, retaining my composure.

He pulled a video cassette from an identical, unlabelled row of black and held it aloft.

'We don't normally film proceedings, but on this occasion . . . Sr Ignacio de Bobadilla, our distinguished visitor from Spain, had finished telling the epic story of the beginnings of Surprise and, with the aid of explanatory graphics, had demonstrated how those who join our company have only one alternative: to succeed. We'll wind the tape forward to the closing sections of his stirring speech.'

He inserted it into the video cassette player's greedy

throat, pressed play and sat down. Immediately almost the whole screen was filled by his voluminous, naked body, save the lower right corner, where an equally naked lady was doing her utmost to hoist his buttocks onto a vibrator that seemed to split the screen in two. Even the whites of Fatty's eyes went puce and, in a frenzy of despair, he started slapping the remote control.

'Your wife?' I asked out of politeness.

Jabbing indiscriminately at the remote, he hit fast-forward instead of stop and his video self began jumping up and down as if riding a highly inflated bicycle fast over cobblestones. Eventually he hit eject and the machine peeled out its cassette with an obscene gurgle.

'This is the one, this is the one,' said Fatty in a barely audible voice, sweating cobs. He looked thinner than he had two minutes ago.

On the screen a well-dressed man with a trim, grey beard strutted self-importantly up and down before an audience of gawping wannabes.

'A mere five hundred years ago,' he reverberated in his Castilian accent, straight out of a Spanish TV series, 'one man, ordinary but for his blind determination to believe in no one but himself, dared to defy two millennia of unquestioned truths and launch himself into the unknown, equipped with just three flimsy ships, a handful of faulty instruments, a rabble from the ports and gaols, and the obstinacy of his erroneous conceits. Paltry ingredients, you may say, for this paella of yours. Yet it is thanks to him that I am here today addressing an audience that doesn't wear feathers on its heads; that I am here to tell you that you too, with what you see as your meagre resources, can all stake claims to greater lands than he did. How much longer will you go on looking for old solutions to new problems? You won't discover new worlds by beating the same old tracks. The only way to stand an egg on end is to change it. Do you really think a man's greatness precedes his deeds?'

'Does Sr Tamerlán know of the existence of this video?' I took advantage of a pause from the marquis to ask.

'Of course. I made copies before I handed the original over to the police. He has one of them.'

'And he let you keep this one?'

'One word from him and the catfish would be watching it at the bottom of the river instead of us.'

The Spaniard's words, meanwhile, were doing their best to crawl out from under Fatty's: '. . . dared to cross a sea that all but he thought endless, and, on the other side, he found the greatest treasure in the . . .' As he spoke, he inched imperceptibly closer to a thick curtain covering the window from end to end, and the camera inched closer to him. 'But you, on the other hand, are a comparatively tiny distance away from glory, and you know for a fact that there is terra firma on the other side. You've seen it, you've smelt it, you've desired it all your lives. Yet you remain on this shore, watching the boats set sail and disappear over the horizon – and you know that they won't tumble over the edge; you've seen those who took with them nothing more than the patches on their britches return laden with honours and treasure. What are you doing, standing on the edge of a world you already know like the back of your hand, a world that is too small for you and those around you. Dare yourselves to take the great leap! It isn't as far as you think! Dare. Dare. Ply those seas. Your ideas will become real when your belief in them is blind. Come,' he said, and his invitation wasn't rhetorical. He stretched out his arms. He smiled. He invited them to share in the wonderful world he'd discovered. Accompanying his gesture, the camera, which had gradually been expanding the mid-shot of the marquis to a full one that took in his audience, now panned across their faces, which gazed back like children in a puppet theatre. Hesitant, looking uncertainly at each other, first one, then several, got up from their seats. 'Do you still say you don't know what there is on the other side?' they heard. 'I will show you what there is on the other side. Mark well. Behold your future!' With a magician's flourish he waved his arm twice and the great curtain covering the east side drew back to reveal the enormous window and the golden tower framed in it. 'Come closer. Look.' Oohing and aahing, knocking over chairs and tripping over each other, without looking where they were going, they advanced towards the huge window as if guided by a comet in the night. Some pressed their hands or noses to it, the latecomers tried to peer over their shoulders, until they eventually ordered themselves into a long strip stretching the width of the room.

'Freeze it,' I told Fatty.

I tried to count the heads in the paused, faintly flickering image. Twenty-four, I made it, including the Spaniard, who was out of shot.

'Was anyone else there?' I asked.

'No, I think we're all . . . The caretaker!' he remembered.

Twenty-five. I counted again. One, two, three . . . twenty-five? I nearly slapped my forehead when I realised.

'The one who's filming! That makes twenty-six.'

One of the people I'm looking at, I thought, is the

mysterious witness number twenty-six. How can I tell which one? I asked Fatty to hit play. The camera showed a wedge of river and some viscera-coloured clouds receding into the darkening sky on their way to Uruguay; the dark mattress of trees far below, the lights of the port and their reflections in the water, the long row of people looking out, more perfectly and beautifully recreated in Sr Tamerlán's golden tower. 'Look at yourselves,' said the marquis. 'Behold yourselves. You are part of that same golden substance; you can feel it running through your veins. If you only believe in your own potential, a golden future awaits each and every one of you. Who's to say you're not in there already, watching those still standing outside?' I picked out the clear, gilt features of Fatty in the line of bobbing heads, smiling and waving at himself. Others pointed at themselves, called out, shouted things. 'Mark well,' repeated the marquis. 'Mark well. Behold your future.'

Then everything happened very fast. The reflection of the ones in front seemed to shudder slightly, then the glass cracked into a spider-web and big chunks began to fall towards the street, taking the images of the new converts with them. Someone shouted 'Look, the murderer!' and a corpulent back sheathed in a grey coat loomed into view between the lens and what must have appeared behind the shattered glass of the opposite tower. The camera reeled and dived, and the screen was flooded with crackling snow.

'That's as far as it goes,' announced the fat man, hitting pause.

'What happened?'

'In the scrum to see someone inadvertently hit our video maker and he dropped the camera.'

'So the murder wasn't recorded.'

'The accident,' he corrected me. 'No.'

'How very convenient. And you didn't see anything?'

He was sweating again, and again his tubby fingers started fidgeting, Hardy-like, with the tip of his tie.

'So you *did* recognise Sr Tamerlán's son.'

He pulled himself together faster than I'd expected.

'You can be quite certain, my dear sir,' he said to me, pronouncing the words with self-assured gravitas, 'that if you put him in a line-up with a circus dwarf, two blacks, a transvestite and a one-eyed hunchback, I wouldn't recognise him, even if you made me stare at him for a week. Pass that on to your employer.'

He'd started to get up to remove the cassette, but I stopped him in his tracks.

'I want to watch it again. The last bit. Rewind please.'

He rewound. The camera returned to the grey overcoat, which moved out of the way, the heads bobbed frantically like dice in a shaker and the shards of glass flew upwards to fuse into the window and its still intact promise of riches and success.

'There,' I said to him. 'Now slow forward.'

Once again, the increasingly absurd scene played itself out before my eyes in klunks, like the second hand of a watch: the heads now waved slowly, with all the time in the world, like seaweed in the tide; the spectators contemplated a reflection that had taken on an air of eternity; but that wasn't what had caught my interest: almost imperceptible the first time, the man in the overcoat could now be seen clearly, although he deliberately kept his face averted from the camera, advancing from left to right across the screen, jostling and barging through the crowd which, spellbound, barely noticed him and protested lazily and with infinite slowness. And it was only then, *after* he began his advance through the viscous submarine medium of slow-mo, that the first crack appeared in the window and began to spread tentatively, as if drawn with a nib and Indian ink, and the first piece of glass opened like a door and, before the grey-clad shoulder covered them, gave a dark glimpse of the blurred shapes flapping behind it.

'Spotted anything of interest?' the fat man asked when we finished.

'Nothing,' I answered, keeping my inferences to myself just in case. 'So. Down to business. I want a list with the details of everyone present that day.'

'We didn't get round to taking the guests' details. We usually do it at the end of the meeting.'

'All right then. A list of all the Surprise members in the room.'

'That's confidential information.'

'How much?' I sighed.

'A thousand dollars, and in return you'll receive your first batch of Christopher products, and this badge showing you're a retail partner,' he said, pinning a little metal badge in the shape of a rabbit onto my lapel. I looked at his. He had a similar badge of an Æsop fox in a hat. I signed the cheque and tossed it across the desk.

I asked where the bathroom was. When I got back, I found Fatty raptly piecing together a giant pyramid of Christopher products on his desk. He was taking boxes from the base and trying to stack them on the summit without the whole structure collapsing. I wondered how to break it to him.

'It won't work,' I told him. 'It's a mathematical inevitability.'

'You're mistaking mathematics for morality. I'm not interested in the viability of the system, but my chances of saving my bacon. There are your boxes by the door. One of them contains the list you asked me for. Good luck with your sales.'

'Why don't you get out before things get any worse?'

This time he looked me in the eye. I wish he hadn't. The holes of his pupils were two small to let out all the pain his colossal body had managed to store up.

'I've lost too much. I can't go back.'

'You've invested a lot in this?'

'All my friends. I've next to none left now. I was always one for few friends. Few friends, but good ones, as they say. Should have listened to my wife. In cases like this it isn't the quality of your friends that matters, only the quantity. One friend's as good as another if they're willing to take part in Surprise. The few good friends I had I lost in this business, and now I haven't even got bad friends to invest in it. It's times like this when you learn the true value of friendship. If I pull out now, I'll have lost my friends in vain. It's worth risking a few more to justify the loss of the others. There are childhood friends I still haven't tracked down. Alfredo, for example, who used to tease me when we played football. I kicked his leather casey under a car once, and it burst like a toad. Fucking lard-arse he called me. Do you think he'll hold it against me after all this time?'

'I don't know, Fa . . .'

'Hernán's my name. Hernán Stoffa. Stuffer Stoffa the lads used to call me. It wasn't that long ago we used to get together on Sundays for the match and go for a pizza at Las

Cuartetas afterwards. Now I spend my weekends trying to sell Christopher products door to door; and even if I did have any free time, I'd have to go to the match on my own because they haven't done as well out of it as I have. But you know how it is: no sooner do you get your head above water than they want to cut it off; when you start to get ahead, there are people who try to drag you down instead of being happy for you. Is it my fault I stopped being that idealistic, good-natured local lad? It was the same when I stopped being a Lefty. This country doesn't forgive people that change. Serves me right for being so bloody generous, mind. That's what you get for doing business with your friends.'

'I thought that was precisely what Surprise was all about.'

'A word of advice: only deal with acquaintances; they're more malleable. Only use your friends as a last resort, at the eleventh hour, when you can't scrape any more from the bottom of the barrel. There's always the car mechanic, the butcher, your kids' kindergarten teacher, your old man's friends at the nursing home . . . Yes, indeed, stick to acquaintances; don't repeat my mistakes. Oh, and another thing,' he shouted as I was getting ready to leave, a huge box of Christopher products under each arm, 'don't forget, fifteen per cent of your sales are mine.'

* * *

Skirting the dock, staggering under the weight of the boxes, I stumbled across the unearthly bulk of Columbus's caravel. They'd made quite a bit of progress over the last few days, having completed the hull, deck and masts; with the furled sails lying on one side, it would be finished. From high up in the tower it had looked sturdy enough: capable, if not of sailing to new worlds, then at least of floating about in the docks like a rubber duck; but on closer scrutiny it was quite obvious that it stood less chance than one of those nutshell caravels we sailed on plasticine seas as schoolboys. They'd stained the cheap wood dark brown to make it look sturdier, rigged it with raffia thread, and the aftercastle looked like a shack in the act of being tipped overboard. But the worst thing was the hull: they'd covered the great whale ribs with unseasoned 0.5-mm pine cladding and, with the damp of the first two nights, all the planks had warped in the terrible agony of wrenching themselves free of the screws that held them in place. Screws, on the *Santa María*! Next thing you knew they'd be using them to screw Christ to the cross. I stuck my whole hand into one of the countless gaps between the planks: the ship they were building looked better suited to straining the seas than plying them – a kind of Columbus's egg in reverse. Straining against the four ends of the main and mizzen masts like Tupac Amaru drawn by horses, a banner caught the wind: a swelling sail striving in vain to drive the beached ship forward. Along the length of the torn and frayed nylon banner read the legend: 'The construction of the *Santa María* is sponsored by Spanish Surprise, an independent sales company. Madrid-Caracas-Mexico-Buenos Aires. Set sail for the First World hand-in-hand with the Motherland.'

Chapter 7
PINBALL & TETRIS

I woke feeling pretty lousy: aching joints, tense jaw, breathlessness, burning eyes sensitive even to the dim light, bitter-tasting-snot-encrusted nostrils. Out of anything stronger, I resorted to my pot-bellied maté gourd and its stubby little bombilla, and the caress of the hot sap on my stomach restored me enough to face the exhausting routine of showering, shaving, shitting and sitting down to make the phone calls. I picked up the list and, glancing through, decided to start with Diego Armando Maradona, to see if he'd bring me any luck.

'Engineer Urano, please.'

'Who's speaking?' asked a secretary's voice.

'My name is Alberto Porcel,' I improvised. 'I'm calling from Surprise . . .' There was a silence of hand over mouthpiece.

'Urano here. Who's speaking?'

'My name is . .' I repeated the explanation. 'I wanted to ask you some questions about the meeting last Wednesday 27th . . .'

He hung up, and my string of follow-up calls only met with the answering machine. I had no better luck with the next names on the list: two of them didn't answer, and three of them hung up on me as soon as I explained why I was ringing;

193

only one stayed on the line, just long enough to howl a string of insults at me and force *me* to hang up. This isn't working, I thought. I'd started with the hope I'd be able to sort everything out over the phone; it's not much more personal, after all, than a computer. Was it possible I'd have no alternative but to go out on the street and spend the day *outside*, ringing doorbells, talking to *people* – strangers, probably hostile? What assurance did I have that they wouldn't slam the door in my face the way they'd slammed the phone down? Wouldn't I do the same in their shoes? What they need, I decided, is an incentive . . .

After digging in a drawer, I salvaged a blank chequebook from some obscure, bankrupt provincial bank and, on each cheque, printed the name 'Surprise' and an invented account number with the laser printer; then, in case any of them proved sceptical, I stashed two thousand dollars cash in my jacket pocket. After that, I made a call to hire a mobile phone from a nearby outlet. What followed was a trick of the imagination: flattening the streets and houses of Buenos Aires into a numbered grid like the one in my Filcar guide and then, to negotiate this virtual city, rarefying myself to a sequence of algorithms that could move through it frictionlessly like a ghost. How different could it be? Buenos Aires was a file name, Felipe a search instruction and the cheques, key words to open the doors.

The first of these belonged to a branch of Tamerlán & Sons at the junction of Avenida Rivadavia and Calle Combate de los Pozos, run by one Alberto Palomeque (a.k.a. Sid Vicious). I'd been rather ambiguous over the phone about the purpose of my visit and since, to his penetrating eye, I looked less like a customer than someone wanting to sell him a timeshare, he invited me curtly to take a seat.

'Sr Tamerlán sent me,' I spat back at him.

The change was radical: his eyes opened disproportionately wide, he collapsed to his knees on the carpet and went into a violent coughing fit; I ran to fetch him a glass of water, which fell through his limp grip to the floor.

'I knew it,' he wheezed, his eyes turned towards the glazed shopfront. 'I knew this day would come. Just like in my dream: Sr Tamerlán needed me, asked *especially* for me to go and see him. "The company's in danger, and there's only one man who can save it . . ." he said. And I passed through the mirrors, one after another, until I reached his office . . . What does he need me for?'

'You can start by explaining what you were doing at the Surprise meeting on Wednesday night.'

I never saw such a sudden transformation in a man. It reminded me of one of those little collapsible dogs I used to play with as a boy: it was kept upright by a spring at the base, but at the slightest pressure, the threads would slacken and the little dog would collapse as if its bones had melted. Sid pulled a long face and lowered his eyes to the puddle of water on the shallow pile of his beige moquette. I think for a moment he expected me to rub his nose in it and yell 'What *have* you done, you *naughty* boy!'

'Only for money . . . loyalty . . . ver ppen gain,' he stammered.

I loosened my tie (I didn't need it any more) and made him cough it all up. Yes, he had been there. Yes, he admitted, I took a guest with me, I'll hand him over: Sr Marcelo Rinaldo, 474 Calle Maure, 5th Floor, Apartment C, telephone number . . . I carefully noted everything down. We'd got off to a good start.

Anyone else? Lots of people I didn't know. What episode? I don't know what you're . . .'

'Sr Tamerlán sent me to find out about the episode. That's all he's interested in. The episode.'

'I thought that . . .'

'Come on,' I interrupted him. 'Do you really think Sr Tamerlán would have me waste his time with the likes of you for any other reason? Tell me everything you know.'

He looked at me in childish terror, trying to buy himself some time. Perhaps I'd overdone it a bit.

'It's extremely important to him. He wants to hear your opinion before anyone else's.'

He calmed down a little, but was still eyeing me distrustfully, like a boy being spoken to lovingly after a smacking.

'It was self-defence . . .' he ventured, and watched me to see how to go on. I gave him an understanding look. 'That man was trying to throw him out of the window . . . you know. Luckily, Sr Tamerlán's son managed to free himself with a judo throw.'

'You got a clear view? Was it him?'

His eyes shrivelled in their sockets like raisins, his suit was suddenly three sizes too big for him, even his nails seemed to retract into his fingers.

'Well, clearnnff,' he spluttered like an empty soda-siphon. 'Ffffpp.'

He cast abject glances at me, begging me for a gesture to give him a clue whether he should answer yes or no. But I wasn't about to let him off the hook, and in the end, like a goalie saving a penalty, he had to dive to one side or the other.

'No.'

'That's not what you told the police.' I said, coolly stepping up to the spot.

'They were pressurising me, I didn't want to . . .'

'*They* pressurise you, so you say what *they* want to hear; *I* pressurise you and you say what you think *I* want to hear. We won't get anywhere like that, Sr Palomeque,' I said, leisurely reeling out the words, marvelling at how well I was doing. 'You have to decide who you want to be loyal to: Sr Tamerlán or . . .'

'There is something I didn't tell the police,' he said. 'I also recognised the other one.'

'The man in the grey overcoat?'

'Wasn't it a mackintosh?'

'So you did recognise him'

'No.'

'This isn't working, Palomeque.' (I loved patronisingly pronouncing his surname.) 'You just told me . . .'

'I'm talking about the one that fell.'

'You know who it was?' I almost leaped out of my seat. He shook his head.

'But I'd seen him before,' he clarified.

'How did you recognise him? I thought he fell backwards.'

'Precisely. I never saw him from the front. But the back of his neck was unmistakable.'

'What was so striking about it?'

'It's hard to put my finger on, but believe me, if you put him in a line-up with everyone's backs turned . . . It's like women's arses: you can't explain it, but there are arses you'd recognise from thousands of others. Know what I mean?' he said, in an attempt to win me over with a humble smile. I was starting to like him.

'And where did you see him?'

'In the tower. In the invisibility room.' I frowned, none the wiser. 'There's a point at the top from which you can see all points . . .' he began, pausing out of courtesy for me to put two and two together, and feel suitably intelligent.

'Ergo: there must be a point at the base that's visible to all the others. That's where our friend was?'

'For days on end probably, biding his time. If it hadn't been for his son's heroic intervention, perhaps Sr Tamerlán by now . . .'

'Wait, you're getting me confused. You believe our friend meant to attack Sr Tamerlán.'

'Or rob him. Business secrets maybe. It's a common enough occurrence, between rival firms . . .'

'So why would he hide just where everyone could see him?' I finished saying and fell silent. The stolen letter of course.

'What everyone in the tower wants to see is Sr Tamerlán. It is towards him, who is invisible, that our gazes are all direct- ed. Who wants to look at what everyone can see?' he concluded, his last words reduced to a hush by some indefinable sadness.

'Perfect. But something doesn't add up. How come *you* spotted him?'

'I don't even belong in the tower,' he said without looking at me, and suddenly I *was* able to define it: the sadness of the exile. 'I've only been in there three times in my life. The last time was that morning.'

'Did you mention it to anyone?'

'Not even my wife. Please tell Sr Tamerlán when you see him.'

'What?'

'That he can rest easy where I'm concerned. I won't talk, even under torture. I'm . . . Come with me,' he said, taking me by the arm and leading me to the glazed shopfront. 'Look at them.'

On the imposing white façade of the building opposite, where only the strangeness of the light of day had prevented me from recognising the busy entrance of the Roxy, two enormous, bearded colossi – elbows on knees, heads between elbows – supported the entire weight of the building on their muscular stucco backs. They looked as if they could stay there for centuries, resigned to contemplating the traffic of cars and pedestrians along Avenida Rivadavia, oblivious to the cramp and the fatigue, the tedium, the desire to get up and go for a stroll down the pavement like everyone else while the masonry caved in behind them and the screaming pedestrians made a run for it.

'He'll realise one day. And when he does, he'll send for me.'

* * *

I stopped for a few minutes on the pavement to check my list. Sheltering behind a flower stall to avoid getting caught in the stream of pedestrians, I dialled the next number on my mobile and got through to Dr Glans's house, where a laconic housemaid suggested I talk to his surgery and hung up. I only had his address, so I rang directory inquiries. It was always engaged. I was still trying to get through when I saw them pull up.

They double-parked the blue Falcon, and the one I recognised checked the address on a PDA. They were both wearing expensive jackets of soft, black leather – rich men's leather – and Ray-Ban sunglasses (the driver, gold frames and smoke-coloured lenses; the other, the same mirrorshades as the first night), steel Rolexes, gold chains. The passenger got out – his short, neat, greying hair, again freshly trimmed – avoiding the front bumper, whose buckled left side stuck out like a crumpled horn. The other one, scratching the back of his neck beneath his abundant white hair, adjusted his glasses on his red, carbuncular nose and settled down to wait, heater on, engine running. I had no reason to conceal myself; we were, after all, supposed to be collaborating, but I kept behind the flower stall all the same and, when the chance came, I melted into the crowd and moved on, walking round the whole block to reach the corner.

I took the Subte at Congreso and, once inside the carriage, I looked for the map to check how many stops I had to go. Forced to hang from the chrome bars for lack of any handles (if they were tall enough to reach them), people grumbled and muttered insults as they let me through. I finally reached the map, yellowed and streaked with coloured lines, protected by a sheet of cracked acrylic fastened to the cardboard plaque by ten screws, only five of which were left, and I noticed that someone had torn out the piece I needed through the loose part of the cover. Bored, I started to read the carriage's advertisements attentively: a blonde in a flame-red jacket was hugging a stranger in parrot-green leather, while the print below read 'Afrika Leathers' with giraffe spots on the 'Afrika' as if the 'k' had given it leprosy or something. I was trying to work out the connection between the striking spelling and the even more striking colours of the leather when, segmented between the people waiting on the platform, I spotted the sign for Miserere and, kneeing and elbowing my way through the crush, I managed to reach the door and squeeze through a crack in the mob fighting to board the train.

I left Plaza Miserere after dodging an evangelist pastor, who tried to catch me with his megaphone as if it were a butterfly net, and, crossing the street, I plunged into the crowd of buyers and sellers under the arches and turned onto Calle Mitre to reach the surgery. I climbed to the second floor by a greyed marble staircase coiled like a hungry boa constrictor round the empty birdcage of the broken-down lift, and rang the bell at the side of a bronze plaque which read: Dr. Aldo Glans MD, Pædiatrician.

Inside, two mothers waiting with their children looked at my solitary, suited form with vague curiosity. I approached the receptionist, who dealt with me without looking up from the copy of *Hello!* he was leafing through.

'Got an appointment?' he asked, without bothering to see if I had any children in tow.

'No, listen,' I answered him. 'I've already spoken to the doctor: it's an emergency. Premature ageing . . . It was my tenth birthday yesterday and look at the state of me. A month ago nobody would have said I was a day over twenty. My years are like dog years, you know . . . Hence the urgency.'

I thought it would shake him out of his apathy, but he didn't bat an eyelid; the two mothers, on the other hand, even before I'd finished, had clutched their respective offspring in padlock arms. Coolly the secretary got up and disappeared down the corridor, while the two children kicked to get free, and their mothers hissed at them furiously, pointing at me with their eyes and arching their eyebrows as I leafed through a few back-issues of *Gente*.

'The Doctor will see you in a moment.'

The Doctor was a friendly queer with such a flashy satin tie that I almost shook it instead of the boneless hand he held out to me as he gave me a gentle smile through parted lips.

'How can I help you, young sir?'

'Where did you get the tie?'

I carefully noted down the address – somewhere in Recoleta; might stop by later on – and told him the reasons for my visit.

'The meeting of Spanish Surprise last Wednesday was our five-hundredth, coinciding with the Fifth Centenary, and to mark the occasion those attending were given the sum of one thousand dollars,' I rattled off, then paused, to watch his beady eyes acquire a glow to rival his tie, 'plus another thousand for whoever contributes information to help us locate our ten-thousandth guest, who was present that night, but forgot to leave his details . . .' I went on a while longer, though he'd obviously gone for it hook, line and sinker: for a grand I could have had him listening to stories about my sister-in-law's varicose veins and still asking for more.

'Doña Ernestina Hidalgo! She arrived with a very handsome young man: Eugenio; I don't remember his surname. Then there was Dr Tarino and Dany – Daniel – Tabardo, but they're already members, of course. Give me a second, let's see . . . Can I offer you a coffee?' He opened the door: 'Eduardo, coffee . . . two coffees, please. Perhaps if I describe the people I remember by sight?'

I listened to him in seismograph mode, only paying attention when some distinctive word or other made my needle jump; it only happened twice: '. . . a young woman who was allowed in, despite being in jeans and training shoes, to avoid an altercation at the door . . .'; and '. . . an elderly man in a grey trench coat, who arrived late and didn't talk to anyone, not even when . . .' He broke off. At that moment the miffed secretary came in with the coffees and put them down on the table, spilling just enough in my saucer for the cup to drip on my trousers afterwards; inside the rim was a thick border of froth and, as I couldn't picture him undertaking the titanic task of whipping it, I was probably looking at his spit.

'What shall I tell the patients, Aldo?'

'Tell them to wait. They're all from the social, anyway.'

He waited for the secretary to leave and, seeing that I was writing out his cheque, he paused.

'I'm afraid it's just the *one* thousand. Not even when . . . ?'

'Eh?'

'I thought you were going to tell me about the murder.'

'No, not murder,' he corrected me. How could I think such a thing? He gave me his version. Sr Tamerlán's son was trying to commit suicide and the other man fell, selflessly attempting to save his life. He sacrificed himself for the person he loved. He waxed lyrical, but when I asked him for details, he had none to give. He and Dr Tarino had apparently had a rather unpleasant tiff over who'd go down to see to the body and who'd stay to look after those in shock, until someone exclaimed that the body had disappeared.

I didn't let go of the cheque till he had a tight grip on it in case it started pogoing round the room, then asked him if I could borrow his phone, to save some credit on my mobile (a precaution in case I didn't get all twenty-six names for Sr Tamerlán, because then it was coming out of my own pocket).

* * *

Doña Ernestina Hidalgo was at home: a once stately town house, sandwiched between a video-game store and a Pizzaphone. Tucked away behind the tall iron spears of its railings and the polished leather leaves of two etiolated magnolias, it looked as if it were awaiting the mercy of the bulldozers to recycle it permanently into a rotisserie or a car park. Inside, however, it was impeccably preserved: the light from two sparkling crystal chandeliers bounced off burnished bronzes, skated over polished ebony surfaces, crackled off the silver, shone twice as brightly in the tall mirrors and oozed over the glazes of the vases before combining with the ashen light filtering through the coloured lozenges of the windows and the warm light climbing from the flames of the deep, grey marble fireplace, to be absorbed by the thick oriental carpets and the heavy tapestries hanging on three walls, the fourth being occupied entirely by a vast library crammed with old cloth- and leather-bound volumes. Preceded by a constant jingling of rings and bracelets, floating in a whirlpool of vaporous fabrics that reached down to her invisible feet, my hostess wandered about the few empty spaces in the drawing room.

'A prize you say? How charming. The last prize I received was the National Prize for Literature and that was . . . Guests? The ones I told you. Sr Eugenio Lopatín, who brought a classmate, a Sr Walter, or Nelson . . . some Uruguayan name, I don't really remember, an employee with one of those hamburger chains . . . Yes, I saw him too, a man in a grey capote – the kind the English call a mackintosh – piercing eyes . . . Then, as you must know, a most unpleasant situation, I'd rather not talk about that.'

'You were invited by Dr Glans,' I pronounced, when I'd finished taking everything down.

'Don't talk to me about that man. What a disappointment.'

I stifled a yawn. Tired of bouncing from one reflection to another like pinballs, my eyes had gradually adjusted enough to spot subtle inconsistencies that I hadn't picked up at first, dotted about the room like garden gnomes on a golf course: a framed photograph of Carlos Gardel among the portraits of her ancestors; a seashell sea lion beside a fine, silver-mounted specimen of a nautilus shell; a sinuous marble of a naked goddess and serpentine swan about to be impaled by an imitation-bone corkscrew in the shape of a boy pissing . . . As if noticing the incongruous objects of my attention, her tone of voice changed:

'You must be wondering what leads a woman of my status to patronise somewhere like Surprise. Well now, the answer is simple. I do it for the poor.'

I put on that expression of polite interest I'm so practised at, in the hope that I wouldn't also be required to right myself on the ocean of blue silk in which I was so pleasantly submerged. It seemed to satisfy her.

'The poor,' she went on. 'Ever since I was a little girl, they tried to instil in me contempt for the poor, but even then I was a rebel and wasn't willing to accept the rigid moulds in which my class tries to pigeonhole reality. The poor have so much to offer us.' She motioned in the general direction of the portrait of Gardel. 'Just look at tango, which started out poor and is now played at the Colón. We have so much to learn from you . . .'

One of her feet brushed against me and an unexpected roughness made me look down. She was wearing espadrilles.

'I'm talking about genuine poverty, mind you. Not like that diluted product, servants.' She laughed tinklingly. 'No doubt you think I'd be happy to converse with the maid every day while she serves me breakfast. Far from it! My encounter with the poor has to be full and total; it has to involve not just my soul but my body. I can see I'm embarrassing you.'

I nodded, though I was in fact looking down to check my watch: 11.30. Those guys could arrive any moment. I kneaded my stiff neck. The cocaine, what else. And that door was so far away.

'I . . . believe we all have to find our inner pauper, the taste for the simple life. There are those who call themselves friends of the poor yet at the same time profess that their goal is a world without paupers no less! What would become of us without them? A world without paupers would be like a garden without soil. How long can flowers survive in a Sèvres vase, Sr . . . Sr . . .?'

'Fuolxx' I replied, stifling another yawn in my closed mouth. 'Nwot lwong,' I added straightaway.

'Which brings me to the last and perhaps most important issue.' At this point a faint shell-pink flush began to spread under the pearly gloss of her skin. 'Our men are no longer potent; we have fewer and fewer, and weaker children. We would be engulfed by the inexhaustible proliferation of the poor if once in a while – and quite rationally – we didn't incorporate something of their blood to fortify our own, a task that in my grandmothers' days was exclusively reserved for the menfolk . . . But times change, you know, and the sixties cannot have been in vain.' She'd come and sat on the arm of the sofa, and she was stroking the back of it as if it were stuffed with cats. She fixed her eyes on me, the only part of her face that preserved something of perhaps not life, but . . . moisture. 'That's why I've always dreamed of finding the ideal pauper, a special pauper shall we say, possessed of a degree of nobility even, the nobility of his poverty,' she said as her hand began to play with the hair on the back of my neck. 'I'd be willing to give myself to a pauper like that, to make his wildest dream come true, to toss away two thousand years of civilisation the way you'd throw off a silk shawl, and feel for once what the beasts of the field and the birds of the air feel . . .'

I got out of there as fast as I could, muttering something about millionaire parents and gagging on a silver spoon, and ran down the cracked marble staircase just as Tamerlán's two heavies were opening one of the iron gates. The white-haired one walked straight past me and went up the steps towards the half-open door. The other one put – as I'd feared he might – one arm round my shoulder and invited me to go for a stroll in the garden.

'So, kiddo? How's tricks?'

'Nothing yet. You?'

He shrugged and held up his Ray-Bans to view the irregular domino of visible sky.

'What can I say. This assignment . . . The old man's totally strung-out. What about you? What happened with your computers? Forgotten how to hit the little keys?'

'Hitting the little keys has got me a lot further than you so far.'

'Yeah, sure.' He smiled meditatively, tossing a dead match into the bed of fume-blackened plants growing among the cat turds, and suddenly I found myself pinned against the trunk of one of the magnolias. I could see the butt of his .38 stuffed into his belt. 'If we don't find these missing punters, we're well and truly fucked, you worse than us,' he growled.

'Are you threatening me?'

'Listen, pal,' he said to me almost sadly, 'don't do this to me.'

'I'm not that easily frightened,' I insisted. 'I was in Malvinas.'

He smiled with delight. He let me go, wiping his hands on his trousers.

'The old man likes you. I understand why. You've got a sense of humour. So don't blow it, pull your socks up and tell me what you learned at school today.'

I gave him a round-up and made it as convincing as I could, omitting some facts and inventing others to flesh out the story. If his questions were anything to judge by, they didn't know any more than I did. The white-haired one came down the stairs, the same dozy expression in his half-closed eyes, and pulled out the hand he'd been hiding under his jacket: it clutched a silver candlestick. 'I told her you wanted a word with her as well. I'll wait for you in the car if you want to make the most of it.'

My companion bared his cruel teeth in a widening grin, patted me a couple of times on the cheek and, with a 'Shan't be long!', climbed the uneven marble stairs. The other lit a cigarette, inhaled and pushed his glasses up over his forehead like an Alice band to hold back his thick, white hair. He let out the smoke as he rubbed the bridge of his nose, and contemplated the world through his listless, blue eyes. They didn't include me in their disenchanted tour of the garden, the walls, the street beyond the railings . . . I hadn't made any concrete arrangements with the other one, so I sidled over towards the half-open gate. Without betraying his sincere disinterest with the slightest movement, the melancholy thug smoked on with unfocused eyes. Once on the pavement, I set off at a brisk pace towards Plaza San Martín.

Only when I found myself under the thick, sylvan light that filtered through the tops of the tall trees did I slow down and call Daniel Tabardo's secretary on my mobile; she slotted me in for 1.05 p.m. What precious precision: I had an hour and five minutes. Office workers, shop assistants, young couples and small groups of schoolchildren were beginning to mill around the square in search of a sunny spot for lunch. I stuck Patricio Rey y sus Redonditos de Ricota in my walkman and set off in the direction of the slope. As I made my way down, I contemplated the traffic of pedestrians converging, swirling and issuing on, around and from the gigantic anthill of Retiro Station in ordered columns down Libertador, Alem, Maipú, Florida . . . out from Downtown and the City, the port, the coach terminal, the bus stops; scattering across English Square, negotiating the streets with their mosaic of taxis and buses, single file, kneading themselves into pavements narrowed by street vendors and their stalls. Letting my legs do the walking, I reached the War Memorial at the foot of the slope: twenty-six names on each of the twenty-five black marble slabs, mounted in a semicircle of pink granite facing the nearby English Tower, so that not even dead could they forget them. As always, there were bunches of fresh flowers, though I'd never seen who put them there. Like a blind man, I reached out a trembling hand to read their names by touch; letter by letter, my fingers reunited what stone had parted:

GENTILE, RUBÉN

FEUER, CARLOS DAVID

SOSA, ROSENDO

CORREA, JOSÉ ANTONIO

One of them could just as easily as be running their fingers over the letters of mine, I thought:

FÉLIX, FELIPE

Entering Retiro Station didn't improve my mood. All the big stations of Buenos Aires get me down, with their sad-yet-worldly squalor; but there's something at once more intense and vague about Retiro, something harder to define, that can only be described as belonging to the order of the metaphysical; the pigeons whirling high up in its vast domes looked like the souls of the damned looking for a way out of hell. I took a B-Line train, whose wooden carriage with its worn leather upholstery was straight out of the Far West, and empty enough for me to put my feet up on the opposite seat and have a smoke under the no-smoking sign while I reviewed my achievements to date. I'd started out with fifteen names and had found two more. There were still nine to go. It was slow and gruelling, but it was working, for now. I got off at Tres de Febrero, where the platform is level with the treetops, and, after walking through its wrought-iron Doric columns, I went down a broad staircase to a white majolica-tiled station. I walked along Dorrego for two blocks, under the lofty foliage of the tipa trees before I realised I'd got off one stop too soon and still had another ten blocks to go. The street was empty in spite of the hour, the only sign of life being two riders out on the polo field, appearing and disappearing behind the ivy-covered steps, every now and again the clack of the ball making the silence all the purer. From behind me, getting nearer, came an unmistakable diesel throb and I turned to hail the taxi.

'Ciudad de la Paz and Concepción Arenal,' I sighed, relieved to get in, and slumped back into the seat with my walkman on to underline the fact that I didn't feel a bit like chatting. But there's no one more tenacious than a bored taxi driver full of the joys of morning:

'Cold out, isn't it,' he said, looking at me hopefully in the rear-view mirror. Ah well, what can you do? I thought to myself as I unhooked my headphones; I'd make conversation with the executioner tightening the noose round my neck if I thought he was uncomfortable with the silence. The cabby was dressed in a T shirt and kept smiling. He was up to something.

'Yeah, bit chilly. It's the wind.'

'This is nothing. You should have been in Malvinas.'

Oh no, not today, I thought to myself, feeling the familiar bolus of anguish starting to churn in my guts. Stopping off for a coffee, swapping war stories and phone numbers. Not today.

'Were you in Malvinas?' I asked, all innocence.

'Uh-huh,' he answered me and started telling me about the cold. He was missing two toes from his left foot and three from his right, but it wasn't a problem driving; a friend of his had had his whole foot removed. Gangrene, he said, and me, how awful.

'And don't think we've been looked after; not a chance: we can't find work for love nor money. I did all sorts when I got back. I was even a bear for Frávega – for a whole summer. Makes me come out in a sweat just thinking about it, it does. And me, so used to the cold,' he said and turned left onto Luis María Campos.

'Wasn't it better to go straight on down Dorrego?' I suggested doubtfully.

'It's this way Arenales, isn't it?'

'No. Arenal. Concepción Arenal. It's that way.'

'Oh. Not to worry. I'll turn back,' he said, cutting almost perpendicularly across a roaring 168 and, by the time I opened my eyes, we were meandering down a narrow alleyway of puppet-theatre houses, so incongruous in this part of the city that for a moment I thought the 168 hadn't missed us and that, from now on, I'd be condemned to wander through a celestial, papier-mâché Buenos Aires with this taxi driver who didn't know the way telling me Malvinas anecdotes for the rest of eternity. Two blocks further on we came out on Avenida Santa Fe, which was cut off where it joined Avenida Cabildo by an abyssal trough as deep as the Grand Canyon. 'That's a pain. I forgot all about the viaduct. The roadworks have been at a standstill for like five years, haven't they? Would you look at those potholes. Reminds me of the valley we were stationed in. After the final bombardment.'

'Hard, right?'

'There are no words to describe it,' he said and immediately started searching for them while we reversed. 'Two, no . . . three, four bombs a second were falling, you couldn't put your head out of the foxhole, you couldn't run, you shook inside there, like being in a blender, you felt like the walls were crushing you, your ears were exploding,' he recounted, illustrating his point with the jolting of the taxi over the cobbled crocodile back of Calle Carranza. 'We were all shouting, but nobody could even hear themselves, and the flares and the tracers . . .'

'Turn! Turn on Soler!' I bellowed, but he was already halfway down the next block. 'We can take Nicaragua,' he said, which was, of course, one-way and took us in the wrong direction. 'Does it go the other way this side of the tracks? That's funny, fancy that, I normally have a such good sense of direction, we got lost once in the Islands, night was falling, and we couldn't get back to our positions . . .' Voltaire, a little side street straight out of a Spanish pueblo, led on to Arévalo and, if the cabby hadn't driven against the flow, we'd have been back to where we started. 'Even the sergeant sat down on a stone with his head in his hands, the fog was so thick that even at this distance . . .' (he gestured to the space between us) '. . . we couldn't see each other and night was falling fast, in the Islands it used to get dark by five . . .' Driving down El Salvador we passed the silos on Calle Dorrego and, Filcar in hand, I told him to take the next right. Just three more blocks, I thought gratefully. '. . . And a night in the open over there can finish you off, so I tell the sergeant, sorry Sarge, I know these fogs,' and he braked a few metres from an impregnable wall of stone that blocked our way completely; above us, out of reach, stood the Calle Soler bridge. 'Looks like there's no joy this way. Let's try the next one. They're low fogs, rarely exceeding two hundred metres in height, I say to him, and they last all night.' We never got as far as the next one because there was a dead end at the X of train tracks on Calle Amenábar; going by the frigging Filcar it was impossible to tell where the tracks cut the streets and where they didn't, so we ended up reversing down Crámer to Dorrego, which the taxi driver swung onto with gay abandon, blithely regardless that it was taking us in the opposite direction. 'Our mistake, sir, Sergeant sir, is to assume that going *down*hill's the shortest route; if we go *up*hill, we'll come out through the fog and be able to read the terrain from the surrounding hills like a map, then we can decide which route to take even in the dark.' He was belting down Dorrego now, taking us further and further into the unknown, past the abandoned markets, and I breathed a sigh of relief when he turned onto Avenida Córdoba and followed the caravan of traffic down Jorge Newbery and along Álvarez Thomas to Federico Lacroze, where he turned again. 'So we started to ascend, because we had nothing to lose, and in just over half an hour we reached the top.' We were stuck at the level crossing in Colegiales, with the train blocking the avenue like a rebuilt Berlin Wall. It was one o'clock sharp and I was going to be late for my bizarrely scheduled appointment; it had been twenty-five minutes since I'd taken the taxi to save myself walking eight blocks. 'And was it clear?' I asked him stoically. 'It was completely dark by then and the lowlands were a sea of white cloud, the hilltops peeping out just above them; but you can read the stars like a map – and I know the skies over the Malvinas like the back of my hand.' Suddenly remembering it wasn't a sacred cow in India, the train finally deigned to move on, but the barrier stayed down and the bell kept ringing to signal another was on its way. 'I decided to take a bearing using the Southern Cross. The shorter arm was right over our position, and when we marched back down into the fog, we had to march in a straight line so we wouldn't lose our way again. We climbed more hills, forded more icy rivers, crossed gruelling streams of stone, the streams of stone are . . . oh, you know . . . before we heard the sound of the sea again and caught its salty smell . . .' We were now advancing along Ciudad de la Paz, floating down the street the way you do in video games, all the lights on green. 'But our position was nowhere to be seen, and the sergeant flew into a rage: "What kind of a bloody wild goose chase is this, you stupid prat," you know what they're like – have you done your military service? – and there's me standing my ground, Sergeant Sir, I'm certain, it's got to be around here . . .' Half a block before our destination, we were held up by the long file of cars waiting to cross the bridge over the tracks and I started getting the fare ready to save time. 'Then I feel the ground give under foot, so I jump in the air, and when I land there's this almighty clatter of corrugated iron and our lads underneath it shouting "We surrender, we surrender!" We'd only been standing on the roof of our own foxhole the whole time! Camouflaged with peat it was! The blokes inside thought we were an English patrol, so they hadn't warned us! Then it rained ice all night. If it hadn't been for me, we'd never have lived to tell the tale . . .' At the last moment, just as everything seemed to suggest he was about to turn left on Santos Dumont, he carried on towards the bridge. 'No! No!' I wailed in despair, 'don't take the bridge!' 'Easy, mate; I'm not that much of a prat. Can't you see that little street just to the side? We'll get to Arenal much quicker that way than if we take the other one.' We squeezed down the side street, barely as wide as the car, but the street turned back on itself and we came out on the other side of the road heading in the opposite direction. 'Whoa, this ride's done my head in,' he began, as I opened the car door and got out, thrusting a note at him through the window. Needless to say he had no change and had to cross the road to a pizza parlour with my fifty while a blaring of horns from the long train of cars behind us rose into the city sky. 'Well, it might have taken a while, but you're not telling me it wasn't worth the ride,' he grinned as we parted. 'You'll have some stories to tell the kids tonight, I'll bet?' I said I certainly would and waved as he pulled away.

* * *

The owner of the paddle tennis courts – a pint-sized, lamp-burnt squirt in black satin shorts, a white eyeshade against the fluorescent glare and a fuchsia Lacoste polo shirt to bring out his tan – held out his left hand and offered me something to drink. The receptionist came back with a mineral water for me and a Gatorade for Dany. I poured out half a glass and we drank each other's health (I couldn't tell you why if you twisted my little finger till I screamed): Dany straight from the bottle, which he turned bottom up to quaff the greenish liquid the way they do in the ads, putting it down almost empty with a clean arc of his left hand while his right adjusted the stole of his towel, which matched his wristband. It occurred to me that every one of his gestures was designed to reinforce the contrast between his hale, relaxed life, brimming with health, and my wretched, stressed-out city existence, and, unable to stop myself, I stuffed a finger inside the neck of my shirt, which felt somehow dirtier and tighter, the skin on my hands looking *yellow* beside his tan.

I explained the reason for my visit, asked the question, the answer to which revealed the secret identity of Gazza Gascoigne (eighteen down . . .) signed the cheque under his nose and hand-ed it to him. He took it in his right hand, when I'd aimed for his left. He was starting to make me dizzy. All this time nothing I'd said or done had been able to dislodge the fixed smile of satis-faction on permanent display below his golden moustache, as if the thousand-dollar windfall were just another daily confir-mation that that exclusive service industry called destiny was working away as perfectly as well-chosen health insurance. No wonder he'd earned his fox badge in less than a month.

Nor did I get much out of him about the 'accident' – his word for it – except that the 'unfortunate acrobat' would have managed to grab hold of the cornice had he been in 'better physical shape' and that, for the same reason, he Daniel 'Call-Me-Dany' Tabardo had been the first to reach the window to witness what came before the fall. 'At no time did he show his face,' he assured me. 'He fell out of the window under his own momentum, the young man could do nothing to catch him.' Throughout our conversation (punctured by the monotonous clock-clock of tennis balls from the courts above and beside us, and shouts from the rooftop five-a-side) Dany constantly switched his gold Cross ballpoint from one hand to the other, back and forth, in a short flight with all the regularity and tedi-ousness of a metronome. What *is* this arsehole trying to do? Hypnotise me? I wondered.

'Grey, yes. I remember it clearly. A Burberry. How can there still be people who insist on wearing such uncomfortable clothes in this day and age?'

He windmilled the biro in his left hand from thumb to little finger and back, then did the same with his right. My eyes followed it against my will and he struck.

'You look surprised,' he said.

'No, well . . . um . . .'

'Let me guess what you're thinking,' he smiled. 'You're asking yourself "Is this guy left-handed or right-handed? Eh?" Correct me if I'm wrong.'

I put on an idiotic smile and, as I expected, he took it for assent.

'Well. In fact I'm neither: I'm ambidextrous. Though it would be just as accurate to say I'm ambisinister. And don't think it's a simple privilege I've been blessed with by nature; far from it. From being small I set out not to be half a man the way others are. Human potential is infinite, but the education we receive seems to be systematically directed at frustrating it, reducing it to the poor and mediocre general pattern. Even as a schoolboy I never used to let my briefcase spend more than a minute in each hand, and I used to swap my knife and fork round several times a meal. When playing sports nothing disconcerts my opponents more than seeing me switch racquet hands and smash just when they're expecting a backhand. These trophies bear witness to my persistence and early farsightedness. Once I'd decided to become a complete man, I found nothing difficult. It's like your body being bilingual, see? Few people are as entitled to call themselves "self-made men" as I am. I'm currently devoting my energies to founding the Argentine Ambidextrous Association.'

'Hmm. Like the Argentine Handless Artists Association, only the other way round.'

'Quite,' he nodded. I increasingly find people don't listen to a bloody thing you tell them. I let him prattle on for a little while longer, putting up with coin tricks, paddle tournament

anecdotes, et cetera, then shook his hand – God knows which –
and got ready to leave.

'Ciao. Take care,' he said, without moving from his seat.

By the door was a stand laden with trophies, and a little
experiment occurred to me.

'Catch!' I said, tossing him a green onyx obelisk with a little golden paddle-player perched on top, in an arc wide enough
for either hand to catch. He tried to field it with both, and they
collided beneath the trophy and began to jiggle it about without either being able to do any more than keep it in the air for
a few more seconds before it inevitably slipped through his ten
pleading fingers and smashed to dust on the floor.

As I expected, I thought, closing the door behind me on
Dany's deflated mouth and moustache. Ham-fisted with both.

It was well past noon by the time the bus dropped me
at Puente Saavedra, and I strolled along the broken pavements
pretty much at random, making my way through the winding
queues waiting to storm the buses: maids, nannies, cleaning
staff, gardeners, drivers, nightwatchmen, teachers, all arriving
from and departing for Boulogne, Munro, Carapachay, Banca-
lari, Haedo, Morón, Castelar, William Morris, José L Suárez,
Liniers, Lugano, Laferrere, San Justo . . . puffy anoraks, acrylic
scarves, plastic bags for handbags, on the way to their first or
second jobs of the day, piled on top of each other on the crowded, narrow pavements, squirming like worms in a jar. I walked
a couple of blocks, searching left and right till I spotted it. A
huge red-and-orange poster announced 'Pumper Nic gives you
more. Bogof!'

'Gimme a double Pumper – the bogof; a Coke, a Frenys, a
mobur, I mean a molops . . .'

'Pumper . . . Frenys . . . molops . . . Coke . . .' mumbled the girl into her microphone and held out a ticket. I prefer Pumper Nic's to McDonald's on the whole: there's a more relaxed, almost Zen-like atmosphere in here, maybe because the food's so bad, and the customers so few and so hard up. The poor are less rowdy when it comes to spending their readies.

After my first Pumper I belched and decided to have a nicotine break before attacking the second. 'The Fun Way To Eat', read the paper place mat; I looked round to see if I could spot anyone having any. I pushed aside the tray and, through a hole in the formica table, I could see the toe of my shoe. It was a start. There was a bin nearby, with a green hippopotamus emblazoned on it and a sign saying 'The hippo is happy to eat what you don't!' I wondered at the beast's powers of self-abnegation. It can't have felt as smiley as the drawing depicted when it was being force-fed the tray-loads of cardboard, polystyrene, limp lettuce, rubbery chips, stale mayonnaise and half-chewed Pumper Nics the cleaning assistant was dumping into its mouth. I couldn't read his name on the tag over his pocket: he looked like a Walter, but I needed him to be closer to be sure. I looked at the hole again and stuck my finger through it from below: it looked like a worm poking its head out. I had a brainwave: resting my finger on the formica, I trimmed the edges of the hole with ketchup and called over the would-be Walter with my free hand.

'I know it's the customer's responsibility here to clear the table once they've finished, but you could at least give it a wipe afterwards! Look what I've found. What do I do with this? Feed it to the hippopotamus too?' I protested while checking his name-tag.

Walter *Díaz* (bingo! another one down) looked at the table in annoyance, his face blurred with indifference, but when he spotted the finger, it came into sharp focus. I was about to explain the trick (always my favourite part of magic shows) when he began to shriek, pointing at me – or rather at my finger – and making the whole place stand up as one and run towards us. I pulled my finger out and left before they could reach us, leaving my free Pumper untouched. I didn't miss it, though: anyone who's been to Pumper Nic's knows that one's enough.

Luckily, the bus soon turned off Avenida Maipú and took to the side streets, thick with dark, winter vegetation, striped with sun and shade, still covered by the autumn leaves that no one had bothered to rake up. I tried calling Sr Oroño (a.k.a. Leopoldo Fortunato Galtieri) all the way, but no one answered, so I decided to drop in personally. I got off near Borges Station and walked two blocks to the address I had. From a distance I could see lots of cars at the door – black cars – and when I got nearer I could see the people standing outside and wreaths. I approached a little old man in a cardigan, who was looking on at the scene in bemused amusement from the opposite pavement.

'Excuse me . . . Has there been some . . . mishap?'

'Eh? Mishap? Miracle more like. That bastard Oroño had been diddling half the neighbourhood.'

'They killed him?'

'Unfortunately not. Heart attack. Are you acquainted?'

'Friend of the family.'

'He had no friends or family, that one. Half of them have come to see if they can pinch something back. Fleeced you too, did he? I escaped by sheer luck: got back from the meeting completely convinced and was going to buy my first batch off him when I happened to mention it to that lad over there, the one with curly hair ...'

'And that meeting,' I said, pronouncing every word with infinite care, as if my tongue were a cactus, 'didn't happen to be ...'

'Don't remind me; they had us down the precinct all night.'

I didn't hear his account of his terrible night. I was raising my eyes to heaven and murmuring prayers of thanks. Three witnesses in my lap in one go; the dead man had nearly taken them with him to the grave. I couldn't believe my luck.

'And why are you ... ?'

'Umberto Petraglia, attorney-at-law.' I wrung his unprepared right hand. 'I'm gathering evidence to accuse Surprise of murder. That man they killed paid for his last batch of products with a bounced cheque. Looks like some big stunt to put the willies up the other members.'

'I said it was no accident. And that lad, what's-his-name, Turkestan ...'

'Tamerlán. César Tamerlán. He's the one pulling the strings.'

I had no trouble getting the information out of him after that, though he couldn't remember the name of one of the guests. According to my information, he lived out in the sticks in Tigre and had no phone. Wouldn't you just know it?

'Tell me *your* version of events.'

'...that Spaniard wittering on and on ... those little hand-held cameras ... velvet curtains, eh? ... Would someone committing suicide jump backwards?' The last bit was interesting, so I paid more attention: '... that's why we didn't see his face ...

He was falling for a while, getting smaller and smaller, looked like he'd disappear before he hit the ground, but he didn't. He landed on the grass, bounced once and just lay there. Then someone shouted "There he is, that's the murderer!" Then we all looked up and spotted that Timberland fellow.'

'Was he wearing a . . .' – I thought for a minute – '. . . a grey coat?'

'He was in his shirtsleeves.'

'No. The one who shouted.'

'Oh. A raglan.'

'Not a Burberry.'

'No, no. I'm sure it was a raglan. That Taliban was just standing there . . .'

'Did the one in the Burb . . . the raglan shout . . . *after* he appeared?'

'Well, he wasn't going to shout before, now was he.'

'No, of course not.'

'Now you mention it, I did notice something odd. Talisman was standing there in the broken window, right at the edge, but he wasn't looking down; he was looking straight ahead. At us. And he was smiling. He stood there for about a minute, laughing at us. Now I understand why. You were right. He wanted us to get a good look at him.'

'Didn't I tell you?'

'Then he disappeared into those mirrors. And when we looked down again, the body was gone. All that was left was a dent in the grass. They calculated the whole thing, cold as you like?'

'They're professionals. One more question. What bus do I take to the Tigre Delta?'

'That's easy: the 59 two blocks from here to La Lucila, or to Olivos if you prefer, and from there the train to Tigre, and buy a ticket at the boat terminal to ...'

* * *

'900 River Caraguatá please.'

Climbing over two river-buses moored side by side, I reached the one I'd been directed to. I found a seat by the engine – the only place warm enough – and sat there studying the sparse river traffic: the occasional pensioner in a rowing boat, the odd barge laden with willow-wood, the white hulks of catamarans. Beneath us the thick, black water smudged the varnished wood with a tarry foam, every so often burping detergent bubbles up to its iridescent surface. A bloated catfish, surrounded by bobbing grapefruit buoys, floated belly up, the tips of its long whiskers lost in the depths. Two old fellows appeared, hauling a generator laboriously aboard; then a group of boys and girls in white pinafores and school satchels, who sat down all together at the back, and we set off. The boat chugged along until it crossed the undulating line where the fœtid black waters of the Tigre meet the broad umber of the Luján, then it speeded up, so much so that I had to move away from the roaring engine. After half an hour travelling upriver past weekend cottages, shacks, English-style houses (they reminded me of Stanley), thick undergrowth and, on the widest stretches, waving reeds, the boat dropped me at a crooked, wooden jetty. I crossed an unweeded lawn of Mesopotamian grass, fringed like a barcode by the light of a reddish winter sun shining through a distant wood of bare poplars. Behind a row of cypresses, the tips of whose roots peeped out of the ground like a gathering of pixies, appeared a little two-storey tumbledown, stripped and sanded grey by rain and sun, with every appearance of being uninhabited. At the creak of the first stair under my feet an almost imperceptible whine came from out back, so I walked round to have a look. It had come from a skinny dog with a tawny coat, slumped in the mud, so weak that it could barely wag the tip of its tail when it saw me. A few more bites and it would have gnawed through the rope that tethered it to one of the piles, but you could see that, at the last, it hadn't had the strength; I snapped the rope with a tug. As it couldn't walk, I picked it up in my arms and carried it round to the front, where I filled a rusty tin with brown water from the pump. It emptied it twice, the second time standing on its wobbling legs, then followed me up the stairs to the front door, which opened with a slight push. In the kitchen there was a full saucepan on the portable gas-stove; despite the smell of rotten stew that billowed out when I uncovered it, I put it on the floor for the dog, which began to bolt it down, wagging its tail now in long arcs. There was a cage by the window, containing a goldfinch with shrivelled eyes, lying on its back on the parallel wires, its clenched claws pointing upwards; on the table was a glass with some tarry-looking dregs of red wine and a fly stuck in them, a clean plate, one place setting, breadcrumbs ... The house smelt of bachelor; whoever it was had left unexpectedly, intending to return straightaway, and hadn't come back. In a rickety chest of drawers in the bedroom, which, beneath a hardboard ceiling that sagged under the accumulated weight of the bat droppings, doubled as a living room, I found a shoebox, wrinkled from the damp, and in it the photo of a man in waders and a checked shirt, hugging a young dark-skinned beauty, twenty years his junior, holding in her arms a little girl wearing pink bows, standing on the neat lawn smiling at the camera in front of the recently white-painted house. Beneath that there were some short pornographic novels for the poor: *The Pleasures of the Hammock*, *Horses and Mares* and other such titles, and at the bottom a handwritten receipt torn from an exercise book, whereby one Heberto Luna handed over owner-ship of the house to a Néstor Soria, and a marriage licence, in which the name 'Néstor Soria' was printed in ink in the pains-taking calligraphy of the Civil Registry Office, and the woman's was illegible beneath the biro that had later scrawled 'whore' over and around the crossings-out.

In spite of the cold, I decided to wait for the next boat down at the jetty; the dog kept me company the whole time and I knew it was hoping I'd take it with me, so when the boat arrived, I jumped aboard as fast as I could. Through the win-dow I saw it throw itself into the water and swim for a stretch in the churning foam of the wake; I was about to shout to the pilot to turn the boat around when I saw it double back and laboriously climb up the first step of the jetty, shivering and dripping wet. Fortunately the roar of the engine drowned out its barks.

It was dark when I was helped off the boat by the ticket seller, who gave me a hand to leapfrog the crumbling cement stairs lapped by the Luján's ashen waters. Still numb from the cold, I climbed the steps to the brightly lit ghost of the Tigre Club, glittering eerily in the spotlights against the shimmer-ing darkness of the river and the blind silhouettes of the never-ending islands. The wind enveloped the double row of columns and, turning my back to it, I walked towards the number 60 bus terminal. The first one I boarded was being sluiced down and the wellington-booted driver shouted from the back 'Not this one, son, the one in front there.' The train was quicker, but I preferred the bus so that I wouldn't have to change and could sleep all the way back, and I was still half asleep when I got off at Junín and Charcas over an hour later and made my way with difficulty through the canyon between the twin hulks of the Faculties of Medicine and Pharmacy, through which all the wind in the city seemed to be howling. I was starting to feel ill, kind of fluey, my whole body and head aching; I kept repeating 'I wanna go home, I wanna go home' with every step I took towards the open maw of the dismal Hospital de Clínicas. The only thing I asked was that this Tarino (a.k.a. Carlos Menem) chappie would keep things short and sweet, and wouldn't have another tale of national or personal salvation to tell me. I'd had my fill of those for one day.

Once inside, I was startled by the echo of my own steps in the big, empty corridors, and wandered about for more than ten minutes before I found a haggard-looking nurse to give me directions. (Extractions. 6th Floor.) The lift wasn't working, so I had to climb the grimy granite stairs and walk along another four or five corridors before I found the door I was looking for.

There was something about Dr Tarino I didn't like, or rather there was nothing about him I didn't dislike: he was loathsome in a way at once so general and specific that you didn't know where to start. No wonder he'd got his lion badge in Surprise.

'Clothes off, please,' he said without looking up.

'Listen here . . .'

'You'll already have been informed that this is no normal extraction. You have to take off all your clothes . . .'

'I'm the man from Surprise,' I announced, summoning all my strength, and to my relief (I don't know where I'd have found the energy otherwise) his face widened in a toothpaste smile and he held out his hand. His affability was even more repellent than his indifference, but at least it saved me the extra effort, and his information was sound enough. I already had the details of two of his guests, one of them the lame woman who'd shouted at me down the phone. Tarino had no trouble remembering the name of the third, bringing my total up to twenty-three, although, as expected, the mystery man in the grey coat was one of the two remaining ones.

'Three, yes. An especially good crop that week. It was a gabardine, not an overcoat. No idea. By the time I got back from the bathroom, it was all over,' he lied. 'Magnificent, magnificent,' he remarked, holding the cheque up to the light, so proud that I imagined, rather than cashing it, he'd frame it and hang it up with his diplomas. 'Surprise has never failed to live up to its name.'

'Not everyone shares your sympathy,' I pointed out.

'Envy, naturally. Surprise is nothing more than a scale model of the jungle we live in, and believe you me, we doctors have to fight for survival in that jungle too.'

'I know. I read the life of Dr Schweitzer as a boy.'

'A country doctor. They have it easy in the country, believe you me. They whine and carp and appear on television claiming there aren't enough drugs to go round, but that's because they're all shooting up out of sheer boredom. Me, I'm putting together the capital to open my own clinic and don't feel that collaborating in the sale of quality products is beneath my professional dignity. I'm telling you this in full confidence, because I can see you're clearly an *insider*. You at Surprise have organised something magnificent on the basis of an *idea*, a simple idea, and, in the world of business, having an idea like that is like striking oil in the desert. Oil,' he repeated, and gave a little chuckle that didn't augur at all well for my drained moral resources. 'For thirty years I've been hearing that the oil reserves will only last another thirty, but lo and behold . . . The oil's always there, just where you least expect it. All you have to do is *look*. I . . .' (he paused dramatically, like a business speaker, for the equation oil=I to engrave itself indelibly on my brain) 'have managed to extract it from the dried-up arteries of this comatose city. Yes, *here*,' he said, the vigour of his assertion creating an expectant incredulity that I hadn't taken the trouble to feign.

'And does it pay, this blood business?'

He wrinkled his nose and upper lip as if he'd been asked about his popcorn cart.

'Please. Every morning a couple of my men scour the queues of the jobless, striking up conversations with the most desperate-looking ones, and then, feigning indifference, they mention this place to them . . . The laboratory, as you'll have noticed, only requires the most basic facilities: two trained nurses could perform all the extractions without my participation, except that I have to keep an eye on things to make sure nobody puts their hand in the till, if you know what I mean . . . You realise, of course, that blood is a junk product next to what I'm talking about.'

He was playing hard to get, like a girl at a dance, and

smiled in delight when I asked. Instead of answering, he went off on yet another detour.

'I'm the end product of a long evolutionary chain. And when I say "end" I *mean* "end": you simply can't go any further or any deeper. You lot at Surprise strip men of their money. But money's just the start. There's more, far more to dig out in there. Where others see only useless rocks, the expert eye detects a seam of purest gold. Let me try a little test on you. Where would *you* keep looking?'

'Well . . . after hard cash, I suppose . . . the poor sod's car . . . his house.'

'Furniture, the tools of his trade, wife, the clothes on his back. But anyway. Suppose you took it all away. Suppose you stripped him naked – stark naked. The archetype of the professional con. Is that it?'

'Well . . . yes,' I answered, grinning and bearing it. His worst insults would be more bearable than his palliness.

'Wrong. That's where we come in. Blood. Corneas. Kidneys. What else? We could pare the body back to the skeleton and utilise every last bit of it. Only the bones would be left. Is there anything else after the bones? What is the deepest of the deep?'

He nodded, indulgently, seeing that I'd guessed.

'We harvest it from the iliac crest – oh, I beg your pardon – the hip; and we pay them what they couldn't earn in a fortnight of honest work. Sometimes they aren't as downtrodden as they look and feel encouraged to ask: we assure them the pain won't last long. Ha! Did you know that bone marrow is worth several times its weight in gold?'

I felt a sudden wave of nausea, which I couldn't put down

to my marathon of coke and bad food; a lot of fatigue and a little self-pity. I can't stand Menemists, I thought.

'And that's where the circle of a perfect business deal closes. Before handing over the money, I act the father figure, taking them to one side and speaking to them from the heart: "My friend . . . you deserve better than this. You're about to be given this money, which will disappear on your numerous debts or shoes your children will wear out before the blood's back in your veins. Don't you think it's time to change, turn the page and start a new life? Your problem is unemployment, isn't it. I have a job for you: a job and a deal. No strings attached. If you want to invest your money wisely, turn up this Wednesday evening at this address . . . " Believe you me, not a week goes by without my reeling in two or three for the regular meetings, sometimes more. A great future awaits you.' He slapped me on the back when we said goodbye. 'Trust my clinical eye. Every profession . . . I believe Maradona isn't just a person. He's a concept, and every profession, no matter how humble or how lofty, has its Maradona. Perhaps you'll earn the name of Maradona in yours, as I have, in mine, humbly . . .'

Not him, I thought; you don't touch Diego. I can't say I'd planned it: it was more like my eyes made out his fingers in the door frame and, so fast that it was almost simultaneous, my ears heard a horrendous crunch instead of a slam. Tarino also seemed to be affected by this strange distortion of time because, before starting to howl, he managed to show me his hand, its fingers pointing in different directions like the vanes of a swastika and, as if asking me for confirmation, he stammered out:

'You . . . you've broken every bone in my hand.'

'You can use them as small change,' I replied and walked

away through the empty corridors as fast as I could until his screams had stopped ringing in my ears.

I walked twenty blocks against the biting wind, my head full of noise, loathing the very paving stones I trod on, till suddenly the taxis and buses in the street were replaced by scattered people walking in slow-mo under a neon sky and I realised I'd crossed Avenida 9 de Julio and reached the pedestrian stretch of Calle Lavalle. Cinemas, video arcades, tacky import outlets, ice cream parlours recycled for the winter into purveyors of choripáns belching their greasy breath at the passers-by; couples without two cents to rub together, kids sporting hostile mohicans and shaven heads sitting on the pavement drinking Quilmes by the litre at the mouths of kiosks, a trio of shivering Collas numb with cold conjuring up the memory of Andean snows with their flutes and panpipes . . . over this sad Thursday-evening fauna of Lavalle floated a threatening aura of radioactive waste.

I entered the arcade, with its relief of mountains at the back, complete with artificial lake and working waterfall, plastic plants, blue skies and painted clouds, and I asked Víctor, the bloke in charge, for the 3D Tetris.

'Hasn't arrived yet. Held up in customs. But that one's new.'

I played for a while, the slow rain of bricks from above speeding up as I shunted them around and rotated them to fit them together and leave no gaps, wall after wall after wall. Not for a second did the rudimentary concentration required for the game quiet the roaring in my head and, bored with winning, I handed it over mid-game to the inevitable gawper who, in his befuddlement, let all the pieces pile up and lost.

'Gimme a token for the pinball,' I said to Víctor.

I thought it would be easier to relax with pinball because, being mechanical, it makes you use your body more than your head. Once, taking advantage of the fascination with the first wave of video games, when you couldn't give pinball machines away, I bought a pinball machine at an auction. It worked fine for a while: it was the life and soul of the house and a wonderful way of reconnecting to the real world after one of my cybermarathons; but it soon began to fade and die. The springs lost their spring, the lights were reluctant to light and the bleeps became moans as if it were in pain. I ended up swapping it for a digital one, but that was an anti-climax. A simulation's never the same as the real, live thing; I missed the contact, and the sounds it made were cold and unnatural.

I'd made 573,655 points on my first ball when the fatigue hit me; a collage of desolate, empty maps from my Filcar guide began to superimpose itself over the crazed trajectories of the little silver balls and, disheartened, I left all three to bounce around for a bit, warbling and flashing their little lights, then disappearing into the open jaws of the machine. I did nothing to save them. That night, with the day's images in hot pursuit and that dreadful crunch still ringing in my ears, I was racked with insomnia and, to make matters worse, a car alarm went off under the flyover and I couldn't get to sleep until the battery ran out several hours later, around dawn. By the time I woke up, it was almost three in the afternoon. I'd set my alarm program for ten and, five hours later, the accursed words, which I knew by heart, were still echoing in my ears: 'Wakey wakey. Time to get up. You've got loads of stuff to do. I mean loads. If you don't get up now, you'll spend the rest of the day running around trying to catch up, everything'll go wrong and you'll hate yourself for not getting up early enough. If you get up now, you'll have time for a shower and a quiet breakfast and a read of the paper, and you'll feel really good, walking down the sunny side of the street, seeing people, the whole day ahead of you. If you get up late, though, like you do every day, you'll leave the house dirty and hungry, your beard'll itch and your shirt collar'll feel too tight all day, it'll rain and the buses won't stop when you stick your hand out. If you at least *enjoyed* sleeping in, but you suffer every single minute, and that suffering's nothing compared to what's in store when you get up late, your eyes swollen from sleep, your mouth all claggy, your teeth hurting from grinding them in your sleep: your day ruined before it's started.' The recorded message went on and on, redoubling the verbal lashing every thirty minutes, until after four hours it switched to: 'That's it. You've fucked up again. Forget it. Stay in bed. Wallow in it like a pig then. *Don't* go out. *Don't* see anyone. Tonight, when you're up till dawn with insomnia and you feel as if you're turning into E.T., you'll remember what I've been telling you. No. Don't even dream of getting up. The harm's done. Just enjoy – ha! – your couple of hours in bed.' I hardly ever got up before that part, but I must have been seriously done for today, because only an hour later did I manage to remove the mound of blankets that stood between me and all harm, and stagger to the bathroom.

* * *

The country landscape was bisected by Avenida Chorroarín. On my side of the street, behind a high wire fence under a tepid winter sun, shone a stretch of fertile, productive pampas, with its tender green grass and imperturbably grazing cows; but on the other side, the open country offered an image of the primæval desert, with patches of thistles taller than a man on horseback, weeds and little patches of woodland. A peculiar atmosphere hung about the whole place, as if the ghost of the colossal hulks of the Warnes Hospital, demolished a year earlier, still haunted the blighted land and prevented its regeneration. Lucky I'm heading in the opposite direction, I thought as I negotiated the gates of the Faculty of Agronomy and Veterinary Science, leaving the gloomy post-nuclear landscape behind me. I should come here more often, for picnics or runs, it's almost like the real countryside, I thought, and as if to corroborate, a gaucho went past on horseback – harness, reins, saddle, the whole bit – headed for the tilled fields of Avenida San Martín; not even the white coats of the students who crossed my path could dispel the illusion. 'The Institute of Experimental Medicine,' I asked a pretty blonde, who stuck out a fleshy lower lip to show she didn't know, and I tried two or three more until one (ugly, naturally) offered to escort me. 'It's over there,' she said, pointing to a low casemate at the side of some wire-fenced, concrete-paved yards, at the far end of a lawn where a crowd of her fellow students were chatting in small groups, or having lunch on the hoof, or anxiously reading their notes as they leaned against square concrete pillars. The path led between two huge rocks embedded in the grass by some landscape gardener's dubious eye, and I could barely keep myself from yelping with fright when one of them moved. I walked around them and only then did I see the outstretched legs and the heads trying to raise themselves from the floor. The two cows were covered in purple contusions and coagulated gore; the one that had moved followed me with its liquid brown pupils, its breath audibly bubbling through the light froth of blood around the muzzle.

'What are they?' I asked a bespectacled student with wire-wool hair, looking on imperturbably as she tucked into her ham and cheese sandwich.

'Trampled cows,' she replied, somewhat annoyed at having to gulp down her bite.

'Who trampled them?'

'The other cows. In the truck. They're no good for eating now . . . so they bring them here.'

'Why don't they just put them out of their misery?'

Her mouth being once again full of sandwich, she confined herself to pointing. I followed the line of her finger. In a roofed amphitheatre, exercise books in hand, a large group of students were watching a farmhand (the same one that had passed me on horseback) handling a third trampled cow. As I approached, I watched him stick his sheath knife beneath its spinal column, level with its forelegs, and work it back and forth until he'd opened a button-hole, then repeat the process level with the hindquarters. He and another farmhand in a beret unfastened two hooks attached by heavy chains to the steel roof-joist and ran them through the button-holes. After making sure the hooks were fast, they began to hoist the animal up by pulleys. As the whole of its body left the ground something appalling happened: the animal, which looked dead, opened its eyes and let out a ghastly low, and from the steps of the amphitheatre came a hail of exercise books hitting the floor and the shrieks of male and female students fleeing the scene. The lecturer, who'd been checking his notes leaning against one of the rusting columns, made a gesture of annoyance to the older gaucho, who lifted the beast's head up by the muzzle and cleanly sliced open its jugular. A steaming, red cascade spurted towards the cement floor, spattering several of the students, and in a matter of minutes the place looked as if it had been hosed down with blood. The students crowded together on the highest steps to escape the flood.

I headed for the casemate in disgust, but couldn't go in straightaway because they were unloading a lorry in one of the fenced yards. Standing on the roof, a fat man in blue overalls and an old man in a frayed pullover were shoving in sticks with nooses and, like some fairground game, fishing out dogs one by one: the largest by the scruffs of their necks, kicking and trying desperately to bite the thing that was choking them; the smallest sometimes by one leg, as they howled with the pain, and one even by the tail. As soon as they recovered a little, the animals threw themselves at the wire mesh trying to push their paws and muzzles through; some growled at me as I approached, others poked their tongues through their half-closed muzzles and tried to lick my hand. They must have done a dozen when a shrimp in a white coat and round glasses, with a long nose and shock of grey hair, appeared at the door and shouted in a falsetto:

'No more dogs! Cats! I told you to bring cats! Haven't you got any cats there?'

The two men looked at each other and grinned.

'There was just one, yeah, but we couldn't get it off the roof of the lorry,' said the old man, clawing at the air with his arms and legs to dramatise while the other man's belly shook with laughter.

'Find it and get those other things out of here.'

'What do you want us to do with them, Prof?'

'Take them down to anatomy: they always come in handy there,' he said and disappeared.

Supposing I'd found my man, I followed him through a door that led into a shadowy chamber filled with the smell of cat piss. The room was mainly occupied by fruit crates doctored with chicken-wire to make cat cages, which were piled to the ceiling in towers, walls, pyramids barely separated by corridors and interstices so narrow that only the Professor could move comfortably through them.

'Dr Gobbio, I presume. I'm from Surprise.'

'Dr Rauss sent you, right?'

'No, Dr Stoffa.' My old friend Fatty from Surprise must have been as much of a doctor as I was, but the habit was catching.

'Oh, forgive me,' he said, adjusting his glasses. 'Well. How can I help you?'

When I told him about the prize his eyes lit up so bright I thought his specs were going to slide down his cheeks in two thick tears of molten glass. He cleared one end of the rickety formica table, piling everything on top of the antediluvian Olivetti that threatened to snap it like an old nag's back, pulled up a chair for me and held out three different biros to write the cheque with.

'I've already told the police . . . two bs . . . no, the other cheque in my name too; I'll save Dr Rauss the paperwork. My other guests? Let me see . . .'

With one salivated forefinger he leafed through a rumpled, black notebook, murmuring 'Hm . . . hm . . .'

With nothing better to do, I let my eyes wander over another open one right under my nose:

2/5/92. Some transformations to bring about:
self-interest → self-sacrifice
individualism → obedience
nocturnality → diurnality
instinct → training
3/5/92. 'Like cat and dog': two antagonistic and
irreconcilable principles. No compromise possible.
Opposites even in their semiology: wagging or twitching
tail= happy/angry; growling/purring = angry/happy. How
could they understand each other? No accident that they
have, from the beginning of history, been our two most
common pets. A two-sided mirror, always reflecting back
at us the fatally divided image of our souls.
4/5/92. Locking up the cat a little longer each day: this is
the measure of civilisation.
5/5/92. Training them to lick the hand that beats them.
9/5/92. It is impossible to completely possess a cat.
12/5/92. Adam was the dog of God; Eve, the cat of Lucifer.
X vs Y. Cat eyes =s nake eyes.
19/5/92. Smash the cat to smithereens and use the pieces
to manufacture a dog.
21/5/92. The feline part of man: the source of all his ills.
Whoever masters it will harness an energy greater than
that of the atom.
24/5/92. A country and a decade to feed my nostalgia:
Germany, 1935–1945. If that had lasted, who knows
where we would be now? But no, we had to go back to
the baboons.

Our reading was interrupted by the fat man, who burst

in with a piece of severed hosepipe in his hand and said to him:

'You wouldn't have a thicker one, would you eh, Prof? This one leaks all over the shop.'

'Look over there.'

He furnished me with the names of Dr Rauss (a.k.a. Evita) and Dr Seisdedos (a.k.a. Lady Di). I was only one short now:

'Grey, yes, with a belt. I remember him because I wondered where he'd bought it. There's a place called "The House of a Thousand Waterproofs", isn't there? Or was it just a hundred?'

The cat piss had gone to my head and, outside, the city mist filled my lungs like mountain air. The fat man and the old man had finished their work. Where the lorry had been there was now a tall pyramid of dead dogs, as stiff as wooden models. The carbon monoxide had frozen their last snarls in a final group photo of their mass death. At the apex of the heap, like a cherry crowning a sundae, the two jokers had placed the cat: upside down, four stiff legs in the air, claws drawn.

To avoid the mud, I went back via the side of the shed where the cow was hanging – at least what was left of it once its hide had been removed, its organs emptied, its musculature shredded. In a hurry to get out of there, knowing I should have taken another route, I stepped in a blood clot and found myself flailing, clutching and kicking at the air, as if by grabbing hold of it I could prevent myself falling into the pool of blood. I flew up so high that, while I was up there, I still had time to think 'This can't be happening to me. I don't deserve it,' and landed on my right foot, left hand, left foot and right hand in that order, hanging there with my face to the sky as if suspended by the belt buckle on one of those hooks. I managed to get up without touching the foul ground with anything more than a sleeve and the edge of my jacket, and, swearing like a truck driver, almost weeping with rage, I bent down to pick up a couple of used paper napkins off the grass and, rubbing my hands in disgust, strode furiously towards the exit.

Near the kiosk I was stopped by a girl, holding a biro and some form or other attached to a clipboard. She had bushy eyebrows and beautiful brown eyes that reminded me of the cow's. 'I'm not in the mood for surveys,' I told her.

'It's a student petition,' she replied.

'What are you asking for?'

'We're asking for animals to be killed more humanely.'

'If by humane you mean human, I reckon your wish has been granted,' I answered angrily, pointing to the shed.

'Less cruel,' she corrected herself and held out the biro.

I signed, muttering an apology and trying to look into her eyes, if only once; but she kept her long curved lashes lowered all the time. I gave her a polite peck on the cheek before I went.

When I reached the gate I turned round to see if she was following, but the field was empty. The sun was setting over a horizon broken only by the line of trees and the odd building; in the absence of any wind a column of brown smoke was rising almost vertically from a tall crematorium chimney. The illusion was complete: the gloomy pavement by the grounds of the old Warnes Hospital was a relief as long as it led me as far away as possible from the sunny fences of Buchenwald.

Chapter 8

PARQUE CHAS

Right next to the Faculty of Veterinary Science, where the blocks are a third or a quarter of normal size and separated by toy streets named after European cities, is one of the most extraordinary neighbourhoods in the city (at least for those with more of an eye for the magical than the practical aspects of maps): Parque Chas. In my faithful Filcar I easily located the precise point from which all that enchantment radiated: an oval of concentric streets divided into six slices of pie by diagonal streets meeting at a perfect central egg. What spaced-out architect must have decided, for once, to relieve Porteños of the rigid Cartesian draughtboard that hems them in on all sides, and build in some forgotten corner, between the straight and angular tracks of commerce and industry, this spider-web of streets as slender as silk threads? Just across the roar of Avenida Los Incas, the dark curve of the first lane, Dublin, left the rush-hour city behind me and enfolded me in silence. I walked through the wintry smell of damp gardens, guided only by the islands of light made by the sixty-watt bulbs (every other one burnt out) and the slits of yellow light filtered here and there by the half-open curtains or lowered blinds. I took a shortcut down one of the spokes to reach the hub of the web, crossed the inner circle of Berlín and reached the incredible point where six corners pointed to a void of tarmac lit by a single, solitary mercury street light. Every ring had left a couple of decades behind, and at the hub, every corner – save one – boasted a shop removed from the ceaseless currents of the city by this eddy in time: an apothecary's with remedies in big glass jars, a kiosk with goodies from my childhood, a greengrocer's with yesteryear's prices written in chalk on a clapped-out blackboard; a Peronist Party Office, closed; an empty shop that gave no hint of what it last sold; pavements with no people; streets with no cars; and, bridging the void, between the telegraph poles of the six arrowheads, a tangle of electricity and phone cables silhouetted against the expectant sky. Only one of the corners was occupied by a house, a modest slice of the pie with white brick walls and dark green shutters and a flat terrace, from which a sparse array of geraniums and ferns peeped incuriously. I rang the doorbell, hanging from its wires at one side of the wooden door.

I heard the pattering of feet approaching down the passageway, a muffled shout of warning, strange squawks; then the door flew open and two little girls, looking astonishingly like penguins, threw themselves round my legs.

'Malvina! Soledad!' a voice called to them from inside, and I looked up to see a figure walking briskly down the lighted passageway. I asked her name, and when she'd confirmed it (Gloria) I explained why I'd come. Her expression flicked from alarm to suspicion, then annoyance, then back to suspicion; it was obvious she'd like to have slammed the door in my face, but that would have left the girls on the outside, with me.

'Surprise? Do you take me for a complete bimbo? Do you want to come in and see the number of boxes I've been landed with?'

The question was eminently rhetorical, but as it might be my only chance, I muttered 'Ok' and barged in and, by the time she'd realised, I was in the living room with the two girls, who wouldn't let go of my trousers and had begun to mmmmm with contentment.

'What pretty girls. Are they yours?'

I could see them better in the light of the living room. They were about ten years old, both on the short and compact side, not quite obese, with little almond eyes, cheekbones criss-crossed with purple filigree, and long pointed noses. They walked clumsily on land, lurching unsteadily and lifting their short arms slightly for balance, but even so they clung to my legs and gazed up at me myopically. Twins.

'That's the wrong face you're wearing. Try another one.'

'It's just that it's the first time I've seen twins . . . who both had, you know . . . the syndrome . . .'

'Mongoloids.'

'That's the one. They look like penguins,' I added. If it was honesty she wanted, I had skip-loads for her.

There was a pile of Christopher products in the middle of the living room and my suggestible imagination gave it the shape of an igloo. Looking more closely, I saw that it did in fact form a little house with an entrance at one side.

'That's all they were good for in the end: a playhouse for the girls. Can you see me buying any more?'

I explained about the prize and wrote out the cheque – the usual lie. She calmed down a little, though she still eyed me suspiciously as she invited me to sit down. I chose one of the green-velvet armchairs; immediately, the two girls came over, one on each side of me, and rested their heads on the arms of the chair for me to stroke them. Gloria smiled as she watched them.

'At least the girls like you. Forgive me for being so beastly just now, but I find it hard to believe that Surprise are giving instead of taking away.' She held the cheque up to the light. 'A thousand dollars?' I saw the happiness in her: not a trace of greed, and, for the first time, I felt like a piece of trash about what I was doing. 'At least the girls and I get some of what we lost back. I never had it in me,' she said pointing at the pile of products, 'to screw a friend or an acquaintance the way I've been screwed. Forgive me,' she repeated. 'I've been on tenterhooks for a week.'

'Why a week?'

'A week last Wednesday I went to your company's meeting to see if I could give the products back, and they told me to piss off. It was all the money I had.'

She was, I suspected, elegantly circumventing their real reply, and was back on the alert. She'd had another look at the cheque and put it to one side for the time being, rather than pasting it to her eyes like her predecessors. I knew I risked blowing everything with the next question, but I was so anxious I couldn't delay it any longer.

'Alone,' she replied. 'Didn't I tell you I haven't got it in me to rope other people into this shitty business?'

That's it, I thought. She's said it. The only thing left for me to do now is to think what to tell Tamerlán. Why? Why did I have to come up with Witness No. 26? I'd dug my own grave. Yet again.

'Something the matter?' she asked, startling me. I hadn't thought it showed; poker faces are usually my specialty. 'You've gone all . . .' she said.

'No,' I said, 'tiredness; bad hair day . . .'

I realised I couldn't leave just yet, although I wasn't going to get anything else out of her; but at least another few minutes' grace, the velvet of the armchair, the little girls' beady eyes which, sensing something, watched me inquisitively. I sighed inwardly with relief and said yes thanks, a double, when Gloria offered.

I thought it would take her a few minutes to make the coffee, but what she came back almost straightaway carrying was a Scotch. And a vodka for her. I don't know if the mistake was my transmission (coffee) or her reception (Scotch), but they cancelled each other out in any case and I gratefully savoured the outcome. Gloria sat down on the arm of the sofa, balancing on it, legs crossed in a half-lotus; I had a fleeting vision of something that I couldn't decide was either black knickers or cunt. 'Wanna find out? Now?' a faint voice asked me, barely audible from centuries of fatigue. It was me, trying to talk to someone who'd listen.

'Fox,' she was staring at my badge. 'Aren't you too high up to be going round door to door?'

I unpinned it from my lapel and tossed it onto a cushion on the sofa.

'It's borrowed. Here, it's a present.'

'Don't you wear it anymore?'

'I'm sick of it. I'm going to resign,' I said.

'You can bring your boxes over too if you like. We'll pool our resources and make a city for the girls with them.' She laughed. It was an innocent laugh, childish, as if she were the girl we were going to make the city for.

We started chatting and soon I felt the awful oppression lifting from my chest, as if in the last few days it had become the foundations of both of Tamerlán's towers. It felt good to have lost, to have reached the end of the road, not to be able to go any further. It was what many in the Islands felt when they were taken prisoner. That's it. We're alive, the English are here, we defended our country and we lost. It felt good to talk without a purpose, a strategy, the need to hustle each other, to humiliate each other, to extract the information they don't want to give, to mislead them. Suddenly words weren't just for prising things out of people or imposing one's will; they were exchanged, given, stroked like a cat, given back, rolled on the tongue, and sometimes reached down to the chest. I hadn't realised what I'd lost till I'd started to get it back.

Gloria was out of a job, hence her urgency over the money.

'I didn't know what I was going to do, you've saved us,' she told me, and I seriously considered the possibility of crawling under the sofa and staying there for the rest of the evening. She told me she worked an eight-hour day in the complaints department at the state telephone company listening to people swear their heads off till her smile shattered like glass and the little pieces started hitting the floor, the way they do in the cartoons (her comparison was a delight: someone else who drew those absurd connections; I thought to myself I'm not alone). She was almost happy when the company was privatised and she was invited to retire. 'I let myself be screwed with voluntary retirement. We lived on the severance pay for a few months, but the girls and I are a bit frittery, and blew it all on lunches and theatre and cinema and ice creams, clothes and toys and God knows what.' Whenever she said 'the girls' she looked at them and they raised their heads from the arms of my chair to focus their myopic eyes on her and smile. They had just over a thousand dollars left, she told me, when this boyfriend of hers came on the scene: 'Actually, he picked me up in a bar,' she said shaking her head as if to say what a jackass she'd been, and had talked her into sinking her money into Surprise, while kissing his crossed fingers and swearing blind he'd cover the risk with his own. 'Can you believe it?' Gloria asked me. 'The bastard picked me up and fucked me just to turn up at the meeting with his friend of the week. Whenever I said "See you on Thursday," he'd get frantic and say "No, it's got to be Wednesday, it's got to be Wednesday, I can't stand being apart from you for so long," the piece of shit. When you're past thirty and in my position, you get so afraid of scaring men away that you sometimes end up giving yourself to them on the cheap,' she said with a wan smile, and I felt like smothering her with kisses. I restrained myself. 'Another thing I went to the last meeting for was to kick his arse, but not surprisingly he didn't show up again. And I've had my fair share of dirty tricks, mind; you wouldn't believe me if I told you. But never anything so . . . petty, so . . . pathetic. Being betrayed with something so mediocre, that's what galls me most.' I have to do something about that cheque, I thought, at least ask her to give it back so I can use it to slit my wrists. 'Ah well. I'm getting all whingy,' she said. 'Sometimes, my life, I dunno . . . it hasn't always been easy . . .' she said, staring into the bottom of her vodka-less glass.

'I can see,' I added without a second's thought.

She stared at me for a few seconds, not understanding.

When she finally did, she looked at me less out of anger than something approaching disappointment. Not that much: must have been used to it.

'Meaning what? The girls? They're the best thing that ever happened to me.'

There was an awkward silence. The first.

'It's gloomy in here,' she said, uncrossing her legs so fast that I was left wondering once again, and descending from her promontory and stretching them, she walked over to the stereo. It was a bit cold inside and her thighs were covered in gooseflesh. 'I'll put some music on. What do you fancy? Satie or Guns N' Roses?'

'Not fussed.'

One after another, the compact disc began to deal a series of slow, pure, crystalline notes, which hung in the air for several seconds before being replaced by the next. I pictured someone with all the time in the world dismantling a crystal chandelier, plucking off the cut-glass teardrops one by one and throwing them into a still pond, barely scaring the fish and reciting she-loves-me-she-loves-me-not without moving their lips, till the end. Satie of course. Gloria disappeared to some unknown destination and came back holding a spliff between finger and thumb.

'Smoke?' she asked me, exhaling an endless unfurling of the sweetest, most intoxicating smoke in creation.

'Do swims duck?' I answered, reaching out a hand.

We smoked in silence. It was top dope: resinous and smooth as honey, and after a few tokes I was the pond into which the crystal tears were dropping. The two girls had also closed their eyes, swaying and resuming their mmmmm.

'Musical, aren't they.'

'Actually, they're pretty deaf. They pick up the vibrations I suppose. We communicate more through gestures and looks than words.'

'Don't they say anything?'

'Only from memory,' she smiled, exhaled. 'They repeat stuff like little parrots.'

'Little penguins.'

'I didn't know you could make penguins talk.'

'Maybe a cop could.'

'That would make them stool penguins.'

We cracked up laughing till I got stomach cramps. The two girls were smiling sympathetically nearby. Forgetting the squeamishness I'd indecisively set out to master, I stroked their bright purple cheeks with the back, then the palm of my hand.

'Make them say something,' I asked.

'Their party piece is the National Anthem. Want to hear it?'

'Long as I don't have to stand up . . .'

'No, it's the Charly García version.'

Gloria put Satie on pause and the girls, obeying some gesture I must have missed, skipped gleefully over to her side, each grabbing a hand, and opened their mouths to sing (not bad for those Disney voices of theirs), almost going into a trance over the last lines.

> Let us live with glory, our crown,
> Or swear to glorious death.

'It's the bit they do best; they must think it's about their mum.' Getting up to revive Satie, Gloria carried on to the bathroom at the end of the corridor. She forgot to close the door properly and, to my delight, the whole time she was sitting there I could see her naked right knee and calf, pricelessly adorned with an anklet of skirt and black knickers (at last the answer), the merry tinkle of her pee thrown in for good measure. She came back fixing her skirt.

'You will stay for dinner, won't you?'

Milanesas and chips. The milanesas were very good: the breadcrumbs stuck to the meat, and there was garlic and parsley in the egg mix (the very opposite of the ones my mother makes; when you try to cut them, the breadcrumbs fall off in chunks like the skin of a leper). The chips, however, were flaccid and oozing grease, precisely what chips shouldn't be.

'These chips are awful, aren't they,' she remarked, stuffing a forkful into her mouth. 'Want me to make you something else?' The girls ate quietly, holding the milanesas in a scrap of brown paper, tearing off hunks of bread and wiping each other's plates with them to see who'd win. They drank orange crush; we drank white wine and soda. The kitchen was warmer than the living room, as Gloria had left a couple of hobs on. They hissed faintly as if to reinforce their presence, which in the uniform brightness of the fluorescent tube their pale blue light did little to remind us of.

During dinner Gloria mentioned a town that rang more than a few bells; choking with eagerness I provided the name: 'Malihuel'. We discovered we had something in common that was stronger than blood or sacred vows: the same childhood memories. Thrilled, we played pat-a-cake over the table, the girls clapping to see us so happy. I used to visit that little backwater in the toe of the boot of Santa Fe Province every summer;

she lived there until she was ten. We spent a long time, at least until afters, trying to ascertain if we'd ever met; but we reached no conclusions. Maybe I was the boy who climbed the fig tree beneath her to cop a look at her knickers (highly likely!), but no, said Gloria, disappointed, I remember now, he was from Rosario. And didn't she have a shaggy dog that looked like an inflated possum and played with me one day, fetching sticks from the lagoon? No, she didn't. But the places were still the same even if we hadn't seen each other there: the church steeple, the first thing that poked out above the trees as you approached along the highway; the Tuttolomondo spaghetti factory, which closed at siesta time, where we used to play hide-and-seek; even today the smell of eggs and flour when someone's kneads dough or graduates from university sucks me back down the tunnel of time, and I'm there hiding behind the sifters, the racks of drying spaghetti, the hum of the extractor fans . . . Guido, Mati, Vicentito, did you know them? 'Did I,' she answered, digging a provincial idiom from one of the drawers of her memory that life in the capital hadn't managed to exterminate. 'Guido used to hang out with a friend of mine, and I heard something about Mati recently, let me see . . .' The square on summer nights, enough shady hideaways between the lamp posts for a bit of nooky in the weeds: that was where I touched my first breast, I proclaimed proudly; whose, whose went Gloria, and when I told her she burst out laughing, sure, big deal, her tits were better polished than the one on the Monument to Motherhood. And I once had a wank at the historic watchtower too, I said, just to show her I wasn't messing, and she'd thrown bread at me. The best memories, we both agreed, were of the lagoon and the island off the bathing resort. At weekends families would come from all over Santa Fe and you could barely walk on the island for the number of cars, lorries and vans, and the endless causeway connecting it to the shore was always jammed solid. We waxed nostalgic about dinners at the hotel, with its marble staircases and velvet curtains; there were festivals with artists and musicians from all over the country: Gloria's father took up as an impresario and they once had dinner with Sandro, who gave the little girl an autographed photo. No, I didn't keep it, I've got nothing left from those days, Gloria answered my excited question. That island, I remarked, was just a shell of rubble and flattened dirt barely sticking out above the muddy water, wasn't it? Only the tip of the Yacht Club came off slightly better, sprinkled with sand and protected from the burning sun by the trees that two generations of Malihuenses had gone to great efforts to grow (the brackish water of the lagoon killed everything, even the fish). And yet, I went on, I swear even today that that little island only just delivered from the mud is the most beautiful island in the world and knocks any tourist brochure paradise, with its white sands, palm trees and crystal-clear waters into a cocked hat. Every so often I make plans to go back, spend a few days in the town, visit my friends, swim in the lagoon again. 'You know that other island,' Gloria interrupted, 'the one full of rams' heads? You could only get there by boat, and I brought back a skull, carrying it by one curly horn, and spent the rest of the summer polishing it with Odex and an old toothbrush.' 'And you remember the . . .' I'd say to her and she'd say, 'Yes, hold on, I don't believe it, you saw it too? I thought I was the only one in the world,' and we both talked over the top of each other, about the tiny island of flamingo nests in the distance, a patch of pink in the middle of the water, and when the boat approached, a miracle: the entire island would lift into the air and open like a hundred orchids flowering at once, and above and around us the flamingos blotted out the sky and the air was pink and thunderous, and in our memory we stood hand in hand in the same boat, our hearts stopped at the sight of such beauty.

By the time we met in that recollection of the flamingo island, we were no longer in the kitchen talking both at the same time, laughing at nothing in particular, looking into each others' eyes (or me at Gloria's round arse as she got up to get some ice from the freezer); together we'd put the girls to sleep, sung them half-forgotten songs by Sui Generis, La Máquina, Virus until they fell asleep: Malvina sucking her thumb, Soledad with her head under her pillow, and, leaving the door open a crack, we crept back to the living room with the light off, each sitting at our own end of the sofa and staring at each other without a word, barely able to make out each other's silhouettes in the half-light across the strait that separated us. And when one of us decided to cross it, it was of course Gloria who ventured the first caress; she drew my eyebrows with her fingers, closing my eyes as she went, down the side of my nose to my mouth, which I opened for her to complete the sentence she'd started to write on my lips. I discovered that she kissed slowly, her mouth slack, her tongue lazy and languid, her teeth ghosting the shadowiest of bites. I'd like to see them simulate this on a computer; creating a liquid interface like this will require a qualitative technological leap that nobody's going to waste snogging a mere simulation of a female. Kevin was right: we *are* still too attached to imitating reality. The possibilities of virtual sex are limitless: how about screwing your Harley Davidson or Porsche; or if art's your thing, Botticelli's Venus or, more perversely, the Venus de Milo, or – why not? – an orgy sur le pont with the demoiselles of Avignon (especially the ones on the right). My mind took to wandering the boundless marches of cyberspace, and when I finally re-entered the atmosphere of Planet Earth, I found myself with this strange woman, older than me, the mother of two mongoloid daughters, writhing on a dilapidated sofa in a tastelessly decorated living room. I'm better off like this, I thought; that whole childhood memory game was getting mawkish, now let's get down to business. I slid my hand under her angora sweater, easily reaching her breast because, as my eagle eyes had already detected, she wasn't wearing a bra. One less hurdle, I thought as I twizzled a hard, protuberant, knob-like nipple, far too large for a breast that fitted my cupped hand. To give myself more freedom of movement I pulled her sweater over her head so abruptly I nearly choked her, and began the predictable descent, kiss by kiss, down the ladder of her prominent ribs to her navel. But before I could reach it, she rolled over, forcing me to find new words to tempt her mute back. I stroked it distractedly, even feeling relief at the truce, and contemplated the possibility of a massage till I could come up with something better. Massages had always worked for me, especially since I'd got hold of a bespoke program: shiatsu, Thai, Swedish, energy, relaxation . . . 'You still there?' whispered Gloria suddenly, taking me by surprise (one of the things I find most annoying is having my train of thought interrupted), and I cheerfully chirped yeah, where d'you think, to mask the first stirrings of annoyance at her veiled complaint. Here we go, I thought. I rested my cheek on the curve of her waist and gradually loosened my arms, letting the weight of my body rest on hers. What a shame, such soft skin, I thought. A wave of dope came and went, blowing through my body like a hot wind, emptying me without warning. Such soft skin, I repeated, but the repetition was less in the words in my mind than in the suction of her pores and the static of little tiny hairs between her and me. I took my shirt off to hear better. Immobilised, Gloria squirmed to reach the edge of my jeans and slide a hand inside. 'Hey, kiddo, I'm not Rubber Woman you know,' she giggled softly into the pillow; but rapt in my new discovery I couldn't let go of her or stop rubbing my newly awakened skin against hers. Something's happening here, I felt rather than thought, with some alarm; something's coming through this wrapping of mine, suddenly so thin and porous: it isn't the dope, it isn't the childhood memories, it isn't just feeling horny. I had to find out what it was, this crackling of bubble wrap on my skin when it came into contact with hers, my armadillo carapace suddenly as soft and yielding as a cat to its caresses, and, seeking the answer, I lost myself with no chance of return in the succession of plains and hollows from her nape to her waist. This skin, this beautiful skin, a voice inside me kept repeating as I rubbed my nose, my eyes, my mouth on it the way you do on a sun-dried towel when stepping out of the sea. There were small pockets of energy that alternated with the softness of the skin, points so intense that my fingertips felt almost like reliefs, and I pursued their tracery across every corner of her body, flipping her over to snuffle about in her breasts and armpits and beyond her belly, following the elusive waist of her skirt, which she herself saw to unfastening and tugging off, twisting and turning to free hips and thighs of the trap, and make it vanish beyond her ankles. Her body became vast in the darkness, extending in all directions at once, lost in time as well, and I lost myself and roamed over it with my broken compass, my nameless map and handless clock. They're more different than ever in the dark, I felt as I entered her, her cunt fitting me snug as a cast of my cock, her sigh so deep on feeling it slide in that for a second I wished for some light to see her face by – although the darkness had the advantage that I didn't have to close my eyes to people it with the ghosts who'd lead me smoothly to the finale. It never ceases to amaze me that I'm never satisfied with the woman I have beneath me and that to get aroused I have think of another one, or of the same one somewhere else, in another situation, sometimes even with someone else. On automatic pilot my body dealt the thrusts that rock the world, while I searched the database of my mind for the most suitable images for the occasion. I made do with the first hit, Marroné's secretary, which gave me a new spurt of fire to redouble my attacks; there was even a faint element of humiliation that made me pant more deeply, but then I got this montage with spirals of toilet paper fluttering over her boss's arse, and started shaking my head (which I always keep to one side to avoid distractions) left and right to erase it from my sight, when I felt two hands grabbing it, pulling it to the middle, forcing me to open my eyes and see what lay before them: the eyes of the woman, capturing the reflection of the faint light that filtered in from the street, and gazing into mine. 'Felipe,' she murmured so low it could have been telepathy, and with a shudder, I suppressed a fresh wave of annoyance awoken by her interference. Nosy, I thought, don't you understand what . . .?

'Anything wrong . . .?' she asked, and before she could finish, I said 'Nothing, I'm fine' (Why don't you shut up?). I leaned against the sofa-back to let her move, leaving a corner of cushion for her to sit on while, lying on my back, I occupied the whole sofa, my eyes fixed on the grey light of the ceiling. She caressed me, despite the marble hardness of my tense body, as I pondered the fastest way to get up and go home without offending her. Before I could – slow as ever, timorous, letting myself be outmanœuvred – she straddled me, and, as fragile as the caress of a feather, I felt a glimmer of pleasure when the tips of her bush met my abdominal muscles and her generous buttocks lodged themselves on either side of my dispirited cock. Then it was gone, extinguished (absurdly, at that moment I remembered the wavering blue flame of the pilot light in the boiler when a south-easterly blows) and looked away, letting her get on with it, in the hope that the message would finally reach her, or that she'd soon tire. Still, to her credit, instead of treading the well-beaten paths, she chose to bestow her ghostly kisses and the petal-like brush of her caresses on the curve of my shoulders, my closed eyelids, the hollow of my arms and knees, the line of my throat . . . She squeezed my arms from top to bottom like tubes of toothpaste; she unknotted my clenched fingers one by one, licking their tips like ice creams; her tongue delved into the hollow of my chest, drilling deeper and deeper till it found the nest of all anguish. My hostility, my decision not to collaborate at all, turned against me and left me helpless in her hands, then suddenly Gloria was everywhere, exploring me at will and my skin was a mosaic of match-heads and her tongue the sandpaper lighting roads of fire as it went. The brain, I managed to think, what a

criminal deception; the only erogenous zone is the skin. My
body began to stir, far removed from my will, but I no longer
knew which body it was – the heat fusing them at the points
of most friction – nor who was panting above and sighing below, whose were the kisses that mingled in the total interface
of our mouths, whose the air emptying from our lungs, or how
long this membrane between two soap bubbles would last.
Nothing, nothing, nothing. Only right at the last did I regain
my body, feeling the whole of it liquefy down to the last cell
and eject itself in a gush through the tiny hole at the tip, feeling that it was impossible for that to happen, and, before losing all notion of what was happening, feeling that the
impossible was happening, as the still-uncontrollable judder-
ings of hips above accompanied the broken murmurs poured
in the ear below till the body above moaned and shouted before it collapsed trembling, no bones unbroken, on top of the
awaiting one beneath. For some time Gloria went on biting
and sucking my ear, neck, shoulder, anything she could reach
without leaving the axis on which she turned, while I renewed
the exploration of the mystery which I now felt further than
ever from solving: what was it that my fingers kept detecting
on the inexhaustible surface of her back, the sweet fruit of her
buttocks, the slide of her thighs (climbing up, sliding happily
down, running back up, the way we did on the slide in the
square in Malihuel); I desperately wanted to be blind to feel
her more intensely and, lifting my fingers to break the spell, I
made another discovery: the air felt rough after touching her.
Some part of my body, probably the one that most snugly fitted
her recesses and projections, whispered a corollary: after
touching this, it told me, you won't want to touch anything

else. Learn that now, even if you forget it when you get up: you'll forever be comparing; any other skin will feel like sackcloth; it's going to be hard to live without.

Gloria asked me if I'd enjoyed it and I nodded enthusiastically.

'Wasn't it great? The first time,' she said. 'And we came together.'

'I thought you came afterwards,' I contradicted her.

'What? Oh, right. I meant together, not at the same time. God, what a day. Just when you think the only thing you've got to look forward to is having dinner and watching the telly till you nod off, a stranger rings your doorbell, barges into your house and fucks you like a god. And there are people who complain about life.'

We chatted again afterwards, less anxiously, the stiff cock and the open cunt that lay in wait behind every phrase before, now sleepy and content, leaving us to play with words like two little kids in a sandpit, all wrapped up in themselves and serious with concentration, lending each other toys without knowing whose is which: post-fucking words, another dictionary that preserved the purity of life's first words. They made it easier to find each other at last, at one of those crossroads in our common past where, until now, our paths hadn't crossed.

'Wait, wait. Felix the Cat! Was that you? You once beat the shit out of my cousin Diego!'

'Your cousin? But then you must be . . .'

'We did, we did meet: you ran after me with a squeezy bottle at the lagoon at Carnival! I grabbed you by the hand to stop you!' she shouted, doing so again twenty years later. 'You were just this little kid! My, how you've grown,' she said, shaking my prick, which was awakening from its slumber. 'That's a big one, eh?'

'I was floating on my back naked once in Bariloche and the newspaper published a photo of me with the caption "NES- SIE SPOTTED IN LAKE NAHUEL HUAPI".'

'In that icy water too! Just imagine if it had been warmer!'

'Yours was famous too. Guido told me.'

'What?'

'That you let the boys touch it.'

'The liar!' she shouted, bursting with laughter. 'I only let him look once! The bastard had promised me he wouldn't tell! The whole town . . . oh God, I want to die.'

Then it just started flowing, and we put together a story from the odds and ends of our two separate ones: chance meet- ings a basketball game, the church door, the queue at the bak- ery; sometimes conclusive, at others impossible, but which we vehemently assented to nonetheless, spiting the insipid truth with deception. For her, it also meant additional security: the stranger she'd let into her house, who was banging her a couple of hours later as her daughters slept in the next room, had been transformed into a child in red trunks, chasing her in and out of the picnic tables on the island, squirting innocent yet premoni- tory jets of water at her with his little carnival-clown squeezy bottle. I suppose that was another reason why she opened up:

'You know what struck me about you? You met the girls from the start, but you stayed. With the others, you have no idea; I'd sometimes spend months thinking up excuses for them not to come round, because I don't want to see them pull that face, and the day I do is the last I want to see them. With you I don't have to worry.'

'I want to see you,' I said to her. 'I'll turn on the light.'

'No, Felipe,' she tried to head me off.

I should have listened to her, but she was too late; my hand was already on the switch. She managed to cover herself, but not the way a naked woman usually would: she'd left her breasts and cunt exposed, while her hands had flown to cover perfectly innocent parts of her breast and belly. Immediately I realised why. Ten people wouldn't have had enough hands to hide the marks that swarmed over her body like insects, denser in the parts she was trying to hide.

'Now you've seen me,' she said to me angrily. 'Now turn it off.'

I didn't. I approached the sofa, sat down on the edge and touched one. It was as if they'd pinched very hard and torn a piece out, the surrounding skin then stretched like a darn to cover it. It was these shiny little scars that my fingers had detected, confusing them in the dark with some obscure tactile illusion produced by my enchantment; only now did the map I'd drawn by joining up these dots with my fingers begin to take shape. Gloria stared at me in resignation, waiting for me to make up my mind, and I'd like to have obliged: what, when, who. But I already knew the answers. They did it to this skin, I could feel it in my throat, in my eyes; they were capable of doing this to this skin.

'The lighter ones are cattle prod; the darker ones, cigarette burns. And don't worry: they're more than ten years old. They won't bite any more. Or are you the compassionate sort? Can you turn the fucking light off, now, or do you want to see more? Look.'

She opened her arms, exposing her body. I got up and

turned off the light. Without approaching her body again, which I sensed was as tense, hostile and tight as a shut clam, I spoke without thinking.

'You think you have a monopoly on suffering? I was sent to the Malvinas when I was nineteen; I was wounded in the head and spent a year not being able to speak. Yeah, I know, it doesn't compare. I'm way down the rankings. I have no right to complain.'

I thought that she'd be even more pissed off after that and kick me out, but instead she sat down, hugging her knees, and asked me:

'Where in Malvinas?'

'Puerto Argentino. Longdon. What, you've been there?' I said, a little more sarcastically than intended.

'Not on Isla Grande?'

'No. Why?'

She didn't answer, but I could see her loosen up and propose a truce by tucking away her legs to make room for me. 'You want the details or just the gist?' she said to me after a minute's silence, and I told her there was no need to if she didn't want to, I'd heard plenty of stories like hers. 'I can promise you,' she corrected me, almost disdainful in her self-assurance, 'you've never heard one like mine before. By the time I finish, you'll probably want to leave. So think about it. You still have time,' she finished, and from the way she said it I knew I had no option but to stay. Gloria went to fetch a blanket for herself and another for me; she brought cigarettes and smoked the whole time she was talking, without moving from her end of the sofa (nor I from mine); without touching each other once the whole time, each enwrapped in the cocoon of our own warmth.

'The first time I realised what was going to happen I was eighteen and dating this boy from the Guevara Youth, who loved to talk at the meetings. He wanted me to go and live with him, but I wasn't sure. I'd just started my degree (Law) and, although his passion turned me on, he wasn't very bright; so naïve he was a bit thick, actually. There was a meeting that night in the faculty building, some kid who'd been wasted by the Triple A, and Fabián took to the podium in the street, which we'd cordoned off, and began to mouth off about all the blood spilt, the martyrs, the Revolution . . . As an orator he stank: one cliché after another, nobody took much notice of him except me. But I wasn't listening to what he was saying. He suddenly looked so lovely up there, so full of life, that I felt something here, and said to myself there and then "Yes, alright, I will live with him, yes, I do. As he was climbing down, I waved to him and started to jump up and down to call him over; I could barely contain the urge to shout it out to him from where I was standing. But I wasn't the only one: someone else was calling him from a parked car. His old gesture, as much as to say "Look woman, the cause comes first; you'll have to wait," always used to really get to me; but this time it filled me with tenderness, and I was trembling with impatience as he approached the open car window. Without a word an arm came out and hit him in the forehead with a hatchet. A hatchet: one of those little axes you use to cut the wood for the barbecue, and Fabián fell on his back with the hatchet still stuck in his forehead, and the car pulled off and disappeared before he'd stopped moving on the floor. There was pushing, running, shouting; people opened up to let him die, alone, in the middle of the circle of spooks that materialised out of the rally as it broke up. Me, I was paralysed, I couldn't even shout. A friend pulled me away and I let her without resisting; the only thing I could think of was that they shouldn't leave him there with the hatchet in his head, that someone should show some compassion and pull it out, I couldn't stand the idea of him lying there like that with that look of frozen astonishment on his face and the hatchet buried in the middle of his forehead. That day was like a revelation to me, you see? As if it had been my own head the axe had split in two. I stayed in the movement, even after the coup, but only as a reflex, on automatic pilot, because the other alternatives were even scarier. I'd seen that day that we'd never beat them, that we weren't capable of doing anything like that to them, that if we played by their rules, they were bound to win.

'It took them some time to catch up with me, late in the hunting season, when urgency had become routine to them. They asked hardly any questions: there wasn't much they didn't know by then. They left the hood on the first few times. It was horrible because I never knew what was going on, whether they were about to do something to me or not, my body couldn't brace itself, I lived in a constant state of terror. I know I just blanked out at some point, like they'd pulled the plug: it just disconnected. Sometimes the intolerable thing is the awareness of what they're doing to you, and when I lost that, I stopped caring about it; when the pain gets really bad, you faint and that's the end of it. I lived in a total stupor for months: I suppose I must have been eating and sleeping and shitting, but I can't remember anything, except those moments of pain from another world which, in the otherwise general void, eventually merged into one long howl of pain. They got bored with me in the end – some fresh meat must have arrived – and they threw

me into a corner. One day they stuck my head in a bag, shoved
me up and down the stairs and dumped me on the floor of a
van with others like me. They took us, I found out later, to the
Garage Olimpo two blocks from my apartment – which I never
set foot in again; I think they kept it. They did things differently there: *they* were the ones wearing the hoods. I learned to
recognise their bodies; there can't have been more than four
or five of them, and there was one who was clearly the boss:
they called him "Captain". The others came and went, but he
was always there, like he was turning up for a date. From the
taunts of the others I realised that he reserved this privilege
for me alone. That brought me back. In the middle of nowhere,
there was suddenly something I could hang onto – a ledge. And
when he took his hood off one day, when I could once again put
a face to him, give an identity to the sheer animal panic my
whole world had become, I began to recover my own. You know
who I'm talking about, don't you?'

I suppose so, but the idea was so intolerable that I didn't
even dare to tell myself, and I sat there dumbly waiting for
her to do so. After all, I wasn't the one who'd started this little
game.

'My ex-husband. The girls' father.'

I ought to have got up and split that very instant, but
that's what generally happens with the most harrowing stories:
you're disturbed yet so fascinated at the same time that you
can only listen till the end, utterly in the grip of the teller, who
makes the story last to prolong their control over us for as long
as possible. Most of us Malvinas veterans are old hands at it: we
know all the tricks.

'Gradually my situation improved – between sessions of

course. They treated me, clothed me, fed me. They did it routinely, anonymously, as if it were the same for everybody, but I knew that, if I'd outlived my shelf-life, it was because *he* wanted it that way. They were more careful during the sessions too: they put out their cigarettes and closed their knives, and they were careful to do the picana shocks where they wouldn't leave such deep marks. And I was only scared when I couldn't see him, although he hardly ever let me down. It would have been absurd to: they were our dates, the sessions were. In the few seconds when the total pain stopped, my eyes would search out his. And when they met, I felt as if his hand were holding mine and wouldn't let go. Once – I'll never forget that day – I noticed they were full of tears. I was strapped to the bed-springs, you see; they'd used the picana on me till I'd fainted, then thrown a bucket of water over me. And I was feeling sorry for him. Really, my brain must have been mashed potato by that stage, but at that moment I felt as if my suffering had a meaning, as if I'd be capable of putting up with all that and a thousand times more as long as he was there. It felt like a triumph. Think about it. Him, a man who'd done this a thousand times without batting an eyelid, he was crying now – and all because it was me, not just anyone, tied up there. How could I not feel flattered? There and then I made up my mind not to let him down. I'd put up with any pain, any atrocity to show him I was worthy of him. I smiled, to let him know and, though the smile could barely have been visible through my deformed features, I think he understood, because he wiped away his tears and gave the order to continue. I closed my eyes, bathed in tears too, but tears of gratitude. I was no longer alone. Someone had reached out a hand to me across the darkness; the terror had gone and in the soft, golden light bathing my soul the intermittent shocks of the picana flashed like distant lightning.

'He made me abort my first pregnancy because I'd been raped by so many men that he couldn't be sure the child was his. "If you'd talked earlier, we wouldn't have come to this," he yelled at me, as if I'd held out on purpose so as to have sex with lots of men. There was a grain of truth in it, of course: I preferred the rapes to the picana; I used to thank God when I saw one of them pulling his zip down, although his companions often used to give me more just to watch their pal jump from the shock. It was one of their favourite jokes: they never tired of it. His accusations hurt me because they were so unfair. I have proof that he himself sent them to rape me: by having me belong to everyone he thought he'd be able to loathe and forget me. The result, of course, was just the opposite: the more he gave me away, the sicker his desire became to possess me absolutely. He tried to free himself from my fatal spell and took me on one of those night flights . . . to let the sea take care of me. At the last moment, naked in his arms, drugged as I was by the cold coming in through the hatch or God knows what else, I embraced him tenderly (that's what he told me) and at that moment, when he realised he couldn't let me go, he thought about crossing the threshold with me. What a romantic, right? The sea would have been our wedding bed, he said; he didn't know how much I hate fish. The only result of that flight (I can't remember a damn thing, because they'd used horse syringes on us) was that I caught a dose of flu. I never saw my travelling companions again, of course. After that he moved me out of the cell and took me to his house, locking me away like a nun in a cloister. I'd have stayed anyway: I didn't really want to see my family and told them as little as possible. That he was a soldier, yes. That he'd got me out of there too. They never understood any of it anyway; my mother, the silly cow, no doubt even thought "Well, well, who'd have imagined it? The girl gets herself thrown in gaol and comes out with a real catch?" Did I mention that they'd caught me at my parents'? The men holding their shotguns and my old man puffing out his chest. "If my daughter's done something she shouldn't have, I won't be the one to stand in your way. Do your duty, officer." What could I do in my situation? Call a friend? I did try though, more than once, but I'd hang up when they answered. Once I rang a friend of mine they'd taken in earlier, to see if she was still alive, and without hesitation she asked the silent receiver "Gloria? Is that you? Won't they let you talk?" I stopped calling my friends after that: it only made me suffer. He made me unworthy of them and without them I had no other option but to get closer to him. And when I fell pregnant again, that was it. The friends I have now are all new. I don't have to tell them anything, and if I do, they have nothing to compare me with: the only Gloria they know is this one. Funny, isn't it? Most people who've been through what I have are afraid of bumping into their torturer in the street. Not me. I was nearly nine months when he didn't come home one night, nor the following night either. It wasn't the first time, but he always used to give me some sign: leaving the house full of food or something (I still wasn't allowed to go out alone). Before the week was out, I heard the news about the recovery of the Islands on the radio and realised where he'd gone. Along with the revelation came the labour pains. I could feel them inside me, as if they were trying to peck their way out, and eventually a neighbour showed up with the police, woken by my screams. It was sheer agony, the worst of all. The last pain he caused me.

My two beautiful little girls were born in the ambulance on the way to the Santojanni, and I was born with them that night. They had to give me a cæsarean without anæsthetic on some street corner or other. I was covered in blood. Later they congratulated me on how well I'd withstood the pain. Ha! Mamma mia! They weighed one kilo eight hundred and one kilo nine hundred, because they were slightly premature. It was the night of 2nd April 1982.'

She went quiet, trying to guess from my expression whether I'd had enough, drawing long and deep on her cigarette. Through the half-closed blinds filtered the headlights of a car disconcertedly going round and round the hub of all those streets, trying to guess which one to escape down.

'Did he make it back?' I eventually asked. She nodded as she put out her cigarette in the cone of fag ends that spilled over the ashtray between us.

'He was one of the last. He came straight from the ship. I hadn't had any news of him, not a thing; one hand wanted him to come back soon and look after the three of us, for him not to leave me alone in a situation like that – I wouldn't swap my girls for anything in the world now, but at the start . . . The other prayed – alone – that he'd tread on a landmine and blow himself up, or be riddled with bullets, or captured on a mission (the bastard was a commando), and that they did to him what he'd done to me. Too bad they were English – such gentlemen! The Chileans would have been much better. The Gurkhas were a disappointment, weren't they? Did they cut off anyone's head in the end?'

'Not that I know of . . .'

'I kept dropping things, cutting myself, burning myself

when I was cooking: one hand versus the other; they could barely do anything together when they were looking after the girls. And in three months everyone was back, and there was I hearing rumours of prisoners being taken to England in secret as hostages, getting used to the idea he wasn't coming back and beginning to enjoy it. But the bastard always turns up just when you least expect him. But this time I had a surprise in store for him; this time it was me who'd pulled a fast one on him. It was a night like this, nearly ten years ago, I heard the doorbell go and opened the door. He was still in uniform, carrying his kitbag, and, without so much as a hello, he stared at my empty belly and said "I want to meet my daughters." He was gone, way gone (he'd never really been on the hither side) but this time I knew he'd gone for good; thousands of kilometres out to sea. My letters had fallen into that black abyss staring at me now, along with everything else. When he saw the girls asleep in the light from their night-light, he stood there stock-still, struck dumb. Fifteen minutes, without moving a muscle or making a sound. I was on the verge of yelling at him when he asked me in this neutral drone, still not moving, what I'd called them; Malvina and Soledad, the way you wanted, I told him, digging my nails into my palms to stop myself screaming. But we can change them if you like, there's still time, I began; but he stopped me and held up one hand. Then he said "No, it's fine. It's fine," he said, looking at the girls sleeping together, one little hand on top of the other, face down in their cot. "It's fine," he said, looking dumbly at the room, "It's fine," he repeated, measuring me with his eyes, and again, "It's fine," as he picked up his bag, "It's fine," as he opened the front door, and one more "It's fine" reached me as I peered out onto the pavement, riding on the noise of his footsteps receding loudly on the flagstones, hard with winter cold. He never came back and, a few months later, someone who didn't want to identify himself phoned me to tell me he was dead and that I should never try to find out any more. Can you believe it? The terror of the camps, the hero of the Malvinas, ran away from a woman and two newborn babies.'

'Would you rather he'd stayed?'

A flash of the old pain, still capable of life, like those dried-out fish that gradually revive when placed in water, flitted across her features. She went on the attack.

'What if you lot had won the war? What if the girls graduate as lawyers? Do me a favour, Felipe. Haven't you understood what kind of a creature he is? For Christ's sake don't give me that cliché about the guy who tortures, rapes and murders in working hours, and then goes home and is a loving father and exemplary husband? Bullshit. A torturer's a torturer everywhere he goes. He just changes his style, his instruments. At home he's more patient: he has years ahead of him. A bastard's a bastard and he defiles everything he touches.'

'The girls too?'

'No, not the girls. My body filtered out all the harm. The girls were born pure. Can't you see? What do I care if they aren't intelligent. What I do know is that there isn't a wicked bone in their bodies. That's where I beat him. It was my only way out. If they'd turned out normal and they'd had this much intelligence, he'd have turned them into what he wanted. This way he didn't get the chance. You know what they are, my girls?'

'What?' I asked, instead of giving the obvious answer, out of politeness.

'Angels.'

She said nothing else. When she tired of waiting for a reply, a remark, anything, she whisked the blanket off her with a toreador's flourish and went to the bathroom. The light in the corridor lit the fall of her shoulders, the gentle wobble of her buttocks, her ankles as slender as wrists. Pity, I found myself thinking as I was getting dressed, with such a pretty body as that.

'Leaving already,' she said when she came back and saw me dressed.

'Yes,' I said, trying not to look her in the eye.

'You got scared.'

'No, it's just that . . .'

'What. Got to feed the cat?'

I ought to have gone, I thought, while she was pissing. Done a runner. Now I was trapped again. 'Well,' I said, 'a little longer,' and I sat down on the sofa. Immediately, a shooting pain ran from my arsehole to the back of my neck, and I leaped up and screamed.

'What happened,' she exclaimed in fright.

I pulled out the offending article. It was the fox badge from Surprise. Gloria put her hand over her mouth, but her laugh escaped through her fingers. Still in pain, but seized by the irony of the situation, I chuckled too. The cheque, I suddenly remembered. Gloria had sat down beside me and was eagerly attacking my belt buckle.

'What are you doing?'

'I have to look at it. Surely you don't think I'm going to let you go home wounded in combat.' She laughed some more, flipped me over and pulled my pants down, lightly nipping each cheek. She turned on the light to examine my wound, forgetting her own for the moment. 'It's a deep fucker, eh.' She came back with some cotton wool and hydrogen peroxide. While one hand bathed the affected area, the other tiptoed up and down my crack, brushed my arsehole and toyed with my balls and cock, which it found hard despite myself. She finished and just as I was (kneeling on the ground, my elbows on the sofa cushion) she threw herself on me, running her hands over my chest, the soft brush of her cunt on my arse.

'Don't go, Felipe.' Her tone had lost its sexual insinuation: all of a sudden, she was begging. 'At least not tonight. The girls and I need you to stay tonight.'

Instantly I shrivelled, as if, like a bottle of champagne, my prick had been dunked in an ice bucket. I don't know if it was the position, but I felt like I was being buggered, and did what I usually do in these situations (when pushed, I mean): I lay there, stiff as a statue, and Gloria's caresses began to slide off the 'No' of my body like water off a waxed surface. Eventually giving up, she sat down on the sofa beside me, rigid, her hands on the angle of her closed thighs.

'I don't understand,' she told me. 'Things happened to you too, if you haven't been telling stories. I thought that that . . . And Malihuel, too.' She was doubting.

'Malihuel yes,' I managed to mutter as I adjusted my belt. Then she did something I wasn't expecting. She went down on her knees, hugged my legs, grovelled.

'Please don't go. Look, I'm swallowing my pride and begging you to stay. If you don't want to sleep with me, if you don't feel like touching me, you can have the bed and I'll sleep on the sofa. Or you can take us to your house, we'll get by in any old corner, I swear we won't bother you. Just for tonight. I haven't slept properly for over a week, and if I don't sleep tonight I think I'm going to go mad.'

'He's alive,' I said.

She nodded.

'You ran into him,' I went on, taking my time not because I was guessing step by step, but because everything had suddenly become so clear that I couldn't process so many bytes at once. 'Where?'

'At . . . You know.'

Yes, I thought. Of course.

'There, in the tower. That day.'

Now it was my turn to unhook my poker face from the hatstand and adjust it again, and feigning indifference, to ask name, surname, occupation (ha!), go through the list of witnesses with her and rule out the possibility of mistaken identities. I'd save time if I left right now and barged in on Tamerlán shouting 'I've found him! I've found the twenty-sixth man!' It was as if I'd always known: the pack's incomplete till the death card's been turned.

'He was the last in before the doors closed. After ten years he stepped out of my worst nightmares and walked into that room. I was paralysed, it always happens to me with him, I sat there nailed to the chair watching him approach, his eyes drilling into me. But that wasn't the worst of it. He looked at me the way you look through glass, he walked straight past me as if I wasn't there: he passed through my body like a ghost through a curtain. That more than anything made me certain he hadn't changed: it was his signature, unmistakable, and he was writing all over my body again.

'Was he looking for you?'

'Do you think he didn't know where if he'd wanted to? No. He was as surprised as I was. He probably even thought it was *me* that had finally located *him*.' She choked on the smoke with laughing. 'He went and sat right at the front, lapels turned up, staring at the tip of his shoes all the time. He was there for something else, I assure you: I can tell when he's on assignment. Though something in him *had* changed, that's for sure. Not just the grey hair, the grim mouth, the drooping shoulders . . . He was hesitant, cautious, as if he didn't really know what he was doing there. When he was in the army, he was always the boss, and now – they must have discharged him I suppose, he looked "discharged" – he looked like . . . a clerk. I watched him all the time, and he kept looking at his watch trying to hide, knowing I was watching him; and he was already on his feet when the glass of the other tower had started to crack, get the idea? He knew what was going to happen. He shouted "There he is, the murderer," before anyone appeared at the window. It was all choreographed, understand? Everything except me being there. So when the cops questioned me, I told them I hadn't seen anything. I couldn't care less after everything I've seen in my life . . . Anyway, he never takes risks. Yesterday he sent two guys to check me out. Two heavies, instantly recognisable, they showed police IDs, I had to let them in. We've come to ask you a few questions they said, and me I'm screwed, a goner. Lucky the girls were at school. They started asking me about the day at Surprise, about my guests . . . Just like you.' She paused, enough to make me uncomfortable. 'No guests, I told them. They didn't believe me. One of them kept banging on about a man in a big grey coat with fur lapels and leather buttons; and the more details he added, the more emphatically I said no. If they've come to test me, I thought, they'll get nothing to worry about: all my reflexes, all my resources to come through an interrogation alive returned after ten years as if not a day had passed. He must be laughing in his office, his basement or wherever he is, thinking what a doddle it'll be to get those jackasses off my back. "That's my girl," he'd say afterwards, when they brought him the report. Anyway, he should have known there was no need to send me his messenger buzzards to make me keep my lip buttoned. But that's the way he operates: always overreacts; he'd never put himself at risk over a worm like me.'

She fell silent and sat there looking at me, waiting for God knows what. But I was too bewildered to tell her not to worry, that the two spooks hadn't been sent by her ex but by my lord and master – or perhaps that she *should* worry after all. I was so distracted with what was going round my head that I didn't react at first when she asked me:

'So who sent you?'

'Eh?'

'Come on. Where do you think I was born? Switzerland? You had me going there for a while with the cheque, and then I got the hots for you, which isn't difficult in my case. Did he make you learn the Malihuel bit by heart, or did he choose you precisely because of it, because you knew me from there?'

'Listen to me . . .'

'What are you playing at? The good cop? Pulling that nothing face of yours. Are you the one that looks after the small print? "Fuck her first, mate, because afterwards she'll spit it out without being asked. I know what I'm talking about." Is that it?' She didn't wait for an answer. 'You left me enough clues, mind. Surprise, Malvinas ... Did you do it because of how useless you are, or did he want me to guess from the start?'

'Gloria,' I pleaded. 'I don't work for him.'

'Oh, no? Who *do* you work for then?' She'd stood up without bothering to cover herself with the blanket and spoke to me from above, a female defending the nest. I could have sworn the marks on her skin were beginning to fizz like furious bees.

'I can't say,' came my lame reply. I had to get out of there as soon as possible: the piece of metal in my head had started to purr and in a few more minutes things were going to start spinning out of control. Gloria sat down with a sigh, pulled the blanket over her shoulders, lit a cigarette and swore at her sparking lighter.

'You know what the worst thing about all this is? That – in spite of everything – I don't want you to go. Must be like he said, mustn't it? Deep down I must like it. I'm pathetic, aren't I. Well, that's it, mission accomplished, you got everything you wanted out of me. What are you waiting for? Another crack while we're at it?' She opened her legs in defiance, like two mandibles ready to catch me if I came near. I got up from the sofa and began to walk around the room, clutching my swollen head in my hands, trying to think. The cheque was the only thing that managed to slip under the closed door of pain.

'Have you got that cheque I gave you?'

'What, now you want to take it back?'

'Please. I promise you. Get it for me,' I pleaded.

'They didn't half train you well. You people don't usually know how to inspire sympathy. All right.'

She went over to the chest of drawers and, turning her

back to me, opened a box. She didn't seem to be worried about me seeing her any more. How beautiful she must have been, I thought, and immediately, remembering the little girl in Malihuel, I corrected myself: how beautiful she was. She turned round, waggling it in her hand the way a dog wags its tail.

'Here.'

I ripped the cheque in two, then four. She looked on agog as I pulled out two wads of a grand each and handed them to her. She smiled suddenly. She'd realised.

'It was a fake, wasn't it. You fobbed me off with a piece of toilet paper. You bastard! And what's this? To keep me quiet?'

'No conditions,' I said to her. 'A present. Or compensation, if you like. From me.'

Her sarcasm sweetened to irony.

'Well, we didn't have such a bad time, after all. Just let me think it's for personal services. The door's always open for you if this is what you're paying. Well,' she exclaimed flicking through the notes with her thumb like a pack of cards, 'I think I've found my vocation.' She looked up as I approached the door. 'Do your friends pay as well as you do?'

'I'm going,' I replied.

'Yes, I know. And I wanted you to stay and protect us. You'd probably open the door for him.'

'Think what you like,' I told her with one hand on the door handle.

'Wait. One more thing. I should have waited to tell you, but I suppose I'll never see you again. I do think you're Felix the Cat, but what I can't believe is that that little dream-kid has grown into this.'

She was sitting in the middle of the sofa, under the direct

beam of the night-light, very upright, knees together, arms at right angles either side of her body, hair cascading over her shoulders: a queen on her throne, dismissing a vassal who, forbidden to turn his back, could but withdraw backwards. The blinding points of light glittered ever more intensely as the rest of her body was slowly eclipsed in half-light. She suddenly appeared to me as one of those drawings of the constellations in maps of the sky: the random star groups the only sharp reality, the lines that joined them and the animal or human figures that enclosed them just ghosts projected by the imagination to populate the frozen blackness of space. I closed my eyes, and, piercing my eyelids, the points of light remained there, pinned red-hot on my retinas.

'A few years ago I went back to Malihuel in a fit of nostalgia to regain something of the flavour of my childhood, a time when life was beautiful for me. Don't you know what happened to the town?'

My face must have said no for me.

'It's been swallowed up by the lagoon. There's nothing left, just a few odd houses you reach by boat. They had to move all the public buildings to Fuguet. The water floods the streets we played in as children, Felipe. As you approach across it, the first thing you see in the distance is the church spire. We got as far as the ruins of the altar in the boat. All you can see of our island is the top of the hotel (where I had dinner with Sandro when I was a girl) and the dead treetops of the beach resort. There are no flamingos, no nothing. Malihuel has gone for ever, Felipe.'

Chapter 9
THE VIGIL

They brought the draft round to my house one night in a patrol car (I'm talking of course about the first half of this story, the part that took place ten years ago). Not that I wasn't expecting it: when I'd heard about the recovery of the Islands on 2nd April, I knew that if my bad luck had made my military service coincide with our only war in a hundred years it wasn't just to give me a fright. For a few days I toyed with the idea of dressing up as a Chola and decamping to Bolivia on the Estrella del Norte; only half-heartedly, because I knew my fear and inertia would win the day, so to save time I put the books and notes for my programming degree under the bed (I'd only started the week before) and got down to the only thing I knew how to in these situations: waiting. I remember that night well because I was stroking Ana's naked back (still unused to the miracle), when her skin began to flicker in electric blue flashes and, peering through the blinds, I saw them get out. It would have been around eleven at night and I tore it open in front of them in my T-shirt and underpants. I was to present myself at 0600, and when I'd finished reading, they stood there staring; for several seconds I wondered if they were waiting for a tip.

'You'd better be there or we'll come looking for you and you won't get off so lightly then,' spat a titch with a Chinese moustache, and the three of them turned and left like the Three Wise Men to carry on the distribution, every draft promising a pair of ill-fitting old army boots, a FAL with a bent barrel, a dented helmet without a strap in every little pair of shoes that nobody had left outside, their gifts to receive. Ana rang home to say she was staying the night at a friend's house, while I tried unsuccessfully to explain to my mum but couldn't make her understand or even stop smiling; she told me to wrap up warm and send a postcard (I think she thought that I was off to England for a computing course and, humouring her as I always end up doing, I found myself telling her not to worry, it's summer over there) and not to forget to write to my father (whom I'd never even met). That night was the first time that Ana, softened by the filmic romanticism of the situation ('This could be our last night together'), let me go down on her, and we lay there hugging, wide awake and barely talking, till the time came. At about three in the morning we took the bus to Retiro, then the coach to the regiment, which was out in La Plata, and it wasn't till the belly of the plane, in the darkness and the deafening roar (quite a relief, because nobody felt like looking at each other or talking), that I realised I still had her smell on me, impregnated on my chin and eyebrows, and almost intoxicating under all ten fingernails. The perfume of her cunt stayed with me the whole war: it was enough to catch a faint trace of it flowering unexpectedly amid a thousand others for the whole unbearable reality to vanish like mist, and for me to return to her arms and my bedroom, which shone with colours more vivid than the ones in the Van Gogh painting.

What the war stole from me, greedy for a bit of woman amid the stench of all those men (over 10,000 variations on a theme) it gave back to me with a deceptive composite smell, the substitution so gradual that I went from one to the other without realising: the smell of peat, wood, helicopter fuel, scorched meat, damp wool, the wind blowing from the sea, the collective fear macerating for weeks in the mud of the foxholes, the whiff of gunpowder in the morning air after every bombardment simulated the original so successfully that, two years later, when I caught it again on a woman, of whom all I remember was her smell (I never saw Ana again), I was paralysed, naked, on all fours above her, feeling the weight of the uniform and rucksack on my body, and under my hands and knees the slimy mud and sharp rocks, because all I could smell was the Islands. I could almost smell them now, perched tremulous as a butterfly on the reflection of my nose in the bus mirror. The driver looked at me out of the corner of his eye, puffing now and then on his cigarette despite the 'No Smoking' sign opposite the Malvinas sticker in the mirror. It can't have been his, he was too young to be a veteran; to think that not so long ago we were still the boys of war. Once or twice during the journey I raised my trembling fingers (from the cobblestones) to remember her scent, pursuing the fleeting trace beneath the cheap perfume of the soap I'd used the night before to shower when I'd got home; but it was so faint that I found it difficult to decide whether it was her smell or just the memory of it.

When I spoke to Tomás about it once, he nodded gravely – as if he'd been doing nothing but ponder the question for years – then pinched his tattoo to join the two Islands across the far north of the strait: the contour had barely altered, but there was no doubt that I was now looking at a perfect female sex, complete with half-open lips and a few unwaxed hairs on belly and thighs. 'Get it now?' he said, letting go of the fold of skin and breaking the spell. 'What do you want them to smell of? And they ask us why we want to go back.'

That must have been why in the Islands having a girlfriend was a matter of life and death: we, the lucky ones, felt like part of an exclusive club where we could meet and talk about them, write them letters and share the delight of receiving them, although no one could conceal their initial panic on disembowelling the envelope and skipping the first few lines to make sure we weren't being dumped, sigh and smile, and go back to the beginning, and only then start reading as you should. We weren't fussy: sometimes it was enough to have necked once with them at the cinema; we didn't even need them to like us that much. If the war turned any old cross-eyed, knock-kneed Aldonza into a Dulcinea, it was because in each of us nested the magical terror that only the ones who had a girlfriend waiting would make it back home. Though no letter of hers ever reached me, I have proof that Ana did wait for me; she apparently even came to visit me a couple of times. But I didn't recognise her. At least, that's what I was told several months later by one of the male nurses at the Campo de Mayo hospital, without sparing me the suggestion that he'd taken advantage of what I couldn't. One of the first things I did when I was discharged was to look for her. I remembered she lived in Floresta, I even had a mental picture of the front of her house: a white thing encrusted with porous stones that looked like a meringue pudding, but I couldn't remember the address. Three days running I scoured the neighbourhood street by street, first E to W, then S to N, my steps tracing its grid until I'd exhausted it, but I couldn't find it. I approached lots of people to ask them, but most of them fled: my hair hadn't grown back yet and the scar must still have been very visible. And, of course, God knows what I said to them. Even now, walking down the street, I sometimes imagine I'm going to bump into her, although my fear of not recognising her increases with every passing year. In all probability she'll be an amorphous lump with sagging tits, a kid attached to either hand and another in the oven; when I walk briskly past her with head bowed, as is my wont, it'll be she who stops me and looks at me smiling hesitantly. Felipe, is that you? Don't you remember me? After all, if she went to see me at the hospital and recognised me, she'd have to recognise me now. I've hardly changed.

Some lost their girlfriends before coming back and, if the letters reached them, they were unlucky enough to find out while they were over there, where they were least prepared to deal with it. Others found them still waiting, but it was they who didn't return, their hearts and pricks buried thousands of kilometres away. Even the ones who married them on their return and are still with them today, and tell their children about their war exploits, sometimes dream in deepest night of a bed as broad as the sea and, stretching out one hand in their dreams across the strait to stroke that perfect outline, now lost for ever, they awaken to find only the softness of that warm flesh that destiny has tried to console them with. How could those simple girls from the neighbourhood or school, sometimes barely groped at a dance or beneath a burnt-out lamp post, compete with the Islands? As the letters arrived – or didn't – from the mainland, or when we were defeated by the effort of reconstructing a face and body in that jealous and ruthless land, we gradually realised we were surrendering them in return for a greater love. But we didn't realise just how far we'd come till that day at the end of May, when, after an unusually quiet night, we left our tents and foxholes to find the desolate terrain wrapped in an endless veil of white. The first snow had fallen, thick and spongy, from east to west the whole night, covering the craters and caves and rocks and open-air bogs, the skeletons of the disembowelled machines, and the streets and roofs of the distant town; covering too – as we found out much later – the still steaming and devastated Goose Green, a few hours earlier the scene of the longest and bloodiest battle of the war). Seeing what had become of our lives since, many years later a few of us would recall that day when the Islands had worn white for us and understood what they'd been trying to tell us: that it was more serious than we thought, more final and defining; that we were married to them.

Before I got off the bus, I removed my Ramones and Metallica badges, which with the long hair allowed me to pass for a rocker (people still can't get used to this war veteran thing) and replaced them with the Malvinas badges I had in my jacket pocket. 'God bless you, son!' exclaimed Hugo's mum when she opened the door, although you could see from her face that she hadn't the foggiest who I was. Inside were more uniforms than a parade, and only the presence of wives and girlfriends and children chasing each other with toy guns between their parents' legs lent a touch of colour to the olive green monochrome of the scene. Hugo lived with his mum, a devoted daughter, widow and mother of soldiers, in a dinky half-floor apartment at the junction of French and Uriburu whose décor had evidently been dictated by her son's whims. There wasn't a centimetre of wall that wasn't covered by maps of the Islands, campaign photos, portraits of comrades-in-arms from 601 Commando Company, weapons of war or hunting or collector's pieces, certificates and diplomas accrediting courses at home and in Panama, decorations received in Tucumán and the Malvinas, animal heads so ill-treated by moths and the sun (the most recent must have been ten years old) that they looked not hunted but nicked with a saw one night from the Natural Science Museum; 105-mm mortar and cannon shells on the floor, wrapped in rosaries and prints of the Virgin; model ships and planes hanging from the ceiling or on shelves, assembled and painted with the inexhaustible patience of the crippled. At the centre of this sanctuary and its offerings reigned First Lieutenant (HD) Hugo Carcasa on his wheeled throne, his heavy boar's head turning weightily every so often on his gigantic torso like the turret of a tank.

'Javier! Brother!' he greeted me when I approached him and, after a few minutes of smiling politely at his questions about someone else's life, I negotiated the six pairs of army boots that surrounded him and headed for a table where I could see a few bottles of white sticking out. Cornered, I stuck to my guns and waited for a familiar face, but only managed to catch a glimpse of Verraco captivating an audience of four with his video victories. He didn't call me over, so I imagined he was spreading the word that he'd designed it himself.

By my third glass without ice I'd started to feel the heat and took off my jacket. Hugo's mum offered to take it Huguito's room, but I said don't, I'll take it myself. There were two single beds separated by a narrow corridor, and beneath the hills of great coats and capes, I could just make out the embroidery of the Islands, one on each bedspread. Sergio, who'd once stayed over to sleep, told us that Hugo had a box full of little plastic ships and that they'd stayed up reconstructing the war's naval manœuvres, with Hugo barking the orders and jumping on his bed like a monkey, and Sergio crawling around on all fours executing them. As I was on my way out, something familiar poking out from under the bed around Puerto Howard caught my eye. I squatted down and pushed aside the fringe of the bedspread to check: a box of Christopher products.

'Felipe! Brother!' came a shout, this time getting my name right, as I left the bedroom. It was Sergio, Ignacio and Tomás with a new pair of army boots for Hugo's collection. I was truly happy to see them; they were the company I'd come for after all. After sending Tamerlán the complete list by e-mail and sorting out my fees over the phone, I'd spent the rest of the day in a state of profound malaise, incapable of resting or relaxing or looking forward to the still inconceivable engorgement of my bank account. Not even the infallible Web had brought me the usual solace; I'd had to log off when I caught myself typing with my eyes full of tears and a painful knot in my throat. The joint I'd smoked had made me worse and, after a half-hearted lunch, I curled up on the bed to sleep, unsuccessfully. Spending so much time in contact with the outside world must have thrown you off balance, I told myself to avoid further distress; it'll take a few days to readapt, it's always the same. Company's addictive, you know that; pretend you're in detox and let go a little bit at a time. You'll be back to normal in a week.

Sunk in thought at the bottom of my glass, I jumped when I saw it fill with red; Ignacio was slapping me effusively on the back (he gets bolder when he's had a few) and we drank to the tenth anniversary. I'm a bit hard on them, I thought to myself as I watched them passing the bottle round and grabbing handfuls of Wotsits and saluting every retired officer without so much as a glance. I laugh privately at their crazy plans and the faithfulness of their obsessions; yet they'd been the ones who'd come to get me and dig me out of the hole I'd been dumped in on my return, kept me company and looked after me till I was well enough to look after myself. If it hadn't been for them, instead of this one, I'd now be at one of those birthday parties in the Borda where the birthday boy doesn't have the coordination to blow straight and the male nurse has to puff the candles out.

Hugo's mum came in to general applause with a large, steaming bowl containing the main dish, a meat-chicken-and-fish concoction of her own: 'Three Forces Pie'. It was cut by a helpful sergeant who took a sabre from the wall (laughter from the congregation), and the women helped to serve it. The first plate was for her adored son, and was accompanied by a kiss on the forehead. Approaching with my empty plate, I joined Tomás, Sergio and Ignacio, who were waiting with cheerful resignation at the end of the mess queue. My growing irritation, induced by the wine and one of my headaches looming over the horizon, now spilled over towards them too; however hard I tried, I couldn't forgive them for always talking about the war as some longer, more exciting version of a school-leavers' trip, for getting to stay in the town while we were marched off to the mountain, for being the ones who were with me now. You weren't the ones, I mentally reproached them, whose bodies clung to mine in the wordless fear of the belly of the plane; we didn't jump out together in the last light, running and shouting and taking advantage of the roar of the rotor blades to ask each other at the tops of our voices 'Is this Malvinas? Are we in Malvinas?' because no one had told us, and only when we crossed the town and saw all the traffic signs on the other side of the road did those who still insisted we were in Ushuaia finally fall silent. It was dark when we began to skirt the bay, without dinner, our summer uniforms soaked by the outrageous icy wind, newly torn from the creature comforts of civilian life and suddenly laden with twenty-three kilos of gear; no sooner were the last lights behind us than we began to dump everything and the embankment became so clogged with tents, boxes of ammunition, drums of drinking water and provisions that you could only walk down the middle of the road: we'd just arrived and we already looked like an army in retreat. The NCOs tripped and stumbled in the dark, shouting Who dropped this drum whose is this ammunition if I catch him I'll shoot him here and now you bastards we're at war, and us killing ourselves with muffled laugher and Carlitos saying Brother are we off to a bad start. The three of us had done our obligatory service together – and the day before Carlitos on the phone We're fucked Rubén and I have already been called up see you in the regiment. No one knew the lieutenant: he was from the Chaco, his name was Chanino and he had less idea of what was going on than we did. Intimidated because we were from Buenos Aires, quicker, cleverer and whiter than he was, he gave orders like someone apologising, and was so courteous that we got quite fond of him and sometimes even pretended to obey him so he wouldn't feel bad, like when the sarge ordered him to make us dig ourselves in facing east on a crag of solid rock,

'With picks if need be.' What picks, you prick? There aren't any! hissed Carlitos, Chanino shushing him in a panic. Luckily we were pretty well hidden from the sergeant by the rocks, so as soon as he disappeared, we moved a few metres down and pitched our tents at the edge of a cliff face that seemed to face east, or north: without compass or maps or a single glimpse of the sun, opinions varied. Rubén turned to Chanino, who 'should know about these things, being a country boy'; the corporal looked pensively at the sky for some time (Carlitos: 'Armadillos fly north in the winter; the most reliable compass you can find.'), licked a finger to test the direction of the wind (it was blowing so hard he could have tested it by throwing bowling balls in the air) and suggested south, so we decided to dig where the ground looked softest and hope for the best. The only thing that mattered was to defend ourselves against that wind, and we drove in the posts and weighted down the flapping tarpaulins with piles of stones to stop them smacking the shit out of us. At the foot of the wall, so that we could dive out of the tents if we needed to, we began to dig ourselves in properly, using the articulated shovels we'd been provided with. Mine came out champion, lasting almost half an hour before all I was left holding was the handle; my mates had resigned themselves a while back to digging with just the blades or their helmets, sometimes just their boots. We eventually managed to make a shallow hollow about sixty centimetres deep in which, squatting and crouching, we could just keep our heads below ground. There was barely enough room for the four of us in there, shuffling our bums like broody hens: it looked more like a rhea's nest than a foxhole, but to us it felt impregnable. We spent most of our time in the tent though: we pulled two sheets of plywood off a shed in Moody Brook, and put our sleeping bags and waterproof ponchos on top: the water ran underneath and we managed to keep ourselves as near to dry as possible. Anyway, we all slept in a heap to keep warm, our civvies beneath our uniforms, with two lots of summer gear over them, three pairs of socks . . . The two hot meals a day brought up from the mess at the foot of the hill would have helped us bear the chill if they hadn't been so watery and cold by the time they reached our area. Only when the meals went down to one a day – and that a thin broth from the top of the pot (the contents of the bottom went to the officers) – did we organise ourselves and pay a visit to Moody Brook or the town on the nick. It had taken us eight hours to climb the mountain, but with the help of the wind we could get down in thirty minutes; it blew so hard you only had to open your jacket like Dracula and jump off the crags and down you floated, the way you do down stairs in a dream. The first time, a few pesos to the guard (cash was still worth something in those days) bought us admission to Ali Baba's cave: boxes of food from floor to ceiling, wall to wall, avenues, side streets, alleyways, roundabouts of food, which we explored with eyes popping and broad grins on our faces; that day we ate rice and corned beef with tomato purée and peas and *bread*; we cleaned the pot (an empty yam jelly tin) and then ate the slices of jelly and smoked two packets of Chesterfield between the four of us. It must have been five in the afternoon before we finished: the wind had begun to quieten down and, lighting one cigarette with another to save our lighter, we threw ourselves on the levellest rocks or the grass swept into cow-licks by the ferocious wind and watched the lights coming on one by one down there in the town, all signs of military occupation dissolving in the distance. In every house a thin plume of smoke rose from the chimney – a miracle: a day without wind – against the ultramarine of the sky and the first stars, and we all fell silent, the homesickness so strong we didn't dare look at each other, each of us privately knitting memories of the life they'd left behind, or dreaming of being down there in the town: a mug of cocoa in their tummy, an armchair and a lamp, a pipe, a dog, a crackling hearth and their slippered feet, warm and dry, almost touching it. Right then I never imagined that, of all the group, I'd be the one for whom the dream would come true. They came for me the following morning: they needed someone to listen to the BBC and translate the news and eventually – should they manage to intercept anything – the communications of the English squadron now taking position around the Islands. They were the best two weeks of the campaign: snuggled between the radio and hearth of a requisitioned house, a steaming mug of tea and English biscuits, I spent nearly the whole time watching the raindrops slide down the window, the wind rattle the panes, the watery sunlight that sometimes bathed my legs. Every couple of hours I'd grab the typewriter and hammer out a summary of the information and take it next door, where the communications people were based. I had hot baths, I shaved with shaving foam, I got a winter uniform, I washed my underwear, and I ate desperately, systematically, devoting several hours a day to it. That was where I met Ignacio, Sergio and Tomás, who were on guard duty outside and would sneak in once in a while to thaw out, have a hot cup of tea and a chat. My luck held till the day the English landed at San Carlos, when, for sticking to the facts and translating the information correctly, I got a mouthful for a full fifteen minutes from some crazed lieutenant about being a traitor and a turncoat, and was sent back to the mountain with severe warnings of what might happen if I divulged the false rumours that the enemy were spreading as part of their psychological warfare. With several hours' walk ahead of me and no one to set the pace, I started back happier than I'd imagined, anticipating a joyful reunion with my mates and convinced by my full belly and well-rested body that life on the mountain wasn't so bad after all, taking it for granted that I'd find everything more or less as I'd left it. As I walked, I began to see how things had changed.

The landscape was different, unrecognisable, and I almost lost my way several times. The open country was a no-man's-land: not even the sheep had stayed, and the only thing recognisable in the fog was the occasional cry of a gull. I passed the twisted, burnt-out wreck of a plane – impossible to say if it was one of ours or theirs. Normally people started to appear near the first mountain but now there was no one in sight, no one for kilometres, and yet I could feel dozens of hidden eyes watching me. There were craters everywhere, huge holes where the rocks had exploded out across the grass and peat, broken mouths full of water and mud, excoriations and scars, openings surrounded by refuse, like the mouths of vizcacha burrows, from which, now and then, a pair of fleeting eyes would peep out, then disappear again. The first ones I spotted were three soldiers who didn't fit in their foxhole, their torsos sticking out and waving their arms like creatures anchored to the seabed.

'Oy, mate, got any grub?'

'Come over here, chubby, and we'll scoff you!'

'Food! Food!'

I shook my bowed head at them and began to run, the way I used to as a boy on my way home with Ma's groceries and the gang on the corner used to chase me. I wanted to reach the safety of our position as soon as possible and set off around the hill as fast as I could, running whenever I found myself out in the open, hiding among the rocks from God knows what, because the English planes didn't come out in the rain and the naval bombardment used to stop during the daytime. All the old landmarks had been blown to the point of indistinction, but I preferred to find my own way than approach one of the positions and ask, because, between the rain and the fog and the rumours of Gurkha commandos, some kid from the Class of '63, his brain strained like a rubber band to breaking point, might finally lose it and start taking pot-shots in the fog till he was out of ammunition. Someone shouted something at one point: it might have been halt or a greeting or more demands for food, but by then they all sounded like animals leaping through the fog from cave to cave, alerting others of the in-truder's presence.

Night was falling (the day had been murkier than water from a floorcloth) by the time I reached the first crags of my mountain.

'Felipe! Felix the Cat! It's you!'

He hugged me before I saw him. Only by his voice did I recognise the soiled and shapeless bulk smelling of old dog on a rainy day as my friend Carlitos. The other faces I found by firelight, albeit so black, emaciated and bearded that I had dif-ficulty recognising them: Chanino by his smile, Rubén by his red Independiente scarf (now brown) poking out of the neck of his jacket, the two Cordobans from the neighbouring position by the FAP they always lugged around. There was someone new too, a little guy with frightened eyes who looked at me as if he'd been sitting in my chair while I was away and now expected me to kick him off: but they'd gone on digging in my absence, and the foxhole was now a deep cave with room for all of us, including him. He'd turned up one day, asking for something to eat, and couldn't say which company or regiment he was from. He was a '63 – you could see it in his eyes – and had apparently fled after being mistreated or picked on by some officer; changing position was the nearest thing to deserting you could hope for on these shitty Islands. There had been a debate at first about whether to keep him (they could have been court-martialled, and then there wasn't enough food to go round), but they adopted him as a mascot after Carlos forced the vote, and as he didn't say a word or have any identification, he was nicknamed 'Hijitus'.

They filled me in as we tended the ephemeral little fire like over-protective mothers, shielding it from the wind with our bodies and ponchos, feeding the weak beatings of its tepid heart with wet twigs and peat. They'd killed a cow a week ago and there were still a few bones left with bits of hide stuck to them to warm up in the embers (grabbing them with your hands and feeling them through your gloves warmed you up more than whatever scraps you could tear off). Apart from the wind, all you could hear was the gnawing of tooth on bone and, now and again, the sound of thunder from the coast, invariably preceded by a sequence of powder-flashes lighting up the layer of clouds that hung from the sky like the belly of a dead animal.

It was that night, before I became one with them and their daily routine, that I saw what, not the war, but the interminable wait for it had turned us into: a tribe of savages or cavemen, monkeys or – this was harder to accept – tramps. So this was the lesson we were here to learn; this was what we'd been brought so far for: this, our true initiation. Squatting in a circle around a dismembered corpse, the flames lighting the soiled faces as they chewed phlegmatically, the fingers with their black nails sticking out of open gloves, tearing off strips of meat and carrying them to the mouths, sometimes growling over the ownership of a bone, sometimes sharing the almost non-existent. Now and then one would disappear into the mouth of its lair and come back carrying some damp peat, or water in a halved skull that, laid beside the flame, turned out to be just a tin hat. The clan of youngsters, expelled from the safety of the herd by the dominant males, trying to survive till their time came; taking refuge from the rain or hurricane-force winds, or the dread voice of the lord of thunder, which now sank us every night into the most innocent of panics as we ran in circles or dug with the fire raining from the sky; or organising ourselves in the mornings to go on sorties and hunt or gather whatever happened to be lying around; every other day we'd go and check the rubbish tip in the town, but in the last few weeks nothing edible had been thrown away; once on our way back, with nothing to show for our efforts, we passed Moody Brook and checked the pile of empty pots, a bit of stew had been spilled on the ground, and Carlitos and Rubén had grabbed a spoon without thinking and tucked in, dirt and all, beckoning me to join them; I still had some reserves from my time in the town, and I looked away in disgust (they didn't even notice), but two days later I found myself hungering after that food; or if we'd collected anything worthwhile, spending our evenings bartering with neighbouring clans (food, batteries, helicopter fuel, clothes, empty tin cans, dry peat; everything had a value, except money). The vision haunted me throughout that first night's vigil till the following morning when, perched on the highest rocks of the prehistoric landscape, I watched the first occupants of the neighbouring caves come out, numb with cold, covered in any old rags, cloth, bits of tent, threads or patches they had to hand, and tying themselves up like parcels with the guy ropes of lost or unused tents. Coughing clouds of smoke in the grey dawn, shaking their boots to feel their toes, trying to piss with their pricks barely peeping out of their flies, blowing on the eye of the fire that had slumbered all night under clods of peat, breaking the ice in the puddles for water. I got a few matés: a Coke can for a gourd filled with the same yerba from three days ago, sipped through an empty biro, one end wrapped in gauze. The houses of the Kelpers, and their chimneys, and their teas with scones and strawberry jam were now a world away, one less and less of memory and more of dream; yet, despite everything, I felt a calm, a peace, because I knew that, come what may, I had to be here; this was my place and these were my friends; my passage through the town had only been a truce and now I could pick my fate up where I'd left it.

I soon adapted. The morning mist had turned to monotonous drizzle by midday and rain by nightfall. It rained for three days and three nights, a persistent sleet whipped up by demented gusts that stuffed it down your neck, up your wrists, into your ears; the peat became as waterlogged as washing in to soak, and the mud became soft and slimy, sticking to your boots and clothes like a second skin. The water that fell from the sodden, sagging canvas of the tents filled the ditch in less than half an hour and the four rifles slept at the bottom for a night until Chanino stuck legs, arms and head below the freezing water to fish them out. By the time it had stopped, my fleeting advantage of dry clothing, clean body and full stomach had vanished as if it had never existed and I was one of them again. I don't think we ever recovered from that rain: three days without a minute's sleep, weeping because we couldn't feel our hands or feet, the five of us eating what I'd brought from the town in my pockets: two tins of corned beef, three Namur nougats, a packet of uncooked rice soaked in rain-water. We sang at first: Carlitos and I songs by Charly and Spinetta, Rubén cumbia and tropical, Chanino zambas and chamamés that brought tears to his eyes. Once we'd exhausted the repertoire, we tried telling jokes, but nobody laughed, so we sat there in silence, filling up with the water and the mud, the level slowly rising past our chests, throats, noses, eyes . . . Every minute was spent thinking I can't, I can't stand another minute, and by repeating the mantra, you reached the next, then all sixty minutes of an hour, the hours of a day and the night and another day, without any relief other than the moments of exhaustion and almost delirium when we hallucinated the layer of clouds opening to let the first feeble shaft of sunlight through or four soldiers approaching, dragging over a pot of steaming stew.

It stopped one noon, just as we'd got used to the idea that there was no world but this; we peeked out to see the first light-blue patches of sky, shivering out of control in the icy wind, which soon revealed a pallid aluminium sun, the faded smile of God dosing out His mercy with a dropper. From the other tents and foxholes these dripping scarecrows also emerged, turning like sunflowers to face the light and warmth. Clumsily at first, coming out of our lethargy, we undid our leashes, got rid of our heavy jackets like recently flayed hides, tore off the layers of clothing till we were nearly stark naked, jumping and hitting each other so that the cold wouldn't kill us, wringing out our clothes (one at each end, putting our whole bodyweight into it). Getting out of our sodden clothes wasn't enough; we needed to open our bones lengthwise and dry out our marrow in the sun. Carlitos and one of the Cordobans managed to get hold of a drum of fuel and, ignoring the ban, we lit a pyre of peat and ran around it, drying or at least warming the clothing we'd put back on, dancing like dervishes, our ghostly faces lit up by the flames.

> *Happy birthday to you,*
> *Happy birthday to you,*
> *Happy birthday, First Lieutenant Hugo Carcasa HD,*
> *Happy birthday to you!*

Radiant as a bride, holding the majestic cake aloft in both hands, her face lit by the flickering flame of the ten candles, Hugo's mother processed towards the altar where her son awaited her, rocking impatiently back and forth, his hands clenched on the arms of the chair. She laid it at his feet – correction: hips – and held it there for a few seconds for everyone to admire. She'd really pushed the boat out, it being the tenth anniversary and all: shored up by a steep slope of meringue and surrounded by a blue sea of hundreds and thousands, the green Islands shone resplendent. Numerous little plastic soldiers ran valiantly among the long candles that pointed at the ceiling like anti-aircraft batteries, and, like a nose-diving Harrier, Hugo launched himself at them and blew them out with one big puff. A salvo of applause greeted his feat, but before they could turn on the lights, the candles sputtered back to life. Everyone laughed: Hugo's mother had bought trick ones and, the loving joke on her delighted son apart, we all understood the symbolic intention her gesture entailed. Eventually putting them out with our fingers, we allowed her to turn on the light and arrange them at one side of the tray.

'Now,' said Hugo, cracking the same joke he did every year as a signal to his mother, who held her eager trowel aloft, 'it's time to *dig in* to the Malvinas.'

Everyone laughed and applauded again, and the cake, which beneath the icing turned out to be a common or garden sponge cake (perhaps she'd been trying to imitate the *taste* of the peat too), was passed round. I stood there for a while, my eyes fixed on the ten dead candles piled at one side of the cake, with their charred tips and the remains of icing and hundreds and thousands at their bases, and only then did I remember that what Hugo celebrated year in year out was not his birthday, but the day when, landing on the wrong beach, his dinghy brushed against one of our own mines and the bow blew into the air along with both his legs, slicing them off at the knee. Now, his mouth full of cake, he was shouting, once again we shall leave our mark on the earth of Malvinas, trample the English underfoot and recover everything they took from us; as if, by merely the changing colour of the map, the earth could reverse its natural tendency to putrefaction and give him back the legs that it had kept intact as hostages in some secure facility: all that would be needed was his return in order to recover them and march them to victory. Perhaps in the razor-wired minefield of his brain he'd come to identify them with the Islands plain and simple, and every night dreamed of awakening one morning to headlines announcing Argentina's recovery of the Malvinas as he threw back the sheets and blankets to find a pair of soft, rosy legs, like those of a newborn babe, instead of the intolerable folded precipice of his pyjamas.

Meanwhile, the wine had flowed and, one after another, everyone began to sing:

> 'Neath your blanket of mists
> We shall not forget you,
> The Malvinas, Argentina's . . .

I barely moved my lips, discreetly altering the second line to 'We shall all', and I too jumped up and down when we finished and started up with 'Fee-fi-fo-fum, whoever isn't jumping is an Englishman.' The whole apartment shook to the rhythmic tramping of thirty pairs of army boots; the women jumped too, clacking their heels, and the children screamed with joy (save for three or four – the littlest – who sheltered under a table, crying), and even Hugo bounced up and down on his chair like a ball with arms. Brandishing a bottle of national Scotch that had materialised from somewhere, arms locked in a square, Verraco and my three friends leaped highest of all, making the line of glasses dance on the white tablecloth. It's been a long time, I thought, and at that moment the doorbell rang. It was the downstairs neighbour, in dressing gown and slippers.

'Now listen here, this is outrageous; one of our pictures came down, what do you mean jumping about like this and . . .'

He was so wound up that he said it all in one breath before

he noticed the thirty-odd pairs of eyes trained on him like rifles. When he turned round, the one who'd opened the door
to him, an air-arm lieutenant I didn't recognise, had shut the
door behind him. Hugo advanced ominously along the corridor that opened in the crowd, spinning the wheels of his chair
like the drum of a revolver.

'And where are you from?'

'I, I . . .' he stammered, 'I'm your new downstairs neighbour.'

'Ah, the new guy. You lot change as fast as chicks do.
Didn't the guy before tell you?'

'I . . . it's just that I arrived in the country not long ago
with my family, and then the children, it's late . . .'

'Of course, you arrived not long ago and you're already
ordering us around. If you don't like life here, why didn't you
stay in . . . Where the fuck are you lot from?'

'From . . . real near, Valparaíso.'

Now all he needs to say is that his wife's English, I thought,
holding my head. In the silence you could hear the hiccups of
one of the children, who was still crying.

'Real near. And for you lot real near will soon be Mendoza,
right? Then La Pampa. And Tandil. And you'll decide this apartment's yours too any moment, won't you?' And, as if spitting
out a piece of chewing gum, he added: 'Chilean. You're sure
you're Chilean? You know what we do to Chileans, here?'

The neighbour scanned the wall of stony faces and moss-
coloured uniforms. Bulging, his eyes ran across the collection
of weapons on the wall and returned to Hugo's.

'So you decide. Let's see, lads.'

As before, but this time without his feet leaving the floor, standing to attention as if for the National Anthem, they began to sing '*Whoever isn't jumping's a Chilean,*' without taking their eyes off the neighbour, who turned this way and that for some hint what to do. He lifted one foot, his slipper hanging at an angle, shuffled a bit, then jumping out of his slippers, took his first hop. Two or three more and he was flying, knees to chest, his faded brown dressing gown flapping about him like the wings of a duck trying to take off from a pond. Unmoved, without the slightest twitch to suggest he was doing it right, the others went on:

'*Whoever isn't jumping's a Chilean! Whoever isn't jumping's a Chilean!*'

A few years ago, I thought, I'd have been singing along. As long as it wasn't me doing the jumping. Taking advantage of Verraco and my friends being occupied, I nabbed the Scotch, poured myself a double and downed it in one without ice or water.

'Feel better now you've been nationalised? Hop it, or next time we'll be the ones dropping in on you.' They sent him packing with a slammed door and, sure enough, the conversation turned to Chilean designs on our territory, Chilean tactical support of England during the war, Chilean plans to replace Argentina in the Malvinas–Mainland link, laying long-term plans for the Islands to become sovereign Chilean territory. Tomás and the others nodded as Verraco explained. They looked so at ease with each other . . . They'd waved me over a couple of times, come here, be friends, but I'd just raised my wine or whisky glass and sent them an indulgent smile and they'd given up without much interest.

'You off already?' crowed Ignacio when he saw me with my jacket.

'Deserter! Deserter!' hooted Sergio through cupped hands.

Verraco stood in front of me, crushing my chest with his open palm. Beneath his obscene moustache he was grinning happily.

'Don't you know the penalty for leaving your post in wartime, soldier? Well, Company?'

'Death!' they chorused.

'Can't hear you! Louder!'

'Death!' they roared.

I smiled, said all right lads and threw my jacket over a chair. Verraco slapped me hard on the back, making sure it hurt, and went off with two other officers who'd called him over. He was spoiling for a scrap, no doubt as payback for the video game (perhaps I had gone a mite over the top). I downed two glasses of wine, one after the other, and resigned myself to listening yet again to Hugo's exploits, as narrated by himself – provided his mother was at hand to hear.

'Malvinas? Malvinas? In that terrain, with that technology, you had to be queer or crippled not to win the war. The terrain of the Islands is just like England, they know it better than we do. But you know what? I'd like to have seen the English with their radar and their night-vision goggles and their body-warmers in the Tucumán jungle. I'd love to have seen them there! Day after day without a glimpse of the sun, advancing across unknown terrain almost blind, every second the possibility of an ambush by a faceless enemy without uniform or flag! The English wouldn't have lasted two months in Tucumán! Like the Americans in Vietnam! They'd have lasted less than the guerrillas in Tucumán! Did I ever tell you about the time in Acheral when we got them with the helicopter? The whole Che Guevara bit was nothing next to that!'

Had I come to listen to this all over again? I sidled away and began looking at the campaign photos to see if there was anyone I recognised; but officers apparently don't hang photos of privates on their walls. But I did come across the white mare, a sight that filled me with joy; I'd forgotten all about her. We found her waiting for us at the foot of the hill the night we arrived, watching with docile, incurious eyes the inferior beings writhing under the weight of their rucksacks and dropping at her feet; and when, raising our eyes towards the hill now the size of Mount Aconcagua, Rubén asked the sergeant Sir Sergeant Sir shall we start loading up the horse, Sir Sergeant Sir had him doing frog-jumps for half an hour for being a dickhead and a pussy: dogs are for burden, horses are for riding, he yelled at him, when the mare suddenly lifted her tail and aimed three or four steaming balls into his bag. From that day on we declared her our official mascot, named her Pampera and brought her grass, especially Carlitos, who grew very fond of her and walked her with the reins whenever he could, peripatetically unravelling philosophical reflections that the mare would nod to: 'Yes indeed, old girl. We've been screwed, we're prisoners before we start. If the war had been with Chile, you and me would be in California by now,' he told her, 'but unless you fancy swimming there, we're never getting out. What kind of war is it if we can't even *fantasise* about deserting?'

Rumours were something else we found to entertain ourselves with. There were rumours about the negotiations: the United Nations had intervened and declared the Islands a nature reserve; the Pope had intervened and declared them an earthly paradise. The Peruvian fleet, the fourth largest fishing fleet on the planet (or the third, or the second, depending how hungry we were that day) was on its way, laden with tuna to solve the food shortage. Catastrophe rumours started flying as soon as the English fleet surrounded the Islands: from the nuclear missiles that would wipe us out in seconds (the Kelpers had had fallout shelters for a while now) to the Gurkhas who could advance underground like moles and eviscerate soldiers in their foxholes, sucking up their entrails and leaving just the empty shells behind them. Then up popped an NCO with an optimistic version to balance things out: the English didn't have our main ally, 'Admiral Winter'! Psychologically worn out by the long wait on their ships, into which they'd been forced by Argentina's resistance, they'd reverted to aberrant practices such as the inordinate consumption of alcohol and drugs, sodomy and continual masturbation. They don't know what they're fighting for; they're mercenaries, unemployed kids picked up on the streets to defend their country for a scrap of stale bread! (Carlitos: the poor English, going crazy in their narrow bunks, suffocated by the heating, nothing to do all day but watch videos and play ping-pong, while we're here having a great old time in the open air, playing cards every night and guitar sessions till dawn.) Another one that kept us entertained for several days was about English commandos strolling about the Islands in Argentinian uniforms, speaking perfect Spanish. If you wanted to unmask them, you had to ask them something that only an Argentinian could answer. We had a lot of fun with that: two days chasing each other around the mountain, shouting 'Famous football teams!' ('Boca, River, Independiente, Huracán, Racing, San Lorenzo . . .') 'Argentinian inventions!'

('buses, biros, dulce de leche, barbed wire, finger-prints . . .') 'Ingredients of a parrillada!' ('sausage, black pudding, chitterlings, sweetbreads, kidneys, brains, udder . . .'). We once cornered an NCO who'd lost his way and tested him at gunpoint.

'Flora and fauna of the Pampean region!'

'Colour of the Pink House!'

'First article of the National Constitution!'

'Main crops of the Antarctic!'

Our man almost started crying and only when he got one right ('pink') did we lower our FALs and let him go.

The other rumours touched on events on the mainland. By the end of May, prevented from landing on the Islands by our dauntless air force, the English had landed on the shores of Buenos Aires, where the citizens had driven them back by pouring boiling oil and water on them from the rooftops. And one day a lad from C Company ran up the mountain panting that they'd bombed the city. 'Bid to assassinate Galtieri, bombing of Pink House. Noon yesterday, city centre full of people. Nine English bombers, cloudy sky. Dive-bombing, one after another. Pink House roof collapses, civil servants dragging themselves across the glass, dead colleagues and chunks of masonry blown across the square littered with exploded cars, uprooted trees, scattered corpses, mutilated survivors begging for help. A scatter bomb hits a full bus driving down Paseo Colón, ripping one side clean off like a sardine tin and spilling a horrific cargo of dead and wounded onto the street. Galtieri manages to escape through secret tunnels down to the river and takes refuge in a gunboat that whisks him away north, so many dead in the square they have to be lined up for the ambulances to get through.' The images were so vivid, the details so minute, that no one doubted the bombardment had in fact taken place, and there were scenes of weeping and despair until a lieutenant popped up and slapped us out of our hysteria: 'Listen, you dick-brains! Do you honestly think we're going to leave the capital defenceless? No foreign power has or ever will bomb our Republic's Capital! That's our job!' We weren't completely convinced, but then someone picked up the radio and it was playing folk, tango and national rock all the time – no word of any catastrophe – so we breathed a sigh of relief: the English were only bombing *us*. By then they were doing so for a few hours a night to 'soften us up', as they say. In the town you slept fairly peacefully because you had the shield of the Kelpers, but on the mountainside there was nothing but sheep, and they fired on us with the patience of a housewife tenderising milanesas with a meat hammer. The blows smashed our heads against the walls of our cave, hurled us one on top of the other, sucked us down or pulled us out, as if, chewing us up, the foxhole couldn't decide whether to spit or swallow. Carlitos swore at his folks for abandoning him here, Hijitus covered his ears and we had to tear his hands away and force him to shout to stop his eardrums bursting; Chanino wept and begged us not to make a noise, as if the bombs had ears, Toto, the skinnier of the two Cordobans, who'd muscled into our foxhole because it was deeper, shouted with the impotent fury of a child to get the fat boy off him, but never explained what he meant. I was revisited by the terror of the dinosaur from the ends of the earth. As a child, it never entered my mind till I laid my head on the pillow: then one, and another, I could hear its tread, thundering its way to my ears across the thousands of kilometres that separated us. Nothing could stop the enormous legs making the earth shake (one alone could squash a car); yet, however hard I tried to stay calm and tell myself they were far away and would take years to get here, the same voice that told me I was right would add yes, its steps sound a long way off but tonight it's closer than last night, tomorrow closer than today, and one day they will reach you. But they didn't; they eventually disappeared the night I realised they were the beatings of my own heart; I never remembered them again, till now, when, drowned by the same beating, waiting for the first bomb to fall in the frozen calm of the night, I realised I'd been deceiving myself, that the dinosaur had gone on advancing all this time and finally arrived, only to find the frightened little boy of fifteen years ago.

My reactions came in layers, like one birthday present wrapping another and another and another: the skin outside becoming a carapace, fancying itself less vulnerable, the throat itself threatening to drown us, tongue rigid, wooden, stopping us talking; beneath it, the pointless alarm bells of adrenaline, maddening in the immobility and impotence of mere prayer: let the bomb fall a little further off, not bury us alive, let it hit some other hole; deeper inside, the flesh and viscera twisted in pain, head throbbing, the nausea churning furiously in an empty stomach; even deeper, all the hatreds, guilts, regrets and accusations of imagination and memory, the furious search for real or invented culprits, the urge to die, the abject promises to a God that, if he ever looked at us, would be zapping to another channel in His boredom – and finally, the long-awaited tiny present at the core: a fear so pure and perfect that a single drop falling on the surface of the soul annulled your identity and conquered your fear of death, because at the point of impact you stopped praying 'I don't want to die' to beg the last, tiny alms of existence: 'Yes, I do, I do, but not here. Not like this.'

Some time later the English must have occupied the surrounding hills, because the land bombardments began, no longer to a timetable, and we never went out other than to find something to eat, follow some order (ever fewer) or take a dump. We began to become part of the foxhole, we couldn't imagine being separated from it, like those worms that spend their whole lives in tubes at the bottom of the sea. Our human form had morphed into that indiscriminate crust: hunger, cold and fear had secreted a second skin, a callus of leather, canvas and metal that covered us like a carapace. Would we be able to shed it when this was over, and would there be a new pink skin beneath, the kicking and wailing of a newborn? Or would it all be one and, on tearing it off ourselves, we'd be left like a skinned sheep, our eyes bulging, twitching in our death throes? If this was the crust of a pupa spending the winter underground, what kind of insect would emerge come the spring? What metamorphosis might await the larvæ that writhed in the open wounds of the earth? We'd almost stopped talking to each other; we passed each other like shadows, our fixed gazes passing through the bodies, always focused far beyond, at the point where parallels meet. A sergeant whom we'd christened Wally Walrus once came looking for men to haul some boxes of ammunition (they weighed as much as a man at the start of the war; now, as much as two) and Rubén left the foxhole to beg him to kill him: kneeling on the ground he shouted at him 'Come on, you fat prick, kill me, you fat queen, eh? eh?' and the fat slob, eyes like blind moons, backing away going 'No, no, go back to your post, soldier' with both hands, and Rubén advancing on his knees 'You fat fuck, you're no use even for that, kill me, kill me,' and in the end the sarge turned and legged it, his big arse wobbling, and Rubén goes 'Why won't they kill me?' and there's Carlitos dragging himself over to him and dragging him back into the foxhole. He was always the strongest. We all leaned on him and the weight threatened to knock him over: his shoulders sagged and his skin hung off him like wet clothes from the pegs of his cheekbones. But it was he who had the best chance of coming through alive and in one piece, he who had most right to survive. And he probably would have, had the English been the only threat, had Verraco not been there too. I swore at myself mentally for having come, for having had so much to drink, for having believed that the accumulated fright of the last few days could be neutralised by the fright that surrounded me. Now I was condemned to remember.

The day had dawned clear, perfect for sheep-hunting, and after opening our eyes to the first ray of sun (I don't say waking up, because by that stage we never slept at night) we got up, making the frost that soldered our ponchos to the ground crunch. Carlos and I, the only ones with anything left, went, or rather fell, down the mountain. The sheep turned out to be wilier than usual (or we were clumsier from our exhaustion) because, zigzagging, it dodged something like five shots and when it finally went down, it did so on the inside of what looked very much like a minefield. The beast thrashed about there, trying to stand up, and I grabbed Carlos by the arm, but he wriggled free and, treading as if he were crossing a rotten wooden bridge, approached till he could reach one outstretched leg. When he was at my side, carrying the sheep on his shoulders, I reeled back when I saw the thick, black blood oozing from its nostrils like blackberry jam. We'd killed so many by then (sometimes with a knife) that it seemed ridiculous at this stage to be shocked, yet the sadness that flooded through me when I saw the hanging head of the dead sheep, coupled with the oppressive sense of foreboding pouring from the rarefied blue sky and the stillness of the yellow grass, was so strong that it tore the sobs from my chest.

'Leave it,' I think I said, softly, and then ludicrously: 'Let's go home.'

Carlitos had started walking, the sheep slung over his shoulders.

'What?' he shouted to me without turning round.

'Let's go home,' I repeated, even more softly, and then I followed him.

He lugged it all the way by himself, the last stretch in his arms like a baby, covered with his jacket to hide it from view (Wally Walrus, especially, seized all the packages and rations that reached us whenever he could; the bastard was getting *fat* on this war). The sheep kicked and writhed when Chanino and Rubén skewered it to skin it, and we realised that it had only been half-dead all along. 'That's why I didn't want to give it to you, it was still nice and warm,' smiled Carlitos. Judging by the light, it must have been about four in the afternoon, and we hadn't had anything to eat since midday the day before yesterday; only with difficulty, due to the pain in my hands, did I approach the recently opened sheep and with the others plunged my fingers into the warmth of its guts. We stood there like that for a while, without saying a word or looking at each other, until the numbness abated and we could feel our fingers again. When he got his breath back, Carlitos got up to go and see Hijitus. He was lying at the bottom of the foxhole, wrapped in wet canvas, and had gone dead. Not even the smell of the lamb beginning to roast brought any reaction.

He was the only one. The two Cordobans had emerged from their cave, sniffing the air like hairy armadillos, and came to sit on some rocks that marked the boundary of our territory. After a while four blokes from the forward positions also came over: the wind was blowing their way. They sat down to wait. But our unwelcome guest dropped in just as the first slices (we carved it up as it roasted) were ready to eat. Like a lion lolling nonchalantly towards a pack of hunting dogs, Verraco arrived with his faithful Wally Walrus on a leash.

'Sergeant, confiscate that animal illegally slaughtered by your troops.'

Had the bastard at least been as hungry as we were, it would have been understandable: the survival of the fittest. But no: his boots were polished and his body generously filled out his warm, dry uniform. No, the fucker was just passing through and had caught a whiff that had whetted his appetite (that word, here!) before dinner and came over and said it's mine and 'Fetch' to Wally Walrus.

'No,' said Carlitos and took the safety off his FAL.

Wally Walrus realised immediately what was going on, and his whiskers and chubby, stubbly cheeks started trembling. But Verraco was slow to cotton on.

'Not ready yet?' he asked innocently, scrutinising the barely seared meat. 'Not quite.'

'The food's ours. We hunted it. We're past expecting anything from you, but at least let us eat in peace.'

'In peace? In peace?' replied Verraco, beginning to smile

as his pupils narrowed like a cat's, his whole face taking on an expression of intense happiness. 'What do you mean leave you in peace, soldier, when we're at war? Let's see Corporal, Sergeant, and you two, seize the conscript and disarm him for me. We're going to teach him some discipline.'

'You two.' Rubén and me. No one moved . . . Verraco whipped out his standard issue. He picked Rubén and jammed it into his neck.

'Corporal . . .'

Chanino began to weep. He looked at Carlitos, pleading. Wally Walrus had taken out his gun too but was pointing it at the ground. Carlitos lowered the FAL then dropped it. It fell and broke a puddle of ice with the butt.

Everything happened very fast after that. Verraco, savouring every syllable as if it were a mouthful of the lamb he was looking forward to, ordered Carlitos to strip. As Carlitos didn't move a muscle to obey, but just stared straight ahead (if only looks *could* kill), he ordered Wally Walrus and Chanino to do it. It took them some time because they had to peel him layer by layer, till he was left standing in his underpants at the side of a pile of clothes taller than he was.

'Those too,' said Verraco, pointing at the dead-mouse-coloured underpants, and it was Wally Walrus who had to approach and pull them down with two fingers, exaggeratedly averting his gaze to show he was a proper little macho man and wasn't interested in what lay underneath. For a moment I felt more like shooting *him*.

There was no birthday party any more, no apartment, no city around me, there was nothing but that glint of death in the island's hills, Verraco's grinning face, both eyebrows raised in mockery of the sergeant, Carlitos as stiff as a stake, hugging his body to keep it from shivering, my finger clenched on the trigger of my FAL, Rubén huddled on the ground, Chanino trying to avoid my gaze, the hungry dogs sniffing about on the fringes at a safe distance.

This is the one, this one and no other, I thought as I watched him laughing and tossing peanuts down his craw, washing them down with a beer and wiping the foam from his moustache with the back of his hand, this is the one who made Wally Walrus, Chanino and Rubén stretch Carlos out over the rocks and frozen puddles, tie his wrists and ankles to the tent pegs, nearly tearing his bones from their joints; but, even though it all flashes before my eyes again, I can't remember what it was I was doing. I suppose I must have obeyed and pulled on the ropes too, jamming my foot against the rocks, pulled with all my might, for that fraction of a second that condemns me for the whole of eternity, hating Carlitos for making us do this, hating his arm for resisting my tugs. Or maybe I wriggled out of it somehow, just played dumb, blended invisibly into the landscape, losing density and clarity as I have so many times since, managed to disappear – a survival trick – in front of everyone instead of picking up my weapon and pulling the trigger to cleanse the world of the beast that had now become part of my life for ever. It would have been easy: he wasn't looking at me; he couldn't see me as he paced smugly around the taut X in the mud that was my friend; but if I did it – if I even thought it – I'd become visible again, and then they'd come for *me*, then they'd do it to *me*. There was a moment when I thought I was for it: when Verraco was squatting beside Carlitos' face (who kept his eyes fixed on the sky), gazing pensively at him as if pondering what was needed to make his work perfect; but the moment passed. Straightening up again, he shouted something to Wally Walrus, who grabbed Chanino by the arm and dragged him towards the forward positions. After a while – it could have been ten minutes or an hour – they came back carrying a heavy machine between the two of them and put it down by Carlitos' body. At the first contact of the two bare wires he writhed and contracted like a worm pierced by the tip of a hook, and every one of his shrieks hung there above the trenches in the windless air, repeating themselves in echoes until relieved by the next. Five or six times until a jab of the wires brought nothing but blood. Minutes passed, captain and sergeant effing and blinding what the fuck's wrong, checking parts, until Verraco got up and wiped the grease off his hands on a few handfuls of grass. 'Looks like the generator's fucked. Just as I was getting warmed up. Ah well, you'll have to get by without radar till it's repaired. Sergeant, double the guard; no one's to sleep tonight. Let's see if you lot learn your lesson.' But he wasn't done, and without taking his eyes off the body prostrated at his feet, he asked the sergeant something and repeated it twice before the other man understood.

'Pliers! Those things for pulling out nails! Pliers! What am I talking in, English?'

The sergeant passed the order to Chanino who, like a sleepwalker, went to rifle through his things.

'Oh, and in the meantime keep an eye on the barbecue, soldier, because we'll be here for a while and I'm not about to go hungry,' he added, and while Rubén readjusted the lamb skewered on the two stakes, a replica of Carlitos' naked body in miniature, Chanino approached with a pair of black pliers (it was me who'd nicked them from the town, waving them proudly, the day I got back) and placed them in Verraco's open hand. Gripping them carefully, as if about to dismantle a delicate piece of machinery, Verraco bit Carlitos' upper lip with the tip and began pulling upwards, forcing him to lift his head till his chin touched his chest, and then held it there. In a few minutes the pain of the posture became intolerable, and his whole body arched upwards, tugging at the tent pegs till they bent, but he couldn't lower his head, which hung with his full bodyweight from the lip that Verraco held in his grip. And Verraco smiled smugly at the touch of originality he'd added to that most traditional of Argentinian tortures.

'Sometimes you have to think before you speak,' he whispered into his ear, almost intimately. 'An open mouth is the best way to get hooked, soldier,' he said to him, giving him little tugs with the pliers as if the fish had taken the bait. He was starting to feel uncomfortable, and with the sergeant busy turning the lamb, he ordered Chanino to take over.

'All right, corporal, hold this for me.'

He handed him the pliers and got up, pulling a pained face as he straightened his knees. Once he was on his feet, he began to harangue us.

'Look and learn, soldiers. Did you think that all you had to do to defend the Fatherland was shoot guns like they do in the movies? Learn how to win the war, then we'll teach the English too. All manuals and maps and blackboards the English are. Think they know it all. But we,' he said, beating his chest to emphasise the fact he didn't include us, 'are veterans of a war they've never seen in the textbooks. Let's see what all that theory's for when they're tied up down here! Just give me some old bed-springs and a well-charged battery, and they'll see how the war here is over in two shocks of a lamb's tail! They come on all macho with their body-warmers and night-vision goggles and tracer ammunition, but dripping wet and starkers on a set of bed-springs even the toughest of them will loosen their bowels, you'll see! That sorts the men from the boys! Face to face! Without all their fucking clobber! Let's see what they do with their night-sights when their balls are sputtering like a couple of fried eggs! They can stick 'em up their arse and then tell us what they see,' he yelled, cracking up at his own joke, without realising that the weeping Chanino, whose arm shook uncontrollably, had lowered his iron grip until Carlitos' neck was resting on a tussock of grass. The harangue had only whetted Verraco's appetite, and he made for the lamb, cut off a rib with his knife, and started tearing and slicing at it gaucho-style.

'Come over here, Sergeant. I apologise I can't offer you the glass of red this deserves, or even salt, criminal,' he said with his mouth full of lamb, and having stripped a rib, he'd toss it away and the men in the neighbouring positions would crane to see where it had landed, while Verraco smacked his lips and licked his fingers. It was the same face I saw now and the same hatred that I felt. What had I been doing with it all these years? What parts of my life had I had to amputate to stop them rubbing against this hatred, what percentage of my body had I turned into dead meat, the only kind that can store it without writhing in agony? 'You killed him,' I mouthed. 'You killed him,' I said, not knowing if I was saying it to Verraco or to myself.

'Felipe, are you feeling all right, mate?' Tomás came over to cover me.

'What's going on?' asked Verraco.

'Nothing,' he said jovially. 'Reckon he's had one too many.' Indulgent laughter. 'Soldier . . .'

'*He* killed him,' I said, louder now, and tried to stand up. Several hands, it must have been Sergio and Ignacio, forced me into a chair.

'No wonder the first game you gave me was all over the place,' said Verraco, coming my way. 'Been at the bottle, have we? You should see me now. I finished the last level yesterday.'

'You killed him. You bastard.'

Again, he took his time understanding. And when he did, he raised his eyes to heaven and huffed in annoyance.

'No, not today. Not another one.' He turned to his comrades-in-arms to recruit their understanding: 'Boys, wasn't this all supposed to be over?' Then he turned to me and said, 'Well? Who?'

'He doesn't know what he's saying, Lieutenant Colonel Sir . . .'

'It was you. It was you. You had him out there all night, staked out in the frost! For stealing food because you lot were starving us to death! Say it was you!'

'Listen, mate, if I had to remember every Tom, Dick and Harry I've had staked out . . .'

'Carlos, his name was Carlos Feuer! He was from La Plata, he was twenty-three years old, he was about to graduate in psychology!'

'Terrible memory for names. If I could just put a face to the name.'

'He's dead, you sick fuck!'

'You bet,' he said with a smile. 'Otherwise, it definitely wasn't me.'

My three friends had to drag me to the door while Verraco, also being restrained, yelled at me insanely, his red neck exploding with veins in the tatters of shirt I'd left him. Hugo, who'd wheeled in on Verraco's behalf, tried to grab me, shouting, 'If I had my legs, if I had my legs,' and in the ensuing brawl I knocked him over, chair and all, on the leftovers of the Three Forces Pie. In the confusion my friends managed to drag me out and shove me into the lift. Back on the street Tomás slammed me against a wall and held me there until I stopped kicking.

'Are you mad? You just beat up Lieutenant Colonel Verraco! You know what can happen to us?'

'I don't care! I'll kill him!'

Sergio stepped in.

'If they come down, you're a dead man. Get a taxi,' he said to the other two. Ignacio ran towards the avenue.

'Listen, Felipe,' said Tomás, slamming me against the wall again. 'I don't care what happened up there with Verraco. We're all on the same side now. Him, you, us.'

'Not me,' I said, feeling as if my throat was being torn apart.

'You too. Look, we all know Verraco's a bastard. But we need him. Otherwise, who's going to take us back?'

'We have to rise above personal grudges,' chimed in Sergio. 'Can't you see that if we fight with each other we make it easy for the English?'

'What English? What English!' I yelled at him.

'The English,' repeated Tomás, and there was something in his tone that silenced me: it was the same one I'd heard upstairs, and his eyes were small and cold like Verraco's. 'You know who the English are better than us. You speak very good English, don't you?'

'Listen,' said Sergio, grabbing Tomás by the shoulder to loosen his arm, which was starting to squeeze too hard, 'go home. Or maybe not today. We'll try and sort out this fucking mess. We'll tell Verraco you made a mistake, you were drunk, the shrapnel in your head makes you hallucinate stuff. I'm sure he'll forgive you in the end, but you have to give it time, right?'

I nodded. And it was true. I did fucking understand. Tomás let go of me.

'Like he says,' he said. 'I guess you deserve another chance. But I'd be watching out if I were you.'

'Felipe,' Sergio went on, 'we're so close. Don't go and ruin it over something like this. It's the future that matters, not the past. Our home awaits us in the future. When we get there, none of this will matter. Only the chosen get to go back to the Islands. Don't fail us now.'

'You'd better go. We'll be waiting for you. After all,' said Tomás, patting me on the cheek, 'where else can you go? We're your family.' He was in the middle of the street by now and his breath steamed in the cold air under the street light. I realised I was wearing a T-shirt: my jacket was still upstairs, as spoils of war for the enemy. A pair of yellow headlights with a little red dot floating above them bobbled towards me over the cobblestones. Sergio pointed:

'Your taxi's here.'

Chapter 10
EL DORADO

I'd given him my home address, but as we drove around Retiro it was the last place I felt like going. Rather than cure me of my need for company as I'd hoped, Hugo's party had awoken a greater eagerness. I desperately needed some contact, but where to find it at two in the morning and in such a condition? 'Take Córdoba and I'll direct you,' I told him; if only I could find a little something for the dizziness, to restore a bit of lucidity, I prayed as we started to cross Avenida 9 de Julio. We hadn't got halfway when Archimedes leaped out of the bath and began to dance about naked in my brain.

'Yrigoyen and Cerrito!'

A heaving crowd was jammed like a champagne cork into the entrance of El Dorado and I found it hard to get close enough for one of the bouncers to spot me and, his arms acting as power shovels, open a channel for me to get in.

'Wotcha, Felipe?' Slap on the neck, kiss on the cheek, tongue out at the people shouting 'Queue-jumper!' and I was in, the rubbing of bodies upholstered in leather rayon moiré silk cotton quilting velvet sackcloth denim studs feathers vinyl rubber polyester linen cellophane wool lace nylon wire suede sequins organza lamé returning the heat to my cold, numb body in minutes. Behind the river of disconcerted first-timers who, overflowing its banks, milled among the columns and eddied around the bar, and the regulars who would float over them every now and then like ducks on water, rose the dancing swell of raised arms and heads, most in 3D specs. Just then I caught the profile of Cayetano over the human dunes, as imperturbable and distinguished as the head of a dromedary, and launched myself after him before the wake of his passing closed behind him.

'Is Moisés here?'

He raised his thick, black eyebrows over his shaven head, bluish with the first growth of hair.

'Saw him in the kitchen, I think. But listen here, darling, I've de-fi-nite-ly given up, so I don't even want to find out if he's got any or not,' he delivered his Saturday speech and, with an elegant swish of the hand, whisked me a gin-and-tonic off the tray, which his other arm held aloft like the stalk of some aquatic plant.

On my way into the kitchen I bumped into Horacio, who was balancing a giraffe of dirty glasses and had thrown togeth-er an outfit of Flecha trainers (the ones with the jagged toecaps and diamond-shapes on the soles), fishnet stockings, hot pants and blue sports top.

'What's it like today?' I took a sip, wrinkling my nose, from my glass.

He pulled a face:

'A downer. Cristian's singing some slowies. But then James is performing something with . . . oh, I forget. With that one.' He pointed to a group talking enthusiastically over the table and passing round a bottle of Chandon Extra Brut. I made a gesture of interrogation that, in this place, could only mean one thing.

'There,' he pointed out

Silent, a full glass in his right hand, a smoking cigarette in his left, dark glasses and broad-brimmed black hat covering what his beard couldn't conceal, leaning on the sink, which brimmed with towers of unwashed glasses, stood Moisés.

'At this time of night?' he replied, looking straight ahead like a blind man, barely moving his lips. 'Acid, only thing,' he said and pointed to the dance floor. We went out.

He held out a tab wrapped in cellophane for me to examine. I don't know if it was the drink or the combination of the darkness, black light and stroboscopic flashes, but what I saw on the tiny cardboard square was the outline of the Islands.

'What is it?' I asked, looking at him in terror.

'Butterfly. Why?'

'No, nothing.' My heart pulsed in my neck. 'How much?'

'Twenty-five.'

'Deal.'

Anything, begged my mind, to split my head in four and chuck it in a corner so I'd forget to pick it up on my way out. I couldn't stand any more reality on an empty brain.

To kill time before it took effect I borrowed a pair of 3D specs from three girls dancing on their own by the VIP curtains, and started moving my head up and down to see how everything became disjointed like a Cubist painting, flattening the disco into a mosaic of hanging fabrics, flat-flamed candles, faceted mouldings and sweating blue-and-red faces. I danced for a while with a braless brunette in a fishnet top, but as she was wearing specs too I didn't know whether she was smiling invitingly or because I looked so ridiculous, and then she was gone. I downed my drink and got myself another, then checked my watch to see how much time had gone by. Shouldn't it have begun by now? It wouldn't be the first time I'd been fobbed off with a dud. My fears were allayed when one of the eddies on the dance floor made me brush up against a circle of ten, shouting 'Freak out! Freak out!' and flipping in perfect acid-choreographed synch. I snatched a couple of tokes of Jamaican sense in the DJ's booth and ran downstairs (it felt like I was on a slide) to dance to a Prince number that had just started. They don't exist, they don't exist any more, dance and shake them all out, all those inconceivable monsters of the last week, that knot of parasites that invaded your body, get them out, now that *was* a ride on the ghost train. My relief wilted a little, however, when I sensed something odd about the two identical-looking chubbies in black and white dancing next to me and, giving them a proper look, I saw they'd grown these long beaks, and I let out a cackle. A colour stirred within me, like a cloud of Indian ink in water and, expanding my chest as it went, it climbed in a long stalk to the holes of my head and unfurled like a flower above the heads of the Corybants. It had begun. I danced to four or five numbers, delving deeper and deeper into the giant intestine that coiled and writhed in its erratic disco peristalsis, until I suddenly started to feel dizzy, as if I were in a ship on choppy seas. For all the holes in my tank-top, the superheated atmosphere, electric with the evaporated sweat and genital lubricants in a permanent state of high excitement, was beginning to suffocate me. Just like that taxi driver who was in Malvinas. I couldn't adapt to the climate and sought relief under the fan that hung like a giant bat high in one corner. In the roaring wind, a pouting girl in a black PVC top and matching shorts that dug into her labia minora was drying her hair, raking her fingers through it again and again.

'How's it hanging?'

'There are fleas,' she answered me. We both stared in silence for a second at the fake Persian carpet.

'Can't see them.'

'One bit me twice: once on the waist, once between my legs. Here, feel. Weird, isn't it,' she replied to my probing hand, which lingered incredulous over the two lumps.

'It was doing its best to dance the lambada with you.'

She didn't get it. Hanging from her hand was a small fake white leopard-skin purse, which gleamed phosphorescent in the black light. I asked her if I could stroke it.

'Geroff! What's wrong with you?' She switched hands, probably thinking I was going to snatch it, or to protect me from its feline zipper teeth. There were animals. A good moth, the size of a Boeing, piloted by two little Japanese girls wrapped in cellophane, was fighting to save the city from a clumsy, rubbery dinosaur that spat blowtorch fire from its drooling jaws. Thousands of Japanese fled in horror before the wind wafting from the moth's wings, ripping off rooftops and toppling trees onto pagodas in its eagerness to drag the monster by the tail, airlift it Chinook-style away from the city and drop it into the open mouth of a volcano. I wept tears of grief for the moth in its death throes on the plain, moribund and seared by the flames – the tragic lot of all moths – expelling its death rattle and an egg from which would emerge the next saviour of humanity, and when the screen turned to a dead-mouse grey,

I looked around in confusion, without recognising the place. I touched my face and it poured over my fingers, my mouth had widened as if stretched either side with hooked forefingers: I caught my reflection in the mirror and I had zebra teeth, striated and yellow, and pink gums two centimetres high. I felt like running, leaving my grimace behind. How had this happened? I was so happy a few minutes ago . . . I sat down and, once seated, I committed the irreversible mistake of closing my eyes and the darkness was ripped up into slaughterhouse colours as the butcher carved and tossed the bleeding cuts on the counter. I felt hot and cold at the same time, like a deep-frozen chicken in the sun.

'You feeling alright?'

A hand on my shoulder. Human eyes before mine.

'No,' I said with some difficulty. 'Far from fine.'

'Little butterfly fluttering about in your head perhaps?'

'No,' I replied, 'but the egg . . . the egg.'

'Moisés bought a batch of five thousand past their sell-by. Everybody's flipping. You're Felipe, aren't you? Love your clothes. Who designed them for you, Beto Bora?'

'No. Mario Menéndez.'

He laughed with delight and more teeth than usual. I shook my head as if I were mixing a cocktail in it. The floor was crawling with fleas as big as chihuahuas running between people's legs.

'There are fleas,' I pointed out, because no one seemed to realise.

'Don't tell me. We have the place fumigated once a week.'

I clicked my fingers to call one, but it merely growled at me, its hair standing on end, sheltering between two black army boots. A Gurkha! I sensed in horror, but when I looked up all I found was a teenager in a virginal white dress. I could see her cunt through the material. It smiled at me.

'I want to play hopscotch,' I told my companion. He laughed again, rakishly. We weren't communicating. My fault, as usual.

'Drink?'

'Water. Cold.'

I ran an ice cube over my forehead till it hurt. 'What am I doing?' I managed to form the thought in the seconds of cold. 'What is this?' But I was no longer alone. A hand was holding mine, an arm curling around my back. 'Glad you're looking after me,' I stammered. I was naked and cold, everything was bad and fine at the same time. 'I've been hurt,' I entreated, 'they broke my . . .'

'Heart?'

'Arse. I mean my soul.'

'A woman?' He smiled at me, longing to know, his blue eyes and black-tipped lashes as wide as a doll's. I mattered to him. I shook my head vehemently.

'A man. Lots of men. Women aren't so bad, even if they do give birth to penguins. You know what I mean?'

'Yes, of course. Me too, the other day I had a fight with Marcelo . . .'

He understood me, and suddenly I had words, I wasn't alone: confessing before the crystalline altar of the night, I told him everything and as I spoke it all became so clear, at last I could see the light, life in neon; years of groping in the dark and now my eyes were reaching the secret cogs and gears that moved the world; I'd been advancing unawares towards them, down a long, dark corridor and, at the end, a light barely filtered through the cracks and at the touch of my magical hands the doors of perception were flung wide and there on the other side were Bugs Bunny and Woody Woodpecker in the colours of childhood, with a big mirror globe at the centre; understanding dawned on me in Technicolor and for the first time in my life I could talk about my dead friends and those who'd killed them, about a year as blank as a vampire's mirror, about the subterranean existence of a mole, scenting the presence of other tunnellers but never ever tunnelling into one, so much grief stored . . .

He must have been talking to me for a while, but only now did the words penetrate the painted paper walls and reach me:

'All right! But you're taking things too far too! You're a pain! You give me all that dense stuff, you . . . bore me! I come to you full of champagne sparkle and you pop all my bubbles, like . . . like . . . You think I spent hours getting myself all glammed up to listen to your blubbing? I can do that in jeans and trainers! You get me down . . . with your dead men and your wars and your diseases and . . . your disappeared! You sound like an old man! And me . . . and me . . . You just don't get it, do you? What the fuck do you come here for?' He held up his hands and waved them about in exasperation: 'The night . . . the night wasn't made for *this*.'

He walked away, or I did. Meanwhile, on the dance floor, all that Cristian's slowies were missing was a piano accompaniment from Freddy Krueger; he was singing a duet with Rosamel Araya, who, a good head shorter, looked every year less and less like Clark Gable and more and more like Charles

Bronson. Hanging from the chain so as not to fall into the open white maw of the toilet, I calmed its thirst with a hot, thin, yellow jet. 'SAY NO TO LIFE AND YES TO DRUGS', someone had written on the wall, and I pushed my way between three guys spasmodically pinching their noses in front of the mirror. Staggering in the sand beneath an implacable sun, I walked over to the black prophet.

'You ripped me off,' I spat at him. 'You boosted me a bad tab.'

'Don't talk so loud,' he pronounced calmly, exhaling dragon smoke.

'Bad tab,' I repeated defiantly. 'It didn't turn me into a butterfly. Get it? It's still me. See? Me! Where's the butterfly?'

'You're flipping. Piss off or I'm calling Timoteo.'

'It was the Islands, wasn't it. You lied to me. It was the Islands.'

He made a faint gesture over my head. A Michelin Man began to advance towards us. I plunged into the thicket of arms and legs, advancing with difficulty for lack of a machete, and reached the bar, where I ordered a glass of cold water. Despite the blond wig, the succulent cleavage and the glass of champagne in his hand, I had no trouble recognising him as he leaned beside me.

'Hi, how are you, what a coincidence,' I ventured in a friendly tone, happy to be with someone I knew.

'No coincidence. Daddy sent his boys to look for you and I was getting bored at home, so I asked them to bring me along. Look, there's Freddy.'

I looked. Beneath the mirror-ball he was raising his arms and repeatedly licking his moustache, while James's snaking fingers discreetly stroked his sweating, naked chest inside his open shirt. Freddy responded to my frightened glance like a laser sensor and winked at me. Owl-like, I turned my head through 180°. The white-haired heavy was chatting with the bouncer at the only entrance, the space between the two narrower than between the bars of a railing. I'd have to start a fire, or something, if I wanted to get out that way.

'Found all the nosey parkers yet?' he asked.

'Yeah. The lot.' He had weasel teeth. 'What are you going to do to them?'

'Don't you know what happens to people who see what they shouldn't?'

I nodded.

'Lady Godiva,' I muttered. He let out a cackle, shaking his long hair, as blonde as wheat in a shampoo ad.

'It wouldn't be at all difficult to disguise myself now.'

'You have no sense of privacy, you lot.'

'Oh, what,' he laughed nervously. 'You're talking about the other day. You really fell for it! Didn't you realise, you of all people, that it was all just a trick with mirrors? It's an act we put on sometimes, like the turd, to test people. Daddy and I just love it. You looked so hilarious, your eyes popping out, not knowing whether to believe what you were seeing, when all the time we were the ones who were watching you, front-row seats for that poor sod's face of yours,' he reeled off, although his voice went up a tone on the last few words, like a butcher's saw when it hits the bone. 'Well, now you've bored me,' it said, recovering its feminine timbre of control. 'I'm off for a bop. Say hello to my old man.'

He was swallowed up by the compound mollusc of the

dance floor. Several flashes froze it white and I could see him tossing his hair in the wind, rubbing shoulders with James, who was no longer dancing with Freddy but with a grinning skull; nor was the craggy red-nose guarding the San Carlos Strait, down which I charged, emerging into the blinding clarity of first light at the other end, from which not even the 3D specs could protect me. The cold dawn embraced me shivering and, amid the ruins of the city, which had been shelled during our distraction, I searched for one of those black-and-yellow animals that take us home, but found two hands instead, each perched on one of my shoulders like friendly vultures.

Bolívar – Belgrano – El Bajo: I thought they'd turn at the port and take me to the tower, but they carried straight on down Avenida Libertador. Sicked on by the crop of panic, the acid whizzed faster and faster round my bloodstream like Scalextric cars: the rampart of apartments grew skywards, warping into a tunnel over the avenue; the myopic spectacles of the traffic lights nailed me to the centre of the earth with their red eyes, then forced me to run rabbit-like with their green eyes until the next red; cars buzzed around us, looming hugely before us and vanishing into wind at the sides in a video-game race; sitting in front of me the pair of backs and necks bulged by the second, threatening to fill the entire car and smother me. I lunged at the handle and managed to open the door enough to glimpse the ribbon of grey tarmac bristling and buzzing, but a crane seized me by the scruff of the neck and plunged me into the ditch, while the other one locked the doors. I tried to get back to my seat but the man with the white hair turned round, looking for all the world like a clean-shaven Santa Claus, and gifted me a slap on my left ear that left me with a shrill buzzing in my head; and as I couldn't see anything except some tipa branches against the clouds, I spent the rest of the journey hypnotised by that splinter of sky from which the worst thing in the world was about to descend.

We turned off Libertador and drove one or two blocks over some cobbles, down a slope so steep that I was thrown against the front seats, then finally pulled up on the pavement. I heard the crunch of tyres on gravel and, leaning out of the window (this time they let me), instead of encountering the wide open space of the river among whose willows and rubbish heaps I was to be executed, I realised with relief that we were crossing sprawling grounds with trees neater than those in an English landscape garden, heading for some phantasmal Roman temple that flashed its tombstone-white columns (now you see them, now you don't) through the dark foliage.

Sitting on a stone bench so clean that it looked recently carved, isolated by his wooden body from the piercing cold filtering up from the ground, Dr Canal sat reading a book before the imposing Roman façade – so realistic that for a moment I expected to be greeted by Victor Mature standing between the columns in chains and Vaseline.

'Sr Tamerlán is expecting you in the pheasant cage, Sr Félix,' said his talking head, swivelling on the pivot of its neck, the lower jaw rising and falling vertically like an old codger chewing his pap. 'Escort him, Sr Tornero,' he uttered, before sealing the exit for the enervating voice of the stone ventriloquist that supported him on its knee. Using my triceps as a joystick, Sr Tornero manœuvred me around the building towards a huge Victorian cage, almost identical to the condors' cage in the zoo. Before I could determine what was going on inside it, a deafening report blew the leafy calm around my head to pieces, and from the big cage came a flapping, squawking pandemonium of panicking birds crashing into each other and the wire in their directionless flights and hanging there, flapping frantically like live butterflies on pins. Without any consideration for my feet, which were tearing up clods of grass in their urge to flee in the opposite direction, the white-haired man dragged me to the cage door and, shoving me inside, locked it and stood outside on guard.

Pacing about between the potted ficuses and palm trees and gargoyled white-plaster rocks, to which the generations of bird fæces had lent an almost natural appearance, Tamerlán didn't come over to greet me, or give any sign of having noticed my presence. A shotgun rocked in his left hand, but instead of hunting gear he was wearing a slaughterman's plastic apron, spattered with drops of blood like a mac on a rainy day, and yellow wellington boots.

'Hold this for me,' he said, proffering a glass from which I took a tentative sip (Scotch), and inserted several cartridges in the gun. He snapped it shut and, aiming with one hand from less than two metres, emptied both barrels into one of the hanging birds, sending most of its fragile mortal flesh through the wire; what was left on this side was little more than its spirit: a delicate ikebana of pheasant feathers.

'Hunting,' snorted Tamerlán's clenched features, distorted with the contained fury that was released drop by drop with each shot. 'A sport of hypocrites practised unceasingly by my class throughout the centuries. As if it would change anything to pretend the prey stands any chance of escape. Besides, in what forest of the world can you find such a variety of targets?

This cage contains practically every known species of pheasant in the world, or did until just now at least: the Common Pheasant, the Impeyan Pheasant, the Tibetan-Eared Pheasant, the delicate Lady Amherst's Pheasant, the Golden Pheasant, the Silver Pheasant, the Pearly Pheasant, the Diamantine Pheasant, even the extremely rare Great Argus Pheasant, almost impossible to find in captivity and on the verge of extinction in its natural habitat. Watch it go,' he said before turning it into a collage of blood and feathers on the rocks, whose rusted wire frames peeped out of the holes made by the shotgun.

'I wasn't wrong about you, Sr Félix. You're a capable man, you can't conceal it, even if you do try and hide behind that failed hippy disguise. You alone, with your meagre resources, managed what an entire team of professionals couldn't.' He diverted his gaze slightly towards the white-haired thug, who was grinding into the tender lawn a sole accustomed to breaking the resistance of lives more tenacious than a cigarette's. 'Ah well, that's professionals for you. Perhaps your wartime experience hasn't been so unproductive after all. My father valued his military past and was always sorry we'd landed in a country so timid about international wars. Parents, I suppose, always want the best for their children, and sometimes it pains them when they can't get it.'

He'd recovered his composure now, his clenched finger resting loosely on the trigger, his breathing issuing silently from his nose rather than whistling through clenched teeth. And judging by his shining eyes, he seemed to be moved – though it could also have been the effects of the tab on my own.

'There's a problem with the last information you brought us, Sr Félix – or rather two problems: either it's untrue and there's still one name missing from your list; or it's true, and is therefore truer than I'm prepared to tolerate. I have to know your sources. To make myself perfectly clear, I want to know who gave you the information about Captain Arturo Cuervo.'

Suddenly Gloria was walking towards me over the prop-room rocks like the Virgin of Lourdes in her grotto and I started desperately signalling to her to hide, until I realised Tamerlán couldn't see her. For now. I have to keep her invisible to his eyes at all costs, I managed to tell myself in a moment of lucidity. The whole situation had suddenly become deadly serious, more serious than it was a few seconds ago, when all that was in jeopardy was my own life.

'My sources are very indirect,' I began, to buy some time. If at least I hadn't dropped the acid, if it would just abate a little . . .

'Sr Félix, those mediæval slaughtermen out there know tortures that not even the Inquisition dared to implement, and Sr Canal is an expert in highly subtle forms of psychological coaction. It would take them no longer than it would take you to break into a video-club computer. There isn't a scrap of information, however insignificant, nor a corner of your body secret enough to stuff it in, that they can't find with a bit of a rummage.'

Now that he'd calmed down and was speaking so articulately, choosing his words with such care, combining precision with expressive force, he was even more frightening than before.

'Why?' I began to ask.

'He's dead, Sr Félix,' he spat at me like a spitting cobra. 'The man's been dead for almost ten years. Missing in action in

June 1982 to be exact. Just like my Fausto. And now you claim that he – he of all people – has been resurrected from that pile of mud and bones to come for my other son as well?'

He held out a piece of continuous feed just like the first one. His eyes had grown as grey and dark as the sky they reflected. I began to understand something, just a glimpse, and I desperately needed to understand more to keep them away from Gloria. It was all that mattered now. So I read:

> *Where art thou, Fausto? Wretch, what hast thou done?*
> *Damned art thou, Fausto, damned! Despair and die!*
> *Hell calls for right, and with a roaring voice*
> *Says 'Fausto! come! Thine hour is almost come.'*

'Sr Tamerlán, I understand your pain,' I improvised.

'Have you ever been a mother?'

'What?'

'I asked you if you'd ever been a mother.'

'Not that I know of.'

'How *can* you understand then?'

'You're right. I don't.'

'Of course not. I'm not talking to you about any old son, you understand. Sons are ten a penny. *You* might have sons and not realise. You might be *my* son, come to that. So what? Are you going to come to me with demands? Because one night, thirty years ago, instead of coming in the dry, I came in the wet? No! I'm talking about *my* son, my one and only. More mine than the Son of God to God. You don't understand, do you.'

He was pointing both gaping barrels at me. If it goes off, I thought, at least Gloria and the girls will be safe. No, I corrected myself. It's not enough for me to disappear, this time.

I've already ratted them out to him. I have to stay alive to protect them.

'No,' I answered.

'How can the relationship that keeps the world going be so flimsy? How can the whole edifice of civilisation be built on something that may very well have been a mistake? We never truly deceive women because we can never make them believe that their child is someone else's. What comparable weapon do we have to instil in them the terror of the beyond? I was tormented by thoughts like these in the days leading up to my marriage. For two months I kept myself pure – except my arse, which will never be very pure anyway – without touching her – it didn't take much effort; it was worse than stroking a plucked chicken. In the end it was Dr Wigenschaft who helped me find the solution. Dr Wigenschaft had also emigrated from Germany after the war, when he had to interrupt his promising experiments into fertility and inheritance. The ideal thing would have been to clone myself, but even in Germany experiments brought no conclusive results; even less so here, on the edge of the pre-adamite forests. The path we chose was as follows: we waited for the night of greatest fertility, when, after checking her to confirm her virginity, he inseminated her with my recently extracted seed (all before my eyes: the certainty I needed was so absolute that not even in him, a man of trusted loyalty to my father, could I fully trust) and then he closed her up, stitched her like a roll of stuffed pork and, hermetically sealed, we sent her to my house to rest and incubate my heir while we celebrated with a bottle of Ruhr wine and some boys. Two months later, when there were no doubts about the pregnancy, the doctor unstitched her and let her go about her life; she could do it with the Bolivian gardener now if she wanted to: as a sexual possession, her value to me was always less than nil. The months of pregnancy were no less feverish. I could do little more than lie in bed thinking all day, with dreadful dizziness and headaches. I thought and thought and thought, I did nothing but think over those nine months, and at the end of them my head felt bigger than my body, like a fœtus's, floating in space, trailing its tiny doll's body behind it. How, I thought, can the divine substance pass from father to son without being corrupted in the process? How to neutralise the call back to nature that maternity opens the door to generation after generation? Because your problems are just beginning with conception. It may not be some other fellow's, but it *is* hers. That little dribble in the pipette is the full extent of your contribution. Look at her holding her belly and smiling at you. What was the use of two months of wire fences when she had nine to drown with the litres of her circulating blood, with layer after layer of her enfolding female flesh, every last vestige of your evaporated signature? Three times I emptied her of every last drop of her blood and filled her with mine until it came out of her ears. In the meantime I pumped hers into my veins and, though its scarcity and wateriness left me weak and wan for days afterwards, they were the happiest of my life because I could feel my son's blood running through my veins. I even begged Dr Wigenshcaft to join us at the hip like Siamese twins until the moment of birth, and only separate us after the umbilical cord was cut. I only gave in when he explained it might involve a risk to the child. Do you know the theory of the homunculus?'

'Yes.'

'Yes?'

'No.'

'People in the Middle Ages believed that the spermatozoa was a little man, tiny but fully formed, issuing whole from the father, and that the mother was merely the vessel where it grew until it was big enough to join the world. You understand? It was a theory that *worked*, like that of the Sun going round the Earth. They saw the world not as it was but as it should be. And so, after all those centuries, their dreams come true. The homunculus will be the torch that the one and only immortal superman will hand on to himself! He himself will gestate it in his belly; after all, what matures in mud can just as well mature in crystal!

'In the days leading up to the birth I felt ever stronger pains, but I assumed they were hysterical and didn't consult the doctor. On the last night the ambulance that came for her ended up taking me and they had to send another for her. Peritonitis it was, and as everything was performed at Dr Wigenschaft's clinic, they operated on us side by side, a local for me and a general for her: for a moment – the happiest moment of my life and of all mankind – I raised my head to see the blurred vision of my open belly and, suspended above it, the clenched and bleeding figure of my immaculate son. Who has ever been more entitled to call himself a father than I? Only someone who has carried his son in his very own innards all nine months, but that man doesn't exist – yet. One Italian assures me that in five years he'll be able to clone me, implant me with my own embryo and carry the pregnancy through to a happy term. But he may just be a quack; my father always warned me: "Don't repeat our mistakes: never put your arse in the hands of an Italian." Anyway, I digress. But you do follow, don't you?'

No one could follow him where he was going, but I nodded anyway.

'I'm not content to achieve the superman in here, in my head, as Dr Canal sometimes tries to console me. I only hope I live long enough for medicine to bring me all the mutations necessary. If I do achieve it, the boy this time will probably come out just like his father and, though his father may not live to see it, he *would* die a happy man. But why keep dodging death when I know there's a younger, stronger, more passionate version of myself burning to live? Sons . . . should fit like a glove, a glove we don to grasp time – and run it.

'My first desire was for them to bring me my son, to cradle him in my arms, to confirm that he was in every part as perfect as I had conceived him in my mind. Seeing him lifting his little hands, shutting tight his beautiful eyes the colour of cloudless skies, shaking his blonde mane soft as down, my eyes filled with tears, but they were tears of pain. How could I manœuvre him through the obstacles of the next twenty years to prevent him colliding with others while skilfully steering away from me? How to secure in the blood everything the blind eye of genetics cannot hold? Everything that matters passes from father to son, and we're forced by dumb nature to play Chinese Whispers with our most valuable thing. The very concept of education, something so precarious and humiliating! Social insects, with their genetic patterning, are more advanced than us. What's the use of fighting for our freedom when it's going to last so short a time? You might think I'm rebelling against society and its rules, but that isn't true. The present-day order gets by pretty well, though it could do with a little touching up. It's nature itself that's out of joint!' he said, stepping with his unfeeling rubber sole in one of the messes of blood and feathers that decorated the ground. 'Is there nothing but void between us? And how can that dream of the imagination that we call fatherhood leap the abyss instead of navigating the dark streams of the bloodline? The one thought that kept me going during my captivity was that I, or someone who to a great extent was me, was out there to carry on if I never emerged from that pit. Canal was a great help to me in that difficult period, and even more of a help in the other infinitely worse one, following my release. Because if the torture's inside you and you carry it around with you everywhere you go, where can you escape to? My son's blood had clotted in my veins. The son rises up against the father. You understand what that means, don't you? A toenail growing in on itself, digging itself into the flesh that gives it life, is no more painful. And it wasn't his political or ideological motivations, as people were wont to call them in those days, that made his betrayal any less bearable. It wasn't his ideals, it wasn't his adolescent delusions of grandeur (I'd let him put up his Che Guevara poster if that was what he wanted). No. He swapped me for the lowest thing in creation: the cunt of that little whore. His father, more of a father than any father ever has been, for what can be bought new or second-hand on any street corner or any whorehouse! The tarantula leaped on its prey and devoured it in one gulp! They weren't ideas! It was the black blood of woman manifesting itself again despite my best efforts, disfiguring the purity of my creation with its stain! The viper paid dearly for her sin, but the evil was already done! My son began to spread inside me like a cancerous growth, growing arms and legs like polyps: the same betrayal, the cells of my body agitated against me, the profusion of life become death; a child romping through my body as through a garden all his own to destroy.'

He gazed at me as if trying to explain something with his eyes, but when they began to multiply on my retina like the facets of the eyes of an insect, I had to turn away. Being in that cage with him was like being locked in a microwave oven.

'I got him out of the way, sent him to live with relatives in Braunau, my home town in Austria, to get in touch with his roots. Know it? Delightful place. And then to Vienna to study. Besides, the dogs here had taken advantage of their momentary ascendancy over their weakened master and wanted me to hand you over in exchange for having rescued me. They wanted to have you!'

His switch to the second person had been fleeting, but not so fleeting that it hadn't thrown all my senses into turmoil again. He fell silent for some time, the V of one hand slotted under his lower lip, and when he spoke again he picked up the thread of his monologue at another point.

'The guerrilla, I could live with that. I was willing to forgive and forget, and I thought the contact with his roots might have straightened him out. But it hadn't. He comes back and volunteers, for a war, without asking my permission. A losers' war. Pathetic! What was he trying to prove to me? We'd only been together a few months. To Malvinas! As a volunteer!' he said, raising his arms in a gesture of perplexity, and stared at me as if waiting for an answer.

'I was drafted,' I clarified.

Once again Tamerlán's contained anger passed like the

shadow of a cloud across his shifting states of mind, as changeable as the sky when the south-easterly blows.

'Malvinas. That was what I found most bemusing. Why did he do it? To get even? Just to prove to me that such an idiot couldn't be my son?'

'It was a gesture,' I suggested.

'A grimace,' he corrected me, puffing at a pheasant feather stuck to his lip. 'I'd rather he'd stayed a guerrilla. Some of the guerrillas from back then are wealthy and successful today. How many successful ex-combatants from Malvinas do you know?'

I totted them up. Sergio, Tomás, Ignacio, the taxi driver, Hugo, me . . . He was right. It had never occurred to me.

'Actually . . .'

'Not one. It's obvious. Failing in a worthwhile venture like the takeover of a country tempers the spirit for more feasible ambitions. Failing in an utterly pointless venture only produces losers. War? A badly told Argentinian joke.

He was pacing up and down between the cardboard rocks like a king in an opera, hands behind his back, grey wrinkled face turning left and right. Now that there was nothing of the pheasants left but carrion, he'd become the old condor in the cage at the zoo.

'When he got to the Islands, he was assigned to A Company, Fifth Regiment, posted at Puerto Howard, Isla Gran Malvina. Owing to a communications error a fraction of 601 Commando Company was stranded for the whole war at the same place. In charge of that group of men was the newly appointed Major Arturo Cuervo. The idiot! To think I gave him my backing! There wasn't a single idea in his head that I hadn't put there! So I tried to play Pygmalion to the military! My father's naïve ideas! He and his friends wasted the best years of their lives trying to civilise that stupid, uncultured peat! *That's* the real tragedy of Germany! Instead of educating Alexander the Great, Aristotle teaching Galtieri to read! Tragedy repeats itself as farce!' I heard him yell without being able to pay too much attention, for once again the Tetris screen had filled right to the top and as a reward we were moving on to the next, harder, more complex than the last. And the first new pieces were already descending, a slow rain of bricks from the sky.

'Felipe,' I heard all of a sudden, and an unexpected shotgun blast couldn't have made me jump any higher. 'If anyone knows what happened to my son, it's that man. If he's dead, it will be satisfaction enough for me to make sure. But if he's alive, then he *knows*, because whatever it was that happened to my son, *he* did it. He'd been waiting in vain to get even with me for too long to waste the perfect opportunity that fate had dropped in his lap. And if that was him that night in the silver tower, there's no doubting he's the one behind all this. What happened in the Islands was just the first step. Ten years later he's back, looking for checkmate. That's what you're going to do for me, Felipe: find out what happened in the Malvinas ten years ago, or – which amounts to the same thing – that man's whereabouts. Then you can cash in your chips and I'll let you go.'

Without another look at me he began to undo the stiff, plastic apron and picked up the shotgun and box of cartridges he'd put down on one of the pheasants' nests. From where I was standing I caught a glimpse of movement in the darkness behind him, and a pinprick of white light revealed the frightened eye of a pheasant that had managed to save itself from the

holocaust. Don't move, I begged it mentally, just sit there nice
and still for a few more minutes.

'Morning exercise always gives me an appetite. Care for
some breakfast?'

'Pheasant?'

He looked at the blasted paradise around him with something approaching sadness. The wind was carpeting one side of
the cage with floating feathers.

'Only in burgers. It's a weakness I admit to; when I get
like this, I can only wind down by destroying beautiful things.
And, unfortunately, those tend to be the most expensive.'

'I'm not your slave,' I remarked coldly, trying to buy the
pheasant some time. 'I can't be at your beck and call all the
time.'

Tears welled up in his blue eyes. He came over and put one
arm around my shoulder.

'I know. And, believe me, I've never thought of you like
that. That's why I'm taking the liberty of asking you this favour, although of course, as you'll understand, I can't allow
you to refuse. Try to understand me. Try to understand a father's grief. If you get me what I ask, you can have whatever
you like. Remember,' he said winking at me, 'I'm Father Christmas. I don't quite know how to tell you, but in these days we've
shared, I've grown very attached to you . . . Felipe, I hope you
won't be offended if I tell you that I . . . I love you like a son.'

The arm draped over my shoulder bore the whole weight
of the world. The colossi of the Roxy would have collapsed under it like sugar lumps.

'I've even afforded myself the luxury of dreaming, these
sleepless nights . . . What if this unexpected visitor turns out to

be a messenger from heaven instead of hell? Think about it. A whole group disappears without trace in the defiles of the Isla Grande, never to be heard of again; nobody but that friend of yours in the madhouse who left his mind over there for good and brings only his dead meat back. And now ten years on, it turns out the officer who was in charge is alive and well. Isn't there a chance, a one-in-ten-thousand chance, that he wasn't the only one to make it back? My son's body lies in no known grave. What if . . . what if . . .?'

I tried to say something, but, trapped by the rigidity of tongue and palate, the words wouldn't come out. The rigidity also extended down to my pharynx, like a big ball of phlegm and cocaine; any minute now my throat would shut as tight as a sphincter.

'I suppose you've heard the legends too. The Island that never surrendered, the ghost platoon still out there fighting the English, the officer who wouldn't accept the cowardly surrender . . . What was it they called him, Sr Canal?'

Colourless, odourless, noiseless as usual, the supreme bodyguard had approached us, nodding at old Lumpy Nose to take a break.

'Major X,' he informed us.

I tore my tongue from the roof of my mouth like ripping off a plaster.

'Major X doesn't exist,' I managed to say. 'It's just another daft story from Malvinas. A losers' fantasy. Losers like us are always making up stories like that. If they told them all, they'd fill more books than true ones. You won't find anything in that direction. You're wasting your time.'

'I've already wasted ten years.'

'How will I manage? Not everything's inside a computer, you know.'

'You've already shown me – though perhaps not yourself – that you can get by without them. If you don't take care of it, *they*'ll have to do it.' He pointed vaguely in the direction of the grounds, but I understood perfectly well what he was referring to. Those in power are always clear even when being vague. 'They'll start by asking you where you got the information that eluded them; then, they'll go and ask that person, and a third person if need be, leaving their muddy footprints on every doorstep. That's why I prefer you. You're capable of proceeding with delicacy, like saying your rosary, counting off each bead till you reach the cross. That's where I want you to get to. The cross. And if that cross is in the bleeding Islands, that's where you'll have to go to get it.'

He turned his back and took off his apron. The meeting was over, and Canal – who else – was waiting for me outside to finalise details. We walked through the grounds while Canal gave me my instructions. Only the last vestiges of the acid were keeping me up on my feet.

'One last question,' I interrupted when I no longer understood what he was saying. 'Has it never occurred to you that your patient is madder than a box of fucking frogs? He's a spoilt brat who still thinks reality's just another word for your parents. Now he wants to play at doing natural selection. And tomorrow what? Why should I be the one to bear the burden of his frustrated motherhood?'

'The mind needs new structures, Sr Félix,' he began. Cracking jokes to him was like tickling a woolly bear. 'Our current psychic framework is from a primitive stage of the species, but only a few chosen ones have started to go beyond it. Little by little they will build the immaculate crystal and multiply its facets. And in the meantime the masses will go on wallowing in the dark sludge of dreams and the unconscious until extinction puts them out of their misery. The vulnerable, archaic formation based on Œdipus and the sinister triad will become the tar pit of millions. The strong will move on to the next stage: the colonisation of the entire psyche by the conscious mind and the direct line of father to son. The female mutation will disappear, in time, save for a few specimens preserved in zoos and nature reserves.'

We heard a loud whistle and for a moment I looked up, thinking it was God. Tamerlán was beckoning to us.

'Will it be easy for you to find work? I mean, when everyone's perfect and there are no more sick people,' I asked my companion, for the sake of saying something, as we approached the cage.

'Every great athlete needs a trainer. Only with a trainer can they reach perfection. That's my job. I don't look after the sick. They make me sick.'

After the air of the grounds, the smell of gunpowder and scorched flesh was so strong that I'd have turned the clock back ten years if I hadn't closed my eyes. I didn't. With one finger on his lips, Tamerlán was pointing at one of the nests; the scratching of claws on wood could clearly be heard, and the tip of a feather fleetingly emerged like a tongue of flame from the circular entrance. What a shame, I thought; I hoped this one would make it. I assumed Tamerlán would simply shove the barrel of the shotgun into the opening and pull the trigger, but instead he shoved his arm in up to the elbow, like Sylvester looking for Tweety Pie, and groped around till he found what he was looking for. To my surprise, it wasn't the pheasant. Cupped in his hand was a speckled chick, as fluffy as a dandelion clock, a bubble of down barely anchored to the earth by the weight of its trembling little wire feet. It lifted its head, turned it one way, then the other, and went 'Cheep!' as if to express its approval of the world it was seeing for the first time. When I looked up from his hand, Tamerlán was smiling, his two rows of perfect teeth shining on the punished land like a rainbow of covenant.

'See that? Life goes on regardless.'

Chapter 11

CLUB MED BORDA

A barely comprehensible gargle answered the phone, like someone strangling a drainpipe in the dead of night.

'Hullo, Soledad?'

'Ooooooooooo.'

'Malvina?'

'Eeeeeeeees.'

'It's Felipe. Remember me?'

'Eeeeeeeees.'

'Is your mum in?'

'Felipe, is that you?' Gloria's voice came on the receiver and sat there waiting quietly. How do I tell her, I thought, running my free hand over the weed patch of my skull.

'I wanted to know . . . how you were all doing.'

'Fine, fortunately. A little quieter, you know. I'm sorry if the other day I . . . you know. Where are you?'

'On a public phone. In San Isidro.'

'Fancy coming for lunch? Promise I won't make chips.'

'I'd love to. Another day. Today . . .'

'It's a Sunday, in winter. What better day is there? A grey Sunday.'

'I'm seeing everything in colour. I've got an acid hang-over. I'm dropping.'

'Come and drop here. My bed's nice and comfy. I promise I'll let you sleep and all. It's horrible to be alone on a Sunday.'

With an obscene crunch of mechanical mastication the public phone swallowed my second token and began its swift digestion.

'Listen to me. This phone's going to cut us off any second. I rang because . . .' I drew in breath. 'I have to talk to your hus . . . to your ex-husband.'

'Yeah, right, I'll just put him on.' She paused. 'You're a fucking bastard, you know? A complete fucking bastard.'

She hung up. It was my last token. I looked around me, devastated. Not a kiosk, not a news stand, not even a bar open: just the empty pavements and the traffic lights and the indifferent Sunday traffic of sealed cars rumbling north. Even inside the duvet jacket Tamerlán had lent me (it had been his son's: maybe he thought contact with it would help me find him, like I was a psychic not a hacker) I was numb with acid cold, my head throbbing painfully, my stomach churning and churning like the drum of a washing machine. I had a vision of paradise in the shape of a welcoming little Porteño bar where you could get a latte and medialunas and watch the dead day go by from a window table while the espresso machine hissed cosily in the background. But the only thing I found after walking and cursing for three blocks was en enormous, empty Freddo ice cream parlour, gleaming with polished marble and dark glass, where some bloke in a short-sleeved shirt, numb with cold, stood behind the counter waiting for impossible customers. In the end I stopped a lone 168 approaching in the empty lane heading downtown, and crouched like a sick animal in one of the back seats, nodding every so often and hallucinating in dreams, vexed to nightmare by the exasperated rocking of the huge cradle of glass and steel. I got off at Constitución, where I had some breakfast at one of the local greasy spoons and, fortified in body and soul, walked the six or seven blocks separating me from the gates of the Borda mental hospital.

The night they took us – those of us no relatives had shown up to claim – out of the military hospital, they made us stand at the side of our beds, holding up the ones who couldn't, threw civilian clothes over our hospital gowns, loaded us into a lorry and rolled down the canvas. Only one of us howled – the whole journey – that he didn't want to go back, that he didn't want to go back to the Islands; the rest of us sat there in silence, not even bothering to keep him quiet. When they lifted the canvas, we could see massed clumps of trees and bushes, a park yellowed from repeated frosts, wet metal street lights and a foggy background of low-lying houses on one side and an endless wall on the other. Once we'd all helped each other out into the square, the lorry pulled off and disappeared round the first corner. I don't know how our whispering little band gradually broke up: a couple of us crossed to the first street and were lost among the houses; others headed straight for the trees; some began to look for something to dig foxholes with. I remember the plaster statue – ghostly it was so white – of an Indian from a raiding party, his horse caracoling fierily beside a pond full of dusty pieces of cellophane, shaking what must once have been a spear at the narrow city horizon hemming him in there; nothing but a rusty wire remained, hanging from his hand as if he were about to unblock a pipe. I must have stood there all night staring at it, because I remember nothing else, and that must have been where they found me, warming my bones after the night-time dew in the first weak sun of the morning, the male nurses of the Borda (for the sad walls that stood behind the trees were those of the asylum) sent for by the neighbours, who on their way to the baker's had found themselves surrounded by these crouching shadows among the wet tree-trunks, alerting them to the imminence of the English attack.

Nothing much had changed. Only the Sunday radio station was new, set up in a dusty patio surrounded by dormitory wings, its microphone fought over by the more active inmates to broadcast their cries for help to the outside world; after an initial second of smiling happiness, the ball of wire mesh finally in their hands, they'd be overcome by the anguish of not knowing what to say and look around in fright until encouraged to go on with smiles and pats on the back:

'Today's as cold as my mother's tit but us loonies are having fun in here; it's Sunday, the day the outside world remembers us, brings us presents and the family comes to . . .'

The one with the mic looked around him as if expecting to see them come round the bend any moment. Another seized his opportunity and the mic, and the two of them began talking at once like a badly rehearsed music-hall double-act, their haloperidol-laden voices slipping on the elusive vowels and clinging to the consonants, rising and falling like a cassette tape when it starts to drag. One boy, who can't have been more than fifteen, his naked legs covered in gooseflesh, his fat whitish body wobbling with every jump, was dancing around two awkwardly smiling women.

'Auntie! Auntie! My aunties have come to see me! Auntie!'

A young couple (visitors) were pulling second-hand clothes from an imitation leather bag and pushing them into longing arms that stretched like bicycle spokes from the surrounding ring of crazies. After his aunts had taken flight, the white-skinned boy had clung on to the girl and was edging towards one of her tits. I approached and, being more alert than most of them, managed to get hold of a burgundy sweater I'd had my eye on, and immediately pulled it over my head. Beside me a little old man, thin and stiff as a board, had procured a blue towelling dressing gown for himself. After doing up the belt with a simple knot and plunging his hands into the side pockets like two plummets, he looked at me and we both smiled in satisfaction. A man with a big nose and a government suit, whom we dubbed The Bard, read one of his compositions through a megaphone:

> We all dream,
> perchance, of the prince
> who never comes.
> We all dream,
> looking through the mirrors
> of solitude;
> death can drive
> on to a careless end.
> Or we aren't all terminals
> but gods
> of the world
> we couldn't create.

'Let go of the microphone! Let go!' burst in the one looking for his family, elbows flying. 'Nobody's going to come for us!' he yelled. 'Nobody's going to get me out of here! I'll never leave the Borda!'

The radio people tried to calm him down in case the din brought the male nurses, but he went on yelling at the towering dovecotes of identical square windows; the mic, forgotten in the confusion, returned to the hands of the poet, who crooned to him in a calm, almost absent voice:

> *Summer traffic jam.*
> *On the taxi antenna*
> *A dragonfly lands.*

His companion's shouting stopped at once. Sane and insane alike stood there in silence for a few seconds.

* * *

Emilio was entwined in the bedspread: they looked plaited together; the white loincloth over his squalid nude body (actually, an adult nappy) made him look rather like a fakir. He wasn't the only refugee from the bleak Sunday-afternoon excitement: inmates sleeping or smoking or simply staring at the ceiling occupied a third of the flaking iron beds, wrapped in sheets as thick as restaurant tablecloths frayed in long jellyfish fringes, which our self-guiding fingers endlessly plaited and unplaited to the rhythm of the identical days and nights; others were covered only by moth-patterned blankets, under which the madmen laid their naked skin on mattresses saturated with the sweat of the countless loons that had gone before them, or the bed-wetters on thick polythene covers. The bed next to Emilio's – my old bed – was unoccupied, and I sat down on the edge and heard the familiar groan of the worn-out springs accommodating my buttocks to their familiar bumps and hollows, the memory of my body finding again – without surprise, as if no time had passed – what my mind had gone to such lengths to forget. Emilio never took his eyes off the angle of the wall and shuddered and stiffened when I touched him, only slowly returning to his customary slackness.

'Emilio. It's me, Felipe. Emilio.'

He opened his mouth as if to speak but could only produce a few strangled noises from the back of his throat. He had fewer teeth than last time, and the ones he had left were encrusted with scale and close to falling out. I ran my hand over his hair, sticky with a patina of filth, like the stuff that accumulates in the nooks and crannies of badly scrubbed kitchens, but again I failed to get through. So I got up and took off my jacket and pullover and, in what was left of my combat uniform, I went and stood between the wall and his eyes. The voice sprang from his lips as if inside him it had never stopped:

'Thanks to our tong taker, my known ledge of the naivetes and their curstoms has incrazed conshudderably. They can them save by the name of culprits, which in their tongs singefries something like "marr" or "mess" . . . The world scalp is all supplied by them to a certain long slithery sea-weird, most abundaunt in these wartears . . .'

This is it, of course, I thought, sitting down on the edge of my bed in fresh defeat. What else did you expect? There's all the data you need, the facts, the dates, the names; a tale told by an aphasic with a bullet in his brain who wasn't as lucky as you were – or maybe luckier. Who knows? *You* ask him.

'Their reeligion is suppressingly like our own, as if both

stunned from a commun trunk; or, more pro Blabely, it washing stalled in them by some messinary and, over the sinturies,
the lack of guiddance and their nurtural tenduncy to priggan-
ism have removed it form its original from; our Chaplin con-
shivers the passivility of accomplicing a vapid conversion as
being veery high . . .'

What was I to do now? Go home for my walkman and
tape him, and then play Tamerlán the tape and tell him 'Somewhere in this Blabel you might find the information you're
looking for about the fate of your son or Major X. Enjoy yourselves.' Could I really have come all this way, in my state, in
the hope of getting something out of him? Only the vestigial
effects of the acid could explain such stubborn stupidity.

'They seem to be fame liar with the conscript of dog, as
they are with the scared book, which they call *Babel* (end be the
similitary to the orang in all). Leafang through its tin pages, I
noticed a scimitar arraignment and the recruitance of names
in which, with a little effart, it was passable to detract the
echoes of the origin ale, the phony tics of their rouge tongue
having gradually defirmed them to pronuanceable varrants: *If,
No Arse, Messes, Dalai La, Ma, Ark, Punctuous Piles Ate*, etc . . .'

I'd never felt this tired in my life, or maybe just once before. Unthinking, I lay down on the bed in the same position
as Emilio. I unfocused my gaze on the same corner of peeling
wall, trimmed with mottled patches of damp, on which his
eyes were fixed: once the eddies in my brain and those of the
flaking plasterwork had combined like one river flowing into
another, I recognised, without too much effort, the outline of
the Islands. They'll follow you wherever you go, a weary voice
murmured in my mind, I don't know if to Emilio or to myself,

while down the whole length of my exhausted body, becoming one with the worn-out bed-springs, the memory occurred. I lit a cigarette and the smoke in my lungs caressed my chest like a calming hand; and so, cradled in the endless sadness of the world, I fell asleep, the lighted fag between my lips.

I started awake in the last light of day from a distressing nightmare in which I was back in the Borda, only to realise that it was true. I tried to get up at once but my body wouldn't respond. I couldn't lift an arm or arch a leg. It was as if I'd lain down in wet cement and now . . . From beside me came a barely audible murmur, continuous, fainter and fainter, dying away, getting mysteriously closer, then drifting away, as if travelling on the wind, a little flame at the edge of the candlestick, barely peeping out, while the squares of sky grew darker in the wall and the cold of the night poured in through the broken panes.

'The Malvinas warp . . . the fist bottle of Turd Whorled Wart . . . with the cuntquest of the . . . whirled by Sargentina . . . the corrapt umpyre of the North is no lunger capable of saving it from the commonest ad vans; the thyme to act . . . the I'm to act . . . the time to tact . . .'

The daylight slowly faded until the half-light outside and that inside balanced, when, with a final flicker, the murmuring guttered into silence.

'He always goes quiet when he gets to this part.'

A hazy, white shadow stood on the threshold.

'Are you new?' it asked me as it approached.

'No, no. A visitor. A friend. I fell . . .' I pointed to the bed, stammering that I was about to leave, trying to convince . . . It hushed me with the outline of a hand.

'People often used to come and see him. His old comrades-in-arms. He talked, he was capable of talking for ten or twelve hours running, he even went on talking in his sleep, we had to medicate him to get him to stop. Are you . . . ?'

I nodded, then realising that my gesture couldn't be seen, I said yes through dry lips. It was as if I hadn't spoken for days.

'You can barely understand a word he says now.'

'Did you know he's here by mistake? He became aphasic and, because the military didn't understand what he was saying, they dumped him here.'

'Yes, I knew. I came in with him.'

'Hang on a minute. You're not the one with the computers? What's your name? Fernando?'

'Felipe. Am I still talked about?'

'You're a living legend. Every time we're accused of being nothing but a dumping-ground for the walking dead, someone comes out with the lost case who's now an authority on computers.'

'It's not as if I learned it here.'

'Have you been out long?'

'They took me out without asking me. Otherwise I might still be with you. It's always like coming home though. I sometimes feel I was brought up here. I have memories of my life before, but I don't feel anything; it's as if they belonged to someone else. Maybe that's it: I was born in the war and grew up here; one island was my dad, the other my mum.' It was easy to speak to this disembodied voice in the dark. 'I still have the mark of the forceps on my head.'

'Smoke?'

I took the fag in two scissored fingers. He lit it for me. He was young, younger than us, and married, I discovered in the

light of the flame. We smoked in silence, unconsciously syn-
chronising our embers in the dark. In the bed next to us an inmate ground his teeth and mumbled in his sleep. Another was
weeping and, from the rhythmic squeaking of his bed-springs,
clearly trying to masturbate.

'He never resigned himself,' I said.

'Did you?'

'We all dream of going back. It's hard to explain. I'd be
crazy to want to go back. But I dream of going back.' I paused.
'You all do too.'

'We do?'

'The ones who didn't go. Otherwise, why are you after us?
You're after us and you're afraid of us. You imagine we know
something we don't want to tell you and you don't want to
know; you envy us because we know the way and you're afraid
of us revealing it to you. We left a precise space when we left,
but we changed shape over there, and when we got back we
didn't fit into the jigsaw any more, whichever way you turned
us; ten thousand of us came back – enlightened, mad, damned
prophets – and here we are, roaming free from one end of
the country to the other, speaking a language no one understands, pretending we're working, playing football, screwing,
but never quite here, always aware that there's a precious and
indefinable part of ourselves buried over there. In dreams, at
least, we all go back to look for it. You understand? It isn't the
criminal who returns to the scene of the crime; it's the victim,
in the tyrannical hope they'll change the unfair result that's
damaged them. Ask the English. How many of them do you
think want to go back? It's us, the losers, the crushed, who
shout "We'll be back, we'll be back" to anyone who'll listen.

Why would the winner want a return match? Hell has left its mark on us and we think we can turn it into paradise just by going back; we wake up at night crying "Daddy, Daddy!" at the demons that laughed and speared us with their harpoons. Do you know why we keep on dressing up like this ten years after the event, why we keep meeting to organise impossible expeditions, reconstructing to the very last second all those days we'd do better to forget? We're infected, see; like Chagas victims, we carry them in our blood and die by degrees. You've seen them, haven't you? They're just like polyps. They get a little bigger with each passing year, like those patches on the wall. Shell shock, war trauma; no, it isn't that simple. We're madly in love, yet we hate them. Fetishists that we are, we worship a photo, a silhouette, an old boot . . . It isn't true there were survivors. There are two bites torn out of the hearts of every one of us, and they're the exact shape of the Islands. We try to fill the holes with stuff from over here, but it's like trying to plug them with tow. Do you know how many of us took our lives for that love?'

'About two hundred.'

'Not yet.'

I fell silent, as Emilio had a while ago, feeling as if my words were less intelligible than his. The doctor got up to leave.

'Is there anyone who understands what he says?' I headed him off.

He shrugged his shoulders.

'Nobody cares.'

'But it is possible?'

'I don't think so. There's no stable code, you understand. Although a while back something strange began to happen, I don't know if you've recognised it. He always repeats the same thing.'

'What's that? I thought you said . . .'

'No, I can't *understand* it, but I can *recognise* it. It's like music: the melody's always the same and, if you make the effort, you start to pick out a few words and phrases. After that, even if you splice them and stick them onto others, they keep coming back. Haven't you noticed how he'll say everything in a rush, then suddenly stop?'

'So maybe . . .'

'He's reciting.'

'How long's he been doing it?'

'Two or three months, as far as I know. But the visits may have started before that. Now I come to think of it, this is the first time he's done it without the chap coming.' He looked at me. 'You're the one who came. Did he send you?'

'Describe him to me.'

'Fifty-something. Moustache. Military type. No uniform.'

'Coat?'

'Grey. Do you know who he is?'

'Uh-huh,' I nodded.

'And what does he want?'

'I have no idea. Does he come often?'

'He doesn't have set days. But when he comes, he stays. Sometimes for ten hours at a stretch without even getting up to go to the bathroom. He sits on your bed with a sheaf of papers and a recorder, and doesn't leave until Emilio's gone completely quiet.'

'Does he write down what Emilio says to him?' I asked in astonishment.

'I think so. Once, when I tried to peep over his shoulder, he showed me a glimpse of his gun. Anyway, it seems to matter to him. The problem is that every visit leaves Emilio worse, squeezed like a lemon, he's catatonic for days afterwards. I once suggested the chap should be barred. Everyone just laughed. Ah well.' He slapped both knees purposefully at the same time. 'I'm off home. Can I give you a lift anywhere?'

'Where are you going?'

'Morón.'

'No, thanks. I don't live far.'

'You'd better get a move on. We're about to close. Mind you don't get locked in.'

'Wouldn't be the first time.'

When I was alone again, I lit another cigarette to help me think. Once again my instinct had won out against my common sense, guiding me to Major X along the winding trails of intuition and scent. Maybe Tamerlán was right after all and, despite all my doubts and reticence, I was the only person capable of solving this case. As one of them, only I could get inside their heads. It hadn't been just another manifestation of my monomaniacal fixation; the Islands had been mixed up in this whole business right from the start. But how exactly? Fortunately it wasn't my job to understand, just to find Major X and hand over the information. So all I needed to do now was hole up and wait, instead of bouncing round the city like some crazy ball. That was all I asked, to be able to rest a little, to curl up on my side and tuck my knees under my chin for a little warmth. It took me a while to get back to sleep because the blanket was too short, and if I covered my chest my feet froze, and vice versa. In the end I resigned myself to leaving my boots on, the way we used to in the Islands, but about six in the morning I awoke with a full bladder and cold feet; quite understandably because someone had pinched my boots while I was asleep. Crawling among the coughing bodies I looked for them in vain; it must have been someone from another wing, or perhaps a male nurse trying to make it through to the end of the month. I returned to my bed carrying a pair of hairy espadrilles that fitted me nicely; wrapping them in the blanket and, with my hands tucked between my thighs, enough warmth returned for me to sleep till breakfast: boiled maté and bread. Monday morning seemed like a good time for Major X to drop by, so I went back to bed to wait for him. If he doesn't show up by noon, I can slip back home, have a shower, change into some warmer clothes and come back for the afternoon shift; but I found out there was lentil stew for lunch and it felt cruel to force myself to make such a long bus journey on an empty stomach with it looking so cold out and me barely over my acid hangover and no sleep for twenty-four hours. Everything will be a lot easier, I reasoned, with some hot food inside me; besides, I'll save making lunch at home and can keep a more efficient watch. It must have been a long time since I'd eaten properly; I devoured three platefuls, wiping them clean with hunks of bread, then felt so full that I decided to have a lie down. The calories in the stew kept me warm better than any blanket and by the time I finally woke up it was three o'clock; now it made no sense to leave when visiting hours were so nearly over and I could go back and spend the night at home. The only thing I missed was my cigarettes, but I felt pretty good apart from that. I didn't even need to think about the case. Tamerlán had asked me to find Major X and I had – all but. Now it was just a matter of hunkering down and waiting. I had only a very vague idea what I was going to do when he showed up: race to a public phone (no, better get the Miniphone from home) and call Tamerlán; steal his wallet or a diary; I'd see when the time came. The main thing right now was to remain at my post, get used to sentry duty again. And what's more, without guilt, because I was clearly doing my duty. At some point I fell to thinking about what I'd do if he never showed up. I couldn't stay here indefinitely. Well, I suppose I could. It was an option, after all, and I was a free man.

After they closed the gates, I wondered why I'd been so sure a man like Cuervo would respect visiting hours. Obviously, he wasn't going to show up at three in the morning, but it was surely worth waiting till late in the evening, especially as I had nothing much to do at home till tomorrow morning. After dinner I joined in a game of truco, but my partner had a tic and his signals kept confusing me: I'd play to his seven of coins and it would turn out to be a four of cups, and then no one paid any attention to the rules and called 'envido' on the second round, took threes with twos, got the score wrong (forty-three, one of them called, after adding a horse and a king together) and nobody could remember who'd called 'quiero'. But the worst thing was that they all got on really well together. They had a fine old time and kept going for hours; I was the superfluous one, so the following night, after pudding (an unrecognisable fruit purée, probably flavoured aubergines), I went straight to bed. It was also the last day I managed to keep track of the time, because my watch was stolen in the night and my bad temper lasted halfway through the morning.

As if to a slow waltz, I rocked myself to the regular rhythm of the hours, to the uneventful round, no surprises, placid. Life was certainly easier, its alternatives simplified: like at summer camp, everything was planned. There were no activities, but at least the routine was organised: you had breakfast, you had lunch, you had dinner, and the rest was free time, like on a package tour (the idea of a holiday had stuck for good). The best thing was not having to take decisions. All my life, I finally understood, had been nothing but a heroic struggle . . . against the force of gravity. That was the real enemy. I understood that at this stage I embodied the fate, perhaps even the redemption, of the species. Our great mistake had been to adopt the upright posture, to become . . . bipeds. Dragging yourself along is easier. We'd entered one of those famous evolutionary dead ends, like the one that finished off the dinosaurs and spared the lizards and snakes. Verticality was quite unnecessary; anything that mattered could be done just as well or better in a horizontal position. I'd confirmed this with computers: setting up the keyboard on the breakfast tray did the trick. How I missed them now, after so many days' abstinence. If only there were one here. Just imagine. A terminal for every inmate, or failing that, a little video-games room, and the age-old problem of mental health would be solved. Under the effects of the substance, an inmate could spend eight hours stuck to the colourful screen, for a Pacman makes no practical distinction between a mad player and a sane one. It was worth bearing in mind. A private room with two or three terminals connected to the Net. And – and – and – a telephone, telly, what else, a radio cassette player with headphones – if I'd had all those possibilities nine years ago, they'd never have got me out of here, I muttered enthusiastically; sometimes technology comes too late. I could set up a complete ecosystem, the dream of your very own fish tank;

perhaps even taking steps to get them to install probes to feed and evacuate me. So enthused was I with the idea that I wanted then and there to make a list of everything I'd need, but couldn't find my biro: someone had nicked that too.

To pass the time I started observing Emilio, whose sleeping lips kept up their regular movement without trembling or slobbering or tightening, as if in his sleep he recovered the faculty of speech. Who knows what there was inside there? Someone once explained to me that his ears perceived his own speech flawlessly, that it was ours that had become an obscene blabbering. The time we attempted to bust him out, he'd come back of his own free will after two months trying to communicate with people on the outside, and after that we left him to it. Who was I to judge, after all? It had taken him two months to understand what it had taken me nine years: that this was the only safe haven for exiles from the Islands. They'd busted me out of here too and only my greater inertia had stopped me coming back – until now, that is. They'd turned up for a visit one Sunday, without knowing I was there; they'd only just started doing the rounds to try to regroup the remains of the once mighty Malvinas army. As soon as they recognised who I was, they decided to bust me out, embracing me with tears that I observed with curiosity. They'd come prepared. Without consulting me, they shoved me into a toilet and, while Ignacio stood smoking at the door on lookout, Sergio and Tomás stripped me of my loony uniform and clad me from head to foot in combat gear, just like theirs save for the boots (they were hardly going to lug a selection of sizes around with them). We walked out through the front door, Tomás leading the way, Sergio and Ignacio at the sides to prop me up, and no one can have counted them at the entrance apparently, because we left without a fuss. As I couldn't remember where I lived, I spent a week at the makeshift veterans' centre on Honorio Pueyrredón, in a state of mute, universal, psychotropic-induced acceptance, till the following Sunday, after a rooftop asado with juicy meat and red from a demijohn, the combined effects of which ended up neutralising the residual effects of the drugs in my blood, my brain returned to my body and I looked around me as if seeing everything for the first time. I have a very clear memory of that afternoon: the sticky purple film deposited at the bottom of the hexagonal glasses, the shifting shapes of the clouds and the eddies of congealed grease on the plates, every one of the leaves on the paradise tree that graced us with a chequerboard of sun and shade, the flies balancing like tightrope walkers on the rims of the glasses; the roar of the few-and-far-between Sunday buses and the engines of the different makes of cars and the words of people's conversations as they walked along the pavement, sometimes unwrapping a sweet from its cellophane or jingling coins in their pockets; two sparrows nervously eyeing the crumbs from the cement verandah, uncertain whether or not to approach; the serrated edges of fern shoots striving to take root in the hollows of grey gravel where the tar had come away . . . the world I was seeing was newly created. The next day I laid my hands on a keyboard again and within a week I'd found a job in a computer repair shop. With growing astonishment I realised that this was an area where my abilities had increased rather than diminished; I now got on with machines as if we belonged to the same species and the only possible explanation lay here, in this lump criss-crossed with scars that my hair in the mirror hadn't quite yet managed to cover, a piece of the machine that I'd taken into my body for ever. The first to sense the change had been the doctor from the Campo de Mayo Military Hospital, who'd discharged me to free up a bed that no one needed. He called me to his office, where there was a lighted piece of milky glass plastered with X-rays. The photograph of the poor skeleton on display wasn't exactly flattering; it had something that looked like a cactus growing in its head and I was about to point this out and ask about it when I realised it was me. 'As you can see from this plate.' He'd unsheathed a straight, extendable steel pointer and was touching my naked bones with it, point by point. 'A fragment of your helmet has been left embedded in your skull. It was too dangerous to extirpate it,' he said hurriedly, with evasive eyes, and I guessed he was lying; they probably hadn't noticed it until it was too late. 'And now it's too late. It's been soldered into your cranium, soldier,' he said, smiling, and went on hastily when he saw I wasn't laughing at his joke. 'It's actually now part of your cranium and extracting it would be like removing a piece of you. The metal will gradually be absorbed by the bone, covered over by it,' he reassured me, perhaps fearing that I was expecting the reverse process. 'In any case, you'll be taking home a permanent souvenir of your time in the Argentinian Army,' he said, handing me the X-ray, though I suppose he was referring to the helmet. I must have asked him about something, I suppose (for some reason all I can recall of those days are other people's words), because his doctor's smile returned to his face: 'Don't be impatient, patient: you're not being discharged, just disinterred. From here we go back to barracks and wait nice and quietly, without rushing, for the Argentinian Army to decide to let us go. No, not us; *you!*' He suddenly got

371

angry at something I'd said, thinking I was taking the mickey; though in fact I took everything quite literally at the time. '*You're* going! Not me! I'm still good for something!' Then they sent me to live with my mother, not expecting that in a week at most my headaches would force them to take me back and try out new methods of healing. As a last resort they experimented with fists and feet, because apparently my howls of pain were keeping them awake at night; I was one of the main reasons they'd decided to herd the hopeless cases into that olive-green lorry and dump us outside the Borda. It turned out to be just the place. My headaches began to abate, replaced in the long run by a blank, featureless peace. There were too many . . . things out there, and I needed to get used to them a little at a time. I soon discovered that here inside no one rushed me, that I had all the time in the world – that I could stay for ever. Except for Sundays, when the people from the cooperative came to bust our balls with their fucking workshops, the days were very quiet, identical to each other, no surprises. People sometimes get rather lurid ideas about madhouses from what they see at the cinema, but the truth is that they're quite peaceful places where nothing much happens, as long as the haloperidol's flowing, that is. The male nurses are people who go about their jobs and pick up their salaries and, like everyone else, what they most want to do is to put their feet up. The doctors, most of them unpaid trainees, don't charge, freeze their balls off, especially in winter in those white coats of theirs, and spend most of the time smoking and discussing Lacan round little electric heaters. There's always one eager beaver that pops up, though. And one in particular had taken a dislike – or a liking – to the little group of Malvinas veterans: whenever he came into the wing, he'd shout 'On your feet, company! Ten-shun!' and get us to march around, or he'd sit on a bench out in the garden and shout 'Forward march! Get down! Take cover!' while us nutters, uncoordinated from all the drugs, ran about disorientated among the trees, bumping into each other and howling as he quaked with laughter, slapped his knees and called the others over to watch. When he was brought to heel, he got out the Rorschachs: he found one with such a mesmerising resemblance that you'd have sworn the very Atlantic had been folded in two along the San Carlos Strait to leave those two terrifying ink-blots on either side so that we could read our madness on their open map. Amid the frantic tat-tat-tat of oral machine guns and the explosions of swollen cheeks (they'd kept us all in the same wing at first) he'd stroll from bed to bed, showing those sad blots with all the delectation of a pervert with pocketfuls of pornography in charge of a kindergarten. Those of us who fell into his clutches were more impressiona-ble, less stable, more defenceless. Every response – 'an explod-ing bomb', 'a chest-wound', 'my head', 'claws trying to grab me' – he'd carefully note down on a form covered in boxes. Then he drew up a chart that proved that all the responses invariably referred to the Islands, and that we were therefore all – here he'd give an indulgent chuckle – suffering from PTSD and were condemned to seeing them everywhere for the rest of our lives. He was right, I thought, resting the back of my neck on my pil-low and letting myself be carried away, he was dead right, and as I drifted off, the distant, blurry shape of the Islands on the wall passed with me into half-sleep and spread without hope of containment across the endless plains of the mind.

I was awakened by a male nurse dragging a huge, light

bag; dropping it on the floor, he counted the beds with one finger in the air and consulted his clipboard. Without a word, he pulled the blanket down to the foot of my bed and began to undo my pants. Before I could stop him, they were already round my ankles along with my underpants, and the male nurse was busy opening a nappy and checking the tackiness of the adhesive. Deciding it was too late, I chose – so to speak – to let him, looking the other way to avoid making him feel uncomfortable. I thought he might put on some baby cream on, or a bit of talcum powder at least, which had its pleasant side, but he didn't; with two or three mechanical movements he slipped the nappy under my arse without touching me, adjusted the tapes, fixed them in position and, after pulling my pants and bedclothes up over it, he moved on, ignoring Emilio. What I should have done was take it off and put it on the man it was really intended for, but I'd never changed a nappy in my life, not even a crazy baby's, let alone an adult's. And besides, he might have been covered in piss and shit. I'll inform the next male nurse that goes by, I told myself, and fell asleep thinking about it. I dreamed it was raining and I was on the Islands, my pants so drenched with freezing-cold water that I pissed myself for a few seconds' warmth on my legs. I didn't have the face to give the nappy back after that; luckily, next day they corrected the error on the clipboard and from then on started changing us both.

They also unified our diets: those who couldn't eat under their own steam were spoon-fed with baby food (probably the liquefied leftovers of the others' meals), which they put in a piping bag and squirted straight into our mouths. It was a good idea, I thought, as I flattened it with my tongue to swallow;

when it comes down to it, biting or cutting food, chewing it, tasting the different flavours and swallowing, requires a great deal of effort and energy. Sometimes you don't feel up to even that: a tasteless pap is all you can take; even if the stomach can stand it, it's the soul that isn't prepared for tasty and excessively nourishing food. After a short time on this diet, I started to put on weight and sink into the bed, or maybe it was the pap accumulating on the sheets, because it was becoming increasingly difficult to keep my head above them. I spent most of the day splashing about in this white mud – fortunately, it wasn't as cold as the snow, just the opposite in fact: it had the lukewarmth of the human body, something like warm flour-and-water paste; it even tasted like it. And it was no longer just the food but the whole world that had been put through the liquidiser; walking through the world, now, getting through day after day, dragging myself laboriously to reach the next along paths, streets, tunnels, passageways, corridors, offices, parks, woods, rivers or mountains, had all been reduced and simplified to the same splashing and groping about in this watery mud. I say 'day after day' or 'the next day' out of habit, for the colour of the sky that stretched beyond this horizon of mud was an invariable nightday watergrey. Children at school are taught that the sum of all the colours gives white. White is the colour of colours, so the enthusiastic child grabs his paints – minus the white so as not to cheat – empties them onto the plate and begins to stir and stir the multi-coloured rainbow with his paintbrush, waiting for the miracle at any moment, and, even when his beautiful coral reds and chrome yellows and cobalt blues and emerald greens and purples and carmines have disappeared, forever liquefied into that greenbrowngrey sludge, the child goes on stirring, incapable of believing it: he's been had. Still refusing to accept it, he picks up his brush and, over the beautiful landscape in his colouring book, daubs greenish clouds in the sky, brownish smoke coming out of the chimney of the cabin, mouse-coloured sheep in the field, then in a rage covers it all with the same ashkhakiolive and, when not a single brushstroke of another colour can be seen, he rips the page out of the book and throws himself weeping into the greenish mud.

After a while I discover that, by opening my mouth and swallowing as I go, I can feed myself: the pap that goes through my body and comes out of the other end releases enough nutrients to enable me to go on. Its smell is that unmistakable smell, at once dead and musty, fermented and dulled, into which all smells merge after being kept for long enough in a polythene bag. With no differences to be perceived the smell becomes indistinguishable from its absence, and my sense of smell soon atrophies. Everything gradually homogenises, everything becomes easier and easier. Certain protuberances that obstructed my forward movement are left behind, they wither and fall off: the teeth from my mouth, the hair from my body, my nails, my ears, my nose, penis, testicles . . . My fingers conjoin and my arms shorten to small fins that my body will at length completely reabsorb; my legs join together along their length and I learn to move by snaking through the mud – my eyes of course have for some time been sealed for ever and soon also disappear from my memory. I no longer need to see, no longer need to hear, all contact with the world reduced to two orifices: my mouth the only entrance, my anus the only exit! One day I stop moving and start becoming spherical. Perhaps it's the first stage of a metamorphosis, but it's difficult to tell: my new life is much simpler than my previous one, but not totally predictable. Something new is happening. While I was moving, time went on flowing, or perhaps it was me and my movement that created the march of time. When I stop, space loses all boundaries; my body expands to fill it completely and I am one, indistinguishable from this underlying substance that stretches to the ends of the universe from the beginning to the end of time, and for this conscious, unlimited, eternal cosmic mass there is no other name than – why not utter one last word before doing away with them completely? – God.

* * *

I was dragged back by a stream of pain, intense and local, as if someone were trying to bend my knee backwards – no point arguing I had no legs because it's a well-known fact that amputees feel pain in the absent limb as well. That was what was happening: someone was tinkering with the body I'd left behind; I'd have liked to ignore it but it hurt too much, and if I was to escape or move, I had to come back. The pain was accompanied by an unbearable pressure, the pressure by a claggy taste of sleep flooding my mouth, the rancid saliva and its smell by an audible creaking of the knee, which was on the point of giving completely; the assault of the senses burst all barriers and, defeated again, I opened my eyes to a broad, insensitive back sitting on the edge of my bed, on top of one of my legs. I was about to shout out in indignation, wriggling my leg eel-like, squashed beneath the wall of rock, pulling on it like a jammed corkscrew, but at the last moment I noticed the grey Burberry, big coat, trench coat, raincoat, overcoat, and restrained myself. Emilio was sitting up straight against the bars of the bedhead, his bulging eyes fixed on the nebulous map of the Islands in the corner of the wall, and as if someone had pulled out the stopper from the toothless orifice that opened and closed in his face, now wildly poured the same words that earlier had trickled through his leaking mind:

'Wood it not be bitter to with raw now, befur it was too late, and prey that the Islands should remain under cover for sever all millennui to come, that we should go on leaping in the no ledge, that a beast in a den survived in some distinct carnage of the planeat, even if inexcessible to use? . . .'

Instinctively, like a cat that wakes up with a Rottweiler on its tail, I began to bristle and hunch, drawing my whole body in towards the clenched lump at the core of the bed, save for the one, long, outstretched leg left far out there as a hostage. In the hollow of the sagging bed my body was practically invisible beneath the blankets; only a wedge of face peeped out to watch. A thick wad of papers on his knees and a tape recorder whirring at his side, Major X took notes, crossed out, revised his annotations, put on his headphones and took them off again, scribbled enthusiastically, stood up, crossed out everything he'd written and started again. Poking out of the ferment of mattress and unwashed blankets, Emilio's talking head feverishly held forth, a buzz of words unrolling from his tongue like line from a reel when a big fish bites:

'They say they are discandied from thaws who rearrived from the Norse, bringing the treasore to the Islands, moor yearns Iago than can be canted on the finngears of all the inhabituals' hands. The world they repit, in-gland, seems to be a contraption of the original in gold land, or to give it the name by which it has been killed for sansureties: elder adder . . .'

Major X controlled him with clipped, precise orders, in true military fashion. 'Speak,' he'd say mechanically, and Emilio would speak:

'I turned round to seaweed of my mean was responseable. Nun of them . . .'

'Stop,' he'd interrupt him, and for two or three minutes he'd feverishly write, cross out and erase, and reread everything, all concentration. 'Continue,' he'd say when done.

'It tarned out to be that sold year from yer five, who had approached me on our revel, claiming his newt meat . . .'

'Stop. Rewind.' He'd count the seconds on his watch. 'Stop. Continue.'

'Noon often. It toured out to beta soldier from err five who had pup roast meat on our arrival, clamming he knew men . . .'

'Repeat.'

'Son of Sem. It tired out to be that sold year from er five who had peached on me to my rival, cleaning up no mean . . .'

'Repeat.'

'Noun of theme. It tarred out to be that sell dear former five who had upreached men on our arreveal, climbing the new me . . .'

'Stop.'

Any moment now, I told myself, he'll get up and go to the bathroom and I'm out of here. But he didn't. Menhir-like, he'd settled in his final resting place. Eventually, out of sheer annoyance I tried to pull on my leg without him realising, but it was as fast as a rivet and so dead I could barely even pull. There was nothing I could do. As a last resort I reminded myself that this

was the man who'd done all those . . . things to Gloria, to see if
it made me react, but I couldn't get my head round it; it kept
sliding away down the waxed furrows of my brain and, rather
than an urge to kill him, I ended up feeling an urge to die myself. Why not? After all, what did I have to complain about? I'd
been given a ten-year bonus, God knows why; even without the
will to live, life hadn't been too bad a deal.

It was Emilio who saved me. The taut thread of his speech
slackened, as if the fish had slipped the hook, and Major X got up
and walked stiff-legged towards the bathrooms. I had no time
to think what I was doing before my hands had grabbed the papers, stuffing them under my pullover. I leaped to my feet and
fell flat on my face on Emilio's bed, scattering the papers across
the floor. Starting to weep with despair, I gathered them into
an unmanageable bundle and tried to hop to the door, dragging my dead leg behind me. It felt like it had been amputated,
I couldn't feel it touch the floor, and when I tried to stand on
it, it kept giving, like a slat in a Venetian blind. I only hope he's
having a serious crap, I prayed, and as luck would have it I found
a wooden chair on my way out to the garden that I could use
as a crutch to get to the main gate and out of his field of vision.
Clutching my knee with my free hand, I managed to hobble a
short way and, with a sizzling tingle, the blood began to flood
back into my dead flesh. By the time I'd reached the exit, my
legs were sliding along the tiled passageways as if on air, and
I'd have had no trouble reaching the street had the guard at the
entrance not blocked the way. I can't have looked as presentable
as I had when I arrived and my expression of forced sanity must
have been even less convincing when I stuck my hand down my
pants and started to rummage, all the while looking at him

with a smile of abject apology. He already had one grappling hook on my shoulder when I felt something crinkly and yanked it out with an exclamation of triumph. Unrolling it against the light, he scrutinised it suspiciously, as if the understandable reluctance to believe a madman ought naturally to extend to his money as well, but I'd already crossed to the opposite pavement and was halfway down the block. I barged into a bus queue, from where I watched the entrance. I didn't have to wait long. Major X came bursting out of the darkness and went straight up to the guard, grabbing him by the lapels and shaking him like a country dog with a rabbit. Miraculously, the 95 pulled up, because the guard was already pointing in my direction and Major X's eyes burned into the crowd fighting to board the bus. Too late to reach it, in his despair he went and stood in the middle of the street with his arms outstretched, but the driver, goaded on by the amber light, accelerated straight at him and he had to jump out of the way to avoid being hit. He started running after it, meaning to catch us at the next red light, which turned green at that precise moment, and we stampeded on. Only after three blocks of crush did I reach the driver who, impatient ticket in hand, sat there waiting as I ransacked all my pockets without pulling out more than some fluff and a paperclip. One hand fondling a tyre lever, he suggested I get off. Almost without touching the pavement I dived into a shop, where I pretended to be making up my mind about what brand of yerba maté to buy: Taragüí, La Hoja, Nobleza Gaucha, Flor de Lis, Rosamonte, Unión, I managed to read before seeing Major X go past inside a black-and-yellow flash, and, resurfacing behind him, I waited for the next cab and told it to follow the 95. I improvised: 'My girlfriend's on board with another man.' We caught up with it mounted on the pavement, embedded at a forty-five-degree angle in the taxi, while a whirl of indignant passengers and curious passers-by tried to undo a knot of struggling figures: the bus driver was grabbing the taxi driver by the pullover; the taxi driver was trying to throttle Major X; Major X, in turn, was dragging a startled young man by the hair, who from the hasty description of a Borda guard could easily have been me, then remembering I'd given the guard my last note, I yelled 'There she is! She's wounded!' and, jumping out without paying, I blended into the crowd. As Major X threw the cabby onto the bus driver with a perfectly aimed commando elbow, grabbed the young man's briefcase and wrenched it opened, rifling through the papers inside and scattering them in the wind. Letting him go, he whirled round in a fury, fell on a blind man trying to get through the crowd and started beating him with his stick, without stopping to think that he might have been a rather unlikely suspect, whereupon several burly proles who'd been watching him unsympathetically finally made up their minds to lynch him. After a few random punches, a perfect circle opened up miraculously amid the tangle of bodies, at the precise centre of which stood the isolated Major X, one straight, sleeveless arm brandishing a 9mm with which he speedily opened a passageway through the crowd and walked away down the busy pavement without anyone following him. Except me, of course.

Between the Garrahan hospital and Calle Caseros he stopped at a phone booth, and I went and stood right behind him, trying not to rustle the papers. He didn't turn round the whole time. He dialled a number, which was engaged twice before he got through. I knew that number.

'Hugo. Hugo. They're here, they're already in our midst. Disguised as headcases, camouflaged under the bedclothes, on the buses . . . They robbed me, Hugo, they've got it, it's in their hands. If we don't get it back, we're done for, do you realise! Put everybody on alert! . . . Yes, yes, fifteen minutes at most . . . We'll discuss it later, your phone must be tapped too.'

He hung up and, stepping up to the phone, I dialled any old number – I had no tokens – until he was at a safe distance. I tailed him for two blocks as far as the first stop – no one there – and went and stood close by him again. What would I do if the bus came? If I got on with him and I had nothing to pay with, the fuss might draw his attention to me. Likewise, I didn't fancy scrounging the few cents I needed off him. Keenly aware of how close I was to losing him, I fell back half a block and crossed to the opposite pavement, where I stopped an old woman coming out of a shop with some milk and a little pop-eyed tyke. There was only one spiel I could hand her, naturally:

'Excuse me Señora, I'm a Malvinas veteran,' I said, pointing at my pants, the only thing vaguely military in sight. 'I got the bus here looking for work but when I told them I'd been in the Islands they told me to get lost, and I'd only brought enough for the outward journey . . .'

The old woman looked at me sympathetically and said with a smile of apology:

'I'm a pensioner.'

Another 95 was approaching down 15 de Noviembre. Surely he won't take this one will he, I thought, racing to the corner. This time the spiel came out all garbled, with me glancing over my shoulder the whole time at the approaching yellow beast, but the little pen-pusher, who I almost grabbed by the tie, didn't believe a word, and I was about to suggest he feel the lump in my head when, grumbling, he pulled out three five-cent coins – not a red cent more! – and dropped them into my outstretched palm one by one without touching it. 'Veterans! Two months! Do me a favour! Now we have to keep them for the rest of their lives,' I heard him muttering as I ran for the bus, overflowing with passengers from the one that had crashed. Major X had climbed onto the running-board with ease, the people sticking out of the door like an upside-down bunch of bananas swiftly having made way for him as soon as they recognised who he was; but I didn't have his advantage and had to bob alongside the bus for half a block before it left me behind in the street in a cloud of white smoke. A 50 and a 134 went past – no taxis – before the next 95, which was almost empty, which for some reason I expected would make us go faster, but the one in front must have been driving past the stops, because a mass of swearing passengers was waiting for us at each, slowing us down. As I scanned the streets and pavements desperately in case Major X had got off, we passed Independencia, Belgrano, Rivadavia and Corrientes, and I was just beginning to lose all hope when, four blocks ahead, I made out the broad yellow back of his 95, appearing and disappearing, broken up by other buses and delivery trucks. We caught up with it at the lights on Avenida Córdoba and our two buses sat there for a few seconds, side by side, the drivers leaning across to each other and saying the kind of daft things bus drivers say when they meet. Had Major X looked out of his window, he'd have seen me in profile half a metre away from him. My joy was as short-lived as the red light. The drivers waved each other goodbye and we pulled off down Pasteur at a rate of knots, soon leaving him several blocks behind. I turned round to a little old man with a toilet-brush moustache.

'Can you lend me fifteen cents for the bus?'

'You're already on the bus,' he opined.

'I have to take another one.'

'What's wrong with this one?'

People who refuse to give are savvier than the ones who ask nowadays, I thought to myself, and tried the Malvinas trick on the girl on the other side of the aisle. It worked to perfection, and I pushed my way through to the back door as Major X's 95 approached.

When I boarded it, I took less than a second to see through the compact mass of passengers that he wasn't on it, and jumped off without buying a ticket. It had stopped on Avenida Las Heras and I'd last seen him at Avenida Córdoba: it would be impossible to track him down, however hard I scoured the blocks in between: Córdoba, Paraguay, Charcas, Santa Fe, Arenales, Beruti, Juncal, French . . . French and Uriburu. 'Fifteen minutes at most,' I remembered, feeling throughout my body the familiar, almost forgotten adrenaline rush of the triumphant hacker. Got you, you bastard; I know where you are.

At least there was a bar on the corner of Hugo's block. Sitting down at a table with a view of his door and the two pesos the girl had given me, I ordered an espresso and settled down to wait. To while away the time I started flicking through Major X's papers; I had two hours to read them with the eye that wasn't looking out of the window and had just started to think I'd been wrong when out came the man himself, blinking in the light and striding with military gait towards Pueyrredón, which he crossed with his head bowed so low that he was almost run over by a taxi. He turned onto Agüero and began walking down towards Las Heras, stopping before the corner of Gutiérrez. He lived in one of those tacky, futuristic '70s tower blocks with formica panels and acrylic bubbles, like something out of the set of *2001: A Space Odyssey*, opposite a workers' rotisserie exhaling its breath of endlessly spit-roast chickens at the pavement. From the door, I could see that his lift had stopped at the fourth floor. I looked at the polished brass ranks of doorbells: A, B, C, D, E, F, G. I'd have to narrow down the alternatives.

'Sharpener. Anything for sharpening?' I said in a high-pitched voice.

'Yeah, my prick you dick to stick up your arse,' answered the man in A, making me green with envy at the neatness of his reply; no one answered at B; at C a woman's voice said 'Yes, I'll be right down' and so on till the end. It had to be A or G. I went back to A.

'"O cut over in twenty, sever: The Pulpe blashes the murderniced instilletoes of housewitch" translates as "October 27th: The Pope blesses the modernised installations of Auschwitz", you dick.'

He swore at me again, this time less imaginatively. I was about to press G when a woman in a frilly apron appeared, holding two knives and a pair of scissors.

'Where's the sharpener?'

'He left.'

'But . . . wait a minute, I recognise your voice. *You*'re the sharpener.'

'Bike just stolen . . . grindstone, the works.'

'And you dragged me all the way down here to tell me that?'

'What do you expect me to sharpen them on? My teeth?'

Luckily, instead of going up to her floor she went to ring the caretaker's bell, convinced it was all a plot to mug her; having the lift downstairs suited me fine. I rang G again and repeated the same paragraph. This time the voice that had answered said nothing in reply and, peering through the door, I saw the lift begin to climb; it stopped at the fourth. I got out of there, *fast*.

The rotisserie had its railings down, but the side door was open and, while I gave an evening order for twenty guests and gobbled down the meat pasties with which the jubilant owner kept egging me on (I stuffed down four, desperate, having forgotten how delicious food was), I saw him burst onto the street, beside himself, looking all around him. He ran to the corner, dived into a bar and a phone exchange, then looked in our direction and for a moment I panicked, despite the carrousel of dripping chickens that stood in the way. Finally, he just stood there outside the door to his building and, raising one fist at heaven, exclaimed in English to the sheer wall of balconies with their potted plants and their clothes-lines and their parrot cages:

'*I get you suns of the beaches! I get you!*'

I realised then that he'd become pretty harmless.

I called Tamerlán from the phone exchange and gave him the exact address. Fortunately, as I had no money left for the bar and it was fucking freezing outside, they didn't take more than half an hour. I stamped on the tiles to thaw out the soles of my espadrilles a little, telling myself it was all over: I'd done my duty like the star pupil and could go home at last. Whatever happened from now on was officially none of my business. I suppose what I was really waiting to see was the two of them marching briskly out with Major X sandwiched between them like the sausage in a hot dog, the barrels of their guns for toothpicks to stop him slipping out. But what if they decided to stay up there all afternoon, the three of them chatting, swapping stories? They might know each other from their truncheon and hood days for all I knew. What I *didn't* expect was to see Tamerlán's two goons come out laden with towers of paper so high they could barely see over the top, tip them into the gaping boot of the Ford and set off in a cloud of white smoke. They hadn't been in there more than fifteen minutes.

Like someone resigning himself to an unjust fate, I pressed the button for the fourth floor. A straight beam of light filtered from the end of the passageway. The door opened with a gentle push, though its lock and latch looked intact. Arturo Cuervo was stiffly seated in a chair at the exact centre of the only room, only the chair had tipped over, its back and back legs, to which he'd been tied by the wrists with wire, on the floor; its front legs in the air, holding his ankles. Quarter of his left temple now formed part of the yellowish wallpaper and the indistinct pattern on the carpet, while his naked, white bulk covered with grey hair was marked and scored like a map by the knife, his eyes fixed on the brownish ceiling, the Ls of his legs in the air, like in some exercise to improve the circulation. I stood there beside him for a while, I don't know how long, unable to take my eyes off him. Seen from above like that, he didn't look so terrifying, and even the once fearsome picana of the flesh, the raper of millions, now lay to one side, almost lost in the patch of grey fuzz that cushioned it. There were tiny droplets of blood everywhere, even still floating in the air, like an almost invisible drizzle barely perceptible to the eyes and nostrils, making you itch and feel like sneezing; it was lit up in the shafts of light coming in through the half-open blinds and clung, still dancing, to the dust in the air. It must have been vaporised by the explosion inside his head; ever since I came in, I'd been breathing in his blood. I had to step over him to reach the kitchenette, where I borrowed a greasy tea towel which I used to pick up the phone – not because I was worried about leaving prints, but to avoid getting the blood on my hands – and dial Gloria's number. The moment she recognised my voice, she lashed out sarcastically:

'Oh. Felipe. So, did you find my ex?'

'Yes.'

'Are you having me on?'

'No. I'm with him now.'

She went quiet for a few seconds, which my eyes put to good use to turn and look at the skin on which the sweat hadn't yet dried. When she spoke to me again, her voice was trembling uncontrollably.

'What is this, another torture session? If you work for him, why don't you just come and kill me instead of playing with the phone? Don't you ever get bored of it, you lot?'

'He's dead.'

This time it was longer before she spoke, but when she did, her voice was neutral, cold and utterly distant.

'Did you kill him?'

'No.' Was I lying? But I didn't feel like explaining. 'I found him like this.'

'Are you sure?

'Half of his brain's on view and the other half's decorating the walls.'

'I mean, that it's him.'

'How can I tell?'

'Do me a favour. Undo his shirt. Has he got a white scar under his left nipple?'

'White as the driven snow.'

'What's his big toe on his left foot like? I mean, if it doesn't bother you to take off his shoe.'

'No need, he's naked.'

'What, they buggered him as well?'

'I don't think so. His arse looks well protected at least. He's missing a nail and a good slice of the toe.

'It's him. Fucking hell, it's him. It's him, Jesus Christ, it's him.' She seemed incapable of saying anything else.

'I thought you'd want to know,' I said over her litany. I wanted to say more, or the same thing in another way, but all the compassion got stuck in my throat, from which all that escaped was an emotionless, bureaucratic dribble. It would have been better not to call. I let my eyes wander around the room. They hadn't left a drawer unopened. And all in fifteen minutes. If not exactly efficient, they certainly were fast workers.

'Gloria . . .' I began.

'Wait, at least tell me where I can find you!' she managed to say before I hung up. Something bothered me. I squatted down at the dead man's side. Except for the small amount that had oozed out of the switch-blade slashes, there wasn't a single splash of blood on his whole body, but there *were* speckles on the side of his face, the lampshade next to him and, a little smudged, the backs of his hands. I checked the heap of clothes, unmistakable after following them for so many hours. That was where all the missing drops of blood had gone. Why, I wondered, would someone stick a bullet in his brain and *then* strip him naked, tie him to a chair and torture him? If what Tamerlán's men were after was information about the prodigal son, they hadn't exactly followed procedure – unless Cuervo had squealed straight off. But he didn't look the type: he looked like he'd take some working over, if only for form's sake. Ah well, maybe Tamerlán had all the answers. I'd call him later.

Something familiar peeped out from under the sofa-bed. 'Christopher Products', I read without having to bend down. 'So you finally found Sobremonte's missing treasure,' I said to him, without finding myself amusing. Out in the street, I scraped my soles several times on the paving stones as if I'd trodden in dog-shit. But what's the point when you're wearing espadrilles.

* * *

Home felt like a stranger's apartment. Even my face in the mirror looked like someone else's. Luckily Martita, the neighbour from 1H who cleaned for me, had stopped by in the week and everywhere was gleaming and well-ventilated. I turned on my computers one by one to feel at home again, then peeled off my sticky clothes, binning each item in turn, espadrilles and all. The almost scalding water and the soap burned on contact with my skin and I cut myself shaving more than once on the week-long stubble. Groomed, perfumed and wrapped from head to toe in freshly washed clothes, I had a cigarette and a cup of coffee before calling Tamerlán.

'Félix. What do *you* want?' he barked impatiently.

'Just to see if everything went all right. You found him, didn't you?'

'Yes, yes. He was where you told us. I suppose I should thank you. You can call Marroné and sort out the money now if you like, then . . .'

'Did he tell you what you wanted to know?'

'Yes. No. It's rather delicate to talk right now . . . Oh well, I suppose you've a right to know.' He turned away from the receiver: 'He croaked on you? Where did you two learn to torture? Pitman's?' He came back on: 'They say he had a dicky heart.'

'Did they kill him?' I asked innocently.

'He told them my son was still alive. Or at least that he got back from the war alive. Do you believe that, Félix? Could it be true? We're frantically going through the papers they brought back. Eh? You've found something. Oh. I have to go, Félix. Talk to Marroné. I'm hugely grateful . . . Goodbye, goodbye.'

He hung up. I'd been about to tell him about the bullet-hole, but he'd soon find out in the papers; or maybe he wouldn't. It was nothing to do with me after all. I was just curious to work out why his thugs had told him such a barefaced lie. Ah well. There were so many possible explanations . . .

Knowing I wouldn't be able to put the affair out of my mind, as so often happens when you finish a long and complex job, I went back to the dead man's papers, riffling through them fairly randomly at first. A superficial glance through while I waited for him in the bar outside Hugo's had been enough for me to get the gist of what they were about. It was nothing too complicated. What Arturo Cuervo had been going to such great pains to decipher was what he himself had written ten years ago, the mythical and untraceable sacred text that held the secret of the war, all the answers to the numberless questions that ten thousand damaged minds had conceived in ten years: the infallible plan to wrest the Islands from the usurping claws of the English and reunite them once and for all with the soil of their native land. What I had in my hands was nothing other than Major X's diaries.

Chapter 12

THE DIARIES OF
MAJOR X

May 21st 1982 – We decided to make our base in a building that we came to call 'the school', for its likeness to
our own, though I fail to understand what function it
can have for the natives. First contact: I tried to speak to
them in all the principal languages, including Castilian, Portuguese, Italian and, thanks to a soldier from
R5, even Hebrew, which, to my great relief, they did not
comprehend; I had come to fear that this colony would
be one of the dreaded kibbutzim mentioned in the Andinia Plan. It was while I was in this state of perplexity
that I heard some guttural sounds behind my back, so
dissimilar to those of any known human language that
I at first supposed the intrusion to be that of a prank-
ster; but imagine my surprise when I observed the glum
faces of the natives light up in reply and begin speaking all at once in the same uncouth accents. I turned
round to see which of my men was responsible. None of
them. It turned out to be that soldier from R5, who had
approached me on our arrival, claiming he knew me.
On being questioned, the soldier explained to me that a

similar tongue, which he had learned on his travels, is spoken on some islands in the North. Incredible though this news may seem, the unquestionable fact is that he can communicate with them, and I have, as of today, had him transferred to my company in the capacity of tongue-talker.

22nd May 1982 – Thanks to our tongue-talker, my knowledge of the natives and their customs has increased considerably. They call themselves by the name of *Kelpers*, which in their tongue signifies something like 'man' or 'men'. Until our arrival, they thought they were the only men on earth! The word *kelp* is also applied by them to a certain species of long, leathery seaweed, most abundant in these waters, hence I surmised that they see themselves as men made of seaweed (before we laugh at their naivety, let us remember that we ourselves seek our origins in a material still less apt – clay – and that the Ancient Maya believed themselves to have been kneaded from corn). The name might also signify 'seaweed eaters', though I never saw them ingest it howsoever, either raw or cooked; perhaps they keep it in reserve for moments of extreme scarcity. Considering how central sheep are to their way of life, it is at least curious that they have not taken to calling themselves *sheepers*. But these animals were no doubt introduced into the Islands in much later times by seafarers, changing the life of these peoples as the horse did the savages of our South.

The base of their society seems to be, as among ourselves, the monogamous family, which proves the universal character of this association. The number of children rarely surpasses two, which explains the scantiness of the population: more would be hard-pressed to survive, given their precarious means of subsistence. Their religion is surprisingly like our own, as if both stemmed from a common trunk; or, more probably, it was instilled in them by some missionary and, over the centuries, the lack of guidance and their natural tendency to paganism have removed it from its original form; our chaplain considers the possibilities of accomplishing a rapid conversion as being very high. They know the cross, though they do not associate it with Our Lord Jesus Christ, who is not depicted on it. Nor do they recognise the Virgin or the principal saints, though they do respect the Sabbath Day and gather in a small building that attempts distinctly to ape – albeit with the candour of a child raising a castle in the sand – the great churches of Christendom. They seem to be familiar with the concept of God, as they are with the sacred book, which they call *Bible* (N.B. the similarity to the original). Leafing through its thin pages, I noticed a similar arrangement and the recurrence of names in which, with a little effort, it was possible to detect the echoes of the original, the phonetics of their rough tongue having gradually deformed them to pronounceable variants: *Eve, Noah, Moses, Delilah, St. Mark, Pontius Pilate*, et al.

These people do not know money and may not even practise trade, other than some elementary form of barter (which, rather than our complex institution of exchange, calls to mind the image of innocent chil-

dren exchanging cards or little balls of coloured glass).
Husbands and wives are faithful to each other their
entire lives and both take part in caring for their young;
adultery or sexual aberrations are unknown, as is stealing or any form of deception. The idea of law, such as
we conceive it, is unknown to them: they are each their
own judges; they live long (one need only reckon up the
high proportion of elderly people in relation to the total
population) and free of disease, in spite of the rigours
of the climate and the arduous struggle for sustenance.
Their system of government, if such it can be called, is
of the most primitive kind: the republican; the perfect
equality among the individuals must for a long time
retard their civilisation. As we see that those animals
whose instinct compels them to live in society and obey
a chief are most capable of improvement, so is it with
the races of mankind. I have seen with my own eyes how
even a piece of food given to one is torn into shreds and
distributed to all, for all that no one individual be satisfied. It is difficult to understand how a chief can arise
until there is property of some sort by which he might
manifest his superiority and increase his power. Moreo-
ver, their thirst for change, the need to shake off the
yoke of centuries, manifested itself no sooner had we arrived. It was a sight to behold how tamely they accepted
our dominion, becoming accustomed to authority as if
their form of organisation were no different; as if, rather
than imposing on them a foreign order, we had come to
fill a vacuum that they could not remedy on their own.
Whatever their rank or authority, they have, from the

outset, rendered us the respect and fear accorded to gods rather than to men. There exists in man a natural tendency to obedience, which freely manifests itself as soon as it is given opportunity, just as domesticated animals, unlike wild ones, naturally adapt to the demands of the service of man, and training has merely to accompany instinct, rather than combat it. Rather than our arms, it was the example of our organisation and discipline that opened the doors of their island to us.

25th May 1982 – A glorious national holiday. We celebrated with a barbecue, which much improved the morale of the rank and file, in spite of the two sheep that we sacrificed barely satisfying our hunger. The scarcity of provisions is alarming. Later, after handing round some steaming mugs of boiled maté, which the *Kelpers* eagerly drank, I made a short speech declaring them full Argentinian citizens.

26th May 1982 – In the afternoon, with the aid of our tongue-talker, I continued my studies of the local tongue. If, of course, it is possible to give such a name to the barbarous agglomeration of sounds that serves the most basic ends of communication among them. According to our notions, the language of this people scarcely deserves to be termed articulate. It could be compared to a man clearing his throat, but, certainly, no South American ever cleared his throat with so many hoarse, guttural, and clicking sounds. The verbal system is rudimentary to an extreme degree, each verb presenting three or four forms at most, barely enough to account for the distinctions between past, present, and future. One need only compare with the one hundred and fifty forms that any of our Spanish verbs possess to become clearly aware of the inequality between their tongue and our own. The subjunctive modes and the preterites are confused in the same verbal form, as if that which does not present itself to the senses should not be susceptible to analysis or differentiation. It is common for the same term to stand for the meaning of several, such as *ask*, which merges in ideas so dissimilar as those of 'begging' and 'enquiring'. Another token of the primitivism of their tongue is the astonishing (for a Westerner) abundance of onomatopœias, which must inform ninety per cent of it, thus disqualifying it as a potential vehicle of abstract or even rational thought. We need only cite a few examples, such as *caw* (the cry of a bird, esp. that of a crow), *splash* (to spray with water), *crash* (to collide), *kick* (to strike with the foot), *stillness* (the absence of motion), *taut* (tight), *slack* (loose, e.g. of a wire; by extension, of a guard or watch), *whimper* and *whine* (two types of sighing sounds made by a puppy dog: the former broken; the latter continuous), *bang* (the noise of a shot or report) or *ooze* (to flow, of a thick substance, e.g. honey or treacle). But far from dismissing their tongue as coarse or deficient, we dare claim it to be admirably adapted to the practical needs of their daily lives. Is there anything in their existence that might cause the higher powers of the mind to be brought into play? What is there for imagination to picture, for reason to compare, or judgement to decide upon? They have nothing to imagine, nothing to compare, nothing to decide. To slaughter a sheep requires not even cunning, that lowest power of the mind. Their tongue remains sunk in the primordial humus, for which they have as many terms as we do for the elevated fruits of thought; so it is that our 'mud' is said in ways as diverse as *sod, slime, sludge, muck, silt, slough, scum*; or our 'marsh' in ways as varied as *bog, peat, mire, swamp, grimpen, quagmire, quicksand, cesspool, moor, morass.* Where we see a single object and denote it with a single word, e.g. 'snow', they have available a battery of terms to characterise it in its most minute variations: *flurry, blizzard, hail, sleet, flake, ice, frost, hoar, rime.* Not to mention the various names for water, which reigns over the Islands for the three seasons that the snow does not own: *shower, drizzle, deluge, flood, rain, downpour, soak, drench, inundate, lake, lagoon, pond, pool, tarn, stream, creek, brook, spring, rill, rivulet, streamlet, runnel, torrent, rapid, current, waterfall, cascade, linn, cataract, fountain, eddy, swirl, flow, run, issue, gush, pour, spout, drip, dribble, drain, trickle, percolate, bubble, gurgle, spurt, spill, flow, sea, wave, surge, roller, surf, breaker, sprinkle, drown.*

Whilst beholding these men – though at times one has to struggle to remember that we belong to the same species – and their habits of life, one inevitably asks, whence have they come? What could have tempted, or what change compelled, a tribe of men to leave the fine regions of the North, and then to settle on one of the most inhospitable countries within the limits of the globe? It is difficult to conceive, even with a supreme effort of the intellect; and yet the evidence of the senses

defies the reflections of our mind: for they are here, and
their number seems to increase, albeit slowly, from generation to generation, therefore we must suppose that
they enjoy a sufficient share of happiness, of whatever
kind it may be, to render life worth having. Nature by
making habit omnipotent, and its effects hereditary, has
fitted the Islander to the climate and the productions of
his miserable country.

27th May 1982 – On inspecting the dwellings of the natives,
I find remains of what might have been an infinitely more
developed civilisation than the current one. Automo-
biles, refrigerators, fire-arms, books, tools, and cutlery
bear witness to a Golden Age, from which, fall after fall,
they have reached to this wretched present. The study
of this ancient civilisation under the virtual laboratory
circumstances provided by the isolation of this island
will perhaps serve to dispel one of the most absurd and
corrosive ideologies to have undermined the foundations
of our civilisation: the one that would have the only being
created in the image and likeness of the Lord descended
from the wild beasts of the wood. How can we explain the
presence of these people more than a thousand kilometres from the nearest civilised coast, unless we suppose
that the Creator formed us all alike and all at once,
distributing us uniformly and at his discretion across all
the regions of the Earth, and that it is those who have not
learned to worship him that have degenerated until they
resemble the monkeys and lower animals?

28th May 1982 – In the morning a couple of enemy planes

overflew the area at low altitude, and the two soldiers
on guard fired on them with their automatic rifles, but
failed to shoot them down. The most striking thing was
the reaction of the Islanders: some ran outside, waving
their arms aloft at the planes and pointing to the shed
building where the rest were housed. I cannot find an
explanation for their behaviour: perhaps they consider
the plane – which they may well be seeing for the first
time – an irascible deity from heaven, whose power has
to be placated with supplications and invocations. I have
heard of similar cases in the South Pacific.

29th May 1982 – Dawn breaks with warmth and radiant
sunshine, so much so that I order the *Kelpers*, after their
breakfast of boiled maté and bread has been served, to
be brought outside under guard. It was a sight to behold:
the smiles of the old folk, the forays of the children, the
embraces of the couples, all enjoying themselves just as
we would do on a family day out in the country. Having
imparted the necessary orders and seen to other duties,
I sat down on a sun-baked rock to smoke a cigarette and
observe them. I gazed at the faces, lined and inexpres-
sive as though carved in granite, furrowed by cracks
and crevices like the steep crags of the surrounding hills
and covered with bristly beards that made them look
more like foxes, bears, or boars than human beings; the
hardy bodies clad in *tweed* (a coarse material, similar to
our burlap, but of woven wool), just as their lands are
clothed in a blanket of peat, the pale, milky-blue eyes
that reflect the perpetually washed-out skies of their

island home. Men and women of the land, their bones
the stones, their pulse the pulse of the island torrents
and seas, in harmony with their environment for generations. Was it not a mistake to come to change all this?
What could so-called civilisation offer them, other than
to complicate and dilute their simple way of life? Would
it not be better to withdraw now, before it was too late,
and pray that the Islands should remain undiscovered
for several millennia to come, that we should go on living in the knowledge that at least Eden survived in some
distant corner of the planet, even if inaccessible to us?

30th May 1982 – Today I have made a discovery that may
change the course of the war. I was making my evening
rounds of the shed, where the various families have
recreated their precarious tribal order, gathering round
their wretched belongings and plotting imaginary
limits with stretched ropes and hanging blankets. The
stench is unbearable. On my rounds, I discovered in the
mouth of an old man with thick, white whiskers the
gleam of gold, and also in the ear-ring of a young girl
with hair of the same colour. Questioned by the tongue-
talker about the provenance of the precious metal, some
of them pointed to the North, repeating a word that
sounded like *ingo-land, ingo-land*. I found the tongue
talker's explanation profoundly irritating. They wished
to have me believe that it came from a far-off country
in the North, beyond the Equator. I informed him that I
would execute the *Kelpers* one by one until they told me
the truth, and that, being of no further use to me, he

would be next. He conveyed my reply to them, stammering over the translation, and I heard them gurgling in their dialect and glancing furtively at me. The tongue-talker took a long time to translate what I said and, sensing that he was concealing something from me, I shook him until he talked. He did so post-haste and his story has had such a powerful grip on my imagination that I have been able to think of nothing else ever since. The Islanders, so it seems, have been trading for centuries with smugglers from the mainland, who know the secret sea routes dating from colonial times: they bring them the most advanced products (the true native technology has barely advanced beyond the stage that we know as the Stone Age: not even a simple steel knife can they manufacture by themselves), and in return, the Islanders . . . – and here he fell silent. When I pressed him, he confessed the reasons for his reticence. He thought it pointless to fill my head with absurd legends. 'All primitive cultures have such myths of great treasures, sir,' he added. I shook him until he talked. 'What do I care about your opinion, fool, tell me what treasure they're talking about!' I screamed at him. 'The *Kelpers*,' stammered the tongue-talker, 'they claim that in the centre of the island, many *miles* (1.6km) distant, an incalculable treasure is to be found, and that they take from it what they need to barter. They say they are descended from those who arrived from the North, bringing the treasure to the Islands, more years ago than can be counted on the fingers of all the inhabitants' hands. The word they repeat, *ing-land*, seems to be a corruption of the original *in gold land*, or to give it the name by which it has been called for centuries: El Dorado.

31st May 1982 – On the arm of the old man with bushy whiskers, I glimpsed a strange tattoo, which seemed to display a heraldic armadillo rampant, and at night the memory of it would not cease to work on me, as if it concealed some vital secret or message. Intrigued, I urged the tongue-talker to ask him what it signified. They spoke for a long time and, when I began to get impatient, the tongue-talker told me what he had learned. The treasure, so it seems, had been brought from the mainland in colonial times, concealed inside the shell of a giant armadillo. As I listened to him, I felt my heart beat faster: the size of those animals is comparable to a large chest; the value of the treasure had to be incalculable. The tattoo, he went on to explain to me, was in some way related to the location of the treasure: just as we charted the immeasurable sky with our constellations, these people drew their terrestrial maps using human and animal figures; and rather than trace them on parchment, which might be spoiled, or stone, which might be broken, they recorded them in the most secure of places: their own bodies. Thus, there was no way to lose one's way while every father recorded on the body of every son the route to the treasure on which depended the material and spiritual survival of all the *Kelpers*.

The story of the armadillo and its treasure began in 1806, during the first English invasion of Buenos Aires . . .

What followed were the pages telling the Legend of the Cordo-bese Armadillo, which I'd already read. My veins were bubbling with intuition and, unable to contain myself, I dialled Tamer-lán's number.

'Félix. What do you want.'

'Just one question. Did your son speak good English?'

'Word-perfect. What's wrong? I thought we were done with you. If you've got something to tell me . . .'

'Nothing for the time being.'

'We've found incontrovertible proof that he got back from the war. That he's alive and possibly very close. If you've found out something that'll help me to find him . . .'

'It's about something that happened to him in the Is-lands.'

'I'm not interested. My son will tell me all about it person-ally when I find him. Goodbye.'

I went back to my reading.

1st June 1982 – We feel the absence of provisions more
with every passing day, though the morale of the troops
continues to be high. The worsening of the living conditions tempers the spirit of the strongest and breaks that
of the weakest: unlike my men, the natives are beginning
to show all the symptoms of degradation. A fortnight is
all it has taken to turn the idyllic community of brothers into a horde of surly and isolated beings, who barely
speak among themselves, or wash, or shave, or change
their clothes. The only thing they seem concerned about
is food: they have become dreadfully demanding, and the
lowliest private need only enter for the phrase to rise up

from all points, repeated like a litany: *Give us food, give us food*. They repeat this in every tone possible, tilting their heads to one side as birds do to observe the effects of each on our faces, and after *giveusfooding* most eagerly, but in vain, they would by a simple artifice point to their young women or little children, as much as to say, 'If you will not give it me, surely you will to such as these.' This is as far as their deep-seated communism extends: their empty stomachs always remind them that they are never sated by their neighbour's fill.

2nd June 1982 – A technical problem that had disabled the Blowpipe missile-launcher was solved in a manner little short of miraculous. An officer from R5 approached, leading by the arm a soldier who was able to recite the instructions manual from cover to cover. Questioned about his astonishing feat of memory, he replied: 'I never forget anything I have read once. Test me if you do not believe it.' So test him I did. I ordered Lieutenant Trejo to bring me a copy of the *Malvinas Gazette*; the soldier leafed through it superficially and handed it back to me. 'Shall I begin?' he asked me, mildly defiant, and without waiting for an answer, 'La Gaceta Argentina Year One Issue One creation Puerto Argentino 8th May 1982 by order of the Joint Military Commander of the Islas Malvinas Brig Gen D Mario Benjamín Menéndez La Gaceta Argentina was created in this capital Padre Father Salvador Santore OP being appointed as editor of the same and as sub-editor Captain D Fernando Orlando Rodríguez Mayo Press Officer of La Gaceta Argentina's Military Editorial

Board has grounds to cover an informative need among the members of the Armed Forces consequently our first objective will be to report the truth that comes from the real and gives a new historical and social meaning to these Malvinense lands falsity in information creates absurd or imaginary illusions on the contrary informative news-broadcasting cleanses our horizons and maintains in us the virile alert of the just and noble light that we have lit and must not . . .' Before he reached the end, I had reached my decision. At this very moment, as I write, I am dictating these lines to him, after having made him read and memorise in its entirety every page of my diary, a feat that took him not above two hours. I shall now destroy it to prevent the risk of its falling into enemy hands. The mind of Private Emilio Beltrán shall hold every word of it, and no one shall be able to read it without my permission.

4th June 1982 – I heard voices last night. They spoke to me with utter clarity. I awoke in the southern silence, amidst the sleeping bodies of my growling men, with the words 'Abandon the school!' whispered in my ear. Cursing and kicking them, I forced them to wake up and herded them into the foxhole seconds before the naval bombardment reduced the school to rubble. From that moment on no one dared call into doubt my visionary powers ('God's radar' they have taken to calling me), and when the following morning I drew a line in the earth and planted a firm boot on either side, they all understood that the moment to choose had come.

'On that side of the line,' I pointed to the indifferent sea, 'you can return to your houses and families,
but as prisoners in an enemy ship, and you shall for ever
bear the bitter taste of defeat on your backs. On this side
of the line,' and, arrow-like, my arm pierced the heart of
the dark inland hills, 'you march to your deaths – or to
honour, fame and glory. You decide.'

I myself took the first step, together with Private
Beltrán and the tongue-talker, both of whom I was gripping firmly by the arms, and nine of my men followed
me, their step steady, their heads held high. Those who
stayed behind avoided our gaze, their heads bowed between their sunken shoulders, an instant of indecision
depriving them for ever of their status as soldiers and as
men.

'Anyone else?' I boomed. The only reply was the
echo of my own words. 'Quick march then. To conquer
glory.'

6th June 1982 – Yesterday, shortly after crossing the first
hills, we entered a zone of eternal mists, and since then
we have been roaming aimlessly in a milky light, without colour or form; only by continually shouting can
we keep together. The cold is intense. The supplies are
enough for only two more days and, in such conditions,
living from hunting, as we had planned to do, is quite
impossible. The old man with the tattoo, whom we had
brought with us as a guide and interpreter, has taken
advantage of the fog to escape. Enraged, I set about the
tongue-talker with blows, he having been charged with

looking after him, and he can now barely stand. I must learn to control these accesses of rage that still dominate me. No harm done this time; after the flight of the *Kelper*, he is no longer of any use to us.

9th June 1982 – We are lost still in the interminable fog, wandering aimlessly, our eyes seeing only the infinitude of the colour white, a thousand times worse than the black stain of darkest night. This is how the nightmares must be of those born blind. Today the head-count gave ten; we have lost two men: Sergeant Peña and Corporal . . . The cold prevents me from sleeping, which is now doubly demoralising, because only in dreams do my eyes recover their sight. I am writing blind.

7th June 1982 – Yesterday we had to cross a river of stone: we dragged ourselves over rocks taller than a man standing, groped our way forward or fell and hurt ourselves. Lieutenant Bermúdez broke an arm and lost all his equipment. The other nine of our party are battered and bruised but still in one piece, though only three of us still possess our full armaments and munitions.

9th June 1982 – I have found an infallible method to prevent myself losing count of the days. With my knife I make a notch in the butt of my FAL, then count the notches on my fingers.

9th June 1982 – We no longer feel hunger and have grown accustomed to the cold and the eyelessness. And we have learned to love this fog now that we know it is the hand of God that covers our eyes the better to guide us.

14th June 1982 – I know not where to begin, I know not
where to begin. I have seen more things in these last
two days than in the whole of my previous life, and, if I
write, it is not in the hope of passing it on, but merely to
discharge the pressure that boils within me and threatens to make me explode. Two days ago Private Beltrán
and I, the only survivors of our heroic platoon, were
advancing through the frozen desert of perennial fog
when my outstretched hands came across a solid wall
so smooth that there was no doubting it was a thing
of human manufacture. I brought my eyes as close as I
was able, to see of what material it was made, and my
surprise knew no bounds when they met only with a
boundless transparency, as if the clean air had candied
to solid rock to halt the fog's advance. From within that
rock, a deep, gravelly voice, the likes of which I had
never heard before, greeted me in perfect Castilian, pure
and distilled like the air that bore it:

'Major X. We have been expecting you. Welcome to
Invisible Argentina.'

I found what followed less interesting, so I skipped over it. If
the dates were correct, Cuervo had been whiling away his days
in the San Carlos POW camp, composing an alternative version of the end of the war to the exact measure of his teenage
fantasies, but God only knows if this was what he'd written at
the time or only what his ravaged mind had managed to scav-
enge from Emilio's damaged words. An impeccably costumed
gaucho had opened the doors of the Great National Estancia
to him, where the last two starving survivors were welcomed

with a sumptuous ceibo-wood-smoked barbecue served on grills of silver. Dozens of men in traditional dress shared the long carob-wood trestle tables, at the centre of which, majestic, stood the Cordobese armadillo. These were the true natives of the Islands: they claimed to be direct descendents of the *Homo argentinus* described by Florentino Ameghino, thus confirming the genius of the patriotic scientist's theory: man had had his origins in Argentina, though not, as he had once thought, in the River Plate, but on the Islas Malvinas. Uncontaminated by immigration or foreign influence, they had distilled the essence of the Argentinian race and maintained its purity to the present day.

'These savage tribes that surround us,' his guide had explained to Major X, 'serve multiple purposes. Their primitive techniques for working the land provide us with necessary raw materials, and are a convenient route for dealings with the mainland, enabling us not reveal our presence. The bellies of their women incubate our cloned embryos and the commerce of their meat grants us the necessary quota of pleasure, as you will notice the absence of women in our number. With women, duplicity and dissent make their entrance, and we must do without them if we wish seamlessly to consolidate the great Argentinian family. This fog, which we generate with our climate control machines, protects us both from unexpected visitors and from detection by enemy planes or satellite. Only those whom we call can reach us here. Our voices have been guiding the great men of the Fatherland from the beginning. They spurred San Martín to cross the Andes, Rosas to fight the French and the English, Uriburu and Aramburu to discipline the plebeian rabble, the Armed Forces to take power on 24th

March 1976 and the Islands on that glorious 2nd April 1982; and they spurred you, Major, to leave Puerto Howard and seek us out. We knew you were the man for the job. The Malvinas war is simply the first battle of the Third World War, which will culminate with the conquest of the world by Argentina. The corrupt Empire of the North is no longer capable of saving it from the Communist threat; the time has come to act, we were only waiting for the right man to guide us, the new San Martín. You, Major X, are that man.'

My God, I thought as I read; this is worse than James Bond. There were even secret weapons that reduced entire cities to rubble in a matter of seconds, satellites that blocked international communications and computers that deposited the world's monetary reserves in the Central Bank of the Argentine Republic. Free of the fetters colonialism and imperialism had imposed on the continent, Argentino-Malvinense civilisation had outstripped all the nations of the globe and, after the defeat of the English, its imperium spread day after day across the world:

> *20th June 1982* – A glorious national holiday. After the capture of the Little Prince in his flagship, the Task Force surrenders to us in full. Belgrano's ensign flies over the enemy's ships, which now turn their prows north.

> *9th July 1982* – A glorious national holiday. Surrounded by their own fleet, the English choose to surrender. Argentinian troops enter London in triumph.

> *12th July 1982* – The EEC accepts the terms of unconditional surrender. All European states are immediately

annexed as provinces of the Empire, with the exception of Spain, Italy and West Germany, whose federated status is recognised.

24th July 1982 – The wheat of the great Fatherland shall grow on land manured with the traitors' ashes. When we complete the conquest of the world, the opponents will have to go into exile on the moon. Ha! We'll see how well they manage to organise the anti-Argentinian campaign from there.

2nd August 1982 – Chrislam, the unity of Christianity and Islam, is now a fact and the days of the Zionist enemy are counted. We shall crush the head of the Serpent forever. South Africa is granted permission, as an allied nation, to invade India, Australia and New Zealand.

20th September 1982 – Ultimatum to the Soviet Union: it must withdraw all its troops from Eastern Europe.

21st September 1982 – Spring Day. The Soviets comply with the ultimatum and fall back to the Gates of Moscow. Reunified Europe celebrates its liberation.

23rd September 1982 – The Berlin Wall falls.

12th October 1982 – Columbus Day. Slavery is reintroduced across Africa. With the presence of the Holy Father, in a heart-felt ceremony in Saint Peter's Cathedral, the Inquisition is reinstated.

25th October 1982 – Revolution in the USSR. Communist leaders are executed and the brand-new Russian Republic applies to be formally annexed to the Empire as an associate state. Formal initiation of World Reorganisation Process.

This was as far as he'd got. The rest was palimpsestuous gibberish, a garbled transcription of Emilio's garbled words. That's it for me too, I thought, closing it. Life's too short. As soon as I muster the strength to see them again, I'll call Sergio or Tomás and tell them to take it with them. They'll get far more out of it than I will.

Together with these papers there was a 'Gloria Brand' notebook with orange covers and a sun and Argentinian flag. How nostalgic, I thought. I opened it, noticing that only the first few pages were written in; the last annotation was dated only yesterday. Major X had clearly been a man of deep-seated habits.

6th April 1992 – I am working rain or shine on the transcript of my diary, like an archæologist extracting fragments of marble from the rubble to reconstruct an immaculate statue. When I have achieved this, when I have managed to refine the mad language of war into the pristine original utterance, I will have only to recite it to wipe away ten years of spurious reality with a stroke of the pen, abolish this grimace of fate, this wound in the mind of God through which the Divine Word bleeds into unworthy stammering. When that is done, the Islands shall fall into our hands under their own weight like fruit from a tree.

15th April 1992 – I force him to repeat each sentence ten, twenty times, until he has exhausted all the possibilities.

The very slightest chance of error is hateful and perhaps fatal. An approximate version, a copy, is of no use to me; it is the original, word for word, letter for letter, that I have to recover. I sometimes wish I possessed an instrument capable of piercing all that disturbed flesh and truly reaching the untouched diamond hidden within, yet . . . The goose that lays the golden eggs. Ha! Prudence. We shall not commit the sin of impatience. Two Islands. Left and right. Two wars. Defeat and victory. It is *that* simple . . .

The day is near at hand. Now they tell me the end of May. I hope I shall have finished by then.

26th May 1992 – Tomorrow the first stage of the plan will be complete. The curtains will open at the exact moment and all will see the body fall. If everything goes to plan, I shall, in short, have the necessary funds to finance the expedition.

27th May 1992 – Tonight is the big night. Hugo has found that soldier's telephone number for me, the one apparently linked to the traitor Verraco. Tomorrow, at the latest, when the name of Felipe Félix is whispered into the ears of the tower's owner, begins the next stage of the plan.

Can't say I was surprised. I'd entered this nightmare with such effortlessness, walked its corridors and opened its doors with such familiarity that I'd felt part of it from the start. *But it wasn't just a feeling.* Was Tamerlán right? Was this all an act of revenge by his old enemy Arturo Cuervo? If it was, Tamerlán had beaten him to it, and the spider that had woven this net so subtly around my client and his son had been caught up in his own web. It was the most reassuring explanation, but it didn't reassure me. How, through whom, had Cuervo croaked my name to Tamerlán's ears? How did he and his accomplices, whoever they were, intend to use me; or worse, how had they been using me so far?

There were too many unanswered questions, so to keep myself entertained I turned on the telly in the rather naïve hope that they'd found Cuervo and it was on the news. I switched to Telefé, then zapped to ATC during the adverts, but they'd just started and it was all politics and international news. I turned up the volume and went to the kitchen to make myself a coffee. I hadn't had anything for dinner and couldn't be arsed going out. I detached the Pizzaphone magnet from the boiler and took it to the phone. I turned down the thundering volume of the television several notches and dialled. Large Neapolitan with anchovies and pepperoni and – I deserved no less after a week of Borda food – two helpings of fainá . . . 'What do you mean you have no fainá?' I exclaimed, muttering damn American chains to myself, when I saw it on the screen, captioned below the image of a familiar façade:

FRESH REVELATIONS IN TIE CRIME

I dropped the receiver and hammered the volume button: '—veloped in mystery the murder of Dr Aldo Glans . . . aberrant sexual practices . . . scarfing . . . his male secretary . . .' The images showed him (presumably) being escorted by police out of an unidentified building with a jacket over his head. Next they showed a photo of Dr Glans in the flesh, lamp-burnt and smiling, sporting one of his unmistakable shining satin nooses.

It took me less than five minutes to break into Clarín's police files and check last week's cases: gunned-down rowdies, confiscated drugs, rioting reformatories, stabbed lovers, abused children: the usual litany. The first one I found was dated 10th June: 'SUSPECTS ARRESTED IN DELTA CRIME' read the headline, and I skipped through it '. . . at first . . . asphyxia from submersion . . . absence of water in the lungs . . . the wife, Lucila Romero de Soria, and her lover . . . the little girl's grandparents . . .' Bastards, I thought, my eyes injected with tears, reliving the dog dripping with water, barking noiselessly at the empty river; they killed this one outright just so they wouldn't have to make another boat trip. And the heart attack of that other guy . . . Oroño? That made four at least. And this, of course, was just the beginning. Cuervo hadn't been an isolated case. From the very start, the monster had planned to kill all twenty-six witnesses one by one.

Chapter 13

HOMO ARGENTINUS

The answering machine message began with a Pink Floyd number that went on forever, then 'You're through to Sole, Malvina and Gloria's. If you want to leave a message . . .'

'Don't stay at home!' I shouted. 'Get out of there now with the girls and call me from wherever you are; it's Felipe . . .' I hung up. What if they were inside, waiting for her? Now they knew I knew. What if they'd already been and I'd left a message for a corpse? There'd been nothing about Gloria and the girls in the papers, but what if they hadn't found her yet? And the girls? Would they be capable of killing them too? What a stupid question. Of course they would. They denied themselves no luxury.

I pressed the doorbell till my finger went white. The blinds were down and the bell made a hollow sound as if the house was empty. But wouldn't it sound like that if the occupants were dead? I rang the neighbour's bell. The door opened a crack and a face peered out at me suspiciously.

'The lady next door, isn't she in?' I whimpered.

'Good evening, young man,' she pulled me up short.

'Good evening. Is she in or not? It's urgent.'

'That one?' she said, pointing in disgust. 'Haven't seen her for days.'

It was the worst news I could have heard.

'Is she out or in?'

'Out, I suppose, with one of those . . . gentlemen.'

'What gentlemen? What were they like?'

'And who are *you*, may I ask?'

I said the first thing that came to mind:

'The husband. I mean her ex . . .'

'Ah.' I thought I saw her smile malignantly, as if pleased. 'It's about time you showed up. The whole neighbourhood's up in arms about your wife's behaviour. Men all hours of the night; sometimes they only leave the following morning, and those poor girls at home all the time, listening, perhaps even seeing it all. It's just as well they're simple-minded and don't understand if you ask me. They're *your* daughters! You can't leave them in that woman's hands!'

She wouldn't let me get a word in; that really drives me mad, and I had to control myself.

'Was it two men who came?'

'No, just one this time. Young fellow, looks like she's developed a fancy for young fellows.'

'Did she leave with the girls?'

'*You* work it out: you're the father. They might be anywhere now. Anything might be happening to them. I sincerely hope you'll be taking her to court over the custody . . .'

'I need a phone.'

She started to close the door on me.

'There's a public telephone five blocks away.'

That was it. I pushed the door as far the chain would go

and my right shoe made contact with her left shin through the gap. I closed the door behind me to shut out her screams and walked away.

I could warn the other witnesses from the public phone, but then I wouldn't be able to keep an eye on the entrance to Gloria's place. They'd have to wait. I'd have a couple more deaths on my conscience, but it wasn't my conscience I was worried about now.

I put down my bag and sat with my back against the door on the marble steps, which soon froze my arse off. I lit a cigarette. The usual Saturday night excitement hadn't ruffled Parque Chas's calm surface of tarmac, tiles and terraces, and the streets were empty because of the cold, save for the dry leaves dragged along by a wind that raked the tarmac with the rattle of tin claws. Several cars went by – sometimes reappearing, spinning round and round like a top before finally plumping for one of the six streets and getting lost again – till eleven at night, when they disappeared. At one in the morning a group of four girls in miniskirts went by, clicking their heels to announce that they were off dancing and, down to two, came back at six-twenty, trying to scare each other by saying there were 'fellas' out there in the dark and giggling nervously. At seven the paper man went by but left nothing at the door. I'd promised myself that, if they hadn't turned up by half past seven, I'd break in regardless, but at eight I still hadn't made my mind up, and by then a few doors had been opened and blinds raised, so I couldn't very well shin up the drainpipe. I was in despair, dead from fatigue and hunger, my bones drilled with the cold and one of my dreaded headaches trepanning its underground tunnels through my brain. I stood up and shook the ash off my body. I'd even run out of smokes. How many more hours could I stand it? If she'd left the city . . . Resigning myself, I followed one of the old women who passed with their empty bread bags, giving her a good head start so as not to have to dawdle behind her, till I spotted the bakery and, in four bounds, overtook her to get there first. I bought half a dozen medialunas and a bag of milk, and clutching the lot in the hand that wasn't holding the bag, I ran out without waiting for the change.

There was a taxi parked outside the front door with its engine running and, tottering, with one leg still inside, Gloria was rummaging blindly in her handbag while arguing with the driver. Then she spotted me, turned to me, forgetting her trapped leg and would have fallen flat on her face if I hadn't caught her. I hugged her, feeling as if all the dead in my life were falling back into my arms.

'Gloria. Are you all right?'

'Yes,' a gust of alcohol answered me. 'What are you doing here? Have you been waiting for me?'

'All night.'

'Does that mean you're in love with me?'

'So? Are you going to pay me or what?' yelled the taxi driver with exaggerated hatred. Waiting obediently in the back seat, the two girls watched me, still half asleep. I got them out, paid the cabby, who pulled off without a goodbye, and supported Gloria until her high heels attained an unsteady balance on the grooved flagstones. She was wearing a short, white, tight-fitting dress embroidered with imitation pearls; a black, quilted PVC jacket; green resin earrings and a white shawl that hung down her side.

'Where have you come from?'

'Dancing.'

'With the girls?'

'They stayed at Mum's. I went to get them in the . . . Where is it?'

'It's gone.'

'He wanted to fuck me.' She looked again in irritation at the void left by the taxi. 'I'm runk,' she told me. 'Been out celebrating. Roy's fault: took all the charlie . . . on's own 'e did.'

'Celebrating what?'

'My'usband, 'e really is dead this time 'sn't 'e? You 'aven't come to tell me he's risen . . . from the dead 'ave you?'

She made to sit on the ground, and I had to hold her up by the armpits. Two neighbours stopped to watch.

'Help me get inside, Elipe.'

She was beginning to slip from my arms, along with my bag, the milk and the medialunas.

'We have to leave. You can't stay here. It's dangerous.'

'No. There's no more danger. Don't you understand? He's dead. You killed him, didn't you? Go on, tell me you killed him.' She remembered something and looked around the street in fright. 'The girls! They're in the taxi!'

I pointed to them standing by the door and waiting for someone to open it for them.

''Ave to give them brea-kfast.'

I shook her.

'We can't stay here. Those two heavies will be back. They're killing all the witnesses,' I spelt it out as I shook her.

Gloria went pale and I thought she'd understood, but a second later she doubled up and heaved copiously on my shoes.

There were four neighbours watching by now.

'M'alright. I can walk . . .' She wiped her mouth on the back of her hand. 'I was sure I'd never see you again.'

'They'll kill you if you stay here!'

'Me?' She smiled up at me, trickles of drool and vomit running from the corners of her mouth. 'How? I'm already dead.'

I had to put her down to look for the key in her handbag. The twins waited for me to drag her inside and then followed. I made Gloria comfortable on the sofa – the same sofa – and, leaving my bag in the girls' bedroom, I went to the kitchen to put the kettle on the hob. I looked for a milk pan and, tearing off the corner of the bag with my teeth, poured the contents into it; they hit the hot aluminium with a hiss. The girls had sat down at the kitchen table to watch.

'Do you like medialunas?'

They nodded and I opened the packet on the PVC table-cloth. They each grabbed one and bit the ends off.

'Would you like coffee, or tea, or milk . . . ?'

'Ocolate,' said Malvina.

'Ilk and oney,' said Soledad.

'Where does your mum keep the chocolate?'

Malvina pointed.

'Let me know if the milk boils.'

I grabbed a blanket off Gloria's unmade bed and carried it to the sofa. I took off her shoes and jacket, and wrapped her up as best I could. I heard the girls shouting to me, 'Flipe! Flipe!' and got there in the nick of time to stem the eruption of froth, which was about to overflow. I tipped two spoonfuls of Nesquik into one cup, two of honey into the other, and filled them both to the brim, stirring them at the same time, one with each hand, then put them one at each end of the greasy paper, dotted with medialuna crumbs.

'Hey! You didn't even leave me one?'

They both laughed, shook their heads and started to drink from their cups, holding them in both hands. I made myself a coffee and, armed with a tin of Variedad biscuits, took it into the living room. I sat down by the phone, looking at her. No one was answering at Sergio's; Tomás took a while and sounded half asleep:

'Felipe? Jesus fucking Christ. It's Sunday.'

'Emergency. The English have found Major X's wife. They want to kidnap her and force him to surrender, and I'm here defending her on my own, unarmed.'

'We'll be right over. Give me the address.'

'Listen. Bring me a 9mm.'

'Right you are.'

While I waited for them, I unfolded the list of witnesses. After crossing out four and ticking Gloria, there were twenty-one calls to make; fifteen, as five didn't have a phone, and Tamerlán's heavies weren't going to cross the Atlantic to get the Spaniard. Not knowing what pattern the exterminators might be following, I dialled at random.

'Sr Eugenio Lopatín, please.' The voice at the other end hesitated. No, it couldn't be . . . No.

'Sr Lopatín passed away. His son speaking.'

My knees began to shake uncontrollably, up and down.

'How did it happen?'

'He was killed by muggers. Out walking the dog. He had ten pesos on him. They killed the dog too,' he said, spelling out the syllables as if trying to convince himself. 'It's the funeral today. Are you going to . . . ?'

I hung up. A clean, round drop of water welled from each of my armpits and trickled down my ribs. The line I drew through his name was all shaky, as if done in a moving bus. Was I calling a list of the dead? Could they have been this quick? Sure they could. It can't have been the first time. I dialled Urano's office. Answering machine. Course, it's Sunday, I said to reassure myself. I left a message. Palomeque wasn't at home. 'He's just popped out to the office; call him there in half an hour,' his wife told me. I breathed a sigh of relief: one still alive. I didn't dare say any more, so I invented some excuse about business and hung up. Oroño's neighbour's was engaged, so I called Dany's paddle courts. He picked up. I ticked him. Score: 5–3. I'm getting there, I thought to myself.

'Don't say anything, just listen. I was with you that day in the tower. They're killing us all. Disappear,' I reeled off and hung up. I'd have liked to have given two or three names to everyone I called and asked them to pass the message on, but I suspected most of them wouldn't stick around long enough to hang up. Only by calling them one by one could I be sure.

The girls had finished their milk and came into the living room to watch the television. Malvina grabbed the remote control and put on Cablín. Bugs Bunny materialised on the screen, draped over Elmer Fudd's pointed shotgun and munching a carrot. I'd always envied his composure against all the odds – even more than Bogart's. I managed to get through to five more witnesses – fortunately all alive – and repeat the message I gave Dany. But when Tarino answered at home, I couldn't resist the temptation to innovate.

'I'm ringing on behalf of a group of patients of yours: we're coming round to your house to break every bone in your fucking body; payback time!' I was about to follow it up, but the doorbell rang and I froze. I wanted to peek out of the window, but I couldn't get up. Let them break the door down if it's them, I told myself. The girls were watching me with curiosity, waiting for me to do something. Malvina pointed at the door. Gloria turned over uncomfortably in her sleep and ended up facing the back of the sofa. Whoever it was outside started hanging on the doorbell again.

'Felipe! Open up, mate! It's us, not the English.'

The three of them stood there in full combat uniform, with rucksacks on their backs and FALs in their hands.

'We brought a spare uniform just in case.'

Once I was dressed, I checked the weapon and stuffed it in my jacket pocket. I briefed them about the situation.

'There are two of them; they drive a grey Falcon. They're coming to take her away, or kill her. It would be a good idea if two of you were posted on the terrace with the FALs and one down here. Don't let yourselves be seen,' I said. 'There are potted ferns.'

Sergio and Ignacio went upstairs. Tomás nodded at Gloria.

'She's done-for. Hasn't slept all night,' I explained.

He didn't hear me. He'd noticed the girls. Fascinated, without letting go of his rifle, he knelt down beside them, and they, sitting on the floor smiling, lifted their penguin noses to look at him.

'What's your name?' he asked one.

'Oledah,' said Soledad.

'Malina,' chimed in Malvina.

Two fat tears rolled down Tomás's face.

I called the three vets, Oroño's neighbour and the three from the Surprise team: Stuffer Stoffa, the video-maker and the caretaker. That left Palomeque, and then I'd see what to do about the phoneless five. I called his office. Nothing doing. I rang his wife again.

'No one answers at the office.'

'He must be busy. He's working on a very important job. The president of the company,' she said, gurgling with smugness, 'called him personally this morning he did. My husband has to collate some documents and take them to Sr Tamerlán's tower himself. Only very important people can get in you know.'

I said I did and hung up. I have to save the poor devil, I thought.

'What's going on?' asked Tomás, who'd given the girls a full FAL magazine to play with.

'I'll explain later. And take the bullets out in case they swallow one. I have to go out, and I don't know how long I'll be. Take turns standing guard and stay here till I get back.'

'Are you kidding?' he smiled. 'We ain't going nowhere. We've waited ten years for this.'

I was too late. Palomeque was sitting in the middle of the street when I got there, surrounded by passers-by, who were watching him die, his open briefcase spewing papers around him, on which lay the uncoiled intestines that spilled from his open belly. I squatted down beside him and he smiled when he recognised me.

'You see?' he said to me. 'I was right. My dream came true. He called me personally. "I can rest easy," he said to me, "now that I know the matter is in your hands. No one but you, Palomeque, I know I can trust in you.'"

He looked around him sadly at the scattered papers smeared with blood and shit.

'I can't present them like this,' he mumbled, trying to rescue the only clean sheaf of papers and staining them with the blood on his fingers. 'And I haven't time to type them out again,' he said to himself, trying to gather up the nearest ones. A passing bus blew several into the air and he cried out in despair. I went to get them for him and gathered them into a bundle, then returned them to his briefcase, trying to shake them off my hands. 'I have to let him know about the delay,' he said to me. 'You wouldn't have a token for the telephone? There's a public one over there that works,' he said, pointing. From where I was I could see the ragged spider of cables and the orphaned, dial-less numbers, but I didn't want to disillusion him. At the flower stall a pretty, dark-skinned girl with blonde corkscrew curls held out a token to me and I placed it in his hand, which closed on it tight. 'The company doctor hates me,' he assured me, his eyes wide open. 'And now, on this of all occasions, this has to happen to me. They'll say I did it on purpose.'

'How did it happen?' I asked the girl.

'A car. It was parked over there with the engine running and two men inside. I remember it because it had a twisted bumper on this side. It pulled out as he crossed, gored him like a bull it did.'

'How beautiful the city looks from this angle,' Palomeque was saying to no one in particular. 'You know, I used to look at them every day, but I don't think I've ever really seen them until today. You can only appreciate them properly from down here.

Can you see them? They're beautiful. The whole building rests on their shoulders and they never get tired. They're so . . . white.'

'They don't support anything. They're just decorations.'

'Yes, but look how they strain. Look . . .' he pointed and his body slumped backwards into my arms, his finger still pointing at the torso of the nearest colossus, from whose lap a white dove took flight and was sucked up into the blue. I laid him on the tarmac and slid his briefcase under his head. The flower-girl leaned over him and put a rose on his chest, taking care not to get blood on it. I walked away, with one of the 'important papers' stuck to my shoe for two or three steps, pushing aside the onlookers, who were now blocking the whole of Avenida Rivadavia, leaving the funeral oration to the chorus of bus and taxi horns and the wailing of the ambulance, which couldn't get through for the traffic. This is no use, I told myself, supporting the weight of the gun in my jacket pocket from the outside. They've got the edge on me; I'll always get there too late. I have to go straight to the root of the problem.

* * *

Something had happened to the tower since I was last there. The lawn that surrounded it looked not just unkempt but wild, as if the undergrowth from the nature reserve had worked its way in from below, and here and there were yellow patches, burned by frost and parched by lack of water. The marble base was now dingy-looking, a second marbling of dust and earth, scrawled on by the rain, superimposed over the first. Inside was no better. There was no one at the entrance to sign me in, no one in the enormous hall where my steps echoed like in an empty crypt. Of course, it was Sunday and there's nothing deader and bleaker than an office building on a Sunday – even cemeteries are full of life by comparison – but, although the other times I'd been there when it was buzzing with activity, I still found it hard to believe that it was just down to general wear and tear, and that, polished and tarted up by an army of cleaners tomorrow, Monday, the tower would once again present a resplendent face to the world. There was no such army of cleaners in existence; there was nobody, and the exponential build-up of dirt and disorder was at least a week old. Footprints, papers, even gobs of spit rubbed in by anonymous feet had dulled the polish of the floor to such an extent that all it reflected of me was a vague, blurry form, featureless and subhuman, a degraded doppelgänger hanging upside down from my feet, like a dead pig on a butcher's hook. The potted plants were as withered and dusty as in a drought, the cracked soil in their pots overflowing with old butt-ends and pebbly chewing gum; the mirrors on the walls were pocked with fly-droppings and it was repulsive to see yourself reflected in them. None of the lifts worked, so I resigned myself to making the laborious ascent into hell up the stairs, the gun in my left pocket feeling heavier with every step. At first, sure I'd find him there, I'd thought of going straight to Tamerlán's house in San Isidro, but fortunately, I'd had the foresight to ring first. 'He's been in the tower since Friday,' a dry, bad-tempered voice had answered, 'look for him there.' Evidently, I thought as I climbed floor after floor, which were in no better state than the ground floor, things at home weren't going as they should either.

Somewhere around the fifteenth I heard laughter coming from one of the offices; snaking through the mirrors I could just see the reflection of two conjoined members of the cleaning staff, unmistakable in their open, mustard-coloured jackets and matching trousers, rolled up to their ankles. The woman – I guessed it was a woman from the naked thighs and the position – was moaning with a wet, grey floorcloth over her face; the man, however, noticed me – or my reflection – but, instead of standing and pulling his pants up over his hairy arse as you might have expected, he smiled mischievously at me and beckoned to me to come over, lifting a corner of the floorcloth to murmur something in the woman's ear that made her take it off, let out an obscene cackle and also stare in my direction. I turned around clumsily, like a boy who's just entered his parents' bedroom at the wrong moment, bumping into a mop and knocking over a bucket of dirty water they'd left in the way. With one floor to go my nerves had filled my bladder so full that I plunged back into the hall of mirrors in search of the bathroom I'd shared with Marroné's secretary, but the floor was covered in sticky patches of half-dried shit and I could go no further for retching. I could have pissed in any old corner, but I didn't want to feel like part of the general degradation, so I looked for Marroné's private bathroom. There was a light on and the unmended frosted-glass door was open. Sitting on the toilet, a square book with a white cover open on his lap, five gleaming ones piled by his left foot and one well-thumbed one by his right, Marroné just looked up and smiled at me, raised his thumb and went back to his reading. A mobile phone rested on the tallest pile; plastic pop bottles, and empty boxes of pizza and assorted delivery food spilled outwards from the bathroom floor towards the office. He lifted up the book for a second and I caught sight of the cover: *In the Shadow of Young Girls in Flower*. I tiptoed away reverently so as not to distract him and ended up going in a plant pot.

A reddish mist, the last glow of a dead sun, was still floating above the surface of the river by the time I reached the top floor. It was the only light there was in the succession of empty offices and, using it to guide me through the silhouettes of indistinct hulks, I reached Tamerlán's office unimpeded. When the echoes of my cautious steps had died, a voice filled the twilit room.

'That river,' it rang out, 'has seen more things than the whole succession of civilisations: geological cataclysms, ash clouds, mud slides; had to branch, a delta, to get through and rejoin its course. Colossal fish have plied his waters, reptiles with sabre teeth, amphibians that hauled themselves onto the land and left their tracks in the mud. The monkeys that came down from the northern jungles had to become flesh-eating hunters to avoid extinction on the awesome plain. Try to picture the moment: an evening not so different from this one, two or three million years ago. The river still unnamed, still unthought, merely felt and feared; not a river but a god. Mud, crabs, spiky grasses that cut like a knife. The figure of a monkey crouching in the undergrowth, clutching a bone, waiting for some piece of vermin to wander by and snap its spine and tear it to pieces with its peg-like teeth. Something more than a monkey. The first man. An Argentinian.'

A lighter flame flickered at the centre of the room, lighting up the whole desk as it bit into a sheet of paper and began to climb, warm and yellow, up its edges. Squatting naked on the glazed surface of his desk, his chin between his knees and buttocks, millimetres from the cold, glass surface, Tamerlán was holding the burning piece of paper in one hand and an open book in the other, his eyes contemplating it in intense perplexity, baring his teeth under curling lips to show the edges of the double row of teeth. He kept hold of the paper until the flame caught his fingers; only then did he drop it, still burning, into a large glass ashtray that brimmed with identical dead, black moths. Before the last orange tongue went out, he tore out several more pages and dropped them on it, putting his palms to the flame to warm them. It was very cold in there. Almost all the windows in the room were open and the wind from the river blew through it unchecked.

'That was the starting point of a diaspora that would cover the planet. The men born on the shores of the river, men with his colour in their skin, invisible when bathing naked in his waters, multiplied and organised. The waters of the oceans they crossed and the crystalline mountain torrents gradually washed and whitened them, bleaching their hair to yellow and their eyes to blue, until they forgot their ancestry. But the river didn't forget, he waited: a brief wait for him – a few hundred thousand years – until the ships appeared on his back, loaded with men with white skins and yellow hair, thinking they were discovering when they were merely returning, not recognising their grandsires in the copper-skinned men with coal-black hair. The river witnessed the encounter, impassive and remote. He hasn't changed a bit since then. His murky waters still carry the taste of the red earth, the pristine jungles, the putrefaction of the tropics, to the European city at its mouth. We built this watchtower in order to observe it; but it is he, with his patient eyes, that will see it fall. Do you see? He has all the time in the world.'

He rested the knuckles of both hands on the desk and

nimbly lifted his back legs to turn and face me, his flaccid, balloon-like belly resting, along with his testicles, on the glass surface, his long simian penis overhanging the edge like a pendulum at rest.

'I am the first Argentinian,' he said.

'I thought you were German,' I answered. It was the first time I'd spoken, and I jumped at the sound of my own voice. Tamerlán dismissed my objection with a gesture.

'We're all Argentinians. It's all in here,' he said, holding up the book whose pages he'd been burning to keep warm. 'Do you realise the genius of this man? He wanted the human race to have had its origins here, right here, in this last, forgotten corner of the planet. A bold, almost inconceivable gesture: only an Argentinian could come up with that. This man is the true father of his country.'

I moved a few steps closer to peer at the cover: *The Origins of Man in the River Plate* by Florentino Ameghino.

'Do you understand? Our true homeland is the imagination. Earth and flesh are revoltingly female. Now I see the error of my ways. I wanted to build a bridge of flesh between father and son, instead of calling his name across the void. Only in it can we men engender. The void, that is the substance . . . That's why the Malvinas matter so much. Now I realise my son wasn't wrong, but continued and extended his father's vision. He knew that only in the void of Malvinas could Argentina realise itself in its full purity. Ten years it's taken me to understand, ten years he waited for me to understand before deciding to return.'

He'd turned his pale, darting eyes away from me and now trained them on the dead pages in the ashtray. It looked like he was talking to them.

'You know, in some cultures the punishment for murder is to take the dead man's place. To bang his widow, for example, and look after his kids. The murderer has to leave his old house, you understand, his wife and his children, and live the life of the dead man, the life that the dead man would have lived had he not killed him. *His* wife is the one who is widowed, in the end, and *his* children orphaned. My son César will do that very same thing for his brother. From now on, it will be as if Fausto had never left and César, never been born.'

'Is that what happened?' I asked disinterestedly. 'Little Abe came back and little Cain pushed him out of the thirtieth floor?'

He nodded, smiling.

'Can you understand my joy? My son has come back to me, at last. Everything will be the way it was before. Isn't it wonderful, isn't it a miracle, that a father's love can vanquish even death?'

'Is that why you've started murdering all the witnesses?'

'I'd decided to right from the start. Come off it, Félix, don't tell me you didn't see it coming. Did the dollar signs stop you from seeing straight? Why do you think I paid you a hundred grand for a job that wasn't worth ten? Your looks?'

We were now little more than two silhouettes in the half-light. The twilight had thickened round the tower as we talked and become night; the light from the monitors, like weak reflectors, was all that lit the sad simian perched on the glass, projecting across his skin a green and gold mosaic, like sunlight through forest leaves. The same information shone on all the screens: a list of twenty names that had once been twenty-six. Tamerlán scratched his groin in discomfort, then an armpit.

'These carpets are full of fleas. That's why I spend most of the time up here. Come over here, Félix; you can groom me as we talk.'

'I've come to kill you.'

'Yes, I know; otherwise you wouldn't be looking at me with those big sheep eyes. Think hard about what you're about to do; don't regret it later.'

'I'm protecting someone.'

He smiled as if he'd always known.

'Of course, of course. I realised the day you came pheasant-hunting with me, when I asked you to . . . It never fails to amaze me that young people can go on falling in love in this . . .' He made a sweeping gesture of disenchantment with his hand, despairing to define it. 'I recognise your urges, I understand your motives, I share your reasons, but . . . You don't have what it takes.'

He squatted there looking at me to see if there was any need to go on arguing or if we could move on to the next point. He decided there was still a way to go.

'Survival, Felipe, starts out as an art, but if you don't know how to stop, the day comes when it gets to be an addiction. You can never be sure of having survived, not completely; you always think you need a little more. So everything that appertains to life appears as dangerous, implies a risk to our chances of survival, and has to be curbed. Living becomes a means and survival its end. We're more alike than you think, Felipe. Look at us: Darwin would be proud of us.'

That was it then; he too had realised, as I had, though he probably hadn't made the same effort to deny it. In both of us, the same hunger that no food of this world could appease:

survival at all costs. Both of us had responded in opposite, but complementary ways; the same fear of the world had led me to withdraw from it and try to cling on in its margins; and him, to swallow every last mouthful of it so that nothing was left outside to threaten him. In one of the mirrors that framed us, we were the inverted reflection of each other.

As if to afford me the freedom to decide, he'd turned his back on me and was now gazing out of the fateful window. Down there in the landfill site, one solitary last late lorry arrived with its load of rubbish and rubble, tipped it over the felled willows and headed straight for the exit, the bobbling yellow cones of its headlights lighting up the mountains of trash.

'We're reclaiming land from the river. Reclaiming. Ha! So much effort to buy space when what I need is time,' he sighed, exhaling an infinite weariness. 'If only my father had called me something inglorious like Raúl, or Roberto.'

A light, the first we'd seen, appeared on the distant shore of Uruguay. Between it and us lay nothing but an empty, black expanse.

'The river's very dark at night. When there's no moon, it feels like there's nothing more than a void in its place. It must be cold now. Cold, misty and lonely.'

'I'm willing to let you live if you promise not to kill anyone else . . .' I managed to say. It sounded so pathetic that I already felt embarrassed by mid-sentence and dried up. Tamerlán wasn't listening though. He was still looking through his window, though there was nothing to be seen now. His eyes were turned inwards as if he'd discovered a mirror-world at the back of his skull and he was smiling, his face softer, the reflec-

tions showing something inestimable. He looked released, innocent. His voice came from the distant land on which he had
once again set foot:

'When we lived in the country, my father would bring me
toys. Almost every week, in a brown leather suitcase with gold
catches, and I'd throw myself on them before I threw myself on
him. From far away I'd recognise his silhouette, his stiff-legged
gait when he was in uniform, the suitcase bumping against his
left leg under the weight: I learned to guess how full it was by
the way it bobbed up and down as my father walked down the
gravel drive, past each of the identical houses and their flowerbeds before he'd reach ours. I was especially happy in summer
because Mutter would let me wait for him in the garden, and
we'd open it on the green grass and its contents would spill out
everywhere when he popped open the suitcase lid: teddy bears
with thick, silky fur, glass eyes and happy smiles, and with
them, all the animals of the woods and jungles for a child to
populate his world with: pink elephants and light-blue giraffes;
squirrels with eyes like drops of pitch and real walnuts in their
hands; rubber ducks that paddled on the pond with legs that
really worked; lions and tigers with toothless, pink babies'
mouths; a fox and a bunny-rabbit hugging . . . Then there were
building kits: tall houses with prominent wings, low shops
with their counters and shelves, staircases and columns; trains
with tracks and barriers, and stations with benches and ticket
offices; cars of all colours, and mechanics' workshops, and lorries loaded with bottles of milk, demijohns of wine, packets
of sugar, coffee, chocolate; horses and carts, fire engines with
ladders and extendable hoses and firemen clinging to the sides
. . . There were dolls, too, all shapes and sizes, girls and boys,

with hand-sewn suits and porcelain faces, eyes that opened when you picked them up, and smiling or serious mouths. My favourites, of course, were the little soldiers in their hand-painted uniforms on their lead bodies; the tanks with hidden wheels that turned, the propeller-planes with bombs hanging from their wings . . . My father used to pull them out of the suitcase by the handful and I'd already be playing with all of them at once, weeping in anticipation at the loss of those I couldn't keep; and he, smiling and crouching beside me, with one hand resting on the floor from the pain of his new boots, would stroke my hair and say "You know the rule: one toy at a time. Play with them all a little bit, touch them, press them to your heart. Then close your eyes and picture which one is clearest in your mind. That will be the one to keep," and he'd carry on down the flagstone path to the front door, where my mother would sometimes be waiting for him, wiping her hands on her apron, without looking at him or me and my toys. Did you know I was a country boy at heart, Felipe?' he asked, smiling open-mouthed, and I noticed that the caps had fallen off two of his teeth to reveal the sharp, black pins on which they'd been inserted. 'Those landscapes are never wiped from the memory: the landscapes of childhood. As with the houses, the gardeners had done everything possible to reproduce an Alpine postcard over that flood-prone plain swept by the north wind, damp and smelling of the sea. They'd brought rocks, mountain flowers, small fir trees that took well thanks to the abundance of fertiliser; and the gardeners, dark men in grey uniforms with sunken eyes, who spoke a language I couldn't understand ("Polish," my mother told me when I asked) came twice a week to keep it in shape. My father would allow no

changes, save the natural ones of the seasons, and wouldn't let
the trees exceed a certain height without replacing them so as
not to lose the effect of his miniature native Bavaria, his own
private Zwölfkinder. I suppose that's where I get my taste for
bonsais from,' he said, pointing without looking to the bare
ombú and the withered leaves scattered on the dry soil at its
base. 'I spent my childhood in that garden, separated by the
wire from the oceans of mud that stretched out to the horizon,
in that oasis of order and neatness, with no more contact with
the outside world than the nocturnal glow of the ovens (which
my mother's fables transformed into friendly dragons lighting
up their walks in the woods), the noise of the bulldozers and
the smell of ash when the wind blew in our direction.

'When playmates were available, I'd often ask them to
help me choose the toys. My father wouldn't let me keep them
long, perhaps fearing that, like the fir trees, they'd grow too
high and be out of keeping with the landscape, or possibly to
stop me growing too fond of them and suffering unnecessarily
later. The life of a soldier is made of losses, he'd tell me, and one
had to learn not to get too attached to anything – except the
Army, the Fatherland and the Family. They'd invariably arrive
walking beside him, trotting to keep up with him and dragging the suitcase with great effort but not a word of complaint.
My father used to bring them straight from the station, where
there were lots to choose from. They were usually children
with dark skins and eyes, very skinny and dirty and always silent. He wouldn't let me touch them when they arrived: "He's
crawling with lice," he'd tell me, "we have to give him a *shower*
to *disinfect* him," and, on pronouncing these two words, he'd
unfailingly wink at me. My mother, without saying a word,

would take the boy by the hand and, speaking softly to him, lead him inside, where she'd bathe him and give him clean clothes. With her round, red, Dutch face and resigned smile, my mother had something about her that used to soothe them. She'd often forbid me to treat them badly and I knew that, when she was watching, there were certain games I couldn't play, such as "Guards and Prisoners", "Out of the Hole, Rat" and "Digging your own Grave" (I'd been taught them by other children, officers' children, before the camp began to empty and I was left alone). Once, when I was hitting one of them with a rock because he hadn't said a single word in three days, my mother gave a cry from the house, leaped on me and twisted my arm till she bruised it. That evening, when my father came home, they took him away, in spite of my mother's pleas, and at night I heard her weeping and the powerful words of my father, in his harsh highland German, warning her of what could happen to her. I became very close to many of them: Simon, the pampered son of an influential Danzig tradesman, who'd swear every time I hit him that his father was coming to punish me – in the form of acid rain, I suppose; I wept into my mother's apron the morning I awoke to find his bed empty. There was Hilman or Hilborn, a delicate, fair-haired, pale-looking boy with the body and manners of a girl. His whole family had been musicians and the day he arrived he had in his suitcase his father's violin, which he could play almost as well. After dinner he'd entertain us with Mozart, Beethoven (I've never heard a performance of his D major concerto as pure) and Schubert. Later on, when they made us go up to our room (he slept at the foot of my bed), I'd disguise him in my mother's clothes and make him suck my dick; I'd urinate on him and force him to eat my excrement;

442

once I tried to stuff his violin bow up his arse – without much success I have to say. He never once complained or resisted, forcing me to devise ever more extreme ways to test him. He was with us for quite some time, until he inevitably began to repeat his repertoire so, tiring of him, my father had him taken away. That day my mother made her first suicide attempt, shooting herself in the temple with the gun we kept in the house and opening up this long groove. Her head in a bandage, she ministered to me for days without a word and I felt guilty without knowing exactly why. The most problematic of them was a gypsy boy, who on the first day, when we were out of sight of the houses and I tried to mount him like a horse, dealt me several punches to the stomach and, when I was down, held a piece of broken glass to my throat and told me he'd kill me if I told on him. From then on my life was a constant terror: I had to steal food and money and clothes for him, which he passed on to other gypsies on the other side of the wire; he beat me every day, and at night, when Mutter left the bedroom, he'd climb onto my bed and sexually abuse me, then make me sleep on the floor. I don't think I was ever so afraid of anyone as that little boy with the fierce eyes, except perhaps of my partner – in his good old days, of course. Now,' he said, putting the acrylic prism to his eye like a monocle, 'he doesn't frighten anyone much. Eventually the thefts came to my father's attention and he decided to take him away. "Wild animals don't belong in houses; they belong in the countryside," he said, pointing to the frost-covered plain that stretched to where the horizon met the sky, green and black with the clouds of smoke and the floating ash. They never brought me a little girl to play with, perhaps to avoid racial contamination, and in a way it was better. For me there was no other woman than my mother, with her big breasts and her butter-coloured plaits and her strange accent whistling at the back of her throat when she forgot her hatred of me and sang songs from her country, songs that, with the little Dutch I knew, evoked pictures of mills and polders with placid cows and a sea always black and threatening and tall, thin houses lined up like wafers in a packet. The last day in the camp, in an end-of-holiday confusion, with everyone running disorganised back and forth hurriedly packing their suitcases selecting only the most valuable things to carry and running after lorries that left without waiting for stragglers under orders that nobody obeyed, their guns drawn as they went from room to room in their own houses, my mother took advantage of the prevailing confusion to disappear with my last companion, a little Dutch Jewish boy so young (towards the end there wasn't much to choose from, and my father had been forced to take whatever was going) that I used him more like a dog than a playfellow. In his search for them, my father went in and out of several houses, dragging the brown leather suitcase with gold catches along the floor for the weight of it, shouting orders and questions to soldiers who took no notice, threatened at gunpoint a group of prisoners who'd crossed the fallen wire and were standing wide-eyed on one of the Alpine flowerbeds . . . Eventually the roar of the planes flying overhead almost without interruption in the stormy sky forced him to give up the search and we got into a jeep with some other officers abandoning the camp. That was the only time I saw what lay on the other side of the triple barrier of barbed wire. Some were still trying to conceal the high stacks of corpses, which yielded before the onslaught of the diggers, as soft and flexible as boiled vegetables. I peeked out of the side, incapable of taking my eyes off them, recalling the rivers and woods and peasants with cows, waving from the door of their cabins that my mother's voice had so often raised from the sea of ashes. It was as if a long spell had been broken, the palaces opening like shells to show the rows of barrack huts, the vineyards coming into focus as coils of barbed wire, the lofty minarets resolving themselves into watchtowers, the mossy paths of the wood into caterpillar tracks over human bones, the carriages into lorries piled high with bodies, the knight errant into a sergeant trying to finish off a survivor with a table leg and his companions shouting "Get a move on!" from the running lorry, the chests of priceless jewels into piles of gold teeth, and a mud-covered boot forgotten in the headlong flight waiting for someone to find its rightful owner. Midnight had struck for everyone, taking them by surprise and forcing them to run around a world where they no longer recognised themselves. My mother wasn't there to cover my eyes with her hands and whisper in my ear what she was seeing, what only then I realised she had never seen. "It's better like this, mein lieber Faust," she'd say whenever I asked to look. "The eyes of the imagination see prettier colours." I thought that I might be able to recognise one of my playmates in the pile-up of unknown faces, but I soon gave up trying. All the faces were the same: they all had the same expression of exaggerated laughter and even the bodies of men, women and children had become indistinguishable in the general shrinkage of starvation.

'For several nights that merged into the darkness of our daytime concealment we travelled north, fleeing from the spring across a Europe of puddles and rubble, dragging the suitcase that at the last moment my father had forced me to empty of its toys to load it with the jewels and little pieces of gold he'd managed to amass. For several days we lived in the hull of a bombed-out boat, drenched by the drizzle and the grey swell of the sea, until one night, some men as frightened as we were helped us to embark. The ship was bound for Argentina and, when we arrived, that suitcase was the only luggage we brought with us.'

He paused, conclusively. The story was over. I looked around me in confusion. The sky over the river had filled with aggressive stars that looked down on us in scorn from their niches on high. It was as if the last floor of the tower had detached itself from the rest and, like a satellite, was floating out of orbit, all contact with the Earth lost. With an effort I fixed my eyes again on the creature perched on the desk. Perhaps it *was* better to kill him after all. He was like a dog with a broken spine: irretrievable and capable of snapping at anyone that tried to help him.

'If you take the brightest star as the centre and draw radii like the spokes in a bicycle wheel to the edges of the sky, and draw a spiral away from the centre through each of the surrounding stars, what shape are you left with?'

'It's hard to picture it.'

'A spider-web. A spider-web stretched across the black vault of the heavens, the constellations caught in it like insects sucked dry. And at the centre, at that point of maximum light . . .'

'What.'

'God. The spider.'

'Haven't you found out who was sending the anonymous letters yet?'

He'd stood the acrylic prism on end, like a bonsai mono-
lith, and was leaning towards it slightly, in an attitude of rev-
erence. He picked up a few dry leaves from around the dead
bonsai and piled them at its base, as if preparing an offering.

'That man, Cuervo, no doubt. His messages keep arriving
like the light from many of those stars up there that no longer
exist. Have a look at his swansong.'

He was holding out a piece of continuous feed, identical
to the other two.

> *Farewell, my boys! My dearest friends, farewell!*
> *My body feels, my soul doth weep to see*
> *Your sweet desires depriv'd my company,*
> *For Tamerlán, the scourge of God, must die.*

'Did he confess to your men?'

'No. He didn't have time. You know.' He blew a raspberry.
'We found that in his things,' he said, pointing to it. 'Same
handwriting.'

It was peeping out of the pile of papers I'd seen them carry
out of Cuervo's, just by what was left of the Zen garden, which,
with half its sand tipped out and the other half scratched as
if by a cat and full of fag ends and balls of paper, looked more
like a common spittoon. It was an orange Gloria Brand exercise
book, identical to the one in my possession, but much newer
and shinier. I opened it and examined its pages in the light of
the monitors. It began at the same date as the other one, 15th
April 1992, and went up to 28th May, the day after the crime:

> *15th April 1992* – We spoke at length of our days in the
> Islands. When he was lost in the mist, he wandered

aimlessly until he came across a smallholding, where, thanks to his mastery of English, he was able to persuade the Kelpers to take him in. He spent several weeks fighting for his life, cared for by the couple's young daughter, who remained by his bedside day and night, watching over him, restoring not just his health, but his will to live, which his father had mutilated to the point of leading him to seek death in the war. The couple had accepted him at first thinking to ingratiate themselves with the Argentinian authorities, but they soon grew genuinely fond of him and began to treat him as one of their own. There is no need to say what this meant to our young hero, whose father's slights and insults had been the only domestic warmth he had ever known. Providentially, the farm's radio was broken, and this gave them the time they needed to warm to the young man before they found out that the war was over. One day they saw a group of soldiers approaching along the road, but imagine their surprise when they realised from their uniforms and faces that they were English. They did not hesitate. The enemy soldiers were deceived by the young Argentinian's fair complexion and excellent English, and the couple introduced him as their son-in-law. In a few short months he was. It was some time since the English ships had left the last load of prisoners on the mainland, and he decided to stay. Free at last, in this new land he would give his children what his father had never given to him.

28th April 1992 – Fausto went on telling me about his life

in Malvinas. Catherine's fertile womb soon bore him
two infants: Nigel, in 1984, and little Cynthia, two years
later. He adopted the Kelpers' customs and dress and, as
he adapted to his new world, the pain the memories of
the old one brought him faded. With time, he thought,
surrounded by so much affection, perhaps he would
manage to forget and, perhaps, even to forgive. But fate,
as cruel as the man who had taught him what pain was,
did not wish it so. The plane carrying Catherine, Nigel
and Cynthia back from a trip to England crashed in
the Atlantic and disappeared without a trace, a victim
presumably of some fundamentalist attack.

1st May 1992 – 'I prayed for death,' Fausto told me during
those days, 'but my prayers went unanswered. When I
managed to pull myself together from the madness of my
early grief, I realised I would no longer be able to remain
in that land. I shall go back one day, I thought at that moment, but shall not do so alone. I shall come back to my
own kind and show them the only real way to make the
Islands ours. Cathy, Nigel and Cynthia will not have died
in vain. Their love will close the wounds and bring peace
to our two warring peoples. I shall return to Argentina
and organise the ultimate recovery of the Islands.'

16th May 1992 – 'When I reached my country,' Fausto told
me last night, 'I almost didn't recognise it. It had changed
so much. While I lived happily on the Islands, I would
refuse to read the news that sometimes appeared in the
local newspapers; I would cover my ears when they said
something on the radio. My imagination had filled in the

gaps. In my innocence, I had supposed that the experience of war would have been of some use to us, taught us a new love of country and of the brave officers and men who had given so much to defend it. Instead I found a land devastated, as if the war had taken place here and not there, with a society undermined to the core by petty vengefulness and the excesses of democracy, where the heroes of my youth had been first vilified and ridiculed, then – more cruelly still – forgotten. Therefore my first objective was to seek you out, to meet you all again, for I knew that no one else would want to hear or help me. You, Major X, had been like a father to me during the days of the war and, like a father, you were the first I sought out on my return. Apart from that experience, unshareable with others, we had something else in common: hatred of the same man and the desire to wreak revenge for the many wrongs he had done us: the man that had the effrontery to claim to be your friend and my progenitor.'

A spicy, autumnal smell tickled my nostrils. I looked up. Tamerlán had added some screwed-up pages from Ameghino to the pile of ombú leaves at the foot of the erect prism and had set fire to them. The acrid smoke from the bonfire filled the room and, as the tongues of fire began to lap at the corners of the prism, was joined by the more nauseating smell of burning plastic. There was another page to read.

> *25th May 1992* – I am certain that Divine Providence has mediated in this encounter. Together we shall make Tamerlán pay for everything he has done, then we shall use his millions to organise the recovery of the Islands.

Fausto, whom I now love as my own son, the boy-child I could never have, has told me that, once he takes control of the company, he will take my surname. Only one obstacle stands in our way. Fausto's long disappearance has meant that he is considered legally dead and it is his brother César who will inherit after his father's death. We cannot see our plans delayed by legal complications that may take years, so Fausto will speak to his brother and try to convince him to join us: from what we know he has more affronts to wash away than all of us together. But perhaps he will put the ambition of inheriting everything before his desire for revenge. We shall see what happens at the meeting. We have arranged it for the day after tomorrow.

28th May 1992 – All is lost, all is lost! I saw him fall with my own eyes and carried his broken body in my arms, far away where they cannot touch it. But his death shall not be in vain. I shall confront the treacherous father and his murderous son, I shall make them destroy each other and then, then . . .

The writing stopped there. After that the exercise book offered nothing but the virginal white of blank pages. I snapped it shut.

'Finished?' he asked me.

'Finished.'

He nodded as if to show he understood my silence, or assuming I understood his.

'Now I need to find out what happened at the brothers' meeting. It isn't difficult to imagine, is it? Horrified at such a monstrous proposal, César defended his father and sent the traitor to his death. Then, knowing the grief could kill me, he unselfishly kept quiet, preferring humble silence to recognition at the expense of my pain. How unfair I've been on him. I feel so ashamed. I haven't dared to ask him in case I can't look him in the eye. Canal's with him now. They'll be along any moment and then . . . I'd like to love him now with all my heart, but it's still weeping over Fausto, the fruit of my womb. Where did I go wrong? Everything is so confused inside me. I try to see, but all I see is me. My heart is . . . covered with mirrors.'

He's caught a dose of Major X's purple prose, I thought. I have to tell him before it's too late.

'It's a fake,' I said. 'You've been sold a cheap soap.'

'What?' Some of the old fire returned to his eyes. 'How can you . . .?'

'I've got the real diary.'

'And this one?'

'It doesn't say a word in mine about your son. Only that they found the perfect fall guy to take a dive out of the tower.'

'And make me think it was Fausto.'

'With the fake diary,' I completed.

'I want to see it. Now.'

He jumped down off the desk and walked towards me with one hand held out. Naked and upright, humanly erect, he was even more obscene than as a monkey.

'We have to negotiate.'

'Don't be a fool, Félix. Give me that diary this minute.'

'The tower's empty. You're alone and stripped to the bone, and I've got a gun. You don't know where I've stashed it.'

'What do you want.'

'A piece of paper signed by you, saying you had those six

witnesses killed. If you leave the rest alone, your confession will rot in a bank vault; one more dies and I'll take it to the pol— the television,' I said, correcting myself. 'Oh, and let's not forget. A cheque for eighty thousand dollars which, give or take the odd cent, is what you owe me.'

'All right, Félix, if that's how you think you'll be able to sleep at night. You've gone all sentimental on me.' He tore out the double page from the middle of the Gloria exercise book and snatched up a Mont Blanc from the accumulated flotsam on his desk. 'What do you want me to put?'

'Buenos Aires, 14th June 1992. I, Fausto Tamerlán the First, hereby . . .'

He scratched the blank page, swore, and shook the fountain pen several times over the paper without blotting it.

'Why not write it on the computer?' he suggested.

'No use to me. It has to be . . .' I said, checking my pockets for a biro. 'Shit, I remember to bring a .45 and not a fucking . . . Haven't you got any cartridges over there?'

He spanned the room sadly with his arms.

'Behold the ruins of the century.'

I had to rifle through the drawers myself while he looked on in amusement. I found a broken Bic and, after rubbing it between my palms as if making fire and breathing on the tip for a while, drew the first little stroke of viscous blue ink.

'Now put the names,' I told him when we'd finished the introduction.

'You think I know them by heart? Dictate them to me.'

He signed it and held it out to me with a tight-lipped smile. It was surprising how quickly practical matters had brought him out of his mystical delirium.'

'Well. Shall we go?'

'Like that?'

'True. It might be cold outside. What about you?' he said, fixing his eyes on my combat uniform as if he'd noticed it for the first time. You're walking around dressed like that? You should be ashamed at your age. Did you come in a car?'

He was putting his first leg into his underpants when he remembered something.

'Cuervo wasn't acting alone, was he? Do you know who else . . .'

Then something strange began to happen. A distant murmur like the wind of an approaching storm through a wood came from the floors below. I looked down. Something was happening down in the bowels of the tower, as if the light were getting brighter and the visibility more complex at the same time. Whatever it was was climbing towards us, and with it, growing louder by the second, the rush of the wind. I looked at Tamerlán and the change in his features frightened me more than the uncertainty. His mouth hung open and his bulging eyes fixed themselves on the depths as if the worst creature to walk out of his nightmares were approaching, the dinosaur from world's end. Only when there were six or seven floors left to go did I realise. As if obeying some powerful sorcery, the mirrors had started to turn and *we* would soon be the ones trapped at the point where we could see no one and everyone could see us.

Chapter 14

THE PAIN DRUG

Tamerlán had sat down on the glass, his arms and torso hanging down as if dripping through the trapezoidal gap between his crossed legs. From his flesh, which ran like melting wax, only the two weak, blue flames of his eyes rose to cast me a look of abject entreaty. I had to put my ear next to his mouth to hear his words, which were barely distinguishable from his breathing.

'They can all see me. Everybody's eyes . . .'

He was trying to cover himself with his big-boned arms, but there was no surface, no corner, no atom of air that didn't reflect his sagging, naked body, multiplied millions of times in the mirrors that hemmed us in. It was then I realised that I hadn't given him everything, that I had one last, futile sacrifice to lay at his feet. What he'd lost for ever in the dark labyrinths of the blood came back to him by the less tortuous paths of chance.

'Don't worry, Dad,' I said, pronouncing my own sentence once more. 'I won't let them hurt you.'

I put the gun down next to the keyboard and began to surf; the seconds magically became hours now that I was back in my element. I knew they were coming for us, but even if they started up the lifts again and ran down the passageways, they couldn't move as fast through their world as I through mine. I found the commands that controlled the mirrors almost immediately and introduced a random sequence that would turn windows into mirrors and mirrors into windows in one continuous, maddening braid throughout the tower. No sooner did it start than I had to close my eyes to stop myself falling off the chair and rolling about the floor vomiting, as in the worst, most terminal of binges: it was like being locked inside a kaleidoscope that was spinning at the speed of a centrifuge, caught in a jumble in which whirled the river, the city, the floors of the tower and my body parts, sliced and diced, as if my brain and all its contents had been thrown into a blender. Crawling on all fours, shouting out his name, I tried to rejoin Tamerlán, whom I'd lost in infinite space. What a bad trip, I thought as I dragged myself blindly along, bumping into pieces of furniture or columns, what a bad trip.

The first shot rang out just as I found his knee, followed by a cataract of broken glass. The second sounded closer, and the glass, in my blindness, seemed to cascade into my ear. When he felt me, Tamerlán clung compulsively to me, like a drowning man to a bather only to drag him with him to the bottom like a lead weight.

'What is it? What is it?' he sighed.

My darkness had filled with its own ghosts.

'The English,' I replied idiotically.

The explosions were getting nearer and nearer, the thud of each detonation like the leg of the dinosaur as it climbed the mountainside and got wind of our fear to guide itself in the night. The last shot exploded in my ears, just as before the world had been blown to pieces in my eyes, and I heard the bullet whistle over us and shards of glass stuck to my face like stingers.

'Are we interrupting something?' came a shrill voice.

I opened my eyes. Framed by broken glass in the mouth of the long bullet-blown tunnel through the mirrors stood César Tamerlán looking at us mockingly. Behind him, with his usual wind-up-toy precision, Canal was removing an empty magazine and replacing it with a fully loaded one. He spotted my gun by the keyboard and gestured to César.

'Keep an eye on them while I sort this out.'

He sat down in front of the screen. In seconds (but far longer than I'd have taken), he stopped the mirrors whirling. The city levelled off, the river and sky separated like oil and water, and assorted body parts assembled like the pieces of a doll. With the same ease he closed all the windows, bolted all the doors and trained a thousand spotlights on us. Exposed, Tamerlán let go his drowning embrace and pushed me away as if I'd been taking liberties with him.

'Fausto, my son!' he exclaimed with the eyes of a dazzled hare, looking in the direction of César. Shuffling on hands, feet and buttocks, I put a couple of metres between us.

'Fausto my arse,' the other replied, his knuckles white on the gun, luckily with the safety catch still on. 'It's me, César, understand? César! Your little Fausto is good and dead. Your little Fausto wanted to kill you and keep the lot.'

'You're mistaken, mein lieber Faust.' Suddenly he was speaking German, tears pouring from his eyes, his hands outstretched to César who, shaken and bewildered, turned towards Canal.

'What the fuck's he saying?'

Gun resting on his crossed legs, swivelling to face us in

the chair, Canal contemplated the scene with clinical interest.

'That you suffered shell shock and think you're your brother César. I knew it would come to this. It was only a question of time.'

'Why don't you explain to him . . .?'

'It's not worth it any more.' He pointed the gun at Tamerlán, who was watching in silence on all fours. 'Time for the next stage.'

César looked at him, then at his father. His voice shook when he spoke.

'Now?'

Canal gave him a wan smile and pointed with his trimmed beard.

'What better time. Look at him.'

'Wait a second,' said César eventually, looking again at Tamerlán when he was sure their eyes wouldn't meet. 'Before I do, I want him to understand what's going down here. It won't be any fun if he doesn't understand. Thirty years this shit's been building up. Or have you only just realised?'

'We've talked about this.'

'We've talked! And talked! That's right! Every single day, two hours repeating the same thing at the wall while you stared at the ceiling! Till all the hatred turned into boredom, and back to the beginning the next day! No, I've waited long enough. Now I want it all.'

'All right then. Go on. Treat yourself. Begin.'

'Something to say to me, mein lieber Faust?'

'Yes, you old fool, of course I've got something to say to you! I've got everything to say to you! A lifetime of stuff!'

'Did you miss me?'

'I am not Fausto!' He screamed so loud I thought he was going to spit blood. 'I'm César! Won't you ever see?'

'César? César? I don't know what you're talking about. I don't know any . . .'

'See?' the stranger exploded in Canal's direction. 'See what he does to me?'

'We're not getting anywhere like this,' Canal opined.

Tamerlán looked up at us both from the floor. Then, with difficulty, he stood up straight and entered the cold cone of light from one of the dichroic lamps in the ceiling.

'I had a son, Fausto, once. Your mother once had a son, the one you mentioned. It was her idea to bring you into the world. If you don't like it now, you can go back where you came from. Don't come complaining to me. If you want to be my son, my son's name is Fausto.'

'Shut up!' howled César pointing the gun at his head. 'Shut up! Shut up!'

'And who's going to make me? You?'

César looked at Canal again.

'Make him shut up! Do something! He won't even let me speak now! See what he's like!'

'I want to know what this ridiculous stunt is all about right now,' Tamerlán began, staring him in the eye until he made him divert his furious gaze to the floor. 'My son wanted to come back to me, didn't he; he approached you for help, and you murdered him so you could keep the lot and kill me with grief. You sided with my worst enemy, you both tried to trick me with the fake diary. Didn't you!'

César, disconcerted, looked at Canal. Canal just smiled and looked at me.

'How do you know . . .?' César began, and then he noticed Canal, and then me. 'See?' he said to Canal. 'I told you that one would fuck us up.'

'It was Cuervo's idea to hire him, not mine. And you went along with it,' the other stated flatly without defending himself.

'You too, Canal? All these years of trusting in you, pouring out my most intimate secrets to you . . .' Tamerlán began to chide him.

'Precisely. It was starting to bore me.'

'So what happened to the superman?'

Canal pointed to César with his open palm.

'That one? He wouldn't even pass for Supergirl.'

'Give me that tape! Now!' screeched César.

Canal produced a thick roll of duct tape and a pair of scissors, snipped off a length and stamped it over Tamerlán's mouth, unwinding the rest several times round his head, neck and down to his wrists, which he made fast behind his back. Never had he looked more like a spider. He struck him once with the butt of his gun in the pit of his knee, and Tamerlán fell to his knees.

'All yours,' he said.

César entered Wonderland in a single bound.

'All my life you never wanted me for anything but to compare me with Fausto and choose him over me. You made me think it was all my fault, but you thought everything I ever did was a fault because I did it. I was closer to Mummy because she protected me, but she was only playing along with you. She was the good cop, you were the bad cop. I once heard you shout at her that after Fausto she should only have given birth to girls. It didn't matter to me if I was a boy or a girl. All I wanted was for you to hold me and carry me in your arms. Then Fausto suddenly disappears and from one day to the next you want me to start acting all butch. "I don't want a mincing queen as a son!" you used to say while you abused me. If I at least thought it had given you some pleasure, but no, you only did it to humiliate yourself; I'd see it in your eyes afterwards: you despised yourself, you made yourself sick, you promised yourself this time was the last and then half a bottle of whisky and two or three grams of coke and there you were, back degrading yourself all over my body. Don't make me do it, you'd shout, don't make me do it, as if I were the one to blame! I never meant anything to you; I was just a diversion for you to despise yourself more! Then suddenly you want me to be like Fausto, like you! Take over the company, have *children*! Can't you see what a walking contradiction you are? Can't you see I couldn't give you what you wanted, Daddy? That even if I wanted to, even if I tried as hard as I could . . .?'

'You're pleading,' Canal intervened. 'Remember what we talked about.'

'You're right,' said César, wiping the sweat from his face with one hand. 'I'm talking about the past. This is the present. So many times I dreamed of having this big talk with you, Daddy, before you died and we wouldn't be able to any more. Telling each other everything.'

His words were losing their marrow, becoming dry and hollow. He looked around him for professional guidance.

'Am I doing all right?'

'Not bad.'

'You'll tell me if you think I'm doing anything wrong, won't you.'

461

'You're doing fine, you're doing fine. Now ask him to dandle you on his knee.'

'Now *you're* going to start criticising me? Thirty years, thirty years and I finally say something to him without him criticising me, and you honestly think I'm going to let you? Nobody's going to criticise me ever again, understand? All my life, "Look at your brother Fausto, look how your brother Fausto does it, Fausto knows how!" If Fausto does it so well,' he said, bringing the bared teeth of his weasel's snout close to his father's face, 'so how come he's been eating penguin shit for the last ten years while I'm still alive and kicking?'

Perplexity made Tamerlán's eyes grow wider. César realised he'd hit the target.

'He never came back. We made it all up to drive you insane.'

Tamerlán's convulsive answer came across merely as faint undulations over the surface of the silver tape.

'It was brilliant, you understand? One day in a session I happened to say "If only Fausto would come back so I could kill him properly" and I hadn't got to the end before we knew what to do. Easy-peasy. We picked up some piece of offal from the street and disguised him as a person. When we finished, he looked a lot like what my brother might look like today; then we prepared his ritual death. A revolutionary therapeutic approach. You don't know the things I said to the poor man before I pushed him out! He was so pissed he didn't understand a thing. Remember, Cleo?'

'Yes, I remember.'

'If you swallowed the bit about Fausto the murderer and César the saviour, we were going to wait a few months before the next phase. Enjoying your adulation. But your friend here forced us to speed things up. Fat favour he did for you. Can't you see, Daddy? It isn't enough for me to kill you here, in my heart. The chain has to be cut, Daddy. The chain has to be cut!'

He went quiet, swallowing hard, his Adam's apple working like a misfiring piston. He went up to his father and ripped the tape off his mouth so violently that Tamerlán's pores filled with blood.

'And what are you going to cut it with? This shitty plan? Only a silly prat like you could come up with something like that. The only thing you're proving is that your brain's in your arse, as I've always said it was.'

'That's a lie! It was a brilliant plan! Doing your utmost to save me, drawn in deeper and deeper with every step till you fell at my feet. And only then, more out of compassion than anger, would I finish you off and clean up.'

'Really? So if everything turned out so well for you, why are you the one trembling and not me?'

'I'm stronger, you understand! You need me and I don't. Need *you*, I mean! Not any more! Without me your life is over, without you my life . . . begins.'

'Like fuck. I don't need *you* to be my son. I'll adopt one – this guy, for example,' he said pointing at me, 'and he'll be a lot better son than you.'

'This one? This one?' he said, pointing at me with the gun.

'César, don't get distracted,' chimed in Canal, my saviour.

'Wait. Wait. I have a better idea. A clean slate. I'll separate from your mother and inseminate some hungry little bitch. I've got all the balls you haven't.'

'Oh yeah?' César snatched up the scissors that Canal had

left on the desk and, clicking them like castanets, began to flamenco round his father. 'What if I snip them off, eh? What if I snip them off?'

'Why don't we all calm down a little?' intervened Canal, his self-assured double bass beginning to slide audibly towards the violins. The session was starting to get out of hand.

'Acknowledge it. Acknowledge I'm right,' stammered César in supplication. 'For once in your life you have to acknowledge me!'

'The one who has to acknowledge you're a useless piece of shit is *you*.'

'Don't delay any longer. The time has come to act,' Canal urged.

For a moment César looked at him with more terror than at his father. Canal had taken a contraceptive out of his jacket pocket and was holding it out to him. César watched him, transfixed:

'But . . . I'm the one with AIDS . . .'

'It's for the DNA, you stupid cunt. You don't want it to come out in the papers that you fucked your old man – before you killed him.'

César took the contraceptive as if it were a gun for his turn at Russian roulette. He tried to tear it open with his fingers, then lifted it to his mouth, tugging at it with his teeth, but managed nothing more than to bite off a couple of scraps of plastic and spit them out to either side.

'I can't,' he said eventually, letting the arm holding the contraceptive fall to his side.

'What do you mean you can't?' For the first time Canal looked disconcerted.

'I won't be able to.'

'But we've been working for months on this. Your therapy . . .'

'What therapy, Cleopatra? You spent it wanking at all the most morbid bits! Look, you convinced me and I agreed to everything, but now . . . I won't even be able to get it up. Why don't we just chuck him out and get it over with? It makes no difference,' he begged.

'It does make a difference! It makes all the difference! It's something that's never happened before. For the first time in history we're about to kill the father! You have to drive a stake through his heart, like with vampires! Otherwise he'll always come back to life! I've been training you to commit the most enormous act in Human History! We're on the threshold of the superman and you want to turn back! Didn't you want to be the superman?'

'No. *You* wanted it. The only thing I want is the money. Oh. And to see him dead. If you're such a sucker for the superman, why don't *you* fuck him?'

'I've grown out of that,' he said without thinking. 'César, please. Listen to me, it'll only take a minute. Remember. "A few small inches for a man . . ." You stick it in, you pull it out. Just the tip. You don't even need to come. Go on. Just do it for me. It's no big deal'

'I hate it when you grovel.'

'Hey, while you sort out your little tiff can someone untie me and bring me my clothes? I'm cold.'

'You'd better start bracing yourself for the big jump. You know where.'

César was pointing at the window that Fausto – the fake

Fausto – had fallen through.

'And who's going to throw me? You? You haven't got what it takes.'

'I won't need it. You're going to do it yourself. Don't you see what's happening? Like in a game of chess, I've been cornering you till you have no option but to throw yourself out. Checkmate, Daddy-o. You're finished.'

Tamerlán kicked the board.

'*I'm* not throwing myself out! Chess my arse! You want the king, you'll have to take it!'

'That's what I've been saying,' intervened Canal, addressing Tamerlán and referring to César.

'See how pig-headed he is?'

'Don't talk about me! I forbid you to talk about me in front of me!'

'How easily he gets offended.'

'He always was highly susceptible. Once, when he was a boy ...'

César emptied the magazine into a mirror to one side. One less reflection in the countless ones around us, like one less number in an infinite series.

'That's it. I want to get this over with, I want to move on, I want to start my life. Humanity will have to wait a bit longer. It's already waited this long ... Window, move.'

'I've told you, I'm not jumping.'

'You have no alternative.'

'Maybe not. But I'm not jumping and that's that. Eh?' he said, his chin jutting defiantly at him. 'What are you going to do about it?'

'I can't stand it any more. This is so like you! You're only doing this to spite me! If it isn't your idea, it's no good! You won't let me have any ideas of my own!'

'You never could do anything right.'

'You have to jump!'

'What for? To make you happy? That would be hypocritical. The fact is, sonny boy, that your plan's a pathetic piece of shit.'

'Just this once, Daddy, Daddy. Don't ruin it for me again.'

'You always were a spineless wimp.'

'Cleo!' bleated César, his jaw so tense I thought it might break.

'See? You have to grab him from behind. Look what happens face to face.'

'He won't jump.'

'He's right in a way. I think we've grown a little overfond of the geometry of the plan. Why would he indulge us when we're going to kill him anyway?'

'What then?'

'If we shoot him, the bullets will show up in the autopsy. You'll have to push him.'

'Why me?'

'You know I hate physical contact.'

At César's first step Tamerlán ran for the tunnel of broken glass, which he'd never get through in bare feet, his hands still tied behind his back, bobbing along heavily like a rhea, then fell flat on his face as if bolassed.

'Where were you going?' His son strode confidently forward until he caught up with him. Turning quickly like a cornered cat, propped on his elbows and back, Tamerlán began to launch kicks at César's shins and landed two that made him sit down. For several metres, more sure-footed now, Tamerlán ran at his son, who only escaped his kicks by scuttling away on all fours.

'*You're* throwing *me* out! You and whose army? Look, look at me trembling!' he shouted, with the desk between them. César was on the verge of tears.

'Help, please! Help!'

The voice came from the tunnel of broken mirrors. It was Freddy. Almost carrying his mate's prostrate figure, manoeuvring it through the narrow gap of bristling shards, he approached from the shadows. He was carrying an Itaka in one hand and had the other round the waist of his wounded partner who, like his shirt front, was so red with blood that his nose looked white in comparison.

'Help us, doctor,' he pleaded.

'What happened?' asked Canal without approaching.

'They were waiting for us. Threw everything they had at us. Machine guns, FALs, I dunno what. We had to cut and run. They got Tornero in the guts. He'll die if he doesn't see a doctor.' He set him down and Tornero collapsed without opening his eyes. His feet moved slightly, then stopped. Very soon a double pool of blood had formed on the mirror of the floor.

'What about the others?'

'There was nobody in two of the houses and they were waiting for us in the third. Someone had warned them, I tell you. Him,' Freddy pointed at me. 'It was you, wasn't it, you little shit?' he said to me, starting to raise his shotgun.

'Not yet,' Canal stopped him. 'We have bigger fish to fry.'

'Yes, he's bleeding to death.'

'Bigger. Actually you've arrived just in time.' He pointed at Tamerlán. 'He won't jump. He needs some help.'

Freddy smiled.

'Pleasure.'

Tamerlán and Freddy began to size each other up from opposite sides of the desk. Freddy ran to one side, Tamerlán to the other. Freddy went round to Tamerlán's side, Tamerlán to Freddy's.

'Et tu, Brute?' Tamerlán shouted at him in mockery.

'Fuck Brute!' answered his ex-bodyguard. 'I've had it in for *you* for a long time.'

He took a flying leap and, rolling across the glass, fell on his ex-boss and pinned him beneath his bulk. Tamerlán swore at him and Freddy grabbed his arms and wrung them like a wet floorcloth. Tamerlán began to squeal like a hog.

'Shall I throw him out now?' Freddy panted.

'Better take the tape off first. It won't look good in the autopsy,' said Canal.

Tearing it off like women's clothes, Freddy freed him of his bonds. Quick as a pit viper, Tamerlán's first free hand plunged between the henchman's legs and, turning with the full weight of his body, twisted his balls into a bow-tie. Using the fallen pachyderm's bellowing body as a ladder, Tamerlán clambered up onto the desk and started jumping up and down, chattering and baring his teeth like a defiant monkey. Freddy's eyes peeped over the edge, and Tamerlán tipped the contents of the Zen garden into them, missed him with the ingot of acrylic and hit him in the forehead, edge on, with the ombú pot. Freddy toppled backwards, the withered bonsai rooted under his nose like a second moustache.

Tamerlán seized his chance and ran to the other end of the room, where he again sought out the high ground, this time the model of the future Buenos Aires. He trampled the convention centres, the shopping malls, the diplomat's residences like some movie dinosaur. This time Freddy got it right. Grabbing one end of the wheeled table on which the model was mounted and pushing it as if in a trolley race in a supermarket, with the shrieking Tamerlán on top, he headed for the place of execution, gathering speed until it crashed into the window frame, where, taking half the city with him in his arms, Tamerlán went flying towards the thick glass which, though it shattered and fell, halted his momentum sufficiently for him to grab the outside of the frame. The model, table and all, flipped over his head and, without touching him, began its long descent through the void.

'I'm alive! I'm alive!' yelled Tamerlán, trying to reach the edge with one of his legs and climb back in but only managing to slash it on the broken glass. Freddy squatted down beside him and tried to push him out by his head, but Tamerlán sank his teeth into his hand and latched on to him like a bulldog. Freddy had lost his gun in the battle of the desk and, howling like a wild animal in a trap, began to grope around him in desperation, until the fingers of his free hand closed on the acrylic prism. He landed it once, twice, three times on his ex-boss's skull until Tamerlán began to gape, then set about hammering his fingers against the frame until the ingot broke in two. Like a genie coming out of the rubbed lamp, a nauseous gas hissed into the room.

I watched him fall. He seemed to be floating on his back, getting smaller and smaller, the expression on his face becoming more and more difficult to read, and he seemed to find the current of air against his body pleasant, like when you strip off in front of the fan in summer. He didn't shout or flail. I think around the twentieth floor he actually put his hands behind his head as if the air were water, believing that, if he just lay there suspended, he'd soon be rescued by a passing salt-white yacht plying the blue waters of a mirror-like ocean, and friendly arms would reach out to haul him over the gunwale, wrap him in a blanket and give him a glass of cognac, and friendly ears would listen eagerly to his incredible tale of survival against all the odds. Till a metre before he landed, he must have thought that, in some hitherto unheard-of way reserved by God throughout the history of creation especially for him, he would still be saved. He hit the grass softly, barely bouncing, a boy throwing himself on the mattress to test sprawling postures. Against the distant green lawn his white body looked like a sleeping lamb viewed from the hills.

'The other one now?' Freddy's voice shook me out of the spell. He was looking at Canal; Canal was looking at me.

'No. Go down and keep watch. Nobody's to touch him till the cops get here. Good idea, the model.' Then turning to César: 'I can just see the headlines: MOGUL DESTROYS DREAM, THEN COMMITS SUICIDE.'

César, mute all this time, was looking down out of the broken window, the wind blowing his hair in his eyes.

'Can I go down too?' he asked.

'Not a good idea. They saw enough of you last time. Twice would look suspicious.'

'What about Tornero?' asked Freddy, pointing to his partner, who by now was marooned in his own blood like an isle flottante.

Canal shook his head. Freddy shrugged his shoulders,

once, and his back disappeared down the tunnel. After the crunch of his soles on the broken glass, silence fell. Canal nibbled a cuticle, lost in thought. César had been squatting on the floor. He stood up, holding one half of the prism. He put a hand into it, scooping out a little of its filth and breaking it up in his fingers till it fell to the floor.

'What I always suspected. Another one of his stories. No gold, just shit.'

He picked up his father's pants from the floor and wiped his hands on them, then screwed them into a ball and tossed them onto the desk. He walked round it and sat on the throne, then crossed his legs and rested his forearms on the armrest.

'So? What do you feel?' Canal asked him.

'Nothing.'

César had his eyes firmly fixed on the carpet.

'It all went pretty well, didn't it?'

'Yes.'

'Are you worried about something?'

'No.'

'Are you going to answer me in monosyllables all night?'

'Leave me alone, Cleo. We're not in a session.'

'That's what I thought. I spend months training you for this and in the end you can't do it. I could groom someone to stand in for your father, the way I did with your brother, but it won't be the same now. I'll have to rethink the whole orientation of your therapy.'

'What are you insinuating? That it's my fault?'

'Yet again you've let others do your work for you.'

Getting up from his chair, César retrieved the silver riding-crop from the floor and cracked it several times on the edge of the desk as if whipping it into a gallop.

'Shut up! You sound just like him! That's why I killed him, understand! So that nobody ever talks to me like that again!'

'You see? I'm right. As you haven't reached closure, you still have all the hatred inside you and you discharge it on the person nearest at hand.'

César slumped back in his throne, sulking.

'Well, that's that. Best laid schemes, eh Félix?'

He was looking at me. I was still there. I say 'there', but I didn't really know where. I'd managed to stay out of it so far, keep invisible for most of the time as if watching it all from another room, through the mirror. I don't really know how I do it. What I do know is that I learned it ten years ago: I'm in the thick of it all but everything happens . . . around me, brushing past me, barely touching. A survival trick. It always works, up to a point. As long as I manage to feel nothing.

'So now what do we do? Sit here and wait?'

'I have a better idea,' said Canal. 'We'll find out how much he knows.'

'Shouldn't we wait for Freddy for that?'

Canal smiled.

'Leave it to me.'

He handed his gun to César, who accepted it limply and rested it on the glass, pointing at me. Then he disappeared into his private cubicle. César looked at me with something approaching annoyance, as if we were sharing a long lift journey and he was obliged to make conversation.

'So the old man was thinking of adopting you, was he?'

'I doubt I'd have accepted,' I said to him.

He smiled mirthlessly.

'It isn't that attractive from the inside, is it.'

'It must have its compensations, I suppose.'

'Yes, if you survive the suicide attempts. Ah well. He's dead now. And everything's mine. Wasn't such a bad plan, was it?'

'Your father would be proud of you. Are you going to run the company now?'

'Are you mad? I'm going to flog it. Control will be handed to a plc, and Canal and I will be shareholders. We've already sorted out the restructuring. We're going to rotate all the mirrors so nobody really knows where the boss is. It'll be a democracy. A democracy without the people. That whole personalised, hierarchic deal is too vulnerable. The spider's mistake.'

He paused, waiting for me to ask. He didn't yet have his father's declamatory gifts, but he wasn't wasting a second trying them out. And I, of course, slipped effortlessly into my role as privileged interlocutor, as if he counted me one of the assets of his inheritance.

'Which one?'

'From the centre of the web it can move all the threads. Control all its prey. But it's easy for its enemies to find it there. It occurred to me while I was watching *Caligula*.'

'It's good to have models. Especially when you're young.'

'You're funny. You wouldn't have made such a bad brother. Certainly better than the other one. He was worse dead than alive. You know what inspiration Caligula gave me?'

'You're going to make your horse chairman of the board.'

'No. Something he said. "I wish the Romans had just one head and I could cut it off with one stroke."'

'And?'

'*He* was the one who just had one head. You know what?'

'What.'

'I can't forgive you for what you saw that day.'

Canal came back carrying a doctor's bag in one hand and a syringe in the other. He rested both hands on the desk and took back his gun.

'Do me a favour. Bring the couch in from reception.'

'In here?'

'We won't be comfortable in there. Believe me. It'll be fun.'

'Huh!'

Skirting the pool of blood in which floated the island of Tornero's body, César disappeared into the tunnel of broken mirrors.

'Get undressed, please, Sr Félix,' Canal said in a professional tone.

I pulled a wry face and made a classic Porteño gesture at him, pecking the air with my upturned fingers.

'Don't worry about your pride and joy. It's nothing sexual. Although in a few minutes you're going to wish it was.'

When I took off my jacket, Tamerlán's confession and the cheque fell on the floor. Canal gestured to me to take a few steps back, and went and picked them up. The cheque he barely looked at before tearing it into little pieces, but the document he read with growing interest as César came over, preceded by the tinkling sound of a Christmas sleigh sliding over splintered glass.

'Read this.'

They looked at each other pleased.

'That's the cherry on top.'

'Reads just like a suicide note: he confesses to his crimes, then jumps out of the window. Pure Hollywood.'

'And it says nothing about me.'

'No. It doesn't mention you at all.'

They both turned towards me.

'Actually you've saved us a whole heap of trouble.'

'Yes. There's no way he'd have written this for us. How did you do it?'

'We're indebted to you.'

'What shall we do? Let him go?'

Canal picked up the syringe from the desk, held it up and squeezed. A thin, vertical jet spurted out of the needle and opened into a fountain that nearly reached the ceiling. He kept squeezing until it was half empty.

'He's bound to survive this dose. It's the best we can offer you, Félix. Now finish undressing, please.'

I did so, leaving my underpants on, though I knew what he was going to say.

'Everything, please. Now lie down here. On your back, on your back, I've already told you your privates are quite safe.'

Once I'd made myself comfortable on the couch (I had to close my eyes to the brightness of the dichroic lamps), they tied my wrists, ankles and neck with adjustable leather and aluminium bands, and Canal knotted a length of rubber hose round my biceps. I tried not to watch him, but instead let my eyes drift upwards to my prone body, reflected full length in the whorehouse mirror of the ceiling. I had trouble recognising myself. I'd thinned over the last few days and my skin had gone saggy and yellowish. I'd lost a lot of hair too. I was looking at a mirror image of myself ten years back.

'Clench your fist several times please and keep it clenched when I tell you.'

I obeyed. You always obey doctors. The jab was quick and precise; I barely felt it and it was over.

'You'll see how fast it takes effect,' Canal said to César.

'What effect does it have?'

'Pain.'

First I felt cold. Only natural being naked with a south-easterly whistling in through the broken window. But this was a cold I'd never felt before, no, not even in the Islands, where your flesh ended up dying and falling off your body. It was as if millions of tiny splinters of ice had entered my pores all at once, freezing my flesh as they penetrated, without melting, then entering my guts, my bones, my heart. I was freezing up, freezing up like a corpse in the morgue, but not dying, my eyes froze solid in their orbits, my tongue on my palate; my guts hardened and cracked with unbearable cramps and my blood froze in my heart to a single block of red ice. Yet, even now, I could still move, see, scream . . .

'The window! Close the window!' I screamed. Speaking felt like chewing on barbed wire.

'See?' came the sound of Canal's voice through the oceans of pain. 'It's already starting.'

The light seared through my eyelids into my retinas, as if I was being forced to stare at the sun with my eyes sewn open. I tried to wriggle free, but the straps cut into the soft flesh. Something – something immensely heavy – was crushing my chest. Deformed and monstrous from the unprecedented pain of looking, all I could see was my own jacket. I'd worn it over my naked skin hundreds of times, but its nylon lining was now fibreglass and scorched my skin like a phosphorus grenade in a full cave.

'Get it off me! Please get it off me!'

'Make up your mind, Félix. Are you hot or cold?'

With one tug they tore off the jacket and, with it, all my skin. I was now nothing but a flayed animal, skinned alive on the operating table, thrashing in its death throes, without even eyelids to block out the red-raw body stretched before the hugely bulging eyes. How could I still be alive! How! my brain screamed, spinning in a vortex of liquidiser blades, amid whose roar I could make out and understand every whirring word:

'Know how it works? The drug does nothing to his body that his body isn't doing to itself, all the time. It causes no special pain; it merely blocks the usual pain inhibitors. It is proof that pain is the essence of life, the basic condition of physical existence. The body is a ball of snakes writhing in constant agony. Everything in there operates in a constant state of unspeakable pain: heart beating without a second's rest, joints grinding against each other, muscles stretched on the rack of bones, blood burning within, shit rotting in the intestines, neurons in permanent electro-shock. Germs, viruses and parasites hammering on all the doors, every day massacring the millions of cells that can barely keep them at bay, and those same cells, thrown into civil war, warring with other cells to see who keeps the lot, every tissue striving to be the cancer that devours all the rest. Billions of cells working desperately, howling in silence, writhing in the intolerable fire of life. The human body! A grill of bones with the flesh roasting on it till it chars, every jet of blood stoking the flames like kerosene. We survive day to day because we live anæsthetised, macerated in a soup of endogenous morphines. This is what happens when we neutralise them. And they ask me why I hate the body. A writhing worm cut in two, that's what a feeling human being is. And that's just when we aren't doing anything to it. Just imagine when we do.'

'Can I try?'

'Wait. Watch me.'

Canal had pulled up a chair, its legs grating against the glazed floor.

'Can you hear me, Félix?'

Some part of my body must have said yes.

'Open one eye, Félix. I know it's hard but you have to try. Can you see what I'm holding?'

As intense as sun on water, the light bounced off the wet steel, the curved glass, the translucent liquid inside it. The lethal dose! Yes, the lethal dose!

'Morphine. All for you.'

My eyes must have rolled back wildly, my mouth must have drooled. Like a headless chicken's, my body had a life of its own.

'Not yet. First you're going to answer a few questions for me.'

A thousand red-hot needles drove themselves into my skin from my lips to my groin, a carpet of pins unrolling down my body for people to trample on. Canal had blown on my skin, like someone blowing on a spoonful of soup.

'Can I try?' César put himself between the light and my face, a cloud of unspeakable relief.

'Gently does it. He's fragile.'

He twisted my ear, trying to rip it off at the root; I tried to bite his hand. My effort hurt more than the indignity he was inflicting on me.

'Bitch!'

Canal laughed, shaken by short, dry chuckles like the tick-tock of a clock striking my skull.

'And dangerous. Imagine the morphine, Félix, coursing through your body. No more pain. Nothing, no pain. Here it is, Félix. First question. How did Sr Tamerlán know the diary was false?'

'I told you. It was an accident . . .' Speaking was worse than anything.

'No excuses. Information. How did you find out?'

'I have the real one at home. Please, give me the morphine now and I swear to you . . .'

'It's your time, Félix. If you want to waste it like this . . .' He applied the slightest of pressures to the piston, and the precious liquid began to flow thickly from the hollow, chamfered tip and slide down the straight steel cylinder.

'I stole it from Cuervo . . . Major X . . . but I told Tamerlán straight away, I told all of you. I didn't know you were . . .'

'Don't try and second-guess me, Félix. You're not here to please me, but to tell me what you know. Speak without thinking and let me be the judge. You remember our first session? The time has come to tell me your memories.'

I talked without stopping, I don't know how long for, chewing over the filthy mess of the last two weeks of my life in the open sore of my mouth, vomiting it out every so often in sickening gobbets, choking on my loose teeth which, mixed with the words, lacerated my tongue and throat; and the more I talked, the more excruciating the pain became: it tore my organs from their places and with every retch I tried to expel them through my mouth; all my life it had wanted to escape from my body for good and ooze out over the couch and the floor. I talked until I didn't know who I was, until much later than I would have stopped caring, until I was reduced to a voice that was nothing but one endless vibration of pain.

'What got into you over the witnesses, Félix? First you tag them for death, then you want to save them? What for? To be *God*?'

God, the trampled cow hanging from the hooks in the shed, lowing pathetically, jumps about in its death throes. The veiled globular eye of a slaughtered sheep, sky blue amid clouds of fat and pallid flesh, encompasses a world arched by the meridians of pain. Not God. Worse. Human.

'There are those that experience only destroys. Totally. Longing to redeem the intolerable past, they relive it, but worse. One puff from the world blows them out like a candle flame.'

'How did he find Cuervo? That's what he isn't telling us. That's where he fucked up our plan.'

'Let me do the talking. Félix. Can you hear me, Félix?'

Of course, of course, my whole skin a sensitive eardrum responding to the slightest vibration of the air, but even if you slide in the tip of the knife, crack the oyster in two and delve into the soft flesh, there's something in that mess of your own making that you can slice to pieces and break down, but you'll never find. Plunge your arms in up to your elbows, try to get hold of it, and it will slip through your fingers, you've broken the egg on the floor and now you try to pick it up with your hand, you can't, you can't, ha ha ha, you can't . . .

'Let him go. He can't take any more than this. The morphine, Félix. Concentrate on the morphine. How did you find Cuervo.'

My teeth tried to find each other like magnets, steady side by side, they emerged through the torrent of flesh in two neat rows.

'He's laughing at us. Didn't I tell you? He's laughing in our fucking faces.'

Pincer fingers squashed the wings of my nose and my lungs filled with fire. As I opened my mouth absurdly wide to gulp down the air of the world, an avalanche of used capsules wrapped in a burning cloud of gunpowder fell into my mouth and my lungs filled like the bag of a vacuum cleaner. Canal – it had to be – had emptied an ashtray into my open mouth.

'With the morphine, Félix,' his shredded voice fought its way through the thicket of torn bronchi, retching, coughing and asphyxia. 'Those fag ends will soothe your throat like butterscotch. The ash like fresh water. So tell us, Félix.'

He had difficulty opening my eyes: my eyelids seemed to have sealed over. The direct light crossed them and my whole body shone visible like an illuminated glassworks.

'If I *want* to know, I *will* know. Nothing escapes my sight,' said one eye set in glass.

Nothing, let alone me, this microscopic crustacean trapped between two slides in a thin film of water, blinded by a light so intense that it makes my body transparent, everything, every organ, every cell, entirely on view, uselessly waving my little legs in the water until I give up and keep still, my black eye perplexed in the burning light, not knowing which way to look. Daphnia. Black eyes that can't blink. Nowhere to escape to, in a suddenly 2D universe. The best thing is not to move, to do all you can to still the vibration of agitated gills, to control the tics of a few limbs accustomed to perpetual motion.

It's difficult to observe a living organism. You have to freeze it somewhere, fix it with resins and stain it with dyes, immobilise it forever between two glued slides. Maybe if I don't move, he'll believe this is what I am. Maybe if I don't move, he'll take me for some preparation or other.

'Who told you about Cuervo, Félix.'

It's useless. Through the transparent flesh of which light is master, a tiny opaque stain that refuses to keep still gives me away. I can see it, as clear as a cardiologist holding it in his hand during a transplant: my dark, beating heart. You can see it, but not what I'm hiding there. The light that makes my brain's every neuron transparent cannot pierce it. Not you, nor you, nor him, nor him; I'm the only one who can see inside – only I, I, I . . .

'I.'

'I what?'

'I recognised him. He got us . . . ex-combatants . . . selling Surprise,' I managed to say. I felt like I was floating close to the sun.

'Do you believe him?'

'I don't know. It makes sense. You know Cuervo could never keep his mouth . . . Good thing we shut it for him in time.'

'What if he's lying?'

'It doesn't affect us anyway. I was just curious.'

'What shall we do?'

'Let him go, I suppose. Another body would complicate our script.'

'What came next?'

'The champagne. Let's go. Fetch the chalice. Goodbye, Félix. I hope life doesn't keep putting you in situations where you're out of your depth.'

'The morphine! The morphine!' I screamed, but they weren't listening any more, or perhaps my voice didn't make it out. Theirs deliberated as they receded, and in mercy or economy, one of them turned out the lights. Clods of dark thudded against my wooden head. I would have liked to sleep, but the pain wouldn't allow me. I could feel it growing inside, getting bigger with every beat of my heart, fighting for the surface like a diver with lungs about to burst. None of the other pains, the ones they'd inflicted on me, could compare with this; they'd only been containing it. Trying to escape it, I opened my eyes to the outside world. Instead of the scorched earth of my outstretched body, like a satellite photo of a bombardment, my eyes encountered a clean, cold sky full of stars: when they'd turned off the lights, they'd turned off the mirrors as well. That did it. Lost in the vision of the sky, my body began to spread out like a drop of oil on water. My skin stretched to the horizon and, in the cold wind coming in through the broken window, it began to bristle with buildings, houses, trees, cars, pedestrians; railway tracks ran over me in long scars, grids of streets and motorways cut through the rubble; it exhaled exhaust fumes and exuded the sweat of millions through the cement, screamed with horns and sirens and televisions and refrigerators, and screeching buildings under construction, one after another on my chest, till I could no longer breathe, compressing the air in the underground tunnels and the currents of the sewers and piped rivers. The city's thick carapace of tarmac and cement had protected me, and I'd thought that, beneath that crust, the edges of the wound would have joined, but instead they'd only separated even further and the pain had never stopped flowing through the strait. Ten years I'd slept under the uncertain shelter of the city of pain and now I awoke naked under the lone brightness of the stars. The farce was over. At that moment a giant hand descended from the sky and lifting up one corner, like someone getting ready to pull off a plaster, it tore off the skin of the city to reveal the desolate heath beneath: the wind-swept pastures, the streams of stone, the rocks and mud and bogs of the Islands.

Chapter 15

THE BATTLE OF MOUNT LONGDON

The sky above fumes with stars, but at ground level the darkness is impenetrable, as if we were covered by a cloud of ink; it's easier to decipher the constellations than the lines on our palms. Our ears have become so used to the continuous whispering of the wind that in its absence any noise shatters the icy silence with the crash of breaking glass; the snowfall is heralded by the paralysing cold of the air. Hugging Carlitos to keep him warm, I count the beats of his heart like seconds, as if it my counting were keeping it going – one more, one more, one more – subtracting them from the thousands left before the coming of daylight. If he makes it through the night, we can get him to the campaign hospital at the foot of the hill, or even to the post at Moody Brook, but the night is only just starting. Next to us Chanino twitches and shudders like a dog in his sleep; Rubén, his head covered by his jacket and a blanket, next to the possibly dead body of Hijitus, occupies the other end of the foxhole. I'm the only one who pokes his head out now and then; you could say I'm keeping guard, watching over everyone, although my eyes can see no more in the night out there than theirs can in the depths of our cave. I've been hearing low, indistinct voices for some time, but even when I prick up my ears, I can't make out what they're saying. It takes me a few minutes to work out why. By then the first clickety-clack has reached me and immediately a series of dozens of clacks intermingled, like somebody gingerly looking for something in a cutlery drawer, trying not to waken those sleeping. I feel my pupils open as wide as saucers, only to fill with more darkness. The strangely familiar noise has woken Chanino too.

'What's that? What is it?' I begin to shake him so as not to be the one to say it.

'Bayonets.'

I feel something I've never felt in my life: the skin at the back of my neck contracting into a facial gesture and all its hairs standing on end like the hackles of a cornered cat. Who'd have thought we still had that animal graft back there?

'It's the English,' he adds unnecessarily.

Thanks to Verraco, who's wrecked the radar, they've managed to creep up on us in the night (we'd always been assured they'd attack by day) almost right to the foot of the mountain (we'd always been assured they'd attack from the sea) and would have slipped stealthily into our tents and foxholes and killed us where we slept (standing guard being an old joke by now, when we can barely stand up at all) had one of them not stepped in the wrong place and been blown to kingdom come, his ghastly shrieks mingled with the exploding mine. In answer to his solo a chorus of howls goes up with him, except that these are no longer cries of pain, but the ululations of hundreds of savages storming the hill. Chanino manages to get off the first FAL burst before the night is furrowed by a cage of incandescent wires stretching between the rocks and the ground. Between the blindness of the tracer fire, the explosions of the grenades and the thunder of the rifles and bursts of machine-gun fire our brief initial panic is swallowed whole by the purest, most indescribable terror. As we only had one working FAL between us, I began stacking the magazines on Carlitos's chest before passing them to Chanino every thirty seconds. He fires anywhere: judging by the trajectories of the tracer fire our foxhole is facing the wrong way, but he doesn't take his finger off the trigger until the magazine's empty. The FAL's barrel is red-hot and, when I get hold of it to reload, my hand sticks fast to it; I feel nothing but a slight tug as the skin on my hand comes away. The howls of the wounded ring out now as loud as the war cries of the attacking horde, and still we can't see a single one. Then the flares start to fall: snaking trails of cold mercury light trickle slowly down from the sky, dazzling us like full-beam headlights on the road; they light up the battlefield like a football pitch and down below the English advance in formation like a well-organised team, neutralising the first positions. They come at the open mouths of the foxholes from the sides and the back, not caring which, and stick the barrels of their rifles and machine guns right inside to make sure they don't miss, then drop a phosphorus grenade in to make sure and step aside to dodge the white flash, then move on to the next position to repeat the procedure, methodically, like weeding a field. You might have wanted to surrender, but they aren't asking questions. Thirty metres below us they catch three in their tent, which stands there for a few seconds, struggling and moaning horribly like some new species of mammoth hunted down with machine guns, fighting not to go down, till the bullets slice through tent poles and guy ropes, and very slowly it collapses, bagging the air at first, then letting it out through the holes, and still it writhes on the ground, until the hunters advance towards it and begin bayoneting it, sticking their knives in wherever there's a movement, trampling the canvas until their feet meet with no resistance, bayonets poised vertical in the air, ready to fall the moment their sharpened vision detects the surreptitious movement of a wee mouse beneath the ever more clearly moulded contours of the blood-soaked canvas. Realising I'm about to die, I lie back and begin to admire the beauty of the spectacle, of the mountain frozen in the light of the flares, a hundredfold more brilliant than the moonlight; of the precise, nimble movements of the English leaping from rock to rock, blending into the terrain, crawling beneath the green tracer fire that furrows the brightness just above the ground, ricocheting and outlining the contours of the crags with their geometric tracery, and it's all so beautiful that it makes you want to stretch out an arm and touch it, like when you cross a country road on a summer night and a swarm of fireflies on the wing floats by, their phosphorescent trails brushing the window, and opening it you reach out and feel the occasional bump of one against your open palm and, with any luck, catch it and capture the light in your closed hand, intermittent in the pink glow between your fingers. Since the English appeared in the broad flare-light, we've stopped shooting. I don't know why: firing into the dark was one thing, but as soon as we can see them we stop: I stop passing the magazines and Chanino drops the FAL and the two of us just peep out of the mouth of the foxhole, watching. The shouting and the shooting ring out behind us now, English voices and the heavy rattle of a machine gun, which must be ours, the marine infantry no doubt, because the English immediately go past again carrying a couple of wounded and disappear downhill.

'They're retreating!' Chanino whispers.

For a few minutes all we can hear are the sporadic pot-shots of our FALs and the odd burst of PAM machine-gun fire and wounded howling in either language and I decide to go out and see if there's a way we can cut and run before they get back. In the darkness of mere silhouettes the Cordobans start shooting at me.

'It's me, you bloody fools!' I scream at them from the mud. 'The English have gone.'

'Did you see the Gurkhas? The Gurkhas!' shouts Rosendo.

I hadn't. The ones I saw were all quite fair-skinned, but the short ones, their faces covered in shoe polish, could easily have passed for Gurkhas.

'Have we won?' Toto asks me.

'I think they'll be back to fucking waste us,' I say. 'Why don't we make the most of it and get out of here while we can?'

We all hear the whistle before they manage to answer. I dive into them head first as the first shell falls less than ten metres away and some red-hot shrapnel materialises in our midst and sets fire to our jackets. We roll about furiously like three weasels in a bag, trying to escape from this horrible thing that sears our skins until it falls in the mud at the bottom and sputters out, hissing like a hot coal in water. The shelling we're taking is the worst so far: the shells fall at two- or three-second intervals, shaking us about inside the foxhole and, to stop them bursting our eardrums and from the pain of the burns and the sheer terror, we shout for half an hour or two hours non-stop till we have no voices left, and as the silence flows back a hoarse croak remains floating over the trenches: it's our throats, which go on shouting independent of our wills in the miserable lulls called every so often by the English to see if there's anyone still left alive. I let two or three go by but can't make up my mind; my legs won't carry me. But in the next one I'm making a dash for our foxhole when a blast turns me over in the air and drops me on my back in a puddle, which breaks my fall. The stars above me turn in the imperturbable sky. My outstretched fingers touch others wrapped in wool, I turn my head and see a body wedged between an enormous boulder and a landslide. Beside it a pair of legs sticks out from the churned-up earth. When the hand of the dead man tries to get hold of mine, I give a cry and roll to one side. Just then a flare starts to fall and its light is reflected in the bulging eyes that stare at me without seeing. It's Toto. He opens his mouth, gushing blood, and lies there with his eyes enormously wide.

'The Cordobans. They killed them,' I think I stammer at the edge of our foxhole, and the hands of Chanino and Rubén emerge to drag me inside.

When I wake, I can hear them debating the best way to surrender.

'Wouldn't it be better to shoot?'

'Are you mad? They'll waste us.'

'I mean get the fuck out of here.'

'Where to? They're everywhere. Better to surrender.'

'Don't they kill prisoners?'

'No, they're English.'

'And what do you do to surrender?'

'How should I know? You're the corporal. Didn't they teach you?'

'Someone once asked in training and they drilled him till he dropped. "You fight till you die, dog," they told him.'

'Let's try a white flag. Gimme something white.'

'There's nothing white left!'

'What about the Porteño? Isn't he awake?'

Chanino starts slapping me in the face. 'Cut it out, you bloody maniac, what are you doing!' I yell at him. He slaps me a couple more times and turns away.

'Nothing.'

'We are fucking dead. Carlitos is dead, the Cordobans are dead, Felipe can't speak. Is there anyone left out there?'

'The English.'

I turn my head. Carlitos's face is next to mine. Mouth open, eyes open. I start to scream.

'Don't you know how to say "surrender" in English?'

'They flunked me twice. And you lot up in the Chaco? What did they teach you? Quechua?'

'I only finished primary.'

'Listen, when one of them appears you go out with your hands up . . .'

'Why me?'

'You're the commanding officer, you dickhead.'

'Oh, right, before, whenever I gave orders, you just pissed yourselves laughing; now, when it comes to getting my head cut off by a Gurkha, all of a sudden I'm a fucking general.'

'I'm not going. My surrender doesn't count. You're the corporal.'

'Private Rubén Gentile, I order you to . . .'

'Suck on this.'

'Che, you lot in the foxholes! Get out of there or the

English'll shoot the shit out of you! Get out! We've lost!'

The voice comes from outside. Rubén and Chanino start to whisper.

'Must be English! Let's play dead!'

'He said "che"! He's an Argentinian!'

'I didn't hear him.'

'Get out, che, or they'll chuck a grenade in your foxhole!'

'See? Che! Clear as day!'

There are several bursts of machine-gun fire; the brief silence that follows is broken by shrieks, then two explosions. I manage to turn my head and get a look. I can just make out a shape in the darkness, dragging behind it a taut rope, tethered like a dog's lead to something or someone invisible among the rocks. When it turns side on, I recognise the visor on the helmet. It's Argentinian.

'You getting out or not? You've seen what happens,' it shouts in the direction of the Cordobans' foxhole. It's not at us, I realise, they haven't seen us. 'They haven't seen us, Rubén,' I tell him.

Like a party of mountaineers, the rope is also tied to two silhouettes, who appear at the Argentinian's side: one tall, the other short. Helmets like half water-melons.

'I don't want to die in this hole! I don't want to die in this mud!' Rubén starts to roll around furiously, landing unnecessary punches and kicks on us, though nobody tries to stop him, and sticks his arms outside. 'I'm getting out! I'm getting out! Tell them not to shoot!'

They spot him when he's already outside. He begins to walk towards them. The Argentinian disappears among the rocks. The English train their rifles on him.

'Drop your weapon!' shouts the tall one.

Rubén had gone out with his useless FAL over his shoulder. He stands still and looks at them blankly.

'Your gun! Your FAL! Throw it away!' I shout to him.

'The gun, you fucking arsehole! Drop it!'

He must have understood some gesture or other because he unslings it and throws it on the ground. The Englishmen keep their rifles trained on him.

'Hit the deck!' shouts the same one as before.

'Throw yourself on the floor, Rubén!' I shout to him. Nothing. No one can hear me. I'm dead, it suddenly occurs to me. No one can hear me because I'm dead.

The English soldier fires once, a single burst. Rubén falls on his back in a pile of shit. He starts screaming hideously. The little Englishman gives the rope to the tall one and starts walking in our direction, bayonet pointing at the ground.

'No! Please! Please!' All his forgotten English lessons ring in Rubén's ears at once. 'I love Queen! Freddie Mercury! We are the champions! Please! Please!'

Rubén has both hands raised in a gesture of supplication and the Englishman seizes the chance to jam the bayonet in his stomach, but the clothes he's wrapped in are so thick that he doesn't stick it in far enough to kill him. Rubén starts to screech and kick and spastically flap his arms, and the English also screaming puts one boot on his stomach and starts bayoneting him in the face. When I look again, to prevent him escaping they've tied the Argentinian to Rubén's body, on one of whose feet the Englishman is pulling like an ant trying to drag an insect too big for it. The tall one has him by the armpits and is also tugging, in the opposite direction, the way ants will sometimes before agreeing and pulling together. The little man mutters curses under his breath, snorting, while the tall one laughs at him, using one foot as a lever on a cracked-open rock, which glitters in the light of the flares, veined with silver and delicate traces of pink.

'Put your back into it! You're not fucking pulling!'

'Let's pull a Christmas cracker.'

They ease off a little and then on one-two-three they both pull hard and the little one flies backwards with Rubén's boot in his hand, stumbling and falling on his arse in a pool of shit. The other one doubles up with laughter. They relieve me, the laughter and the swearing, for a few seconds we're in no danger of them hearing Chanino's moans, the uncontrollable grinding of my teeth, my thumping heart as it tries to choke me.

'Shit, shit, we're getting fucking slaughtered for a pile of fucking Argie shit!' he curses, splashing about in the brown icy sludge. Putting the boot down, he wipes his hands on Rubén's clothes and, hopping on the spot, takes off his own and puts it on one side. He stamps several times to get Rubén's to fit him, then starts walking with his weight on one then the other, trying to make up his mind.

'Are they *that* comfortable?'

'Very. Compared to the crap *we* get.'

'Think I'll get myself a pair too.'

'Hurry up, before they get stiff,' says the little one, taking off his other boot and throwing it far away like a grenade. His companion approaches the Cordobans and grabs a hold of one of Rosendo's boots sticking out of the mouth of the collapsed foxhole, and puts it against his own, sole to sole, the way you do in a shoe shop when you can't be bothered taking your shoes off.

'Too small!'

Not to feel completely frustrated he picks up Rubén's FAL and tries it. Nothing.

'Not my night,' he mutters.

He gives a few tugs on the rope and the Argentinian lifts his head sunk in his arms and starts to follow them obediently, stumbling past Rubén without looking at him. They're coming straight towards us. Miraculously, since they killed Rubén, not a single flare has gone up and they walk right past without seeing us. I grab Chanino by the hand, a second before the English stop on the roof of our foxhole. The bowing sheet of corrugated iron rings out with a voice like thunder. But they don't hear it. It's been snowing for a while now: a fine, dry snow, like pulverised ice, which, accumulating on the ground, solidifies into a hard crust that crunches audibly beneath the Englishmen's Argentinian and English boots. They move away downhill and, for some time, against the light of the distant explosions and their brilliance in the snow, we can still make out their silhouettes in the wisps of fog, stopping now and again to check the boots of the dead as if out bargain-hunting in a discount store.

Chanino decides not to risk them coming back and, keeping tight hold of my hand, pulls me out of the foxhole and we start our descent of the mountain, dragging ourselves through the rocks, playing dead every time we hear a shot or an explosion nearby, but the only Englishman we encounter is twisted and black and lying on the ground, utterly absorbed in learning how to smile with a single row of teeth. Eventually the rocks thin and the land levels out and we reach the edge of the plain, a reliefless piece of open ground spread out before us until it merges with the black of the sky. No sooner have we set off across it than I feel an uncontrollable urge to look back over my shoulder. What I see in the intermittent flashes is so bizarre that I think I'm hallucinating at first: under the hail of fire and flames that falls relentlessly from the reddened sky, and the hoarse roar of the explosions, the mountain looks like an erupting volcano, heaving with creatures in motion like a trampled anthill; as far as the eye can see, taking cover among the rocks, jumping over the craters, carrying the wounded and dodging the dead, descends an army of spectres, fleeing the English advance. They look like they're moving slowly, but it turns out to be an effect of the distance, because three, then four, immediately run past me, their blankets and ponchos flapping over their heads and backs as if by hiding beneath them they stood a better chance of dodging the tracer fire zinging between the crags or the shells, mortars and grenades that advanced on them like a curtain of fire caught up in their clothes and drawn by them across the plain towards where I stand and wait. More flares begin to float down from the sky and out of reflex we all do what we've been taught in training and freeze in the position we're in to blend in with the trees, like in a game of statues – except there aren't any trees on the Islands. In the blinding white light the plain becomes a grotesque open-air sculpture exhibition born of the delirium of a demented artist: gargoyles, satyrs, dragons, hunchbacks, fantastic and monstrous beings, alone or in compositions of two or three, standing out clearly against the snow for the English to practise their marksmanship on, which they start doing immediately, breathing life back into one, then another and another, until an NCO's voice finally breaks the spell:

'Run, you silly gits! Run! They'll fucking kill us all!'

We start to run across the plain, which booms and buckles under our feet, flapping our arms in the air like windmill sails, in pursuit of a balance that's always just a few steps ahead, charging at the dizzying darkness amid the explosions that come more and more frequently and dazzle without providing light. Nothing counts in our headlong rush but chance, chance rampant and reigning equally over all, without bigotry or bias: a hooded shadow easily overtakes me – I'm going as fast as my legs will carry me – and enviously now I think to myself that man *is* going to save himself and just then, as if running into its arms, he crosses the path of a grenade, which lifts him up and shakes him in its drooling, rabid jaws of fire and then drops him; the last of a blanket-covered group of four – a Chinese dragon at New Year dancing to the firecrackers! – is hit in the legs by a sweep of shrapnel and falls screaming to the ground, wrapped in the blanket while the front end carries on under its own momentum; two of the men stop in their tracks, then turn back for him; the remaining one, deciding to save his arse, runs on for a few metres and is engulfed by a wave of earth, at which his companions panic and leave their comrade, his arms reaching out for them. I stand there for a few seconds to wait for Chanino to catch up and find myself face to face with a shell enveloped in flames that, with all the time in the world, like a frisbee suspended over the beach, is flying through the sky at me; I tell myself that its leisurely approach will allow me time to dodge it, but to my horror I discover that my movements have slowed proportionally, the air around me acquiring the consistency of glycerine and the mud clinging to my boots like fresh cement; with as much chance as a fly on a sheet of flypaper I throw myself to the ground on my face – it takes me an interminable length of time to fall – before the viscous air disappears in a violent suction of two giant mouths kissing my ears at the same time and a piercing howl replaces my brain inside my skull. The shell sinks into the mud half a metre from my head without exploding. I drag myself away from it and fall into Chanino's arms, pulling him to the ground. I have a vague idea that on either side of us stretches the neatly sown expanse of the minefields, so we have no alternative but to lie here on the ground – if it weren't for the cluster bombs bursting in the air and spitting hails of shrapnel from the sky, we might still stand a chance – or go back to the mountain which, less accurately shelled now by our own artillery, offers better prospects of survival. Through the fog a ghostly hulk is coming our way with inhuman screams, forcing us to make up our minds without thinking, and we run in the direction of the advancing English shells, pursued by the thundering white ghost bearing down on us.

'It's the mare!' shouts Chanino.

The thunder of her hooves passes so close that I'm splashed by her snorts and just catch the tall columns of fire reflected in the hemisphere of her bulging eye. A couple of pieces of shrapnel or bullets have already opened up bloody furrows in her dirty white coat and, adding to her panic, they goad her on more than any whip ever could. For a few seconds, after her rump is swallowed up by the smoke and fog, I can see myself mounting her bareback and riding invulnerable through the curtain of smoke and fire that separates me from our lines, saving myself; until intermingled with explosions a dreadful scream shakes me out of the spell. Piebald with shrapnel, the mare reappears stumbling towards us, dragging a long snake of intestines, the other end of which is lost in the fog, like a rope tied to a post that sooner or later will force her to stop. She falls on one side waving her legs in the air and looks at us over her shoulder with her big, brown, trusting eyes, waiting for us to go and help her. How often I'd pulled up a tussock of tough grass for her and held it to her mouth, patting her strong neck as she chewed; she looks at me now as if she remembers. Chanino leads me away by the hand and soon we can see her no longer.

We sit down among some rocks at the foot of the mountain to wait for the English to find us. They must have cleared most of it because the shots are more and more sporadic and the bombardment's stopped. It's also stopped snowing. A shadow barely emerges from the light reflecting from the snow. NCO voice:

'Every soldier that can, pick up a gun and come with me!' it croaks in a broken voice. 'We're organising the counterattack!'

'Shut up, you tosser!' a voice finally answers from high up. The milico pretends not to hear.

'I know you're out there,' he shouts, as if warned by a sixth sense. 'I'll count to three. One . . .'

Two shots ring out, the bullets fly high above our heads and zing into the rocks. Anyone can see they're from one of our FALs. The officer doesn't speak again and after a while we hear him a long way off: '. . . we have to retake the hill . . . everyone in a condition to fight . . .'

We're beginning to freeze solid from our lack of movement by the time they arrive, and we have trouble standing and putting our hands up. There are two of them and, signalling, they make us line up – a line of five – and march uphill. They're rounding up the prisoners near where the mortars were. The earth and rocks look as if they've been churned up by bulldozers and most of the mortars – lying on their sides and twisted – are still pointing in the wrong direction. All their operators have fled or died, except one, who's dying with a stomach full of iron, and screaming; his cries are making the English nervous. One of them gives him two shots of morphine and after a while he calms down and dies dreaming he's back home. The look on his face was unmistakable: he could already smell the café con leche and medialunas.

'English? Any of you? Anybody speak English?'

They take me to one side, where twenty Argentinians are huddled on the ground guarded by four or five English, who are sitting smoking on the rocks, their disjointed faces covered in mud and shoe polish and ash. Only one, who looks like a corporal or a sergeant, is standing, arguing with an impeccably uniformed Argentinian officer. Verraco.

'Tell me what this arsehole wants before I lose my fucking rag,' he tells me. I translate, partially.

'My gun, tell him he can't take my gun,' Verraco begs without seeing me in his hysteria, looking all the while at the Englishman.

'And why's that?' the Englishman asks after I repeat it to him.

'He wants to know why?'

Verraco looks at me this time, then, still not recognising me, diverts his eyes, trying to take me aside and whisper.

'Tell him that if I'm to maintain discipline among our men, that . . . that I'll give it to him if they hold me separately, because they can't leave me with you lo— with them unarmed, you understand, I'm an officer . . .'

I understand. The bastard's terrified that, without his gun, we'll kill him as soon as the English turn their backs. He's right, I'll be the first in line.

'He says yes if you give him a blow job.'

The Englishman bursts out laughing and, still laughing, hits him in the balls with his rifle butt and brings him to his knees. Immediately he shoves the barrel of his SLR down Verraco's œsophagus and puts his finger on the trigger. Verraco gags, eyes bulging.

'Tell him what to do if he wants me to take my finger off the trigger.'

Verraco nods when I translate for him, at the top of my voice so that everyone can hear, and without hesitating he embarks on one of the most enthusiastic acts of fellatio you'll ever see, while from the group on the ground comes a ripple of applause and shouts of 'Go English! Shoot!' He has to push him off with his boot to make him stop.

'I'd like to shoot him. You can kill me afterwards,' I hear someone say. The Englishman looks at me in astonishment, the smile wiped from his face, without saying a word. It was me who spoke.

'That's why he wanted to keep his gun,' I say by way of explanation.

I don't know if he understood; it would have been asking too much. With a gesture he indicates that I should join the other prisoners and, still looking at me every so often out of the corner of his eye, he leads Verraco away pushing and shoving him downhill.

Two English force us to take off our jackets, which we dump on a stack at one side – if only one could hollow out a den in the centre and curl up to sleep. One holds his nose; the other smiles wanly at his joke. Huddling against each other like sheep in the rain, too terrified to speak, our gazes slipping on things and always falling into empty space, we wait. Burying myself as deep as I can in the group, I hide my face among theirs at the first change of colour in the sky; for the first time I fear the coming of the light, of what it might show. At some point I fall asleep, but I go on dreaming the same thing, the reports of the artillery and the shouts of the wounded English and the silence of our men pass into my dreams, the cold easily pierces my scant sleeping flesh and, though my insides are ravaged by hunger, I can't dream of food, the reality so devastating that sleep is limited to merely repeating it. Only the perspective changes: I can see the defeated heads sunk into elbows and hands, barely sticking out in the biting wind of the morning, I can see them from above, I can see my own among them and watch it with curiosity, one more in the huddled flock that the exhausted English shepherds, without lowering their weapons, stand watch over. A shake forces me back to my body and the mountain, created anew by the ashen light of the early morning, looms into view. A mud-covered Englishman, with eyes like distant depths of blue water in two pits of red earth, gestures to us to follow him. He points a finger: you, you and you. Left out, Chanino looks up in fright and I signal to him that I'll be right back. We're the only ones remaining from the forward positions, where the English took no prisoners, and if we'd known we'd never see each other again I suppose I'd have made my goodbye mean something. But there's no way for me to know that I'm destined to return to the mainland unconscious in the hospital boat, nor that Chanino will get off the train taking him back to his home town at a station somewhere or other on the way – I never found out which – and hang himself in the ladies by mistake, with his civilian's belt. It was when I found out almost a year later, when they bust me out of the Borda, that I realised: I was the only one left alive to tell the tale.

For all we know, he's taking us to be executed, but despite it being four against one, it doesn't occur to us to rebel or even to make a break for it: they know we're utterly defeated. Stumbling in our laceless boots, we pass a row of bodies covered in blankets blackened with blood as it starts to seep through them. Judging by their boots, they're English, killed before they had time to swap them no doubt. There are a lot of them, perhaps ten or twelve, although, as you have to count them by their legs, their numbers double and I get confused; anyway, I'm surprised and wonder whether it was us who killed any of them. We leave the caterpillar of corpses behind and start to climb. I recognise just enough of the terrain to realise that we're heading straight back to our position. Two more English are waiting for us while guarding four Argentinians who have finished their work and are sitting down to rest. In one fairly flat, rock-free hollow there's a square drawn with bayonets in the snow, and beside it, face down, they've piled the bodies we now have to bury. The brilliance of the first rays of sun stings our eyes, reflecting off the white crust that reaches to the edge of their ponchos and uniforms, halted there by the warmth – still enough to thaw it – from their bodies. We're each given a shovel and a sign to start digging. Their spades are much better than ours: they don't have that maddening hinge that absorbs half your momentum, but I have difficulty digging with my burnt hand even so, and by the third shovelful it's red-raw. All the time I try to imagine we're digging our own graves; I find it strangely calming. I recognise in the one digging beside me the face of Martín, who did his military service with me, and he recognises me too, but neither of us can say anything, not even with a gesture. I didn't know he was over here too. A negative coincidence: two months on the same mountain and we never once run into each other. He's weeping; he's been weeping ever since we started digging, without any apparent sadness, as if digging and weeping go together naturally, and he doesn't stop weeping as he digs. We dig for over an hour while the sun rises, blinding us as the snow catches fire. I think I fall asleep a couple of times with my eyes open, still digging. The hole is broader than it is deep and rather irregular owing to the stones that keep surfacing, when one of the English points at the pile and makes a hand gesture as if rolling tree-trunks.

The first one we turn over is Rubén. His quilted jacket is half open and the synthetic white stuffing emerges from the holes like some strange mould. His fists are clenched like a baby's and one big toe pokes from a hole in his sock. I must have done something wrong at this point, because the Englishman on guard hits me in the cheek a couple of times with his rifle butt and I go back to my place, calmed by obedience. I'm bleeding quite badly but luckily he hasn't broken any teeth. I think he'll give us blankets to separate the dead, but no, we have to pile them up as they are to rot into one another. Under Rubén are the two Cordobans, Toto apparently untouched, as if death had come from the inside and out of his mouth in a beard of blood down to his neck. Rosendo on the other hand is unrecognisable; I can't work out what's happened to his face. Closing my eyes, I pull on his arms and repeat to myself he's a box of ammunition, a mortar part, a heavy plank, until he's resting face down. It's more difficult to move Wally Walrus: he won't roll and it takes four of us more than half an hour to accommodate him on top of the Cordobans. Then it's the turn of the marine infantry, one a corporal who once caught me with some stolen food and ground my hand into the stones under his boot while he chewed away at it. I'd wanted him dead the whole war and, now my wish has been granted, I feel nothing, not because I feel sorry for him but because it could have been us instead of him: there was no punishment if this could happen as easily to Wally Walrus and Carlitos, to the marine and Rubén, to Verraco or me. They'd come to kill us all; the English bullets meted out no justice. The other marine had been caught by a phosphorus grenade, probably in his foxhole, and was carbonised like something left in the oven for hours. The last of the pile is Carlitos. I have to put him down, I'm shaking too much and, tripping over the other bodies, I start walking towards the English soldier. He trains his gun on me.

'Stand back,' he shouts.

I move my mouth, several times I think; my voice sticks in my throat.

'You . . . can't . . . bury him. You didn't kill him.'

'What? The fucker's still alive?'

'No. Dead. But you don't . . . didn't kill him. We killed him.'

'That doesn't make him one of us. Sorry. Hey, I thought you Argies only spoke Spanish.'

'We did. Can we bury him somewhere else, please. He was my friend. I'll dig his grave on my own.'

'We'll dig them up and separate them once we've cleared up here.'

I insist for bit longer, but the war has tossed my life at me like a coin to a beggar, and it isn't willing to concede anything else. We're spading the first shovelfuls of peat on the bodies when one of us, feeling dizzy, sits down to rest on the crumpled blankets that cover the pile and shouts.

'There's one here.'

It's Hijitus. It's the only name I know to say goodbye to him. We make room for him – he doesn't take up much – and finish covering them with peat, in a big mound of heavy clods almost a metre high. And there they stay: our friends, companions, foxhole mates, even our hated officers, in the only piece of Malvinas soil they've managed to make theirs. My whole world has shrunk to the size of that pit and, when I finish, I stick the spade in the ground and look for something to make a cross. The Englishman understands what I want.

'A helmet, put a helmet on it.'

He orders us to walk over the mound to stamp it down a bit, the way you do with the soil round a freshly planted tree. Bumping into and tripping over each other like blind zombies locked in a small room, the four of us walk round the metal tree, within the imaginary boundary drawn by the Englishman in the mud, sealing the tomb with the prints of our soles like sealing a letter with wax. The Englishman shouts something, but no one can hear him in the air that disappears and the howling whistle that's perforating our eardrums. Everything happens very slowly. I see the Englishman dive between the rocks; my three companions throw themselves face down in the mud. From up here I watch the motionless bodies with curiosity: erect above the devastation, I might pass for the last inhabitant of a dead planet. The whistle from the shell grows in intensity: judging by the direction, it's one of ours, but I can't see if it's a shell or a 105mm. They must have found out about the storming of the mountain, which, as far as they're concerned, is now an enemy position. This first shot is lucky for us: it falls nearby but the shrapnel doesn't hit us, we're well protected. I feel something hit my helmet, no harder than a rap of the knuckles, but it must have dented it a bit because straightaway it feels too tight and, when I try to loosen the strap and take it off, my clumsy, numb fingers slip on the buckle. Someone once told me that it's as well to leave the strap undone in combat because, if you get hit in the helmet, the jolt can snap your neck. Fortunately it's nothing like that, I'm fine, just a slight dizziness, like when you try to read a book with small print in a moving car, so I decide to sit down on the trampled mound and have another go at that strap. Our artillery keeps on firing, but now the shells are falling behind our backs. The English, it seems, haven't been as lucky as us: one of them's lying on the ground and his companions are trying to open his jacket, their hands slipping in the blood. Now that they're occupied, it would be so easy for us to grab the rifles just lying there and shoot them, but my companions haven't got up yet from the pile in the mud and I'm still busy with this buckle. Maybe if I rest a little first, I'll find it easier; I haven't had a wink all night and it won't hurt anyone if I have a few minutes' kip. Besides, the freshly dug-over earth, though cold, feels quite soft under my legs, and I let myself fall slowly until I'm lying on my back. My helmet feels even tighter than before, as if it's stuck to my skull, and the strap cuts into my Adam's apple and I find it difficult at first to breathe, but I soon get used to it. As I drift off to sleep, I have a good idea: I'll stay here and play wounded till the English come and pick me up. They'll treat me well, I speak their language, and they may even give me a few swigs of the old Gineva Convention and a cigarette; I'd prefer a cigar, thanks. With my arms stuck to my body and my legs crossed to keep out the cold (that particular cold that affects the body when it's gone for many hours without sleep) I could pass for a cigar myself, and I begin to levitate from the fatigue, first my feet, floating up there of their own accord and dragging the rest of my body with them before it levels out. Then, head first, I begin to sail through the air, flying as in a dream, manœuvring effortlessly, like a zeppelin on a windless day. I don't need anyone to lead me, I think to myself, I can find the way by myself, there's no way I can get lost, like an unwanted dog a long way from home, my instinct will lead me straight back. Cruising at this speed all day, I can be in Buenos Aires by nightfall; perfect, I've always liked seeing the city lights from the air, like an inverted sky with the stars on the ground. The war's over, the war's over, I repeat to myself in the lullaby of the explosions and, cradled in that certainty, I curl up on my side to keep the cold at bay, with my thumb for a cigar, and fall asleep on everyone's grave.

Chapter 16

THE RECOVERY OF
THE ISLANDS

I awoke numb with cold, waving clumsy tortoise legs in the still air and getting nowhere. I tried to turn over but only managed to bang my head on the concrete floor. The thud, strangely non-metallic, reverberated in the stillness. I couldn't remember taking my helmet off; perhaps someone had done it for me. Little by little, with an effort that felt like lifting my whole body off the ground, I half-opened one eye. In the distance the steep vertical sides of Mount Longdon rose skywards in shadow, a single light shining at the summit like a lighthouse for navigators. Who was it that had carried me or helped me to walk down? Or had I done it by myself and then passed out from the effort? But then why was I naked when the English had only been taking our jackets and bootlaces? I stretched up one blind hand and it immediately closed on the texture of cotton cloth hanging there in the void. A pair of hands in my armpits helped me to sit up and, raising my weak arms and struggling to get them into my sleeves, began to dress me like a child. As I couldn't raise my chin from my chest, I could see nothing more than the angel's shoes, a pair of dry, cracked boots laced up with plastic string, brushed by fraying cuffs held together by a matting of dirt. He was one of ours then; the English must have turned their noses up at boots in such bad condition. He covered my shoulders with my jacket and then, laying me down again, lifted my legs to pull on my trousers and socks.

'Don't know what happened to your boots,' rattled his familiar voice.

'The English,' I croaked.

He laughed, a low, hollow laugh that ended in a bronchial coughing fit.

'You too?'

I knew that, if I made a superhuman effort, I could lift up my head and see him, but the urge wouldn't go beyond the words in my mind. I only had enough strength left to feel the pain, an old, dull pain, less of a present pain than the memory of a pain so strong it still hurt. Two hooked hands hoisted me up; an evil-smelling body supported the weight of mine.

'Can you walk?'

I discovered that I could copy the other man's steps, keeping my socks on the floor, slumped over his shoulder. A seesawing marine horizon with reflected lights was trying to find its balance before my eyes. We must have been coming into the town then. I turned to my companion for confirmation. Bushy beard, more than two months' growth, peg-toothed smile.

'You? Here?'

'Here where?'

Good question, I thought, looking to the horizon for the answer. The lights of Puerto Argentino curved far beyond the two ends of the bay, their remote brightness lighting up the sky. How it had grown since the last time. I had the vague sensation of having dreamed as I slept, dreamed, like so many other times, of going home; only this time it had been the longest dream of all: a full ten years of illusory return condensed into a few minutes' doze.

'They're all dead,' I said to him.

'Just the old man. They've already taken him away. Let's get out of here before they come back.'

'Where to?'

'Home.'

The silhouette of the containers could be made out in the distance. We must be at the airport, I reassured myself, but instead of the planes an incredible apparition met my eyes, its prow rising triumphant from the mists of sleep: the phantasmal hulk of a Spanish galleon, still intact, as if it had just run aground in the cement. A second later I knew where I was.

Through the rusted corrugated iron they'd opened up a hole that you could put your head through, and in the heart of the container full of compressed paper there was a hollowed-out den with just enough room to curl up and sleep. A tunnel communicated with the other container, where they kept their belongings, he explained; the thick paper walls provided insulation from the cold outside, so much so that I was warm again in minutes. I had a dreadful taste of wet ash in my mouth, a perishing thirst and a real headache that was my own, getting stronger as the one induced by the drug waned. The tramp's rear end disappeared down the tunnel that led to the other container and his head returned, preceded by a tall string of stale bread rolls and a large, litre-and-a-half bottle of water.

'You can't ask for more,' my host summarised as I downed almost half the bottle without drawing breath and immediately set about the fossilised rolls with my molars. 'But I can't enjoy it any more. He, on the other hand, was never happy. When it was fine out, he'd spend it on the terrace, watching them. You don't know how lovely we had the terrace done out. Even had a couple of loungers. Got any cigarettes? I'm dying for a smoke.'

The lighter flame lit up the white walls of the room. It looked like a tattered igloo.

'He never explained why. On a couple of occasions I suggested going away, jumping on a train, seeing the country; but there was nothing to be done. I threatened to go off by myself, and he just said, "Well, go on then." I always ended up staying. I couldn't imagine spending a night alone. What are those furry mice called, the ones that go round and round on their little wheel till they get tired and snuggle up together to sleep in the middle of a nest of paper?'

'Hamsters.'

'That's what we were. Two hamsters that had got tired of the wheel.'

'What happened?'

'They approached him one day when he was out there, working on his toy tower. It was what he enjoyed most, working on his tower, and I used to help him. But he abandoned it on the grass, in the supermarket trolley, and followed them without saying goodbye. I saw them walk through the mirrors and disappear. Hours went by, then days, and I began to push it around its elder sister in the hope that he'd see it from some window, and come out and give me something – food, clothes, a few coins, or at least talk to me. But I never saw him again. Till that night, of course.'

'Which night?' I asked him, just for the sake of helping him in the telling, the answer being obvious.

'The night they threw him out.'

He spat between his feet and put out his fag end, which sputtered in the gob of spittle, to prevent all that paper catching fire. I took another drag and did the same.

'Luckily they didn't take him far,' he added.

'Do you know where he is?'

Instead of answering he pushed past me, digging his way through the papers, which kept collapsing, to reach the exit. I followed him. Opposite us, duplicated in the reflection of the still waters of the dock, the sails of Columbus's caravel blacked out the stars, its voluminous pregnant belly solidly embedded in the cement pedestal the tramp was staring at.

'His dream came true, in the end.'

'Which one?'

He looked at me steadily.

'He was there as well.'

The finality in his tone of voice was unmistakable. For me, of course.

'He always used to say it was in the Islands he became a tramp. And when he got back, it seemed only natural to stay one. He'd come to the port in the hope of finding a ship to take him back. I was ready to go with him. Every now and then we'd do the rounds and ask. The sailors laughed in our faces, though some felt sorry for us sometimes and would take the trouble to explain. The ships that go to Malvinas don't leave from here, they'd tell us. But he never lost hope. And now you see. Finally he found it.'

He pointed at the caravel that had caught the wind of departure in its unfurled sails, straining to tear its hull free of the cement vice. The stars shone through the holes in its ribs.

'It's ready to sail.'

So this was the boat that would take us back to the Islands: a ghost ship, of course. Would I still be in time to board it?

'You can stay if you like,' he said without much hope.

I remembered the Borda.

'I've tried it. It's not my thing.'

He gave a shrug.

'You're welcome whenever you like. Bring a packet of yerba next time and we'll have some matés.'

I was turning away when I remembered.

'Hey!'

'What.'

'Thanks for the help.'

His double row of peg teeth grinned back.

'Don't forget the yerba,' he said.

* * *

I didn't have a single coin for the bus in all the pockets I checked, and I couldn't remember if there was any money at home to risk taking a taxi. It wasn't that far after all and, despite how weak I felt, it didn't seem impossible to walk home. My silent steps led me round the edge of the dock to Avenida Belgrano, which led me out of the port and across Avenida Puerto Madero, empty of lorries at that hour, and reached Avenida Paseo Colón, where the traffic lights blinked their colours pointlessly at the absent cars. Only a couple of taxis went past, stalking the only pedestrian in the sleeping city, more out of resignation than hope. Walking in socks down the empty downtown streets at the deadest point of the week, the interregnum between the long night of a winter Sunday and the reluctant morn of Monday, was no different than in dreams. And it wasn't even my own dream. Only when I reach home, I thought, will I be in a place where the nightmares of the living and the dead can't reach me; I'll turn the keys and pull down the blinds, turn on all the screens and never come out again unless it's through them, leave them all in the street knocking on the doors I'll never open. That had been my first mistake, which all the subsequent ones derived from as a logical consequence: going outside. None of this could have happened to me on the Web.

The pain had gone almost completely. The drug in the end hadn't been any more than that: a little bit like seasickness which, once it's passed, leaves no trace and it's hard to believe it could ever have been so bad, the relief of treading on land again so pleasurable that you even look back with a little nostalgia.

Was this how it was ten years ago? Was this what I'd been spared: this silent, floating moon-walk my companions' tales had allowed me to remember as if I'd been walking with them? Had they plodded on as I did now, drawn towards the plain by the inertia of defeat, descending the mountains towards the doomed capital like a flood, pouring through its streets minute by minute in an unstoppable olive green torrent, knocking down fences, trampling on vegetable patches, lapping against the walls of houses at whose windows the terrified Kelpers dared not show themselves; spreading little by little, milling around till they settled like the waters of a lake, depositing a flotsam of abandoned weapons, ammunition boxes, empty helmets, rucksacks, kicked bags – all useless now that the only thing left to do was to sit down in silent bunches and wait for the English to come? I have to get there before they do, I said to spur myself on down the deserted slope of Avenida San Juan, my steps so silent that not even I seemed to be there; I have to hurry, I repeat to myself, even if I know that I'm ten years too late, that the Kelpers and the English are sleeping safely in their beds and I'm the last Argentinian in the Islands.

I had trouble getting my key in the lock and there was no need to turn on the light to see what had happened. They hadn't been content to take the floppies and the hard disks of my disembowelled computers; if what they'd wanted was information, they could have got it over the Web without setting foot in my house. No, they'd done it their way, the best they knew, with that characteristic blend of method and brutality, reliving the good old days that had never quite gone. I groped about for the phone, which at that moment was the only really indispensable thing and, after scavenging around in my own rubbish for some time, I found part of the casing. I went on crawling mechanically across the irregular mattress of my belongings strewn from wall to wall over the floor, groping mechanically for what I was looking for. Under the collapsed boxes of Christopher products appeared a pair of thick socks into which I stuck my feet, blistered and scratched by the last few blocks, which I'd walked on bare soles and, in a lower stratum, my Topper baseball boots, which it took me some time to lace up; all the while not bothering to turn on the light, or to close the door on my way out.

As if the visit to my house had been just a quick stopover, I carried on walking down San Juan against the flow of traffic. The first few blocks I was too numb to even look when I crossed and in the wide open spaces of Avenida 9 de Julio it was only the time of day that saved me from being run over on the motorway access roads. Only when I reached Avenida Entre Ríos did I feel any emotion: it was hatred. I was crossing Avenida Boedo and I still didn't know what I was doing, so I decided not to do anything, just to go on walking till something happened. All need for a decision vanished, trampled underfoot by the simple fact of walking, sheer stubbornness, the soul's most mechanical faculty. By now the lights were bowling handfuls of cars down the avenue every so often, which, with their uneven speeds, broke up till the next set of red lights marshalled them again. I took advantage of one of these starts to run across to the other pavement, laughing at the desperate flashings of headlights, the sudden meandering brakings and the long, continuous tooting of horns, and I would have done it again had it not been for the breathlessness that clouded my eyes so badly that the buildings began to waver like flames and I had to sit down and close my eyes until the city had settled again. 'Go away,' I shouted at it, trying to sound defiant. 'Get lost, leave me alone. I don't need you, I've never needed you. Why go on kidding ourselves? I never came back. I never left the Islands.'

I turned right at the next corner without knowing why, until I looked up and saw the name of the street: Malvinas Argentinas, what else. When I looked down, they were walking beside me.

They hadn't aged, as I hadn't either: like the clocks of Hiroshima, time for us had stopped at an instant. The time and place were just right for the meeting: the dead hours of deep night, the junction of the indistinct streets of Buenos Aires and Puerto Argentino. Their casualness would have made my astonishment sound rude and, with nothing more than an imperceptible shrug of the shoulders (although who knows what they could perceive?), I walked between them on the pavement, where only my steps rang out. The first to speak was Carlitos:

'City's changed, eh, since the last time.'

'You don't come often?' I asked him.

'Not unless we're called,' he looked at me. 'Which is like saying . . .'

'. . . less and less.' Rubén finished the sentence. The charred rents in the material of his uniform looked like black holes in a sky of dry blood. 'Why didn't you call us before, Porteño?'

I hung my head as low as I could to escape the stabbing of accusing eyes. They still hurt on the back of my neck though.

'I missed you all as well. I miss you more than ever. But I was afraid of calling you.'

I looked up slightly. They were looking at each other, winking.

'Way hey! We're wicked we are.'

'We frighten the little boys.'

'And fondle the little girls.'

They drew a smile from me. Bastards, over there too, against all the odds, they used to manage it. No one had ever done it, against my will like that, ever since. Well, one person had, I corrected myself. But she's further away than they are now. With a supreme effort, more for their sake than mine, I looked up into Carlitos' serene eyes. He was massaging his wrist. He'd let his moustache grow to cover the split lip.

'Do you still hate me?' I asked him.

'Since when did I hate you?' He answered me with another question, like a good Jew. Try as I might, I couldn't detect the slightest trace of irony in his voice.

'Since that day when I stood by and let Verraco do . . . Since that night when I fell asleep with you dying at my side. And all these years for letting the monster go on living. As if that wasn't enough.'

The cars had reappeared by the time we reached Avenida Rivadavia. In the two blocks we'd been walking down the avenue, none of the drivers seemed surprised at the strange patrol of dead soldiers walking the streets of the empty city. Maybe, like me, they hadn't bought the story about the end of the war either.

'Your silence sounds like assent,' I said with relief.

'I'm thinking how to explain to you,' he said, breaking it.

'What.'

'That those things don't matter to us over there.'

'Nothing matters to you then. How nice that must feel. You're making me envious. You always did make me envious.'

'Just one thing does. A lot.' He turned to look at me before he said it. 'You guys.'

We turned onto Donato Álvarez. I don't know who did it first. We were moving in unison, like a flock of birds in the sky. All my tiredness had gone, and my doubts and my fear. This was what I'd been afraid of all along. Now it had come, my fear had been replaced by a calm acceptance.

'All right, I admit it, it's a fair cop. You're right to accuse me. I declare myself guilty; it's quicker that way. But don't worry, it won't last long, this state of things.'

'You still don't understand.'

'I didn't think it was so hard. I thought that's why we crossed the lake: to make it less difficult.'

'Chanino, see if you can make him understand.'

He put a hand on my shoulder. A hand as weightless as a blown kiss.

'Listen to me, Porteño, you know what Hell is?'

'Yes,' I nodded vehemently. 'You bet I do. I could write the book.'

'Ours is different. In order to swim to the other side we have to divest ourselves of what we suffered in life. What we remember, we remember without pain. But there is a pain that comes across with us. Your pain. The pain of the ones still alive.'

Rubén intervened.

'The only thing we ask is that you let us in sometimes. But with you there was nothing doing. We knocked and knocked but you wouldn't open. Only very occasionally, in dreams that you'd forgotten before you woke up. A few days ago we waved to you from the highest peaks of Longdon but you didn't recognise us.'

'You elongated everything there, we looked like something out of an El Greco dream,' Carlitos remarked. 'Is that why you did it, so as not to recognise us?'

'Not even when he's dead will this one cut out the psychology,' Rubén quipped. 'And you cast Chanino as a Gurkha.' The 'Gurkha' in question pulled an offended face. 'Good thing he didn't take it seriously.'

'I didn't dare to look you in the eyes,' I said, my own looking down into the rubbish by the kerb. 'I was scared.'

'What of?'

'Of you all accusing me. Of forgetting you.'

All four let out a prfffff of astonished laughter.

'Forgetting us? You? You've been carrying us around on your back for the last ten years,' said Carlitos.

'For not fighting the good fight,' I insisted stubbornly. 'Because I'm alive and you're not, and that makes me happy.' That's it, I said it, I thought to myself. Let the lightning fall once and for all and strike me dead.

'All these years, we've been waiting to tell you,' Carlitos began menacingly.

'What.'

Here it came. This was it at last. What I most feared.

'Not to feel guilty. It's them, they're the guilty ones. The ones who put us all in that situation. They're the bastards. Not you. You did what you could.'

'And something else,' added Rubén before I could speak. 'We're happy you made it. That's good enough for us. You don't owe us anything else. But you do owe us that.'

'That?'

'We know what you've got in mind,' said Carlitos.

'It's just that I miss you. I'd like to be with you.' I implored. 'Let's stay together, like when we were over there . . . like now.'

'You think it's that easy? You know how long it had been since we saw each other, before you started remembering things?' said Carlitos.

'If you aren't here,' Rubén clarified, 'there won't be anybody left to reunite us. Our families dream of us separately.'

'We didn't come to look for you,' said Chanino.

'What *did* you come for then?'

'To say goodbye.'

The knot in my throat rose to my eyes. They walked beside me for two blocks without saying a word, letting me weep. The tears slid down my cheeks and fell from my bowed head onto the flagstones.

'We don't want you with us,' said a voice so childish yet so sure of itself that it made me look up. It was the first time I'd heard it. Hijitus's voice.

'You won't have any alternative,' I told them all.

'That's your decision,' said Carlitos. 'And it's true we can't stop you. But don't lie to yourself that you're doing it for us. We won't be with you when you do it, so don't bother calling us.'

The street was blocked by a long wall of bricks. The walls of Chacarita Cemetery.

'This is as far as we go,' said Rubén.

'You're on your own from here,' Carlitos completed.

'Chau, Porteño,' said Chanino.

'Chau, Felipe,' said Hijitus.

The mirage of the city had risen again from its ashes in the faint colours of the early dawn and, as its fragile substance thickened and took shape, that of my friends thinned until the bricks of the cemetery walls showed through their bodies. Their hands could barely be seen as they raised them to wave to me, and their hoarse farewells merged with the whispering of the wind. The roar of a passing bus drowned them out and, with the first ray of sun over the wall, they disappeared like images from a film projected onto the blue sky.

I didn't run into anyone in the next few blocks, although I couldn't tell whether it was other people or me who weren't there. I advanced through the current of the ever more tortuous river I'd been swimming against since I'd left the ruins of my apartment and, despite its ever narrower banks closing in on me and the tarmac swirling against my feet, some obscure instinct guided me towards its source. When I got there, reaching the centre of the oval mandala from which all rivers are born, I began to rotate slowly on my axis, my arms outstretched perpendicular to my torso, beneath the only mercury spotlight still on, as if meting out light and shadow in the morning of the first day.

Over the irregular saw-edge of ferns and geraniums, high up on the terrace of a house of white-painted brick and dark green blinds, which still sheltered the faint shadows of early morning from the all-conquering dawn, three figures in helmets and combat gear, silhouetted against the lemon sky, were watching me. More ghosts.

'Here. Felipe,' they called me, raising their rifles in the air.

'We won! I hit an Englishman! I hit him!'

'Come in, come up, they may be back!'

Gloria opened the door to me. I stumbled over the threshold and she had to support me to stop me falling.

'Felipe, my love, what have they done to you?'

She helped me to reach the sofa. She smothered my face in kisses. Hers was running with tears.

'It's over,' I managed to get out.

'But look at the state you're in. They've nearly killed you.'

'See? They never can,' I tried to smile. 'They were here too, right?'

She nodded.

'Luckily the girls were out. As soon as I was back on my feet, I rang Mum to come and pick them up.'

'And why did you stay?'

'To wait for you. Will you explain what's happened at some point? Not now, but some time. Ok? I don't understand a thing. Your friends . . .'

They were coming down as we spoke. Gloria gave me a few more kisses and went to the kitchen to make maté. Ignacio had one arm in a bandage.

'You got hit?' I asked.

'Just a scratch,' he beamed back at me.

He and Sergio (Tomás was still upstairs on guard) filled me in and, although their voices came and went as if they were covering and uncovering my ears with cupped palms, I listened to them patiently. It had, after all, been their first confrontation with the English, and they'd done it for me.

'They swore in Spanish,' remarked Sergio, with more curiosity than suspicion.

'Special commandos,' I answered him. 'You remember how they warned us about them in the Islands?'

The first maté flooded through my body like a transfusion. From a tin between her knees Gloria fed me biscuits, which I ate at first with difficulty, then greediness and soon desperation. In the intervals she handed the maté round to the others, who took the gourd from her hands with shy and grateful smiles.

'Can you tell Tomás to come down,' I exhaled, stuffed. 'There's no further danger of attack. Gloria, are my clothes around?'

She helped me get changed, as I could hardly stand up. The combat uniform ended up in a pile of olive green at my feet.

'I've got some bad news for you,' I announced when I had them all together. Sergio, Ignacio and Tomás looked at me in concern. 'The aim of the English attack – Major X – he fell in the line of duty. He'd come to Buenos Aires to elicit support: they located him.' I looked at Gloria out of the corner of my eye. The back of her neck lodged in the back of the sofa, she was smoking, her eyes lost somewhere in the ceiling. 'It may be of some consolation to know that at least one of his murderers paid – the one you shot. They were the same ones who came here.'

The three of them now looked at Gloria who, only just catching on, sat up in the armchair to accept their condolences.

'We didn't know, Señora, our deepest sympathy,' they muttered softly.

'But there's something else,' I went on when the moment had passed. It was strange: we were all deadly serious, even Gloria. 'He left you something. Gloria, there's a bag in the girls' room. I don't know if you saw it.'

'I'll go and get it.'

I took out the still unmanageable wad of papers and stacked them on my knees. After I'd put them in some sort of order, I handed the sheaf to Tomás, who took it in both hands. The three of them looked at me without daring to ask.

'Major X's diaries,' I told them. 'From now on you're going to be their custodians. It's a big responsibility,' I added, to confirm what I read in their eyes. 'Everything that was ever said is true. They hold the secret of the war.'

Gloria and I got up to see them out. Before they left, Tomás pointed to the pile of clothes on the floor.

'Take them,' I answered. 'Thanks for coming. Lads,' I called to them when they reached the empty centre from where all roads departed, 'there's something I never said to you.'

'What.'

'Thanks for coming to get me from the Borda.'

The three of them answered me with a gesture of that's

what friends are for, and I stood there in the door frame until their backs vanished in the amateur Tetris of morning sun and shade. I closed the door. Gloria was sitting waiting for me at one end of the sofa, patting the cushion of the other end with an outstretched arm:

'Spit it out.'

'I'm wrecked.'

'They almost killed me, they almost killed my girls. I can't wait. I need to know now whether to thank you or to hate you. Come on, kiddo. You've already seen me do it ten days ago – a thousand years ago. You survive.'

'Surviving's shit.'

'Tell me about it.'

I had no alternative then. I started with the day I first entered Tamerlán's tower, or with the day the three cops brought me the draft to rejoin the army, there wasn't much difference. As I went on, I realised the two stories had ended up merging into one like two rivers that join to form a third; or perhaps there'd only been one river all along and it was me who had encountered two separate stretches of it at two moments in my life without realising the water was the same. Gloria smoked the whole time, taking cigarette-long pauses between cigarettes; only from the desolate Zen garden of fags and ash that her almost-full packet had become towards the end did I have some idea of how long I'd been talking. She only got up once, to pee; I didn't even do that and, apart from the odd twitch on her face in the parts where *he* appeared and smiles when it was about her or her daughters, and once when I choked up and couldn't go on till she stretched out a hand to touch my knee with her fingertips, she never interrupted or said a word the whole time. I kept talking, the thread of my story guiding me almost blindly through the dark labyrinth of the last ten years of my life, feeling neither relieved nor liberated nor justified as I advanced, just sadder and tireder, and at the same time loath to finish; I remembered Ignacio and how he'd looked at me that night, standing beside his model, the day it had all started again. Now I was the one in his shoes, delaying the end for as long as possible, because I'd understood that when the words of my story had walked the last streets, when my weary feet had found the green-painted door opening at the centre of the mandala and, walking through it, led me to this sofa where I now sat, the circle would at last have closed and there would only be one thing left for me to do. Now I understood the feeling that had begun to flood through me from the first words of my story, the feeling, not white but browngreengrey that the others had become as the colour wheel spun faster and faster: it was the indefinable sadness of goodbye. Not in another ten years would I relive it to tell the sad story lived twice or add another twist to the Möbius strip that, weaving between two worlds intertwined like two facing mirrors, had ended up merely finding its own tail. Tempting fate, the traveller had tried to cross the bridge again and this time the verdict was to hang him.

'I totally agree with you,' said Gloria when she saw I'd finished. They were the first words she'd spoken since I'd begun.

'What about?'

'Let's top ourselves. It's the best thing.'

She leaped up and disappeared into the bedroom. I could hear her opening and shutting drawers. I sat there motionless, still wondering if I'd heard right. She came back with her two hands clenched into fists, which she stretched out to me, knuckles up.

'Let's give ourselves one last chance. Pick one.'

The tips of three of my fingers lightly tapped the back of her left hand. Turning it, she showed me her open palm on which, side by side, lay two yellow pills, rough-looking, like granite.

'What are they?'

'Cyanide. Ok? I'm open to suggestions.'

I felt a blow to the chest, violent, as if I'd been winded; when I inhaled, I felt my lungs fill with this new, innocent air as the skilled hands of relief caressed my startled heart, un-knotting and smoothing my intestines. A languid sweetness invaded my limbs and I felt them fall, abandoning themselves to the weight of the world. Why not? Why not, after all? I'd been weighing up the options all these years, but in none of them had it ever occurred to me that I could do it with someone else. Maybe that was why I'd never really made up my mind. If I'd had an opportunity like this, I wouldn't have waited so long. I started to open my mouth.

'No, not here. Let's go to the bedroom. These things should be done properly.'

The bed was unmade and full of crumbs in the folds in the sheets. Stockings, knickers, bras and T-shirts hung from various angles of the furnishings as if they'd recently rained from the ceiling.

'Imagine if somebody found our bodies in this mess. How embarrassing.' Gloria flitted about, manœuvring between the narrow spaces, lightly swiping the garments from their haphazard perches, and finally straightened the sheets and the blue quilt. I sat down on the edge of the bed.

'You hadn't seen my bed, had you?'

'What do we do?'

The light filtered through the half-closed blinds. Tiny motes of dust danced in the beams.

'Well, we lie down. Side by side, right?'

'Shall we leave a note?'

'What do we say?'

She was right. I started to lie back.

'Shall we get undressed? It's more romantic.'

'You've got it all worked out.'

'I've been through it a thousand times in my head. I know every step by heart.'

It must have been true, because she was one step ahead of me at every turn. I hadn't finished peeling the shirt off my back before she, leaning on my shoulder to balance, had slipped her knickers over her feet – 'A leopard can't change its spots,' she said as the soft projectile left her fingers and landed on the shade of the night-light. Standing at the foot of the bed, she smiled at me. The constellations shone on her naked body, as if the wind had blow away the clouds of an overcast sky.

'Something's missing,' she said pensively.

'Cigarettes?'

'That's for the firing squad. Oh, I know: water. In case they get stuck in our throats.'

She came back with a disposable litre-and-a-half bottle of Villavicencio and two glasses. What a shame to leave her. When the two of us aren't around, whose dreams will we be able to meet again in? Soledad and Malvina's I suppose. Not such a bad option.'

'What'll happen to the girls?'

'My old lady's looked after them more than I have. I, there were times . . . better not to tell you. And if something happens to her, they've always got an aunt and uncle in Rosario. I always thought a father wouldn't hurt them.'

'What if we go to Europe, or the States?'

'What for? We're fine here.'

Lying side by side, not touching, with just a narrow gap of blue quilt between our bodies, we fell silent for a few seconds, staring at the ceiling.

'Shall we make love first?' I asked for the sake of asking.

'In this funereal mood?' She stretched out a hand, took hold of the flexible dwarf between two fingers and jogged it at the base. 'You don't look very willing to me. Anyone would think you're trying to get out of it.'

'All right, go on,' I said sitting up on the bed. Perhaps the only way was to swallow them without thinking. I'd believe in them when it happened. I grabbed my pill with two fingers, delicately, like a contact lens. It hardly seemed possible that something so small . . . Freedom. This easy? My hands were so damp that a yellowish paste formed on the fingers that were holding it. I licked them.

'It's bitter.'

'Yes. We were going to bring out a fruit-flavoured line, but the lab fell. Try not to taste it. Swallow it whole. But let's have a toast first.'

We clinked pills and, with a sip from the same glass, we both swallowed them. I closed my eyes. Quick, quick. But I opened them and everything was still the same. Gloria looked at me for a second like she'd never looked at me before and gave me a wan smile. Then she became preoccupied with picking at an ingrowing hair in her bikini-line that had escaped the wax.

'It's not working.'

'No, it isn't, is it?' she replied absorbed in her business.

'Isn't it supposed to be instantaneous?'

'They must be coated. Coated ones take longer to act, you know.'

'They didn't look coated,' I said with so little conviction that she didn't bother to answer. 'Where did you get them?'

'My guerrilla days.'

'Won't they have expired by now?'

'Cyanide never expires.'

There was nothing to read on the ceiling; it was impeccably painted, not a trace of damp, like a blank screen on which, miraculously, in those last few moments, the film of my life was mercifully not being projected. A bit of luck: I don't think I could have taken it. Just a few brief flashes on my retinas after diverting my eyes from the filament of the light bulb. The room dissolved around them and, when I tried to get back to it, I found myself staring instead at the light undulations of the Malihuel lagoon, the sunlight ricocheting off its surface and dazzling my eyes. I dipped a hand in the warm water and could feel it holding me, its fingers flowing and interlacing, playing with and between my own.

'Feel it? Feel it?' Gloria's voice asked me.

I felt it. The first time just something moving, expanding, at regular one-minute intervals. My ribs began to bow outwards, to give it space, and my heart began to pulse, rather than beat. Then I was breathing differently, as if I had a hot-air balloon inside my chest and the atmosphere was giving me the kiss of life, forcing more – and more – into my lungs with every breath until, fit to burst, it let me go and all the contained air escaped in gust after gust of unspeakable sweetness. In my surprise I remembered that these novel and varied sensations were those of death; I wouldn't have waited so long if I'd know it was going to feel so good. Gloria's hand was still moving inside mine, as if it had a life of its own, and mine did too. They touched and recognised each other like people. It was as if I'd always been wearing gloves and now, for the first time, had been allowed to take them off. I turned to look at her. Her eyes had become liquid, brimming, like water overflowing a glass, and her smile was the same as the time I ran after her with the squeezy bottle at the carnival in Malihuel. Her chin trembled uncontrollably as she spoke.

'Looks like it's working, doesn't it?'

'What is it?' I asked, enraptured.

'Ecstasy. Never tried it?'

'No.'

'Mmmh. Congratulations. Your new life begins today.'

'Aren't we going to die?'

'Someday, I guess.'

I didn't feel disappointed. It wasn't that I'd suddenly been filled with the will to live, just that, in this state of absolute plenitude, it didn't matter whether I was alive or dead, as long as I could go on feeling like this. 'This is what we were made for,' I found myself repeating without surprise as I slid my hand along the curve of her backwaistbuttocks, recapturing the mystery of the first time – no, realising that the first time I'd done nothing more than brush it. So this was touching? This conviction that my fingers weren't discovering but creating what flowed between them, my hands running over Gloria's skin, dissolving the old scars with the ease of the potter's hand smoothing his clay on the turning wheel?

'Hey, I think these things are the real deal.'

'Where did you get them?'

'Manna from heaven. A friend from Spain.'

'Christopher Columbus?'

A fresh gust of warm air blowing from the new world extinguished the words in our mouths before we could speak them and a drowsy sweetness gripped my limbs, holding them fast, delivering me defenceless into her irreverent hands, which began to knead the clay of my old body. A new identity was being born, trembling as her fingers gradually drew out the forms of the new; the hands of Rodin couldn't have breathed more life into my limbs. Possessed by an ambition for greater plenitude, I leaped on top of her and slid inside her open body but, after the first few assaults, I realised I could barely feel anything. Not that I regretted it too much, because my willie swam slackly between her legs the way as a boy I went skinny-dipping one summer in the warm water of Malihuel's lagoon.

'It's not for fucking, is it,' she murmured without disappointment. 'Everything wants to go out and play. Nothing wants to stay inside.'

I couldn't even if I wanted to; my body was turning inside out like a glove so that the hand of the world, which had taken the form of Gloria, could approach to touch me.

'It's great this, eh?'

'Mmmmmh.'

'Can't you say anything else?'

'Mmmmmh.'

Why when a single sound was enough? With both of us feeling the same, there was nothing left to say. Our words had fallen away like our clothes and in this terrible, fearless naked-ness the voice was nothing but breathing sounds, the words poured into my ears nothing but prolongations of the lips that were kissing them. How wrong I'd always been: it wasn't things that were distanced from words, it was us. In the same way that, for the first time, I was touching what my greedy baby's hands were reaching for, for the first time I was saying the words I'd only repeated until now, saying them with my whole body. Before today, I understood, I'd only lied.

'You're really tripping; I envy you. How long's it been since you had something to eat?'

'Day. Night,' I mumbled.

'No wonder. And no sleep. It's like you've taken three at once. Come with me; let's put some music on.'

In our bare feet on the surf-cold sand that had burst through the scales of the parquet floor, we ran to the living room to put on some Prince. Blindly lying on the sofa I discovered that my whole body responded to the slightest vibration, tibia-femur-hip as tremulous and sensitive as hammer-anvil-stirrup, the diaphragm turned eardrum trembling in wave after wave of pleasure transmitted to the throbbing folds of the intestines. I opened my eyes to Gloria, who was parading her nakedness around the room while tracing arabesques with her arms, plac-ing the soles of her feet with deliberate care – a transported, ecstatic Bacchante.

'What are you doing?' I asked her, fascinated.

'I'm dancing,' she remarked, without looking at me,

bewitched by her own movements. 'Dancing barefoot on the broken glass of the past.'

'How long do the effects last?'

'Six hours more or less. Adam and Eve's time in paradise. The guy who invented it thought of everything.'

Six hours! But what did I care if in these six hours I was going to feel everything I hadn't felt in my thirty-year existence? I found myself repeating a phrase I'd once read in a book I never finished, and immediately forgot, remembered now that I could finally understand it: 'There is another country where one is at home, where everything one does is innocent.'

'Why did nobody ever tell me this existed?' I stammered. 'Is there a planet-wide conspiracy to stop us experiencing it?'

'Maybe you're right. It brings out everything good that's been repressed, it takes the fear out of love. Don't you sometimes get the feeling we're more afraid of showing the good than the bad we carry around inside us? Who knows if the unconscious isn't full of precisely this love? We think it's nothing but a sewer because we've been fed Freud's whole psychic trip.'

'Can you imagine if we all took it at the same time? The concentrated energy would be so great that the whole world would change, and that change would be irreversible.'

'You are a sweetie,' Gloria said to me, reaching out one hand, between whose caress and my cheek an infinitely fine dust had settled, as on a piece of furniture after a couple of days without dusting. 'You remind me of my first time. I also thought that giving my ex an e would turn him into John Lennon. If only. It doesn't work on pricks like him, you know. They drool all over you at best. I've been there.'

A few minutes ago, I thought, I wouldn't have believed

it, but now what she was saying sounded perfectly reasonable. With dawning astonishment I realised we'd started talking in order to communicate again, that a conversation like this one would have been inconceivable until almost a minute ago, and at that precise instant I felt in the pit of my stomach the certainty that Tuesday existed and, in the mere conception that another state unlike this one was possible, I sensed with the most childish pain that the effects of the drug were beginning to fade. Gloria was looking at me with the most intimate love, but over her soft smile the first quiver of still invisible sadness had begun to play.

'You too?' she asked without needing to specify.

'So soon?' I implored and went quiet as I heard the first muffled thud, feeling it directly over my heart from the effects of the pill. The dinosaur from the end of the world, wakening from its brief nap in the sun, was on the march again.

It receded in waves just as it had come. The moments of overwhelming fullness came back at regular intervals, but now there was always the awareness, an awareness that they weren't invincible, that little by little they were losing ground and that at some point they'd be gone completely. I still didn't feel fear, anguish, guilt, impotence. But they were now becoming *thinkable* . . . The clocks had regained their authority over time, minutely slicing it up with their precise knives, objects were again clothing themselves in their surfaces and fingers no longer sank in when they touched them. Knowing, always knowing, the ignorance of anything distinct from pleasure ebbing from the incandescent cells that went out one by one like stars in the light of day, I tried to delay the inevitable by closing my eyes and launching myself in one last assault on the still ductile body yawning and stretching to loosen its joints beneath mine, but my caresses were those of a shipwrecked sailor on the chest that keeps him afloat as the current leads him inexorably away from the promised land.

'It's going, it's going, like grains of sand in your hand,' Gloria kept repeating as it crept hopelessly through her fingers.

'Why won't it go on?' I implored. 'I don't want it to stop! I want to live here for ever!'

'I do too, my love. I dunno.' She stretched out, curved and sinuous, to the upturned alarm clock. Ha! Know what time it is?'

'No.'

'Twelve. Noon, but anyway. Cinderella has to make a quick phone call.'

She dialled while I stroked her, closing my eyes to delay for a few more instants the moment at which they'd re-establish their tyranny over the other senses.

'Hi, Mum. I'm fine, don't worry. Reeeeally fine. Are the girls back from school yet? Put them on . . . Sole, my love, my little chickadee. How's Mummy's little darling? Is Malvina with you? Oh, you were listening. You little snoop! Mummy loves you so, so much, you can't imagine how much. Bet you don't know who I'm with?' She covered the receiver with her hand for a second to talk to me: 'You'll see, they'll guess straightaway.' She went back to them: 'Yes! Got it in one! We're going to take you to the cinema this afternoon as a treat.' To me again: 'Doing anything this afternoon?' 'Going out running on the clouds for a bit,' I murmured, 'but I can leave it till tomorrow.' She gave me a long, liquid kiss on the mouth and went back to the receiver.

'I'll come and pick you up at . . . Put Granny on. Mummy adores you, eh. Muah. Muah. Muah again.'

'They say hi,' she said when she finally hung up.

She began ruthlessly to get dressed.

'Tomorrow's Tuesday, isn't it? I have to find some work as soon as possible, I'm . . .' She checked her handbag. 'I can't even afford the cinema; I'll have to ask my old lady for some. You and I just took the last of what you gave me. Mmmh I can still feel it, can you?'

I was smoking, contemplating in the dead corner of the ceiling the life I had before me, my lungs flooded with smoke, which the residual effects of the ecstasy made silky, caressing. Luckily the comedown was gradual, like a slow low tide of the blood, quite unlike the suicidal precipice of cocaine. Now that would have been too much. I felt prey to a strange lucidity, a blank, empty lucidity, with no other object than itself, a dispassionately contemplated nothingness. Nothing here, nothing there . . .

'I'd like to stay in bed with you, to fall asleep together . . . We never have, have we? But I don't like them travelling in taxis on their own. There are all sorts . . . Are you going home? Ah, right, you haven't got one. Want to stay? You can sleep for a while, while I go and get them.'

She stopped talking when she saw me crying. Without bothering to ask me she got on the bed and made room for my head between her breasts, running one hand – merely a woman's hand by now – over my face and hair, repeating in a whisper 'It won't be all right, it won't be all right,' her heartbeat calming me till I could breathe again with my mouth closed.

'Don't go,' I begged her. I was pierced by a sudden glacial

cold, as if my bones were vibrating inside me. She touched my forehead with the back of her fingers.

'You're burning up, you poor thing. Don't be scared, it's the hangover, worse in your state. You'll be all right after a few hours' sleep.'

'Then what do I do?'

'Well, if you feel ok, you can come to the cinema with us.'

'With my life. You should give me an e every six hours, like antibiotics.'

'That's not a bad idea. A mite expensive, that's all. And then you donate your liver to science. I dunno. Listen, darling, you and me . . . I'm afraid we've been seriously screwed. Happy we'll never be. It'd be a real downer though to be happy in these conditions. So let's think of an alternative.'

'It's just that it's all so . . . fragile. First I fall into hell, then I emerge in paradise, and suddenly . . . here.'

'Know what I think? Want me to tell you what I do when . . .? It's like this. Heaven and hell . . . are just drugs. Understand? Drugs. Nothing else. They stay for a while, then they go away. Know what we're going to do? I'll go and get the girls, and meanwhile you can stay here in bed and sleep. I'll only be a little while, ok? When we get back, I'll make you something to eat.'

'I don't know if I'll be able to sleep.'

'I'll tell you a bedtime story. It's a fairy tale to help you get to sleep. I've got some great ones. The girls love them. They're fairy tales in reverse. In my stories the glass slipper fits the step-sister and the ugly duckling grows into an ugly duck. Ha! And Sleeping Beauty carries on sleeping covered in dust, unhappily ever after. Let's see . . . I'll tell you the one about the Toad King. Once upon a time . . . there was a very powerful king, who wisely ruled over a very rich kingdom that stretched from the mountains to the sea and had in it all climates and all land-scapes, and the land bore fruit by the handful, almost without need for cultivation. This king had an only daughter, whom he loved with all his heart, and he would shower her with gifts and attention. Several rooms in the palace, where all ugliness was banned, were for the princess's sole use: one full of sweets, another of dresses, another of pets, another of toys. Of these her favourite was a gleaming, perfect ball of gold, brighter than the sun. The little princess's life was spent peacefully in the pal-ace's beautiful gardens, without a care other than playing with her golden ball. Until one day war was declared at the gates of the kingdom. The king called his beloved daughter to him and said to her: "Duty calls. I must fight the enemy that threatens our borders. In my absence you may play in all the rooms in the palace, including my chambers; all except the one that con-tains the book in which the fate of the kingdom is written, for what is written in it, once read, can never be undone. This is the key to that door," he concluded and handed it to her. "I give it to you so that you will not use it." The days passed and the girl enjoyed her new freedom so much that she was soon con-soled about her father's absence. One day, while playing in the corridors, the beautiful golden ball rolled up against the door of the forbidden room, as if it had a life of its own. Her curios-ity making her forget the warnings, she took the little golden key, which she always kept at hand in the pocket of her apron, and pushed: inside was nothing but a heavy table, on which, lay a great, closed book with orange covers. As she approached, the girl discovered with astonishment that printed on it in gold letters was her own name. That was why he didn't want me to read it, she thought to herself and, feeling offended by her father's deceit, she opened it without hesitation at the first page. It was covered in tiny letters, but to her surprise the little princess discovered that they turned to bloodstains as she tried to read them. Page after page the same thing happened: seemingly ordinary letters became bloodstains no sooner had she fixed her eyes upon them. She closed the book, recalling her father's warnings and sorry she hadn't obeyed them, although no sooner had she done this than through the window she heard the sound of trumpets and cries of victory. Jumping for joy, she tried to reach it to look out, but it was too high, so she had to climb on the table; she still couldn't reach the window; only by climbing on the forbidden book was she able to peek over the edge. What she saw through it struck her dumb with fright, and the golden ball fell from her open hand to the floor, where it shattered into a thousand pieces. Her father had returned, yes, but not resplendent as he had left on his spirited white charger, but weighed down by chains on a sad grey donkey and surrounded by an escort of ugly toads from the northern marshes, his allies in the war against the neighbouring kingdom; they it was who were croaking out the songs of victory. Leading the procession, mounted on the white horse, which advanced with white mane hanging and head bowed, now rode the Toad King. "Your father has something to say to you," he roared in a voice of thunder. Without looking at her, the king spoke, his voice broken and glum: "You have disobeyed me and as a consequence the commander of the toads has deposed me and is the new king. He has asked me for your hand in marriage and I am in no position to refuse him. But do not despair: if you marry him and obey him in everything, the day you accept him and learn to love him he will turn into a handsome prince who will whisk you away to his kingdom, where you will live happily ever after, and I shall regain my throne and forgive you."

'The wedding bed was prepared in the darkest, dampest room of the palace's cellars, which was the one the toad had chosen, and the wedding was celebrated. At the banquet, held with great pomp and accompanied by music from a choir of frogs and toads, when they uncovered the dishes brimming with flies, the princess realised she was better off dead. But she knew she couldn't let her father down a second time and so, under her husband's vigilant gaze, she ate every last little leg of the flies on her plate. That night, in bed, recalling her father's commandment and full of hope that one night would be enough, she tried to warm the toad's cold, viscous skin by pressing it to her body, but it was her blood that turned to ice.

'Little by little she grew accustomed to her new life: to not entering her private rooms, now full of toad children that broke her toys and pulled her dresses out of shape, to never seeing the sunlight any more. She even adapted to the diet of flies, sharpening her wits to make it more varied: in the mornings she would put milk on them as if they were cornflakes, at lunchtime she would make a pie, for tea she would spread them on toast and at night-time she would make purée. After dinner she only had to put up with the half-hour in which the pale greywhite belly huffed and puffed and croaked over her prostrate body, then turned its green wart-covered back on her, and the princess would delay her sleep imagining in a

thousand different ways the features her husband would have
the next morning, for she kept thinking that this time she had
grown to love him and that tomorrow she would awaken at the
side of the most handsome prince on earth. And every morning the first thing she saw on opening her hopeful eyes was
a mouth stretched wider than the pillow on which it rested.
The princess had never been outside the palace, which in a way
was lucky, because the toads had turned the fertile lands of the
kingdom into an open-air slaughterhouse, piling the corpses
of the animals together with the crops to rot in the sun and
so attract the millions of flies they needed to feed themselves,
the entire population devoted to the job of catching them and
carrying them to the palace in big baskets for the toads to eat.
So she started sleeping, sleeping longer and longer. Every night
in secret she would eat some crimson berries that brought her
a deep sleep so that even when her husband climbed on top
of her, she would go on sleeping, his slobbering kisses unable
to awaken her. Through the lengthening night she dreamed
of her handsome prince, sincerely believing she had come to
love her husband and worrying about the inexplicable delay
in the promised transformation; in her naivety she thought
that if she slept as long as possible her dreams would eventually triumph. Her doubts began the morning she awoke to find
the first wart on her finger. Affected by her long enclosure,
her skin had begun to turn pale and green as if she were ill,
and every morning on awakening she looked at herself naked
in the mirror and found a fresh wart on another part of her
body. It was around that time that she began to be afraid of,
rather than wish for, the promised transformation; she would
awaken screaming in the night from a nightmare in which the

disgusted Prince Charming kicked the toad in women's clothes out of his bed. Several months passed, during which the princess resigned herself to her new life so completely that she quite forgot her old one; when one morning, instead of finding new warts, she discovered that one on her belly had grown more than the others and began to get bigger and bigger from that day on. They called the doctor, an old toad with a briefcase who, after checking her, instead of frowning with concern, he stood up and smiled. "We must congratulate the father," he said. "The kingdom will now have its heirs."

"'This then,' thought the princess, "was the change Daddy announced to me, only I was unable to see it. It wasn't enough to dream it; the dream had to become flesh in my body. They may be tadpoles now, but when they are born they will have changed into little boys and girls just like any others – no, not just like any others: more beautiful than any others, as beautiful as suns. This time everything will be different," thought the princess that night before she fell fast asleep.'

AUTHOR'S NOTE

I have, in different ways, rewritten this novel.

On the one hand, the English-language version of *The Islands* is shorter than the Spanish original by some hundred pages. When I began writing *Las Islas* in 1992, some of its realities required a certain degree of introducing to the reader: the internet, virtual reality, new drugs. Today we take them for granted to such an extent than any explanation or over-insistence would be embarrassingly redundant, so that explanatory material has gone. In other cases, I have let go of elements that I judged would be of little interest to readers outside Argentina.

Turning my 600-page novel into a two-hour play in 2011 allowed me to see how further cuts inevitably increased the power of what remained. At the same time, my work on the adaptation, together with the contribution of director Alejandro Tantanian and our wonderful team of actors, brought new action, scenes and dialogue into play: some of these I found so irresistible I *had* to include them in this renewed version of the novel.

Translation is an exacter science than writing. Ian Barnett's practised eye detected many errors and inconsistencies that I was happy to mend; some of these corrections have found their way back into Spanish, in the new edition to be published this year in Buenos Aires.

I believe, with Borges, that 'the concept of the "definitive text" corresponds only to religion or exhaustion', and that what endures, in art as in life, is not what lasts but what lives on, not what achieves finality but what constantly transforms and renews itself. I don't know if *The Islands* will endure, but I have grown fond of its penchant for mutability, of its refusal to settle down and sit still.

Who knows if there are other versions yet to come.

Carlos Gamerro
March 2012, Buenos Aires

Dear readers,

With the right book we can all travel far. And yet British publishing is, with illustrious exceptions, often unwilling to risk telling these other stories.

Subscriptions from readers make our books possible. They also help us approach booksellers, because we can demonstrate that our books already have readers and fans. And they give us the security to publish in line with our values, which are collaborative, imaginative and 'shamelessly literary' (Stuart Evers, *Guardian*).

All subscribers to our upcoming titles
- are thanked by name in the books
- receive a numbered, first edition copy of each book
- are warmly invited to contribute to our plans and choice of future books

Subscriptions (incl. p&p in Europe) are:
£20 – 2 books (two books per year)
£35 – 4 books (four books per year)

Subscriptions are for books not yet published. Visit our site to see our regularlyupdated publication schedule and to subscribe:
andotherstories.org/subscribe

Thank you!

Contact
To find out about upcoming events and reading groups (our foreign-language reading groups help us choose books to publish, for example) you can:
join the mailing list at: www.andotherstories.org
- follow us on twitter: @andothertweets
- join us on Facebook: And Other Stories

This book was made possible by our advance subscribers' support
– thank you so much!

Joel Love
Jon Lindsay Miles
Jonathan Evans
Joseph Cooney
Joy Tobler
JP Sanders
Judith Unwin
Julian Duplain
Julian I. Phillippi
Julie Van Pelt
K L Ee
Kaitlin Olson
Karan Deep Singh
Kasia Boddy
Kataline Labidi
Kate Griffin
Katherine Wootton Joyce
Kathryn Lewis
Keith Dunnett
Kevin Acott
Kevin Brockmeier
Kevin Murphy
Kristin Djuve
Krystalli Glyniadakis
Larry Colbeck
Laura Bennett
Laura Jenkins
Laura Watkinson
Lesley Lawn
Liam O'Connor
Linda Harte
Liz Clifford
Liz Tunnicliffe
Lorna Bleach
Lorna Scott Fox
Lucy Greaves
Lynda Graham
M.C. Hussey
M. Manfre
Maggie Holmes
Maggie Peel
Margaret E Briggs
Margaret Jull Costa
Maria Pelletta
Marijke Du Toit

Marion Cole
Mark Ainsbury
Martin Brampton
Martin Conneely
Mary Nash
Matthew Bates
Matthew Francis
Michael Bagnall
Michael Harrison
Moira Fagan
Monika Olsen
Morgan Lyons
Murali Menon
N Jabinh
Natalie Rope
Natalie Smith
Natalie Wardle
Nichola Smalley
Nick Nelson
Nick Stevens
Nick Williams
Nuala Watt
Odhran Kelly
Oli Marlow
Owen Booth
Owen Fagan
P D Evans
Pamela Ritchie
Patrick Coyne
Paul Dowling
Paul Hannon
Paul Myatt
Peny Meltmoth
Peter Blackstock
Peter Murray
Peter Vos
Philip Warren
Phyllis Reeve
Polly McLean
Poppy Toland
Quentin Webb
Rachel Eley
Rachel McNicholl
Rebecca K. Morrison
Richard Jackson

Richard Martin
Richard Soundy
Rob Fletcher
Rob Palk
Robert Gillett
Robert Leadbetter
Robert Woodburn
Ros Schwartz
Rose Skelton
Ruth Bareau
Ruth Martin
Said Labidi
Sean McGivern
Selin Kocagoz
Shaun Whiteside
Shazea Quraishi
Sheridan Marshall
Simon Pare
SLP
Sonia McLintock
Sophie Moreau Langlais
Steph Morris
Stephen Abbott
Stewart MacDonald
Sue Mckibben
Tamsin Ballard
Tania Hershman
Tess Lee
Tess Lewis
Thomas Fritz
Thomas Long
Thomas Reedy
Tien Do
Tim Warren
Tom Long
Tom Russell
Tomoko Yokoshima
Tony Crofts
Tracey Martin
Tracy Northup
Vanessa Wells
Victoria Adams
Will Buck
William Buckingham
Zoe Brasier

And Other Stories – 2011 Titles

01 Juan Pablo Villalobos, *Down the Rabbit Hole*
translated from the Spanish by Rosalind Harvey
Shortlisted for the Guardian First Book Award 2011

'A pint-size novel about innocence, beastliness and a child learning the lingo in a drug wonderland. Funny, convincing, appalling, it's a punch-packer for one so small.'
Ali Smith's Book of the Year, *Daily Telegraph*

A popular choice for Book of the Year, including in the *New Statesman, Daily Telegraph, Salon, Stylist, 3:AM Magazine, Guardian* and *Independent*.

02 Clemens Meyer, *All the Lights*
translated from the German by Katy Derbyshire
Winner of the Leipzig Book Fair Prize 2008

'*All the Lights* contains stories of brilliance. "In the Aisles" sees Meyer's Hemingwayesque prose explore the lives of late-night shelf-stackers in Leipzig with marked grace, while in "Little Death" he manipulates time with a fluency more readily associated with film.'
– Chris Power, *Guardian*

All the Lights was one of a handful of short story collections singled out by Chris Power in his *Guardian* round-up of the best short story collections of 2011.

03 Deborah Levy, *Swimming Home*

'*Swimming Home* is as sharp as a wasp sting.'
– Christina Petrie, *Sunday Times*

'Deborah Levy has made something strange and new . . . spiky and unsettling.' – John Self, *Guardian*

'A statement on the power of the unsaid. Magisterial.'
– Abigail Deutsch, *TLS*

04 Iosi Havilio, *Open Door*
translated from the Spanish by Beth Fowler

'Iosi Havilio's remarkable first novel brings news of an intriguing world' – Martin Schifino, *Independent*

'With minimalist beauty and exquisite strangeness, Iosi Havilio offers a mesmerising addition to the literature of solitude.' – Chloe Aridjis

And Other Stories – 2012 Titles

05 Oleg Zaionchkovsky, *Happiness is Possible*
translated from the Russian by Andrew Bromfield

A humorous, even feel-good, Russian novel

Happiness is Possible tells the story of a writer late delivering his novel, unable to write anything uplifting since his wife walked out. All he can produce is notes about the happiness of others. But something draws him into the Moscow lives around him, bringing together lonely neighbours, restoring lost love, and helping out with building renovations. And happiness seems determined to catch up with him as well . . .

'Zaionchkovsky has an identifiably Russian, dark sense of humour. His writing is rewardingly risky, his slow-burn structure even more so. And . . . his novel will continue to make you think after you've finished it: about love, storytelling and Moscow.' – A. D. Miller

'Appearing out of nowhere, this novel shows absolute harmony of style and theme.' – *Time Out*

'Zaionchkovsky is one of those writers with a natural charm.'
– Lev Danilkin

07 Christoph Simon, *Zbinden's Progress*
translated from the German by Donal McLaughlin

The most charming novel about age and long life you are likely to read

Lukas Zbinden leans on the arm of Kâzim, as they walk slowly down
the stairway towards the door of his old people's home. Step by step,
the irrepressible Lukas recounts the life he shared with his wife Emilie
and his son. She loved to walk in the countryside; he loved towns and
meeting strangers. Different in so many ways, what was the secret
of their life-long love? And why is it now so hard for him to talk to
his son?

Gradually we get to know a man with a twinkle in his eye and learn
the captivating story of this man, his late wife, their son and the many
people he has met on his walks. *Zbinden's Progress* is heart-rending,
heart-warming and hilarious.

'With *Zbinden's Progress*, Christoph Simon has produced a wonderful,
touching, beautiful book; multi-layered, witty and moving.'
– *Buchkultur*

'Simon's fifth novel is a polished gem, with insight and perception that
know no cultural bounds.' – *Neue Zürcher Zeitung*

08 Helen DeWitt, *Lightning Rods*

A sharp, uproarious satire on sex, work and corporate culture from the
author of the bestselling *The Last Samurai*

Failing salesman Joe has a dream — or rather an outrageous fantasy.
Holed up in his trailer, Joe devises a jaw-dropping plan that will stamp
out sexual harassment in the workplace and make his fortune.
Win-win? As he turns his life around, *Lightning Rods* takes us to the
very top of corporate America . . .

'A weird, generous, hilarious marvel.' – Teju Cole, author of *Open City*

'The question at the heart of the novel: "What do you want?" morphs
inexorably into its sinister twin: "How far are you prepared to go?" . . .
A masterclass in contained satirical exploration.' – Sam Byers, *TLS*

'Uproariously funny' – *Wall Street Journal*

'DeWitt's wickedly smart satire deserves to be a classic.' – *Bookforum*

Title: *The Islands*
Author: Carlos Gamerro
Translator: Ian Barnett
in collaboration with the author
Editors: Sophie Lewis & Ellie Robins
Proofreader: Wendy Toole
Typesetter: Charles Boyle
Series and Cover Design: Joseph Harries
Format: 210 x 138 mm
Paper: LP Opaque 70/15 FSC
Printer: T. J. International Ltd, Padstow, Cornwall

The first 300 copies are individually numbered.